The Amarnan Kings, Book 6: Scarab - Descendant

By Max Overton

Writers Exchange E-Publishing
http://www.writers-exchange.com

The Amarnan Kings, Book 6: Scarab - Descendant
Copyright 2013, 2015 Max Overton
Writers Exchange E-Publishing
PO Box 372
ATHERTON QLD 4883

Cover Art by: Julie Napier

Published by Writers Exchange E-Publishing
http://www.writers-exchange.com

ISBN **ebook**: 978-1-922233-04-2
Print: 978-1-925574-07-4 (WEE Assigned)

Prologue

D eath is not what I thought it would be.

The priests tell us that when we die we immediately face the judgment of the gods and our heart is weighed in the balance against the feather of Truth to determine whether our bad deeds outweigh the pure nothingness of good action. Should a heart weigh more than the feather, then the soul is eaten by monsters and we cease to exist. Pass this test, however, and our soul journeys on to pleasant well-watered fields where wheat and barley grow in abundance, where the cattle are fat and vines groan under the weight of their produce. There we exist in happiness for eternity or until such time as the gods choose to pass us back into the world.

The truth is very different--or at least it is in my case.

I travelled down from the fields of Kadesh by the sandstone cliffs to the narrow black lands of Kemet, bringing with me the prepared body of the king Neferkheperu Scarab, my beloved wife. That journey, in itself, could not be told simply so I will refrain. Suffice it to say that the passage through hostile lands was difficult and fraught with dangers both for me and my precious cargo. I was no longer a young man when I essayed it, and I could not move swiftly or fight off bandits by the strength of my right arm as once I might have. I had to employ deceit, guile and subterfuge and in this, the gods aided me.

When the days of embalming had passed, performed by other refugees from the hand of Horemheb and his successors, I faced up to the problem of conveying the body of my king-wife to her final resting place and there entombing her with due ceremony and the riches that are her throne-right. I knew it would not be easy. The rule of Kemetu law as enforced by King Usermaatre-setepenre Ramesses is shaky at best in this northern region where the Empire of Hattu threatens. I could not rely on the Kemetu legions to protect me, even carrying the body of the king's grandmother, for if the authorities learned of her identity the best she could hope for was

1

a small rock-tomb in the Lesser Valley where female relatives of the king are interred. On the other hand, I risked the destruction of her body and soul should bandits claim her richly-wrapped corpse.

There are two ways to enter Kemet--by sea and by land. Any of the sea-ports would have ships plying their trade along the coast and down to the mouths of the Great River, but the entrances to these ports are watched closely by the soldiers of whichever king holds suzerainty in that stretch of the coast. The watch is kept not so much to prevent crime, but rather to prevent any expensive goods being traded without the payment of the requisite taxes. I could not risk my belongings being thoroughly searched by soldiers as I entered the port, so I opted for the slower land route into Kemet, bypassing the cities.

An embalmed body is light, all water and fat having been absorbed by the natron bath, and even after the body was wrapped in finest linen and all the proper prayers and amulets fixed in place, I could carry my beloved in death far easier than I could carry her in life. I had a lightweight casket made, seemingly of raw and uncut timber, unprepossessing and ordinary, but it held the body safely and would attract little attention unless examined closely. This casket I loaded onto a camel and packed it about with cheap trade goods. I could not carry gold with me, for I posed as a poor trader, but I would need it when I arrived in Kemet. I meant to inter my wife as a true king of Kemet and that involved many costly items being prepared. I could not carry gold with me, but I knew where I could find it in abundance--the treasury of her long-dead brother Djeserkheperu Smenkhkare.

I traversed the land of Kanaan without major incident, though three attacks by bandits stripped me of almost everything I owned. Luckily, they left me my bulky and almost worthless bundle of timber. I passed the line of forts--now once more firmly in Kemetu hands--and made my way through the rich delta lands to the white-walled city of Ineb Hedj, or Men-nefer 'the enduring and beautiful' as many men now call the city, and the great stone pyramids looming like angular mountains on the plateau beyond. Here I found the first friends who would help me--for Scarab's sake.

I was welcomed--no questions asked--and given sustenance and such help as I needed to further my quest. I made a quick visit to Iunu, where I spoke to the High Priest of Atum, and then back to Men-nefer where I made my preparations. Now that I was within the borders of Kemet, I could travel the King's Roads in safety, and presently attached myself to a caravan heading south to Waset. I left it in Akhet-Aten though, as I had business there.

Several craftsmen and artisans friendly to the Aten belief had fled the enmity of the kings from Ay to Ramses, and some had found haven in the north. They had family still residing in and about the former City of the Aten, and it were these men I sought. I visited the house of Mut after nightfall, identifying myself when he stared without recognition at my ancient visage.

"Khu, by the holy face of the Aten, what are you doing here? Is...is she with you?"

I told him, and after he indulged in sincere expressions of grief, I revealed why I had come. "Mut, I must bury her as befits her station as king of Kemet and sister, daughter and mother of kings. Will you help me?"

"Tell me what I must do."

"I need a sarcophagus suitable for royalty, and moveable cypress panels painted with scenes from her life and appropriate prayers, and also worthy grave goods."

Mut looked worried. "Whatever wealth I have is hers, you know that Khu, but what you ask will cost far more gold than I have."

"I will provide the gold. All I ask of you is your skill and your silence."

"You have it, my friend."

I left Scarab's body in his care and took a boat upriver the next day. At Waset, I sought out a fisherman I knew, old and discreet, who took me further upriver to where a tumbled cairn and a grove of date palms pointed the way to the hidden treasury of King Smenkhkare. I prayed to the king, and to his sister, that no harm would come to me, before breaking the hidden seals and entering the chamber. Light from the torch I carried reflected back off stacked ingots of gold, mounds of ivory, and burst bags of jewels and finely wrought jewellery. I had calculated how much I would need for Scarab's burial and removed just that much, leaving the rest against future need. Later, I would transfer the rest to the tomb that would hold brother and sister for eternity.

By the time I returned to Akhet-Aten, Mut and his trusted friends had made a start on fashioning the sarcophagus and grave goods. The gold, ivory and jewels I brought enabled them to start turning superlative wooden carvings into works of art, and a month later, all was in readiness.

"They are perfect, Mut," I said. I walked around the room, examining the cunningly wrought sarcophagus, the intricately carved and painted panels and the wide selection of grave goods. "May Aten bless you for your efforts."

"Two things concern me, Khu. First, how are you going to transport all this upriver without raising suspicion? Second, if this is to be a royal burial, you need the sanction of the priests. How will you get a priest to conduct the funeral without informing the king?"

"I will need you to make an outer coffin, plain and painted. Then I will take everything upriver quite openly as the body of a minor noble being returned to his family estates near Behdet. As for the priests--I have made arrangements."

"The tomb is near Behdet then?"

"Better you do not know, old friend. What you do not know cannot be passed on, even accidentally."

I sailed again, this time on a cargo boat heading south on Iteru. Soldiers came aboard at Waset and gave the cargo a cursory examination. The officer in charge asked me about the coffin and panels I carried and with a silent prayer to the gods I offered up my explanation.

"The panels and grave goods are of excellent quality," the officer commented, "But the coffin is hardly up to the same standard. Why is that?"

"The furniture was prepared in Men-nefer while the body of the young master lay in the House of Death. I had a fine coffin prepared, but on the day we sailed, the fools carrying it to the boat dropped it and it cracked. This was all they had as a replacement. I will have to have a new one made in Behdet."

"We have some excellent coffin makers in Waset. Why not have one made here?"

"I have my orders, sir. We are already a day late, and I have a hard master."

The officer nodded sympathetically and let me go. We sailed on to Behdet, where everything was unloaded and stored in a small warehouse near the docks. That night, my fisherman friend returned with his sons and we took everything downriver to the track that led to where a pylon sat atop the line of the western cliffs and an arrow of light pointed inland at dawn. A cart was waiting, driven by another son of the fisherman, and by the break of day, everything sat at the bottom of the cliff face up which we must climb. The tomb of King Smenkhkare lay in the desert beyond the cliffs, in the green mountain crowned by light.

4

I dismissed the fisherman and his sons with thanks and a little gold, not because they were untrustworthy but because the fewer people who knew the exact location of the tomb, the better. Others would help me complete my mission, but I would have to wait for them, so I hid everything as best I could and made camp.

My helpers arrived the next day--priests and priestesses of the Nine of Iunu. They helped me carry the wooden sarcophagus of King Scarab up the steep and narrow track to the cliff top, past Khepri's shrine, across the miles to the mountain, open the tomb of King Smenkhkare, and install the grave goods. These included the remaining wealth of King Smenkhkare's treasury, laboriously transported piece by piece amid great secrecy. The Hem-Netjer of Atum led the ceremonies of opening the mouth, of blessing the tomb and uttering the incantations of protection, before each of the priests and priestesses uttered words of praise for the King that had put the Nine before all others.

We sealed the tomb and made our way back down to the river. The priests and priestesses bade me farewell before the Hem-Netjer of Atum took me aside.

"The golden scarab that the god gave to her--you have it?" He held out his hand.

"No. It did not seem right to take it. I left it entombed up in Kanaan where Scarab wrote the account of her life."

The Hem-Netjer frowned. "That was ill-considered. With it, I could have conjured a lasting protection on the tomb."

"I will stay and guard it," I said. "I meant to stay here anyway, for my life's meaning lies up there." I gestured toward the hidden tomb that lay beyond the cliff face.

The Hem-Netjer prayed and inclined his head as if listening to unspoken words. He nodded. "The gods will accept your sacrifice, Khu son of Pa-it, beloved of Scarab. Guard her well until she comes again."

"She will come again? What do you mean?"

He did not answer me, but stepped aboard the boat that would carry them back down the river to Iunu. I put the words from my mind, for I reasoned that if she came again I would know it and if she did not, then his words were meaningless.

I lived there below the cliff face and path that led to my beloved's tomb for nearly twenty years more. I built myself a shelter and grew a little food, catching fish and snaring wildfowl in the reeds. People from villages nearby came to recognise me as a holy man and brought me what I lacked, and in return I offered my medical expertise, saving more than a few lives over the years and easing the burden on many more. The track up the cliff face slowly became obscured and fell away, leaving no trace that men had ever passed that way. I found another path to the top and journeyed inland to the green mountain as often as I could while my strength remained, to gaze on the site of the tomb itself. The guiding pylon at the top of the cliff through which the rising run cast its first rays I destroyed, lest others use the god's golden finger to find the tomb, though I could do nothing about the crown of light. Let the gods look after that.

I died, though at first I was unaware of it. My life was so simple and repetitive that I continued my daily routine for some time before I realised that night and day were passing without feelings of hunger or thirst, and I felt no desire to sleep. I realised what must have happened when I saw the villagers lay a wizened but recognisable body in a shallow sandy grave at the top of the cliffs, near where the pylon had once stood. I prepared myself for what must surely follow--judgment by the gods. I waited--and waited--while days and seasons and years cycled by--a bodiless entity on the edge of the desert, my attention fixed still on a rock tomb carved in the side of a green mountain crowned with light. The words of the Hem-Netjer came again to me--'The gods will accept your sacrifice, Khu son of Pa-it, beloved of Scarab. Guard her well until she comes again.' I realised with some horror that I had condemned myself to an eternity of watching and waiting, for surely Scarab could not come again. She must certainly be in the company of the gods, enjoying the rewards of a righteous life.

I railed at my fate and cursed the gods, but they had turned their faces from me. After a while, I became resigned and a hundred years or so later I came to think of my sentence as an opportunity to serve my beloved from beyond the grave. True, I had always thought that I would serve her in the Field of Reeds, waiting upon her for eternity, but was this so different? I had no need of food or wine, of sleep or pastime. I served my beloved by making sure her tomb remained undisturbed.

Years passed and the world changed. The Kings of Kemet came and went, displaced by curl-bearded foreigners and then the followers of a young man who called himself 'Alexandros, Son of Amun'. They were followed by a hard race from the north who ruled Kemet with iron, and in their turn by followers of one they called 'The Prophet'. Through all those long years I waited and I watched, and thrice had occasion to act.

The first time, some villagers forgot the warnings passed down from their forefathers and attempted to scale the cliff face and cross the desert.

They reached the green mountain and sought to force the tomb entrance, seeking anything of value that they might sell for food. All they found was death. The second time was in the time of the followers of the Prophet, men who hungered after gold and had no regard for the beliefs of others. They followed the trail of rumour and old stories, and came to the same end as the first. The third came much later, when fair-skinned men dressed in clothes that encased them despite the heat, attempted to dig into the side of the green mountain. These ones sought knowledge rather than gold, but I could not allow my beloved to be taken back to a 'museum'. I called on the Nine of Iunu and they came to my aid, driving the fair-skinned men to self-destruction. The mountain got a reputation for being haunted and was shunned--which suited me.

And then came a fourth attempt...

Chapter One

The streets of Damascus were choked with traffic and the hordes of people on the footpaths were a daunting prospect for the five foreigners who stepped out of the foyer of the Intercontinental Hotel. Taxi drivers lounging by their vehicles rushed forward, elbowing their way through the crowd, gesticulating and yelling in a mixture of Syrian, French and broken English, each striving to obtain the fare that would surely yield many dollars from these rich but unsuspecting tourists.

An army sergeant and soldiers, waiting outside the hotel, intercepted the taxi drivers, pushing them away, and formed a cordon around the foreigners, ushering them to two black limousines parked in front of the taxis. The foreigners looked startled and hung back, as if not knowing what to make of the situation, but the soldiers hurried them onward, falling just short of actually manhandling their charges. At the kerbside, the soldiers tried to separate the foreigners by gender, showing the three women to one car and the two men to the other. The older woman remonstrated, and in the face of her determination, the sergeant shrugged and gave in, allowing the foreigners to divide themselves as they wished.

"Marc, look after Angela and Doris, will you? I'll travel with Daffyd."

"Righto, Dani," said the young bearded man. "Come on girls, you heard our beloved leader."

The older man with Dani dropped the stub of his cigarette on the ground and stepped on it before joining her in the rear of the car. The three young people piled into the other limousine, the sergeant and soldiers dividing themselves between the two vehicles. The drivers eased their cars into the traffic, the little flags mounted on the front of the limousines announcing the importance of their passengers. Policemen on point duty signalled the traffic to stop and give way to their uninterrupted passage.

"What's going on, sergeant?" asked Dani. "We weren't told we'd have an escort to the conference."

The sergeant said nothing.

"Perhaps you don't realise who this woman is, boyo," the older man said in a sing-song voice that spoke of green Welsh valleys and black coal pits. "This is Dr Danielle Hanser of the British archaeological expedition to the Orontes Valley. She is here by the express wishes of the Minister of National History. I think the Minister wouldn't look kindly on you ignoring her questions."

The sergeant scowled. "I am only following orders," he said in good if broadly accented English. "I am to escort you to the Ministry Building."

"There, that wasn't so hard, was it?" The dark-haired Welshman took out a tin of tobacco and cigarette papers.

"You need to give that habit up, Daffyd, it's bad for you," Dani said. She rolled down a window, letting in the heat and noise of the city. "And why the Ministry Building?" she asked the sergeant. "The conference is supposed to be at the City Administration Hall."

The sergeant shrugged. "I have my orders."

Daffyd lit his cigarette and blew a cloud of strongly-scented smoke over the sergeant, grinning at the man's obvious discomfort. "Ah, orders. The perennial excuse."

Dani shook her head and opened up her briefcase, pulling out some handwritten sheets of paper, a notebook, and a carved golden scarab. The sergeant glanced at her and looked away again, and Dani realised the soldier had not seen the gleam of gold. She knew that for some reason, the minds of most people failed to register the existence of the artefact.

"You know what you're going to say?" Daffyd asked.

Dani nodded. "Just the plain unvarnished truth. We stumbled upon a series of chambers filled with hieroglyphs that told the story of an Egyptian princess. The account indicated the presence of an undiscovered royal tomb and we, together with the Under-Minister of National History, are going to Egypt to find it."

"Why did you bring the golden scarab with you? Are you planning on showing everyone?" Daffyd saw Dani glance at the soldier. "He can't see it, you know, and I doubt whether anyone at the conference will be able to either. I just wondered why you'd brought it along instead of leaving it in the hotel safe."

Dani turned the heavy golden object over in her hands, marvelling anew at its weight and lustrous gleam. It was perfect, painstakingly carved by some ancient craftsman, showing legs tucked underneath, antennae pressed closely to its head and ribbed wing cases enclosing its rounded body. A representation of the ancient Egyptian sun god, it had the symbol

9

of the Aten carved on its belly. That feature made it unique as the Aten--the disc of the sun--had been the personal god of the heretic pharaoh Akhenaten, and anathema to the ruling priests of Amun-Re.

"I just don't like to let it out of my sight," she said. "You know what it means to me."

Daffyd puffed on his cigarette, filling the interior with blue smoke that eddied and slipped out through the open window. "You really think it came to you on purpose? That it wasn't just a lucky find?"

"You've read the account on the chamber walls. Do you honestly think there are two golden scarabs like this? This is the one gifted by the god Atum to Scarab three thousand years ago...and now it's come into my possession. It can't just be chance...and didn't it help me find the chambers in the first place? What's that if not purpose?"

"Alright, lass, I'm not going to argue. I've seen Bashir handle the damn thing and believe it to be no more than a simple rock. That implies something out of the ordinary is going on, though being a hard-bitten scientist I hesitate to call it supernatural."

Dani returned to her notes and as the limousine sped through the streets of Damascus, the policemen on point duty at the intersections waving the vehicles through without pause, she made a few corrections and additions, honing what she wanted to say to the world's press.

The vehicles slowed at last and turned into a driveway guarded by heavy iron gates and armed guards, pulling up at the rear of an ugly brick building. The five members of the British team were led through a doorway into a dim corridor and thence up flights of stairs and along uncarpeted hallways to a small room. Men and women withdrew as they passed, though a few curious looks were thrown their way. The sergeant and soldiers showed them into the room and closed the doors, remaining outside.

The meeting room was almost devoid of furniture and did not look as if it was set up for a press conference. There were only a few chairs around the edges of the room, a table in the middle of the room, but no podium, and nothing in the way of microphones or lighting.

"What the hell's going on?" Marc muttered. "What is this place?"

"Well, it can't be the conference venue," Angela said. "There are no facilities."

"Speaking of which..." Doris added. "Do you think there's a loo handy?"

Daffyd looked pensive and when Dani met his eyes, he shrugged and looked away. He wandered over to the window and looked out through a grill to a drab interior courtyard. "If I didn't know better," he murmured. "I'd say this was a prison of some sort."

"It can't be," Marc said. "Bashir wouldn't dare try anything like that. If we're not at the British Consulate by five this afternoon, the ambassador opens our letter and Bashir's involvement becomes public. He wouldn't risk that."

"What have we overlooked?" Daffyd asked.

Marc glowered. "Nothing. If Bashir tries anything, we throw him to the wolves. Al, Will and Bob are still out there, remember."

"I remember," Daffyd said. He pulled out his tobacco and started rolling another cigarette. "But they don't have any supporting evidence."

"We've got that, though, haven't we?" Doris said. "All the notebooks and photos."

"Unless Bashir takes them. Then we have nothing."

"Yes we do. We have the letter at the Consulate."

Daffyd lit his cigarette and inhaled deeply. "Our trump card. Suddenly, it doesn't seem like very much. Don't forget, we're in a foreign country, and Bashir holds most of the other cards."

Dani sat down on one of the chairs, out of the way, and opened her briefcase again. She took out the golden scarab and slipped it into her jacket pocket. A presentiment of disaster was creeping over her and she wanted the artefact safe. "Perhaps I should have left it in the hotel safe," she whispered.

The door opened, and Under-Minister Ahmed Bashir entered the room, flanked by his aide Nazim, and two soldiers carrying submachine guns. The soldiers took up positions where they could cover everyone in the room, while Nazim placed a chair for Bashir.

"Good morning gentlemen...ladies," Bashir said. "My apologies for the lack of amenities. The decision was only made an hour ago."

"What decision was that, Minister?" Daffyd asked.

"The decision not to hold the press conference after all."

The five British expedition members stared at Bashir.

"But there has to be..." Angela started to say.

"You have to hold one," Marc stated flatly. "Have you forgotten the letter?"

"Letter?" Bashir asked, smiling. "What letter is this?"

11

"You know bloody well what letter," Marc said. "The one to the British Consulate."

"Ah." Bashir took a piece of folded paper from an inside pocket of his suit jacket. "Would this be the one?"

Daffyd strode forward and the soldiers' machine guns swung toward him. He stopped abruptly, but Bashir waved the guards aside, holding the letter out to the Welshman. Daffyd took the letter and unfolded it, quickly scanning the neat handwriting.

"It's our letter." He handed it back to Bashir.

"You bastard," Marc said, his fists bunching. He took a step forward and the guards' guns came up again.

"There's no point, Marc," Dani said. "How did you get it?"

"Suffice it to say that our Postal Service is atrocious and our Military Intelligence quite efficient."

"So what happens now?" Daffyd asked. "Do we all disappear into some dungeon or shallow unmarked grave?"

"My dear Dr Rhys-Williams, what do you take me for? We are a civilised people in Syria. You will simply be put on a flight to England later today."

"That's it? What's the catch?"

"What's changed?" Angela asked. "Down at the site you were worried we'd tell everyone about your..."

"Shut up, Angela," Marc said quickly.

Bashir laughed. "Come, Dr Andrews, did you think I might have forgotten? I remember your threats of exposure and paid heed to them until I secured the letter you sent to your Consulate. However, I have now rendered your threats harmless."

"You aren't concerned we might go to the papers back in England?" Dani asked.

"What would you tell them, Dr Hanser? A fairy tale about finding a lost tomb? I think you would find very few people would believe you, and when I revealed that you had been deported for scientific irregularities, your standing at your university would reach rock bottom."

"We have proof," Marc said.

"Ah yes, the physical evidence. There are notebooks and transcribed texts from the chamber walls, photographs, and a handful of letters written to your colleagues in England. None of the letters contain proof, and you will not have access to any of the notes and photographs. Without those, you have nothing."

Minister Bashir turned to his aide. "Nazim, have my orders been carried out?"

"Indeed, Minister. As we talk, their rooms at the hotel are being emptied of their possessions, as is the hotel safe. All they now own is what they have on their persons."

"Very good. So, gentlemen and ladies, if you would be so good as to empty the contents of your pockets and briefcase on the table, we can conclude our business today."

"You won't get away with it, you bastard," Marc said.

"Really, Dr Andrews, I thought more of you. Don't the English believe in playing the game? You have played and lost, so grin and bear it in a sportsmanlike fashion."

Marc muttered an expletive but Bashir ignored him.

"Now, I must insist you place everything you have with you on the table." Bashir watched as the contents of pockets and Dani's briefcase were emptied out onto the polished wooden surface. "Is that everything?" When nothing further was offered up, Bashir sighed. "I can always order a strip search to be made. I have no wish to subject you to such indignities, but I will if you give me no choice."

After a long hesitation, Dani took the golden scarab from her pocket and laid it on the table. Although she and Daffyd knew it for what it was, a superbly crafted golden artefact from the time of the Amarnan kings, it was apparent nobody saw anything but a rounded brownish yellow pebble. Bashir knitted his brows and leaned across to pick up what looked to be a small sandstone rock, fumbling it as if it proved unexpectedly heavy.

"What is this?" he asked.

Dani shrugged, fighting to keep the concern off her face. "A memento of our dig, a fragment of the sandstone cliffs. Nothing of any value."

"I can see that. What I'm wondering is why you keep it." Bashir turned the rock over in his hands, examining it, rubbing his fingers over its surface.

"Just as a reminder of an interesting dig. You wouldn't begrudge me a memento, would you Minister?"

"It has a curious texture and weight. I think I will keep it." Bashir tossed the rock onto the small pile of papers that had come from Dani's briefcase, and turned his attention to his listeners.

"You will be held here until this afternoon, when your passports will be returned to you, and you are taken to Damascus airport. There is a flight

13

that will carry you home. I hardly need say that none of you are welcome to return to the United Arab Republic."

"What about our belongings?" Daffyd asked. "We have things that had nothing to do with the expedition--personal items."

"Never fear, Dr Rhys-Williams, I will allow you your tobacco."

"That isn't what I meant..."

"I know what you meant, and it is all forfeit. You will take with you the clothes you wear and your passports. Nothing else."

"Your actions are barbaric."

"And your actions have been high-handed and imperialistic," Bashir retorted. "You British no longer have an empire, yet you try to appear so grand and important. Your posturing comes to nothing, however, for Syria is an independent country and our laws apply here. Now run home with your tails between your legs and be thankful I do not hand you over to Arab justice."

The soldiers ushered the five of them out into the corridor and marched them down flights of stairs again before leading them to small windowless rooms with steel doors. The men were shown into one room and the women into another across the hallway, and the doors locked.

Dani looked around the small cell, its only furnishings being an upright chair, a narrow pallet bed, and a round hole in one corner whence noxious odours arose. She crossed to the chair and sat down.

"You might as well make yourselves comfortable," she told Angela and Doris. "We might be here for a few hours."

"I really need that loo break now," Doris said, her voice trembling. "Do you think they might let me use one?"

"I think that's what the hole in the corner is for," Angela said, pointing.

"Oh, I couldn't...not here...not in front of..."

"It's no worse than the camp latrines," Dani said gently. "A bit less private, but we'll look the other way."

They all had occasion to use the hole in the corner over the next few hours. There was nothing else to do in the little cell except talk or sit and stare at the roughly plastered cement walls. Dani contemplated the loss of her golden scarab, admitting to herself that its absence preyed on her mind and left a void in her being that she would not have thought possible.

"It's almost as if the god Atum gave it to me as well as Scarab," she muttered.

"What did you say?" Angela asked.

"Nothing. I was just wondering what we can do."

"There's nothing we can do, is there?" Doris sobbed. "Everything was going so wonderfully a few days ago, and now we've lost everything."

"Cheer up, Dor," Angela said. "Bashir's taken everything, but it wasn't his to take. It all belongs to Midland University, so they'll kick up a stink and get it back for us, isn't that right, Dani?"

"I'm sure that's right," Dani said.

Privately, she was not at all certain that anything could be done. Even if Bashir and the Syrian authorities played down their expulsion from the country, any attempt to wrest the notebooks and evidence from the Minister would almost certainly lead to charges being laid against the expedition of unscientific behaviour at the least, or even of attempted theft of historical artefacts. As expedition leader, Dani could expect those charges to be aimed primarily at her. The outlook was grim, but she was not going to add to the worries of her companions by voicing her concerns.

The soldiers came for them a few hours later and marched them outside to a small bus. Any attempt at communication between the expedition members was interrupted by loud shouting and some shoving, and on board the bus they were seated as far apart as possible. Nazim was at the airport to meet them and hurry them through to the departure gate. He handed them their passports.

"Do not return to Syria," Nazim said. "You will not be permitted to re-enter the country."

"As if we'd want to," Marc snapped.

"What about our belongings?" Daffyd asked. "A lot of what was confiscated was personal items that had nothing to do with the chambers and inscription."

"Everything will be examined, and if it has no bearing on your...on the discovery, it will be forwarded on to you."

"Including our books and cameras?" Daffyd persisted.

"If they have nothing to do with the inscription."

"What about the rock that the Minister took from me?" Dani asked. "That was only a memento of the dig. It had nothing to do with the inscription."

Nazim hesitated. "Minister Bashir finds the rock interesting--and also your request for its return. I do not think he will part with it, Dr Hanser."

"Please see if you can persuade him. You can see for yourself it has no intrinsic value, but it represents a memory for me."

"I promise nothing. Now, your flight is boarding."

They had no option but to board the flight and endure the many hours of travel back to England. They changed planes in Rome and Paris, and would have liked to sample the hospitality of those cities, but without funds could not leave the airports and were dependent on airline meals to satisfy their hunger. Daffyd and Marc spent the trip plotting revenge on Bashir and devising increasing wild scenarios whereby they beat him to the site of Scarab's tomb in Egypt. By journey's end, though, reality had sunk in and they became morose, staring out of the tiny windows at a featureless cloudscape. Angela and Doris slept most of the way, too depressed to face conversation, but Dani spent the hours in thought.

She felt herself on a watershed, where her previous academic life had led up to the Syrian Expedition, and now a whole new world lay in darkness before her. The dazzling prospect of a search for Scarab's tomb had been cruelly extinguished by Bashir's treachery, but she did not feel totally lost. The future lay in darkness but she had faith that the golden scarab would somehow return to her, lighting her way to eventual success.

Why else did it come to me in the first place, if not to reveal the chambers? And why do that if I wasn't meant to find the tomb?

The thought was foreign to her scientific mind, and made no sense in a materialistic universe, but Dani could not shake the feeling that the adventure was not yet over. The loss of the translations was of great importance in proving the existence of the chambers to university committees, but she could remember whole swathes of the account that she had laboriously translated over the weeks and months. She could probably reconstruct the gist of the account from memory, and probably the descriptions of the tomb's position. Even without the golden scarab, she might be able to find the tomb of Smenkhkare and Scarab once she found herself in Egypt. Dani clung to that thought as they descended through rainclouds into British airspace.

They landed at London's Heathrow airport and changed planes for Derby and thence by bus to Chesterfield of the twisted spire and Midland University, where a grim-faced university official waited for them.

Chapter Two

The official letter arrived a week later, addressed simply to Dr Danielle Hanser and bearing the stamp of the Office of the Vice-Chancellor of the university. Dani picked up the letter from where it had been pushed through the letterbox and stared at the envelope for a minute before taking it back to the little sun-filled kitchen of her flat in the city. The twisted spire of Chesterfield Cathedral could be seen from her kitchen window and not for the first time she contemplated how her life had taken a sudden twist like the famous spire. She propped the letter against a flower-filled vase on the kitchen table and sat down to stare at it with a cup of coffee in her hands and marmalade toast cooling on a side plate.

I really don't want to open it.

After a while--half a cup of coffee and a piece of toast later--she shrugged and slit the envelope open with her marmalade-smeared knife, opening up the folded letter within and scanning it.

About what I expected.

'Dr Hanser,' it read, 'Allegations of scientific impropriety have been brought against the recent expedition to Syria in general, and you in particular, by the Ministry of National History in Syria. An informal meeting has been called to deliberate on the University's response to these allegations and the recent expulsion of the expedition members from Syria. You will be required to respond to these allegations. Accordingly, you are summoned to this meeting, to be held on Thursday next (27th) at a venue to be decided. Please contact the Office of the Vice-Chancellor at least twenty-four hours beforehand to confirm your attendance, or to give good reason why you will not be attending. Please note that if you do not attend, decisions that involve your future at Midland University may be taken in your absence.' It was signed by the secretary to the Vice-Chancellor.

Dani read through the letter again before refolding it and tossing it onto the table. She sipped at her coffee while she digested her first piece of toast and the information from the Office of the Vice-Chancellor. Her eyes

17

stared at the flowers in the vase, but she did not see them or the little pink aphid sitting on a zinnia petal.

At least it's an informal meeting. If it was really serious I'd be hauled before an official tribunal. By degrees, her mind turned to her defence. *Do I have one?*

Dani had to face up to choices made nearly a year ago at the end of their first season in the Orontes Valley. When they stumbled upon the first chamber and recognised its importance, they should have reported their find to the proper authorities and taken a back seat to whatever team was assigned to investigate the discovery. Instead, the eight expedition members had voted to reseal the chamber and return to it the next season, hoping to keep its existence secret and be able to investigate its mysteries themselves.

It was a vain hope, and Syrian Under-Minister Ahmed Bashir had caught wind of the discovery; arrived and taken charge. Only the tantalising glimpses of hidden treasure referred to in the account inscribed on the chamber walls had prevented him turning them in. Instead, they found themselves willing accomplices in deceit. Then, when the account came to an end, and the possibility of finding an undiscovered royal tomb presented itself, they had connived with the Minister to continue the deception, agreeing to a joint expedition into Egypt to track down the burial chamber of a king and its associated treasury.

Bashir had outwitted them, thrown them aside without a qualm, and now had made an official complaint in the hope of stalling any possibility-- however remote--of their interference in his plans. Without a doubt, he planned to find the tomb using the descriptions in the account and plunder it, selling priceless artefacts on the black market without a thought for the destruction of so much knowledge.

But what can I do? I can't prove a thing.

Possibly, Daffyd and Marc might be able to think of something. The letter had named the expedition as co-defendant, but Dani disliked the thought of involving them further. The responsibility had been hers and she intended to admit her culpability, and would try and exonerate the others. She decided she would say nothing for now; just turn up at the meeting and see what transpired.

On the Wednesday morning, Dani rang the secretary and found that the meeting was to be held in one of the top-floor meeting rooms of the administration building.

"Half past two, Dr Hanser, in room 603."

"Thank you."

A pause. "Will you be presenting any evidence or calling witnesses?"

"I thought this was an informal meeting."

Another pause. "That is correct."

Dani hung up and considered her position. The informal meeting was starting to sound like a trial, and she wondered whether she should have someone represent her. The trouble with that was she would appear more aggressive than she wanted, and she still hoped the problem would go away by accepting she had acted improperly and accepting a rap over the knuckles. She did not think the university would do much more. After all, it was not as if they had removed any artefacts or anything.

What about the golden scarab?

That wasn't in the chambers, it was outside...and besides, I don't have it.

At twenty past two on Thursday afternoon, she presented herself to the secretary on the top floor and was shown into an antechamber of the meeting room. Here she was left to cool her heels for half an hour before the secretary came to collect her. She was shown into a well-appointed room with deep carpet and gleaming polished wood furniture. A long table faced her, and behind it was arrayed several men and women, most of whom she recognised.

The Vice-Chancellor, Edward McClelland, rose to his feet as Dani entered the room, though his expression was anything but welcoming.

"Dr Hanser, good of you to come." He inclined his head left and right to include the others seated at the table. "You will know our Dean of Science, Professor Voisey; Professor Roberts, Anthropology; Professor Cummins, Ancient History; and Professor Bielish, Archaeology. The gentleman on the far left is Mr Torby from the University's legal department, and on the far right is Mr Parker from the Foreign Office. If you would be so good as to be seated, we'll get started."

Dani took the only unoccupied seat in the room, a plain straight-backed chair facing the panel of her accusers. She straightened her skirts and looked the Vice-Chancellor in the eyes.

McClelland cleared his throat and looked down at the notes in front of him. "Dr Hanser, you have been accused by the Syrian Government of fraud, in that you claimed to be carrying out an archaeological investigation into Neanderthal migration patterns under the auspices of Midland University and the Syrian Ministry of National History, accepting funding and material assistance from both sources; whereupon you abandoned this enterprise and pursued a reckless and unscientific plundering of a newly discovered Egyptian tomb, destroying priceless artwork and removing artefacts. Further, members of your team, both staff and students of Midland University, did aid and abet you in these crimes. Do you have a statement you wish to read into the record?'"

"I...I didn't...er, no, I don't have a statement to read, not knowing the...er, charges being brought against me, but I would like to answer these points if I may."

The Vice-Chancellor nodded and waited while Dani collected her thoughts.

"All right...first, I want to make it clear that I was the leader of this expedition and that nobody else had any part in the decision to investigate the chambers. I made the decision and everyone else had no choice but to go along with..."

"There I must interrupt you, Dr Hanser," Cummins said. "Dr Rhys-Williams, who is a member of my department, has already admitted culpability in this regard, saying he persuaded other members of the expedition to this course of action."

A smile tugged briefly at Dani's lips. "Daff...Dr Rhys-Williams was subordinate to me. It was my decision."

"Please continue," Vice-Chancellor McClelland said.

Dani nodded. "The purpose of the expedition was to investigate the Orontes Valley and its tributaries for evidence of Neanderthal migration routes. In particular, we dug in a deep cave in an unnamed stream valley. We found very little to suggest the valley had been used by Neanderthals, but in the course of our investigations we stumbled upon what looked like dressed stone in one wall of the cave. We broke through..."

"Just like that?" Cummins asked. "Without thought for the archaeological value of what you must have known was of significance?"

"On the contrary, we took photographs of the wall and broke through with minimal damage. You must realise that this was a site without any historical antecedents. We had no inkling that this bricked area would be anything more than a...than a goat byre of recent construction."

"And was it?" Elenore Bielish, Professor of Archaeology, had a look of distaste on her lean face. "Was it a find of minimal historical significance?"

"No, Professor. Inside the cavern we found plastered walls completely covered with Egyptian hieroglyphs and paintings in the Amarnan style. We explored the chamber and found it to be empty except for a few scraps of wood and rope in one corner."

"At which point, the proper procedure would have been to reseal the chamber and contact the university or the Ministry, telling them of your find and letting them make the relevant decisions," Bielish pointed out.

"I agree," Dani said quietly. "However, we were all professionals in the field and we were naturally excited with our find, so we agreed to try and determine exactly what it was we had found. We didn't damage anything, just translated the text and took some pictures."

"You could read the hieroglyphs?" Professor Roberts asked. "I wasn't aware that Egyptology was your field."

Dani hesitated, wondering how much she should reveal. "It isn't, but I have made an extensive study of inscriptions privately. My family has always..." Dani shook her head and gathered her thoughts again. "We found out that the text was the life story of Princess Beketaten, sister to Pharaoh Akhenaten of the Eighteenth dynasty."

"At which point you must have realised the importance of your discovery," Bielish pointed out. "You should have immediately suspended your work and resealed the chamber."

"I considered it, but the sentence construction and grammar was atypical of Egyptian texts, so I couldn't be certain this wasn't a recent hoax..."

"In such an out-of-the-way place? Unlikely."

"And the personal account of a young girl in the centre of such an incredible period of Egyptian history was very compelling." Dani smiled wryly. "We wanted to know what happened."

"So you stopped work on the Neanderthal dig, which was funded by this university and the Syrian Government, so you could indulge your curiosity?" Dean Voisey asked.

"We had found very little evidence of Neanderthal presence and we were near the end of our time anyway. I made what I thought was a reasonable decision."

"According to the Minister of National History in Syria, you found evidence of a tomb in Egypt, and covered up this information in the hope of finding it yourself and plundering it," McClelland said. "Furthermore, the Minister says you attempted to destroy the inscriptions in the hope of covering your tracks."

"Not in the least," Dani retorted. "There was no suggestion of a tomb in the first chamber..."

"First? There was more than one?"

"There were three. Didn't you know?"

The academics around the table looked at each other, and the Vice-Chancellor shook his head.

"Go on, Dr Hanser."

"There was no mention of a tomb in the first chamber, and there were hints that the inscription was incomplete. We were at the end of our stay in Syria, so we sealed the chamber and returned to England. Some of the students wanted to report our findings but I argued against it as I wanted to find out more." Dani looked around at the Heads of Department and Administrative Heads, making sure she had their attention. "It was my decision to cover up our find and return to it the next season."

"So earlier this year, you and your team returned to the site, ostensibly to further your Neanderthal investigations but really to reopen the chamber, and then you discovered the second chamber?" McClelland asked.

"Yes. The account continued in another, larger chamber..."

"Where was this chamber?" Cummins interrupted.

"Behind the first."

Cummins referred to his notes. "You said the walls of the first chamber were completely covered in writing and paintings. Where, then, was the entrance to the second?"

Dani took a deep breath and exhaled slowly. "We had to cut through the painting on the rear wall."

"Let me see if I have this right," Bielish said. "By now, you know that this is, at the very least, an important discovery, yet you wilfully destroy a unique painting to push on further into this tomb merely to satisfy your curiosity."

"We didn't destroy it. We took out as few blocks as we could in an area that would leave the subject matter intact."

"That is for the experts to determine."

"And the third chamber?" Cummins asked. "Did you damage another painting digging through to it?"

"No, it was beneath the floor of the second one."

"If you did so little damage to the inscriptions and paintings," Voisey asked, "Why is it the Syrian Minister claims you attempted to destroy them?"

"I don't know," Dani said. "Unless he's trying to discredit our findings."

"I think you've done quite enough yourself to do that," Bielish said.

"What artefacts were found in this tomb?" Roberts asked.

"It wasn't a tomb, and we found nothing except a few pieces of wood and rope, and rubble in the shaft leading to the third chamber."

"No grave goods, ornaments, figurines?" Roberts persisted.

Dani shook her head. "Nothing."

"Then why are you accused of attempting to steal artefacts?"

"I have no idea. There was nothing there to steal, and if there had been, I would have handed those over to the authorities."

"Like you reported the existence of the chambers?" Bielish asked.

"In hindsight that was a mistake, but the Syrian Ministry of National History--in particular, Under-Minister Bashir--found out about the chambers very quickly and took over the site. From then on, we were working under his direct authority."

"When did this happen?" Parker of the Foreign Office asked.

"About June this year. We were about halfway through the second chamber when he arrived and took over--at gunpoint, I might add."

"Given that he thought you were plundering a priceless archaeological site that seems quite reasonable."

"Even after we'd shown ourselves innocent of that charge? Minister Bashir made it quite plain he was there to find the treasure referred to in the text and he was keeping us on to facilitate its discovery."

"That is a serious allegation, Dr Hanser," John Torby said. "Do you have any evidence of that?"

"You can ask any of my team members."

"Who would back you up, no doubt, through misplaced loyalty?"

"Or through a desire for the truth," Dani said. "In fact, three of my students--Allan Bryce, Robert Burrows, and William Morrison--considered the danger real enough to flee the country in order to provide some leverage over Minister Bashir. With them out of his reach, his threats to our safety diminished."

"Those three students are another problem entirely," the man from the Foreign Office said. "They crossed into Israel and Lebanon without papers and were jailed. The government has since secured their release, but they have caused a lot of trouble."

"And the university will be dealing with them appropriately," Dean Voisey assured him.

"Returning to the chambers and the inscription," Cummins said. "Do you have any evidence for its existence?"

Dani stared. "I'm not sure I understand. If it doesn't exist, then what's all this about? Minister Bashir can hardly accuse me of damaging something that doesn't exist."

Bielish sighed. "He says it was a tomb packed with artefacts that you tried to steal. You say it was a series of chambers with the walls covered in hieroglyphs telling the story of a young girl. A photograph of the inscription would immediately tell which claim was true. Funerary inscriptions can hardly be mistaken for anything else."

"Everything was confiscated in Syria--notebooks, photos, translations, tapes of me reading out the account--everything."

"So all we have is your unsubstantiated claim?"

"Yes."

Bielish leaned closer to Cummins and McClelland. "Do we need to hear more?"

"Does anyone else have any more questions for Dr Hanser?" McClelland asked.

"I have a question," Dani said. "If I am allowed one."

"Of course."

"You call my claim unsubstantiated because I have no photographic proof, but isn't Minister Bashir's claim equally unsubstantiated? Where is his proof that these chambers were anything more than I have said? He can't produce any because any photos he has..."

Dani's voice tailed off as the Vice-Chancellor opened a folder in front of him and removed a glossy photograph. He slid it across the table, but said nothing, watching her reaction keenly.

"What's this?" Dani examined the photograph. It was a close-up of serried ranks of hieroglyphs painted on a rock wall.

"Can you read the inscription, Dr Hanser?" Bielish watched her with a predatory gaze.

Dani studied the photograph before hesitantly translating the writing. "It's incomplete, but it says 'who give water to the One who presides over the Silent Place. The water of this pool is destined...'--that's all."

"Do you recognise the passage, Dr Hanser?" Bielish asked. "After all, you say you have made an extensive private study of Egypt and Egyptian writing."

"It's a passage from the Book of Gates."

"And where might one find such a passage, Dr Hanser?"

"On the walls of a tomb or a temple."

24

McClelland reached out to take the photo from Dani but she hung onto it. "Minister Bashir took that photo in the chambers you claim were not a tomb." He cleared his throat and glanced at the stony faces of his fellow academics. "Your claim to expertise in matters Egyptian has led you astray, or you are trying to deliberately mislead us, Dr Hanser. Either way, the university does not look kindly on your actions which have brought Midland University into disrepute and we have no other course open to us but to terminate your..."

"That photo wasn't taken in those chambers."

"Dr Hanser, we..."

"Look at the rock wall in the photo. First of all, it's raw rock, undressed, unpainted. The chambers we found were fully plastered and painted..."

"We only have your word for that."

"Then look at the grain of the rock. The Orontes Valley cuts through coarse sandstone in which the grains are clearly visible--sand grains. This wall is made of something much finer. I think it's limestone...maybe mudstone. If so, this tomb inscription came from somewhere else. Bashir is the one misleading you, not me."

Bielish took the photo and studied it. "It's probably just a lack of definition that prevents us seeing sand grains."

"Show it to a professional geologist then, and get him to compare it with a geological map of the area. I'll accept his findings. If it's sandstone then you can...you can do what you like, but if its limestone or mudstone, then you accept Bashir's lying."

The academics leaned together, whispering as they deliberated whether to condemn Dani immediately, or consult a geologist. Bielish seemed the most vociferous in condemnation, raising her voice angrily and glaring at Dani, but McClelland and Voisey spoke placatingly.

"We will consult a geologist," McClelland said. "Is there anything else you wish to say, Dr Hanser?"

Dani thought for a moment, inclined to leave well enough alone, but then decided her career was on the line and this might be her only opportunity to rescue it. "Just that Minister Bashir has made allegations that impugn my professional standing at this university. I totally reject his allegations and ask you to examine the paltry evidence he has produced and condemn his unsubstantiated claims."

"Except you have admitted you acted in a less than professional manner when you hid the existence of the chambers from the proper authorities," Bielish said. "Your professional standing at this university is in tatters, Dr Hanser."

"I think we can reasonably leave the matter here for now," McClelland said. "Dr Hanser, thank you for attending this meeting and giving your side of events. We will consider all the evidence carefully and notify you of our findings in due course."

Dani stood and thanked the panel for hearing her out, before walking with head high and back straight, the length of the long room. Outside, she took a shuddering breath and stood looking out of the window at the university campus and the city beyond.

"Are you alright, Dr Hanser?" the secretary asked. "Can I get you a glass of water?"

Dani shook her head, smiling wanly. "No...thank you. I'll be fine. I just need some fresh air."

She took the lift down to the ground floor and made her way to the student cafeteria. As the day was cool but sunny, she took her latte to an outdoor table and sat staring at the potted plants while sipping her coffee. A few students recognised her and smiled in greeting, but she did not see them, her mind a thousand miles away in Syria, where her golden scarab sat locked up with all her notes and tapes.

"I've got to get it back," she murmured.

Chapter Three

U nder-Minister Ahmed Bashir flew into Cairo a month after he engineered the expulsion of the British expedition from Syria. He felt enormously pleased with himself, and looked forward to his stay in Egypt with pleasure and anticipation. His secretary and aide, Nazim Manouk, had stayed behind in Damascus, compiling the notes on the Orontes Inscription into some semblance of order, and would be joining him in Cairo in a few days. In the meantime, Bashir had a few things he needed to do, a few people he had to meet, and the fewer who knew about these things and people, the better. Trust was a commodity in short supply in the Arab world and, outside of his immediate family--an aged father and a young brother in debt to him--Bashir trusted nobody.

Nobody met him at the airport, and although Syria and Egypt were both part of the United Arab Republic, his diplomatic passport eased him through arrivals well before any of the other passengers from the Damascus flight. Outside, in the heat and stink of a Cairo noon, he threw his single case into the back of a taxi and had the driver take him to one of the large hotels in the city centre. Bashir did not care which one, letting the taxi driver choose. At the hotel, he paid the fare and let a porter carry his case into the lobby, while he watched the driver accept another fare and pull out into the traffic. Inside the lobby, Bashir reclaimed his case, ignored the puzzled protests of the clerks on the desk and marched outside again. Hailing another taxi, he gave an address on the outskirts of the city, on the Giza Plateau.

The journey took close on an hour, and Bashir sat in the back of the taxi, mopping at the sweat that beaded his brow. The pyramids loomed large and drifted away to the north as the road led past them and along the banks of the Nile. Their route led them through drifts of desert, farmland, and date orchards. Presently, they happened upon a walled estate and then iron gates with guards in military uniform on watch. Bashir identified himself to the sergeant of the guard and the gates creaked open. The taxi rolled up to the front of the huge stone house and a second squad of guards. Bashir paid off the driver and only then did he turn to the young lieutenant in charge.

"I am Minister Ahmed Bashir from Damascus. I have come to see Colonel Sarraj. Please announce me."

"Certainly, Minister. You are expected. Please follow me." The lieutenant gave orders for Bashir's case to be taken inside and led the Minister into the house. The temperature dropped as they crossed the threshold, and the tapestry-hung walls muffled the sharp clatter of their footsteps on the marble floor. The house appeared deserted and deeply shadowed, but the lieutenant guided Bashir through to a central courtyard where trees cast leafy shade, flowers offered up rich perfume, and splashing fountains moistened and cooled the dry air. They walked down a gravel path to the central fountain where a tall man in military uniform threw morsels of food to golden koi carp.

"Colonel Sarraj," the lieutenant said quietly. "Minister Bashir has arrived."

The tall man turned, his deep-set eyes scanning the sweating Syrian Minister in front of him. "Minister Bashir. My house is yours."

Bashir plucked at the collar of his sweat-stained shirt. "Is it always this hot?"

Sarraj smiled and addressed the lieutenant. "Azib, take the Minister's case to the guest room and bring us iced drinks. We will sit out here." The young officer took Bashir's single case and disappeared into the house with it.

Sarraj indicated the marble seat surrounding the koi pond. "You had a pleasant journey, Ahmed?"

Bashir shrugged. "Good enough, I suppose. What arrangements have you made?"

"Arrangements?"

"For finding the tomb."

"Ah. Nothing as yet." Sarraj held up a hand as Bashir opened his mouth to protest. "Wait. Some refreshment first."

Lieutenant Azib emerged from the shadows bearing a silver tray upon which was a glass jug beaded with moisture and two crystal glasses. Ice cubes chinked gently against the glass as he walked. He placed the tray on the marble rim of the pond and withdrew, leaving the two men alone.

Sarraj poured them each a chilled drink and passed one to his guest. "From my own citrons." He sipped from his own crystal glass and watched as Bashir greedily downed the drink.

"That's good," Bashir said. "Thank you, Michel, but what did you mean when you said you'd done nothing? We don't have any time to waste."

"Your letter lacked details, Ahmed. You said you had discovered the whereabouts of an undiscovered tomb, but did not say where. It is a little hard to judge what preparations need to be made when I don't know anything about it. Perhaps you can rectify that lack of detail now."

Bashir looked around the courtyard and scanned the blank windows and shadowed porticoes of the surrounding house. "How secure are we?"

"Nobody can overhear us. I have given instructions that we're not to be disturbed."

"You're sure?"

"My staff are all military and under my direct command. They would not dare disobey me."

Bashir nodded, but still hesitated, fiddling with his crystal glass. "Midland University in England sent a team to carry out an archaeological dig in the Orontes Valley in Syria, last year and this year. I won't bore you with what they hoped to find, but they stumbled upon something far more interesting--a series of chambers carved into the sandstone. The walls of the chambers were covered in hieroglyphs and they purported to be the story of an ancient Egyptian princess. The story told of a treasury and a tomb, apparently as yet undiscovered, somewhere in Egypt."

"Egypt is a large place," Sarraj observed.

"Indeed."

"A rich tomb?"

"Fabulously."

"You must have information on the whereabouts of this tomb."

"Yes."

"Then where is the problem? You go there, dig it up and abscond with the wealth. Why do you need me?"

"If this was Syria, I would do just that. As a Minister, I have considerable power in my own country, but here in Egypt, although our countries are joined politically, I am a visiting politician. As such, I am under scrutiny and need the assistance of a powerful local figure."

"Is that why you clumsily attempted to evade notice by travelling to the Cairo Hotel before coming here?"

Bashir shrugged again. "I thought it best not to be too open."

"It would have been better if you had taken a room there and then called me. I would have had you moved to a secure location without anyone noticing. Do you have reason to believe you're being followed?"

"I cannot be sure."

"Who else knows about this tomb? This treasure?"

"The members of the British expedition. My secretary."

"Members of your ministry? Your assistants?"

"No. I was careful."

"A pity about the British. I daresay England still feels it has a right to interfere in our country. Do you envisage they will be a problem?"

"I think I have removed any danger from that quarter. I confiscated every bit of evidence they had on the existence and location of the tomb, and then made an official complaint about their conduct to the university. I have every reason to believe the leader of the expedition, Dr Danielle Hanser, will lack any credibility."

"Won't an official complaint draw attention to the tomb?"

Bashir chuckled. "I said they had already found the tomb in Syria and plundered it. Nobody will be looking for one in Egypt."

Sarraj glanced at his watch. "I shall look forward to hearing more, but I regret to say I must leave you for a few hours. I'd like to resume our discussion after dinner tonight." The Colonel arose and left Bashir sitting by the fish pond.

Bashir found himself at a loose end for the rest of the afternoon. He searched out his room and took advantage of the ensuite bathroom, showering and then changing into casual attire before exploring the house and grounds. The staff was unobtrusive, but whenever he found himself encroaching on the suite of rooms where his host lived, a neatly attired soldier would politely usher him away. He perused the shelves in the small but evidently well-used library but found nothing that interested him--the books were all historical treatises on the military and political life of Egypt.

The garden was pleasant, but small, and Bashir got the impression that Michel Sarraj was not a man that had much time for relaxation. The inner courtyard with its koi pond, and the library, were the only areas that bore the signs of the Colonel's presence and attention. Bashir returned to the courtyard with a cup of coffee and contemplated his relationship with this soldier.

Colonel Michel Sarraj was something of an unknown quantity, both in Egypt and in Syria. Bashir had known him for a little over twenty years, since a visit to Damascus by the recently graduated second lieutenant just prior to the outbreak of hostilities in the Second World War. In those heady days when right-wing governments were in the ascendancy, they had met at a political rally of the Pan-Arab Movement and become firm friends. Bashir had opted for political power within Syria and Sarraj for military within Egypt, though neither had succeeded to the degree they had hoped for, talked about, and striven to become.

Ten years before, Bashir had given up the dream of rising within the government of Syria and had sold out his ideals for a sinecure within the Ministry of National History. He settled for a slow but sure rise within the Ministry, and the opportunity to feather his nest with baksheesh from a hundred grateful black market entrepreneurs. The Minister knew nothing of Bashir's little schemes, though undoubtedly he had his suspicions, and Bashir was prepared to liberally grease the wheels of selected persons high and low in order to deflect attention from him.

Sarraj had risen rapidly through the Egyptian army by hooking his wagon to that of Gamal Abdel Nasser, and when Nasser had taken power five years before, had been promoted to colonel. That had been the limit of his rise, however, and Sarraj had become disillusioned with the new President of Egypt. Sarraj had incautiously let slip his dissatisfaction with the course of his country's internal and foreign policies in a letter to his friend Ahmed Bashir. Nothing more had been said, but Bashir now knew that Sarraj was at least contemplating the toppling of Nasser. However, for this to take place, Sarraj would need backers, and funding far beyond the means at his disposal. Bashir hoped he might have found a willing partner for his plundering of Egypt's undiscovered archaeological wealth.

Sarraj returned in the early evening and over dinner they talked of inconsequential things, keeping the subject away from the topic that preyed on both their minds. Soldiers served the meal and stood guard, but the Colonel was careful to say nothing while he had an audience. They took coffee in the courtyard, and lit cigars, inhaling the rich, perfumed tobacco smoke and blowing it out in pungent blue clouds toward the starlit heavens.

"What is the worth of this tomb?" Sarraj asked.

"Difficult to say," Bashir replied. "Imagine King Tut's tomb at least."

"That is a meaningless comparison. I have no knowledge of the worth of such archaeological artefacts."

Bashir nodded and sipped his coffee. "Very well. A conservative estimate puts the value of King Tut's tomb at about five million US dollars, though if the individual grave goods could be sold on the black market to collectors, one might double that. The problem is that the release of that quantity of artefacts would alert the authorities that something was amiss. It would have to be done slowly, over a period of years."

"Years are no use to me."

"There is another possibility. The account referred to the presence of a large amount of gold, ivory, precious and semi-precious stones. I estimate the worth of the gold alone as close to three million dollars. Naturally, gold has a ready market, so funds could be made available a lot sooner."

"What do you want of me?" Sarraj asked.

"Protection, logistical support."

"In what way?"

"You are military, you have connections within Egypt. You can provide transport, men, supplies, without being questioned."

"I am only a colonel."

"So was Nasser when he took power."

"True."

"So if you desire to wrest control of Egypt from him, you will..."

"Stop." Sarraj turned in his chair and scanned the shadowed courtyard. Satisfied at last that they were not overheard, he turned back to Bashir. "What do you know of this?"

"Only what you have told me, Michel."

Sarraj frowned. "When?"

"Two years ago. A rather injudicious letter complaining of...a certain person." Bashir saw the expression on the face of his friend and smiled. "I destroyed the letter immediately. Your secret is safe."

Sarraj inclined his head in acknowledgement.

"So naturally," Bashir went on, "you will need funds, and I need support. I think we can help each other."

Sarraj poured them both another cup of coffee and offered a fresh cigar. He lit his own and puffed contentedly for several minutes.

"What do you want from me? Specifically?"

Bashir considered. "Initially, river transport, an all-terrain vehicle, some men, and of course, supplies for a month. When we find what we're looking for, I'll need men to excavate the site, and trucks to transport the contents, and a secure storage site before I can get the artefacts back to Syria."

"What do you offer in return?"

"Thirty percent of the contents."

Sarraj smiled. "I supply everything, and I'm the one taking the risks. Seventy percent."

"Forty."

"Fifty, and I leave all the tomb artefacts for you. I just remove any gold present."

"If it's in the form of gold ingots, then I agree. If the gold is in the form of artefacts, then they are my share."

Sarraj nodded. "You're very sure of the tomb's existence?"

"Not entirely," Bashir conceded, "But I think it likely. I believe there has never been any hint of a tomb of Pharaoh Smenkhkare having been found, and Princess Beketaten is almost unknown historically. If the tomb of either of them had been discovered within historical times, there would be artefacts from them in the museums. The absence of such things argues for the tombs remaining undiscovered." Bashir shrugged and drained his coffee. "Of course, if the tombs were robbed in pharaonic times then all bets are off."

"But you think they still exist?"

"Yes."

"Where? Do you know?"

"Approximately. The inscription on the walls of the chambers described the place of Smenkhkare's treasury and pointed toward his later tomb. The treasury was almost certainly looted to provide for his grave goods, but I believe if we find the one, we will find the other."

"The archaeologist Howard Carter took years to find King Tut's tomb."

"He did not have a description of its location."

"You are that confident of finding it?"

Bashir grinned. "Yes."

*   *   *

Sarraj retired to his study after Bashir went to bed. He worked at his desk for an hour, reading through reports and dealing with business arising from them before sitting back and contemplating his conversation with the Syrian Minister. After a few moments, he pressed a button on his desk. Deep within the villa, a buzzer sounded and sent Lieutenant Azib hurrying toward the study. The young officer slipped inside and saluted. He waited silently for his instructions.

"Dr Danielle Hanser led a British Midland University archaeological expedition into the Orontes Valley in Syria last year. Find out everything you can about her, the expedition, and what they found."

"Do you want me to include the Minister in my enquiries, sir?"

"No. Be discreet. I also want to know where Dr Hanser is now. Find me a reliable man at the university I can use."

"Yes sir. What time frame do I have?"

"The agent and Dr Hanser's whereabouts immediately. The main report in a week."

Chapter Four

T he letter came two weeks later and Dani opened it without thinking as she walked back from the front hall to her kitchen. She scanned the contents and felt her face cool as the blood drained away. The room lurched and she sat down quickly, the legs of the chair scraping over the faded linoleum. Her breath came raggedly and she made a conscious effort to control her despair.

"They didn't believe me," she said wonderingly.

Dani sat and stared at the letter, reading and rereading it until every word, every phrase, was imprinted on her memory. Distantly, she heard the telephone jangle in the hallway, listened to it ring and finally fall silent before starting up again, insistent, refusing to be denied. She got up and went through to pick up the receiver.

"Dani? Are you alright, lass?"

She heard the list of a Welsh voice and smiled, forcing away her incipient depression. "Daffyd."

"Marc's here with me. We just got our letters from the university board. Have you heard anything?"

Dani nodded, her mind turning back to the lines of print that spelled disaster.

"Dani? Are you there? What's wrong?"

She heard a faint mumble of conversation at the other end of the line and collected her thoughts. "Yes. My letter came just now. I've been suspended without pay for six months, position to be reviewed after that."

There was a moment's silence from Daffyd, then, "I'm sorry to hear that, lass, but it wasn't totally unexpected."

Dani could hear conversation at the other end, scraping and clunking noises, and Marc came on the line.

"Bloody hell, Dani, that's over the top. How can they do that?"

The indignation in the young man's voice elicited a smile from Dani. "I take it your letters weren't as drastic?"

"A virtual slap on the wrist. Damn it, Dani, I take it you're going to appeal?"

Dani was noncommittal.

"We're coming over."

"No, don't do that, Marc. I really just want..." The receiver burred in her hand and she sighed and hung up.

Marc lived in a flat with another graduate student across town, while Daffyd rented a room in the College Halls, so either way, Dani knew they would be with her in about half an hour. After a few moments of resentment at their foisting of their well-meant support on her, she relented, realising that she would be glad to see them.

She returned to the kitchen and put on a fresh pot of coffee and boiled a kettle in case anybody preferred tea. A plate of digestive biscuits completed her preparations and she quickly visited the bathroom, splashing cold water in her face. She peered at her image in the mirror and grimaced, dragging a comb through her auburn locks. It would have to do.

The doorbell chimed and she went to let her friends in, embracing them each in turn and leading them through to the sunny kitchen and its pleasant aromas of freshly brewed coffee and flowers. Dani refused to be drawn on the contents of her letter until everyone was seated, with a full cup and biscuits in hand. Then, in answer to Marc's repeated enquiry, she pushed the letter across the table to him. He scanned it quickly, snorted derisively, and passed it on to Daffyd.

"They suspended you without pay and with loss of seniority," Marc said. "How the hell can they do that? We have right on our side."

"When did that ever matter, boyo?" Daffyd asked. He took out his tin of tobacco, hesitated, and put it away again. "The word of a Syrian Minister obviously carries some weight."

"Bloody McClelland...and Bielish. It's all departmental politics, you know. You're going to appeal, aren't you?"

"I'm not sure there's much point," Dani said, sipping her tea. "It's only for six months. I can survive that."

"Unfortunately, that's the least of it," Daffyd said quietly. "You'll be up for review, possibly reinstated, but your Head of Department will look for someone else to lead the next field expedition. Graduates will be encouraged to look elsewhere for supervision. If you're happy just to lecture to undergraduates, that's fine, but if you want decent research opportunities in the future, you need to fight it."

"I'm not sure I can--fight it, I mean. I can protest the decision, of course, but I've got no evidence, nothing to counteract Bashir's lies."

"I'll bet you could recite whole passages of the account," Marc said. "That must count for something. Where else would you have come across the story of Scarab?"

"They'd just say I made the whole thing up. Unless someone discovers the tomb in Egypt and the location matches the description I'd given them, there's nothing."

"Perhaps someone will discover it."

"Who? The only person likely to is Bashir, and if he does he'll just plunder it and keep quiet."

"So what are you going to do, if not fight the decision?" Daffyd asked.

Dani shrugged and looked out the window.

"Dani?"

"Enough of me. What did your letters say?"

"An official reprimand," Daffyd said. "I'm to refrain from any public statement of events, and I'm not to discuss it in any way that might reflect badly on the university. Other than that, I can continue lecturing and conducting research as before."

"And mine was even more lenient," Marc added. "I just can't talk about what happened. You bore the whole burden of blame."

"Well, I was expedition leader."

"Yes, but we all agreed on the cover up. We're all to blame."

"What about the others?" Dani asked. "Have the students suffered in any way?"

"They're undergrads. They'll be assigned new supervisors and given a talking to, but no blame will be laid at their door, as long as they say nothing."

"Good. I'd hate it if their careers suffered because of my mistake."

"It was down to all of us, Dani," Daffyd said. "Don't be a martyr to this."

"I'm not, but you know the truth of it. I found the golden scarab and used it to find the chambers. It was my determination to find out what happened that influenced the rest of you."

"We didn't need much persuading, lass," Daffyd said with a smile. "We all wanted to know what happened."

"A pity Bashir took the golden scarab," Marc mused. "That object alone would convince anyone there was something to our story."

Daffyd saw the expression on Dani's face. "You alright, lass?"

"I'll survive."

"Bashir won't do anything to the golden scarab," Marc said. "It's too valuable an artefact. He might keep it, but he won't destroy it."

"He doesn't know what it is. To him it's just a curio, a simple piece of sandstone. He only confiscated it because he didn't know why I had it. When he tires of it, he's likely just to throw it away."

"Would that be the worst thing in the world?" Daffyd asked. "It came to you once. At the risk of sounding dreadfully sentimental and unscientific, if you're meant to have it, it'll find its way back to you."

"Or it may be gone forever. I don't think I could bear that."

The three sat in silence around the kitchen table, the rectangle of sunshine creeping across the floor and walls as they drank their coffee and tea. Daffyd twice took out his tobacco and put it back in his pocket unopened. At last, Marc pushed back his chair and stretched, eyeing Dani.

"I don't mean to sound insensitive, but the golden scarab has gone. If you find it again, that's fine, but if not you have to ask yourself what you're going to do. You can't prove anything against Bashir, so you have to just put up with what the university has thrown at you. You're suspended for six months. Alright, you say you can survive that but what then? What will you do after the six months--providing they reinstate you? Continue lecturing at Midland, or look for another position?"

"It's a bit early for major decisions," Daffyd said. "You need to get used to the idea first. Why don't you take a holiday, get away for a few weeks?"

Dani nodded. "You might be right. There's nothing I can do around here."

"Attagirl. Have you got family you can visit? Close friends?"

"No. I'm going to Egypt."

"What? Jesus, lass, I don't think that's a good idea."

"Why not? Everything that interests me is in Egypt. If I can get down there before Bashir gets his act together, I might be able to get to the tomb before him."

"Why? To prove you were right?"

"To protect the tomb. To protect Scarab."

"Do you know where it is?" Marc asked.

Dani hesitated. "You know the descriptions as well as I do."

"Can you remember enough detail?"

"I think so. I was the one immersed in the account, remember? I translated every word of it."

Daffyd nodded. "I remember, and I still haven't the faintest idea how you did it. I've seen trained Egyptologists, professors who've spent lifetimes with old inscriptions and manuscripts have trouble with hieroglyphs. Hieratic script I could understand, but hieroglyphs? You just read it as if it was the pages of a novel. How the hell did you do it, lass?"

"I told you. I studied and..." Dani shrugged, "...my family comes from there."

Daffyd muttered something in Welsh under his breath. "Sorry, Dani, but I can't accept that. You'd have to be brought up with the language to handle it that well. It's just not possible otherwise."

"Jesus, Daffy," Marc interjected. "You were there. You saw her perform and we know she wasn't born to it. She's just damn good at what she does. Stop giving her a hard time."

Daffyd grimaced and took out his tin of tobacco once more. This time he opened it and added the strong, rich odour of cured tobacco mingle with the coffee and floral scents. He stirred the dark shavings with his forefinger for a minute, before shaking his head, putting the lid back on and slipping the tin back into his jacket pocket. "You're right--I apologise. So, Dani, you think you can remember enough of the tomb description to find it?"

"I think so--yes."

"They're pretty vague, and Egypt's a damned large and mostly inhospitable place," Daffyd said. "Even if we'd ended up on a fully-funded expedition like we'd hoped, it was always going to be a long shot. The descriptions are three thousand years old, for God's sake."

"The golden scarab," Dani said. "I could have found it with that."

"But you don't have it," Marc objected. "Bashir does."

"Then I'll just have to get it back."

"How? Are you just going to march up to him and demand it? He'll either laugh at you or have you locked up."

Dani shrugged. "I'll think of something."

"Lass, think of something else to do for six months. You haven't got a hope in Hades."

"You think I should do nothing?" Dani demanded. "Just give up and let Bashir win?"

Daffyd frowned and pulled out his tobacco tin again. He opened it again and stirred the fragrant flakes with a forefinger.

"If you're going to roll yourself a smoke, I'm opening a window."

"Eh? No, I'll refrain, but Dani, nobody's asking you to give up on this. I think you should protest the university's decision at the very least. We'll help you with that, but...well, haring off to Egypt? I really don't think that's a good idea."

"What about you, Marc? Do you think I'm mad too?"

"No, no, of course not, but...er, you've got to admit it's a bit sudden. You just need to think about it a bit more. Then Daffyd and I will help you any way we can."

Dani looked from Marc to Daffyd, reading concern in the faces of her friends. She sighed and swirled her cup, watching patterns form in the tealeaf detritus in the dregs. "You're probably right."

"No more hare-brained schemes?" Marc asked.

"No more dashing off to Egypt?" Daffyd asked.

Dani smiled. "Nothing precipitate, I promise."

"You'll take a holiday? Relax for a while?"

"I'll think about it."

Daffyd and Marc left soon after, having extracted a vague promise from Dani that they would meet up again in a few days to have a drink and talk about the future. Dani closed the door on her friends and returned to the kitchen where she tidied up, before changing into comfortable clothes and heading into town. She had in mind a certain course of action, and though Chesterfield would not provide the means, it would at least give her the building blocks. Whatever the outcome, she did not want to be too open about her plans just yet. Her trip to town involved a visit to her bank and to the only travel agency, where she made enquiries about a number of destinations. Returning to her flat, she wrote letters and posted them off.

Then all she could do was wait. The British Postal Service was efficient, but she still had to wait on slower moving foreign embassies. In the meantime, she frequented the university library and researched places and events that related to her intended destination. Daffyd called, but she put him off, pleading tiredness. Marc phoned, and she avoided him too, not wanting to reveal her plans until she was completely ready. When Daffyd called again, more insistently, she could only put him off by proposing a date to get together for that promised drink. Three weeks passed, and Dani found one excuse after another not to talk to her friends. Then the postman delivered the letter she was waiting for. She ripped it open in the hallway, dropping the envelope as she eagerly scanned the single page inside. A frown creased her forehead and she read it again, before crumpling the letter and dropping it beside the torn envelope.

Dani was home when both Daffyd and Marc came calling, determined to find out why she was avoiding them. She ignored their knocking and telephone calls for nearly an hour, even Marc shouting through the letterbox, until eventually she gave in and opened the door.

"What the hell's up?" Marc demanded. "Didn't you hear us?"

"It's really not a good time," Dani said.

Daffyd looked at her carefully, noting her unbrushed hair, her crumpled clothing, and bags under her eyes. "What's wrong, lass?" he asked gently.

Dani shook her head. "I'm just tired. I haven't been sleeping well, and I need to... Can you come back later?"

"We could, but I think it would be better if you told us what's wrong now."

Dani turned and stumbled back to the kitchen. The two men followed, and stared at a very different room from the one they had sat around in a month before, drinking tea and coffee and enjoying conversation. The air was stale, dirty dishes were piled up in the sink, and the flowers in the vase on the table were dry and dead. Marc whistled with amazement and started to run water into the sink, opening the cupboard under the sink to take out dish detergent and a scrubbing brush.

"Leave those," Dani snapped. "I didn't let you in to wash up."

"So why did you let us in?" Daffyd asked. "I got the distinct impression at the front door that you didn't want to see us."

"You didn't pay any attention to my wishes then, did you?"

"Dani, we're your friends. If you're in trouble, we want to help."

"You can't help."

"Try us."

Dani collapsed into a chair and ran her fingers through her bedraggled hair. "Look, I appreciate the thought, but just leave me alone, will you? I really just need to get through this on my own."

"When you've told us what's wrong."

"Damn you," Dani whispered.

"Very likely," Daffyd said with a smile. "Now come on, this isn't the Dani we know and admire. Our Dani would let her friends help her, or at least tell them why they couldn't."

Dani did not say anything.

"It's to do with the university decision, isn't it?" Marc asked. "Well, we've already told you we'll help with the appeal."

"I've asked around, lass," Daffyd said. "There's damn-all actual evidence been produced against you. It's all hearsay from Bashir, and the only reason McClelland and Bielish have bought into it is because of interdepartmental politics. We can raise enough doubt to get your suspension rescinded, I'm sure."

"It doesn't matter."

"Of course it does," Marc said. "You can't let the buggers get away with it."

"Hang on, Marc," Daffyd said. "Why doesn't it matter, Dani?"

Dani got up and walked over to the sideboard. She opened a drawer and took out a small folder which she dropped on the table in front of Daffyd.

"That's why not."

Daffyd opened the folder to reveal an airline ticket to Cairo. "You're going to Egypt after all?"

"No. I was refused a visa. Bashir pulled strings and has prevented me from finding Scarab."

Marc picked up the ticket and examined it. "So what now?" he asked. "You're going to give up?"

"What the hell else can I do?" Dani demanded. "If I try and enter Egypt, I'll be arrested and deported. I can't get to Egypt, I can't recover my golden scarab, and I can't prevent Bashir desecrating Scarab's tomb. My whole purpose in life has been shot away."

"Steady on, lass. It's a bit over the top to say that's your whole life purpose."

"No it isn't. Ever since we found the chambers, I've known..." Dani's voice trailed away and she slumped down in a chair again.

"Known what?" Marc asked.

"It sounds stupid."

"Tell us anyway."

"It's as if...no, more than that...I was meant to find the chamber. The golden scarab came to me, just like it came to Scarab..." Dani smiled faintly. "Delusions of grandeur now. Are you going to have me committed?"

"Good to see you smile, lass. It's an interesting concept, though...not having delusions--I don't believe that for one minute--but the golden scarab coming to you."

"Come on, Dr Daffy, you don't believe that, do you?" Marc asked. "I mean, we all know Dani's a whiz at translation and has insights, but really, it's just a coincidence she found an artefact that resembled the one Scarab had."

Daffyd shot Marc a sour look. "Look at the facts. There are three lines of argument I can see. First, Scarab found a carved golden scarab in the desert..."

"Scarab ornaments are pretty common in ancient Egypt."

"Not made of solid gold. It had an Aten disc carved on its underside, where there's usually a prayer or a person's name. That's unusual by itself because at the time of the Amarnan kings the Aten heresy was in direct conflict with the other gods--including Khepri, who was represented by the scarab. Then look at the golden scarab that Dani found. Identical description. Is that just coincidence?"

Marc shrugged. "Okay, I'll give you that one. What else?"

"Second point. In the account, not everyone could see the golden scarab for what it was. Remember how the Khabiru elder...what was his name?"

"Jeheshua," Dani said.

"That's right, Jeheshua. He only saw a rock until Atum lifted the scales from his eyes. The Amorites too--they saw nothing but a rock."

"That's poetic licence..."

"What about Dani's golden scarab? You've seen it; I've seen it, and the other expedition members saw it--but what about Bashir? He handled it and dismissed it as worthless--as nothing more than a plain rock. Another coincidence?"

"You said there were three lines of argument."

"Scarab used it to find things, to produce water, to protect herself, to raise the dead even--and don't call that more poetic licence, Marc. You've seen Dani use it to find the chambers. Those two golden scarabs are more than similar, more than identical even--they are one and the same. And while I think of it, there's a fourth reason. Dani's descended from Scarab."

Dani grimaced. "That's just a family story. We have no proof."

"And with a hundred or more generations between them, there's no way you could prove it," Marc added.

"Dani's a dead ringer for Scarab. We all remarked on her similarity to the pictures in the chambers. And your grandmother was Egyptian, Dani," Daffyd added. "Your mother was her only daughter, and you're your mother's only daughter. The goddess Isis promised Scarab an unbroken line of daughters."

"That's still only two generations--out of a hundred or so. Hardly conclusive."

"No, you're right," Daffyd admitted. "Still, taken with the other arguments, it makes you think."

"I'm not going to say what it makes me think," Marc muttered.

"All right, so you see why I'm shattered that the golden scarab is lost to me," Dani said. "I waited thirty years to find something that meant so much to me, and then it's snatched away. I can't even go and look for it."

"Why not?" Daffyd asked.

"Eh? You know why not," Marc said. "Dani had her visa refused. She can't go to Egypt."

"There are other ways of going somewhere that don't involve walking in the front door."

"What do you mean?" Dani asked.

"A flight into Cairo is not the only way into Egypt." Daffyd said patiently and then smiled at his friends' blank expressions. "Egypt has hundreds, maybe thousands, of miles of border with countries like Israel, Sudan and Libya. If you picked the right time and place, you could just stroll across the border."

"Jesus, Dr Daffy, have you lost your mind?" Marc asked.

"I wish you wouldn't call me that. And no, I haven't lost my mind. It's entirely possible. I've done it myself in Kenya. I was there a few years ago when the Mau-Mau uprising took place. I crossed the border on foot into the Tanganyika Territory. Egypt shouldn't be much more difficult if we plan it carefully."

"We?" Dani asked.

Daffyd smiled. "Well, you don't think I'd let you go by yourself, do you?"

"I haven't even said I'm going," Dani said.

"You will, and when you do, I'm going with you."

"Shit, you're not leaving me behind," Marc said. "I can't let you two old fogeys wander off on your own. God knows what trouble you'll get into."

"Look, I haven't agreed to anything, and besides, I'm the one that has nothing to lose by an illegal entry into Egypt. If you two go, there could be all sorts of repercussions. You could lose your jobs or worse."

Marc shrugged, but Daffyd nodded thoughtfully. "You're right, and if we go it will be with our eyes open. You need to go and look for your golden scarab and Scarab's tomb, and I'm interested in that too, so I'm coming."

Dani sighed and then smiled. "I can't say I won't be glad of your presence--both of you."

"Have you thought about which border we're going to cross?" Marc asked. "Across the Negev I suppose."

"Too public. With Israel and Egypt at each other's throats, that border will be watched much too closely. Libya's better."

"What about Sudan?" Dani asked. "Large numbers of tribesmen wander across the borders down there."

"Not many Europeans though. We'd stand out. Besides, there are some violent folk down that way. No, Libya's the way in."

"There's an awful lot of desert," Marc said.

"I never said it would be easy, and obviously there's a lot we need to work out, but I think we could do that better on the spot. We should head down to Tripoli."

"Just like that?"

"Why not? The only other course is to do nothing."

Chapter Five

Dani was on suspension and had no duties at the university, but Daffyd and Marc needed to make arrangements if they were to take time off. Marc had recently completed his PhD and was looking around for post-doctoral research, so taking a break inconvenienced a few undergraduate students that he tutored, but he felt he could live with that. He had a few other personal details to take care of, but he dealt with these quickly. Daffyd had lectures to give and two postgraduate students to supervise, but neither student was in a critical passage and his lectures could be covered by other staff members. He pleaded the stress of his recent adventures to his Head of Department, and was granted leave.

"We can manage, Daffyd," said the HOD. "It's important you get yourself back on an even keel. Any thoughts about what you'll do?"

"I thought about a holiday," Daffyd replied. "South of Europe maybe."

"Well, enjoy yourself. We'll see you back here in what? Four weeks?"

"Better make it six--after the mid-term break."

Dani had cancelled her ticket to Cairo, and the three of them now booked passage on a flight that took them to Rome. They packed suitcases, as if for a holiday, and took the train down to London, flying out of Heathrow. In Rome, they cleared Customs and immediately took themselves to the smaller airline counters, looking for passage over the Mediterranean to North Africa. They found a flight to Tripoli leaving in a few hours, and by the next day, stepped out into the heat of the Libyan capital.

"You do realise we could have flown here directly from Heathrow, don't you?" Marc asked.

"Very true, boyo, but you never know who might be interested in where we're off to," Daffyd replied. "I thought a cursory false trail couldn't hurt."

"Then it's a pity we couldn't see a bit of Rome first. I've never been there."

"You can go later, when all this is over," Dani said. "Where to now, Daffyd?"

"Search me," the Welshman said affably. "I've never been here before."

"Jesus," Marc muttered.

"However, Tripoli is in the northwest, and we need the Egyptian border in the east, so perhaps we should make our way to Benghazi for starters."

"Back into the airport then?"

"Unfortunately, our funds are not going to run to air travel everywhere. We can probably get a bus to Benghazi if you don't mind mixing with the locals."

"We're all going to get murdered in our beds," Marc muttered.

"Nonsense," Daffyd said. "King Idris runs a tight ship and since they discovered oil here last year, American and British firms have been flocking into the country. Westerners are generally liked, and I'm sure the public services are run efficiently."

Neither Marc nor Daffyd was right. They were not murdered in their beds and in fact the Libyan people generally ignored them, but the bus service between Tripoli and Benghazi left a lot to be desired. The bus they found themselves on was old and in need of repair, as was the road between the two cities. They lurched and groaned over pot-holed roads, gusts of dust-laden heated air turning the insides of the bus into a gritty oven. The motion of the vehicle induced nausea, and the stink of unwashed bodies and sundry farmyard animals on board made them seriously reconsider what they were doing.

Across the narrow aisle sat an old woman in long dress and shawl with a wicker cage stuffed with squawking chickens, and two rows behind was a man with a goat. The animal bleated continually and chewed anything within reach, including the fabric of the seats. A squealing pig or two occupied the rear of the bus and from the stench that drifted down to them; it became obvious the porcine animals had not been able to control their bowels.

"Dear God," Marc protested. "Isn't there some other way we can get there?"

"Open the windows wider," Dani advised.

Marc did so, but dust billowed into the bus in choking clouds and he was forced to close them again. He drew a cloth over his face and closed his eyes, trying to shut out the stink and the dust. Daffyd grinned and pulled out his tobacco tin, rolling a fat cigarette and lighting up. Presently, clouds of strongly-scented blue smoke filled the bus and competed with the stenches of Libya. The Welshman leaned back in his seat and puffed happily, while Dani rolled her eyes and edged away from him.

The trip to Benghazi took three days. The bus stopped at towns overnight, the parlous condition of the vehicle rendering night travel extremely perilous. They were put up in small, dirty hotels and suffered from a lack of water for washing and hard, uncomfortable beds. At least the food was good, if somewhat foreign to their palates. The main course was often the traditional heavy bazin dough in a tasty sauce of chicken, tomato, potato, chili and fenugreek. A small piece of dough would be ripped off the central mound and dipped into the surrounding moat of sauce. Other meals were couscous with vegetables and a variety of meats--goat, lamb, chicken or fish. The dish was served in a large bowl without utensils and groups of passengers sat around and dipped the fingers of their right hands in, shaping a ball of food and popping it into their mouths.

On the first night, Marc was revolted to see the pig herder's dirty fingers probing the bowl in front of him and stopped eating, looking sick, but Dani nudged him.

"Get used to it," she said. "Otherwise you'll go hungry."

Marc did go hungry that night, though he ate some dates and swallowed several cups of sweet red tea. Thereafter, he tried to pick his fellow dining companions and managed to control his rebellious stomach enough to satisfy his hunger.

"Why the hell can't they use individual plates and forks like civilised people?" he complained.

"They are civilised," Daffyd replied. "They just have different customs. It's likely to get a lot worse, so make an effort, there's a good chap."

Dani had no problem with the eating arrangements, and practiced her Arabic by getting into conversations with the other women and quizzing them about the ingredients. Soon, she was chatting away and laughing, with her translating some of the remarks for Marc's benefit. Daffyd understood enough of the local dialects to be able to follow the gist of the conversation, so he said little and applied himself to the tasty food.

On the third day they rolled into the western Libyan city. Benghazi reflected its recent Italian colonialist past, and also the long-lasting effects of the Second World War, with many damaged buildings and vacant lots, though rebuilding was in progress as oil wealth started to flood into the country. The streets were often tree-lined and the stone buildings rose three or more floors with carved facades. Awnings shaded the footpaths as shops and restaurants littered the business area, the streets bustling with activity as the economy of the country roared into action.

Dani, Daffyd and Marc stepped off the bus in the central city, glad to escape from the smells and dirt, and looking forward to re-entering a modern city where they could get cleaned up and take stock of their situation. Marc brushed his jacket down, releasing puffs of red dust and examined the soles of his shoes distastefully, scraping the edges on the footpath to rid them of ingrained pig dung.

"Bloody hell," he growled. "It's hard to know what to do first--a nice hot bath, a decent night's kip, a good meal, or an efficient laundry service. Where's the hotel?"

Dani shrugged, not looking at all discomforted by her dishevelled appearance. "Nothing's booked, so we'd better look for one."

"A fairly cheap one," Daffyd added. "Our finances won't last if we're extravagant."

They picked up their suitcases and set off into the teeming streets of the city, looking for accommodation. After a few hundred metres of lugging their baggage through the crowds and being importuned by seemingly every beggar in the city, they decided to ask the way, and were quickly directed into a side street where they found a dilapidated hotel whose better days, judging by the décor, had been pre-war. The clerk behind the desk looked surprised at their sudden appearance in the lobby, but recovered quickly, donning an ingratiating smile and addressing them in a mixture of Italian and Arabic. Dani answered and entered into a spirited discussion of room rates and services available. After several minutes, she nodded and put five pounds on the desk. The money disappeared into the clerk's pocket and two large brass keys clattered onto the polished surface.

"Two rooms," Dani said. "I'm in one, you two in the other. We share a bathroom."

"For five pounds a night?" Marc asked. "Hell, in this place we should be getting a suite for that price."

"For the week."

The rooms were clean if somewhat Spartan. Two single beds occupied each room, with a nightstand between them and a wardrobe. Curtains hid dusty windows looking out on the street and an iron fire escape outside the windows descended two floors to the ground. A door led to an old-fashioned bathroom with a claw-footed bathtub, basin with a stained mirror, and a toilet. Daffyd leaned over the tub and turned the taps. The plumbing gurgled and groaned, spitting out rusty water that cleared after a few seconds, steam arising from the hot water pouring out. He turned them off and wiped his hand on his trousers.

"Not too bad. Who's first up for a bath?"

Marc opened his mouth and then shrugged. "Ladies first, I suppose."

"Go on, I don't mind," Dani said with a smile. "You need to clean up more than the rest of us."

"Ouch," Daffyd murmured. "You're next then, Dani."

Two hours later, all three of them were washed and had changed into fresh clothes. They arranged for their laundry to be taken care of and set out to find a decent restaurant. In view of Marc's disenchantment with local Libyan cuisine, they opted for a tiny Italian eatery. They sat at a small table with a checked tablecloth in a courtyard at the back, under the shade of a spreading tamarind tree. Ripe pods littered the paved courtyard, yielding a sweet-sour smell when stepped on. They ordered pasta and salad, and even found that the proprietor served wine.

"Libya is Muslim," the waiter explained in passable English, "But the police turn a blind eye if it is served out of sight of the public."

"What if somebody comes in for a meal?" Daffyd asked.

"Few people do, except expatriates."

They tucked into their meal, and after ten minutes of dedicated eating and drinking, Marc threw down his fork and stifled a contented belch.

"Now that's what I call a decent meal. Individual plates, edible food, utensils, a halfway decent wine and..." he lifted his wineglass and examined it critically, "...passably clean glassware. Why can't the Libyans eat like this?"

"You need to get out more, boyo," Daffyd said mildly.

"And you need to adapt," Dani added. "There won't be many more meals like this once we leave Benghazi."

"Speaking of which..." Daffyd speared the last cherry tomato in his salad and popped it into his mouth. "Where do we go next?"

Dani topped up her glass with red wine and then looked around to make sure they were not being overheard. "I'm open to suggestions, never having crossed international borders illegally. The Egyptian border is about three hundred miles east of here, near a place called El Salloum, but I rather think that'll be guarded."

"You think they'll have our names down on some list of *persona non grata* even in an out of the way place like that?" Marc asked. He poured himself another glass of wine and drained it in two gulps.

"Perhaps, perhaps not," Daffyd said. "But we can't risk it. I took a look at a map before we came out here and there's a little village called Al Jaghbub deep in the Libyan Desert. It's right on the border and the Egyptian town of Siwa Oasis is only a hundred or so miles away."

"There's a road to Siwa?"

"No. We'd have to cross the desert."

"How the hell are we going to do that?" Marc asked. "I'll tell you right now I'm not walking that distance."

"I don't see you coming up with any suggestions," Daffyd retorted. He pulled out his tobacco tin and started to roll himself a cigarette.

"Easy guys," Dani murmured. "We're all in this together, so let's see if we can work something out calmly and rationally. Could we hire a jeep from Al Jaghbub...or even Benghazi for that matter?"

"Possibly," Daffyd said. He lit up and blew a cloud of strongly scented smoke into the clear night sky. "I'll look into it tomorrow. Another possibility might be hiring camels..."

"Lawrence of Arabia, forsooth," Marc laughed. "Do you know how to ride one?"

"All right, perhaps not, but we're just exploring possibilities at the moment. It really boils down to walking, riding camels or vehicular transport. I think a jeep might be our best bet."

The next morning, Daffyd set off to explore the car rental firms in Benghazi. Marc insisted on accompanying him.

"Just in case you decide to hire a herd of camels or donkeys."

There were vehicles to hire, but the influx of oil company personnel had bumped the prices up and most firms who had vehicles capable of handling the dirt roads and rough country were reluctant to hire them out.

"I am sorry, sirs," said the clerk in the fifth car hire firm. "If you are not used to driving on country roads we cannot let you have a vehicle. The risks are too great, unless you are willing to pay a much higher rental."

"How much higher?"

The clerk told them. "Perhaps if you could find an experienced driver?"

"Where would we find one of those?"

The clerk shrugged. "You could ask around."

Outside on the street, Daffyd cursed fluently in Welsh. "It's starting to look like a camel might be the only answer."

"Can you drive a camel?" Marc asked with a grin.

"No, but I hear you get many miles to the gallon with them," Daffyd replied.

They stopped off in a coffee shop to consider their next move. The café was crowded with Libyans, but they squeezed behind a small table in one corner and put their order in for two coffees and some sweet sticky date cakes. While they waited, they looked around casually at the other customers.

"Why the hell did we come in here?" Marc muttered. "This lot looks as though they'd be happy to murder us for the price of a coffee."

"An interesting mix of people," Daffyd said. "Mostly what I'd call Coastal Arabs, but there are a few Berbers and even a couple of Sub-Saharans."

"And does any of this interesting mix of cut-throats and murderers actually help us find a vehicle or a driver?"

"I suppose we could ask."

"And let them know we're rich foreigners itching to be robbed and murdered? I think not."

"They can see we're foreigners already, and by their definition, rich, so what have we got to lose?"

Marc gave Daffyd a sour look but said nothing. When the waiter pushed through the crowd to their table with the coffee cups and confectionery, Daffyd decided to risk it.

"Excuse me. My friend and I are looking for a driver. Do you know of someone?"

"There are taxis outside."

"We don't want a taxi. We want to hire a car to go into the desert, but we must find a driver also."

The waited shrugged. "Who knows?" He placed the cups and dish on the table and retreated back into the crowd.

"That did a fat lot of good," Marc commented.

"Drink your coffee," Daffyd replied. "Then we'll try somewhere else." He sipped the strong black brew appreciatively and nibbled on a date cake. "These are actually very good. Try one."

Marc did, and ended up finishing them and dabbing at the crumbs with his forefinger.

Daffyd drained his coffee and pushed his chair back. "I was just thinking that maybe we should ask a taxi driver."

"We can't afford a taxi to the deep desert."

"No, but they're professional drivers. They may know of someone."

They got to their feet and started out of the café. The waiter called out and shuffled across to them holding out a piece of paper.

"Take," he said. "My brother's wife's cousin. He might drive you."

Daffyd looked at the Arabic scrawl on the piece of paper. "Thank you, but I cannot read Arabic."

The waiter smiled. "Is address. You must show to taxi driver. His name is Muammar. Very good driver. You see." He disappeared back into the throng of customers.

There was a taxi stand just down the road, so Daffyd and Marc approached the single car at the rank and showed the driver the piece of paper.

"You know address? You can take us? How much?"

The driver studied the scrawl and named his price. Daffyd reached out to take the piece of paper and the driver held it out of reach, naming a lower price. Daffyd grinned and halved it. The taxi driver threw up his hands in mock horror and countered. They eventually settled on a sum that could be paid for with the loose change in Daffyd's pocket and the two men piled into the back of the car.

"Why don't they just charge a reasonable amount to start with?" Marc grumbled. "Then we wouldn't have to waste time haggling."

"Ah, but that's half the fun for the locals," Daffyd said. "If you don't haggle they'll rob you blind."

"So you prefer to rob him? He's only getting a pittance."

"I estimate he's still getting two or three times the normal fare."

The taxi turned off into a side street and pulled up at a faded stucco house with a cast-iron grill gate.

"There," said the driver, handing the piece of paper to Daffyd. He accepted the fare and grinned when Marc pressed another couple of coins into his palm. "Blessings, effendi. You want me to wait?"

Daffyd declined the offer, and after the taxi roared off, crossed to the gate, reaching through the bars and pulling on a frayed rope. A bell clanged above them and after a few moments an old man appeared in the shadows, yawning and scratching himself.

The man stared at the two foreigners and frowned. He said something in an Arabic dialect, and then in Italian.

Daffyd held up the piece of paper. "Muammar?"

The man peered at the scrawl and then nodded, turning away and disappearing into the gloom. Daffyd and Marc waited, the heat of the day raising a sweat and dampening their shirts. At last, a young man of no more than twenty years appeared. He smiled at the foreigners and spoke in Italian first, and when there was no response, in English.

"I am Muammar al-Hadi. You have a note with my name on it. May I see it, please?" the young man read the note and passed it back. "My uncle says you need to go into the desert and need a driver." He tapped himself on the chest. "I am a superlative driver."

"Uncle?" Marc queried. "The waiter implied a more tenuous relationship."

"My cousin's husband's brother. In my culture, all older relatives are uncles."

"Perhaps we could go somewhere for a cup of coffee and talk business," Daffyd suggested.

"My apologies. I have been most remiss." Muammar opened the gate and stood to one side. "Please enter my humble home and refresh yourselves." He led them through a shadowed alcove into a shady courtyard and sat them down at an old wooden table. Clapping his hands, he told the old man who had answered the bell to fetch some coffee. They waited in silence until the coffee appeared. Muammar poured the black beverage himself and passed a cup to each of his guests before serving himself.

"Now, may I have the honour of knowing your names?"

"Of course. I am Dr Daffyd Rhys-Williams and this is Dr Marc Andrews."

"Medical doctors?"

"Scientists."

"And how may I be of service, Dr Williams, Dr Andrews? You require a driver?"

"Yes. We have to go into the deep desert but the hire companies say we must have an experienced driver."

"I am very experienced," Muammar said. "It is just the two of you going? There is much equipment to take? I ask because I know oil company people have much equipment."

"We are not oil people, but scientists who...who look at ancient peoples. There is a third person, Dr Dani Hanser, and just a suitcase each. No equipment."

"Ancient peoples? Well, that is not my business. Where do you want to go?"

"Al Jaghbub."

Muammar frowned. "You have a permit?"

"Do we need one?"

"It is a military district. There have been reports of bandits. Unless you have a permit, the army will not let you in."

"Can we get a permit?"

"There is much paperwork involved."

"Damn," Marc said. "There goes our plan."

"Unfortunately, it seems we will not need your services after all," Daffyd said. "Thank you for your hospitality, Muammar. We must seek another solution."

"May I ask where these ancient peoples you seek are located? Perhaps there is another way there."

Daffyd hesitated and looked at Marc, raising his eyebrows enquiringly. Marc shrugged and looked away.

"We need to cross the desert border into Egypt."

Muammar examined the two foreigners carefully before speaking. "You are smuggling something into Egypt or out of it? As I said before, your business is not my business, but I must weigh the risks. You understand? I have no wish to cause offence, but the forces of King Idris impose severe penalties on smugglers of drugs or artefacts."

"Nothing in or out," Daffyd said. "Only ourselves."

"The nearest Egyptian town to Al Jaghbub is Siwa. You wish to go there specifically, or just into Egypt?"

"Anywhere in Egypt."

Muammar smiled. "Then there is no problem. You will hire a jeep and pay for petrol, and I will drive you to Al Jawf in the south. All I ask is food and a tent at night, for I desire to visit my mother's people in that place. We will have a great adventure, no?"

Chapter Six

The telephone connection crackled and faded, forcing the man to shout. Luckily, there was no one likely to overhear as the man had placed the call from a call box outside a pub in the countryside near Chesterfield.

"Sarraj."

"Colonel, it is Ali Hafiz. I am calling from Ches..."

"I know where you are. Name no names. What do you have to report?"

"The woman is not here."

"Where is she?"

"Nobody knows. The university suspended her and she booked a flight to Cairo, but then cancelled it."

Sarraj considered this information for a minute. "She will not be allowed to enter Egypt. What of the others in the Syrian expedition?"

"The older man and his assistant have also disappeared. It may be related."

"Find out. What about the junior members."

"Still at their studies."

"See whether they know anything. I need to know where the woman has gone."

Ali Hafiz hung up the receiver and stood in the wooden and glass phone box looking out at an overcast English day. He hated the cold, damp weather and looked forward to the end of his assignment in that barbarous country. However, he knew that he would have to find out where the woman had gone. Colonel Sarraj could be utterly ruthless when it came to failure to carry out his will.

* * *

"Where?"

"Al Jawf. It's a small settlement in the south of Libya," Daffyd said. "Muammar's mother's people come from there so he'll drive us and introduce us to his family."

"I'm not sure it was a good idea to tell a perfect stranger we plan to cross into Egypt illegally," Dani said. "What if he goes to the police?"

"What if he does? We're in Libya legally and it would be his word against ours. We could just say he misunderstood us."

Dani still had misgivings and voiced them, but in the absence of a reasonable alternative, she gave in. The next day, they went to the car hire firm and filled out forms and paid for the use of an ancient American jeep left over from the war. Muammar al-Hadi turned up with his driver's licence and assured the clerk of his ability to handle the vehicle on rough roads. He was surprised to see a woman with Daffyd and Marc.

"Dr Hanser is a woman? I thought you said his name was Danny. That is a male name, isn't it?"

"Yes it is, but her name is Dani, D-A-N-I. Is this a problem, Muammar?"

"You are married to this woman? Or you, Dr Andrews?"

"No."

"You are her guardian?"

"No. She is the leader of our expedition. I repeat--is this a problem? Should we look for another driver?"

Muammar considered the question and shook his head. "No, I am not a strict Muslim. However, if we meet up with desert tribesmen, can she refrain from giving me direct orders? She can make suggestions, and it would help if she was suitably deferential, but a woman in a position of authority is frowned upon." The young man sighed. "Libya is a relatively enlightened country, but some desert people still believe a woman should be subject to a male at all times."

"Not just desert people," Marc muttered.

Daffyd raised an eyebrow at the young man and then turned back to the Libyan. "Why don't you ask her?"

Muammar looked startled, but stammered out the question.

Dani smiled. "I know how many Muslim men view women. I can be circumspect."

Muammar grinned. "Then we have no problem. Let us depart for Al Jawf at once."

"We're going to need camping equipment," Marc said. "I don't suppose there are hotels between here and this Jawf place."

"Not even there," Muammar said. "It is a small settlement and a meeting place for the desert tribes. You will need tents, food, fuel, and especially water."

Under Muammar's guidance, they found and stocked up on the necessary supplies, loading it into their hired jeep before setting off a few hours later.

"How far away is Al Jawf?" Dani asked.

"About six hundred miles."

Dani made some quick calculations. "Two days then--three?"

"More like a week," Muammar said. "These are not English roads."

The first part of the trip led south out of Benghazi, along the coast road that they had travelled on by bus. The road was potholed and in places, drifts of sand had spilled across the surface, necessitating careful driving. Muammar drove at speed, but handled the ancient jeep expertly, increasing their confidence in his ability. Toward the end of the day they came to Ajdabiya, a small village, barely more than a scattering of houses around a crossroad. Muammar slowed and drove around the dirt streets until he found a vacant plot and a lone date palm struggling for existence in a harsh land.

"We can camp here tonight," Muammar said, driving off the road and underneath the palm tree.

They got out of the jeep, stretching cramped limbs and slapping dust out of their clothes before unloading the tents--one large and one small-- and starting a small fire. Sunset came swiftly, the orange glow of the desert sunset fading to reds and purples before darkness descended. A thousand small birds chattered and rustled in the dense dry fronds of the date palm and in the dried litter at its base other rustlings told of less welcome creatures awakening from a day spent hiding from the heat. The temperature dropped away with the setting sun, so they huddled closer to the fire, sitting cross-legged on the bare ground, cooking and eating plain tinned fare and flat bread, washing it down with black coffee. Daffyd rolled and smoked one of his noxious cigarettes but sat downwind of his companions and limited his pleasure to just one.

Marc looked toward the palm tree where the roosting birds were settling down and threw a small stone towards one of the unseen creatures at the tree's base. "What are those things? Snakes?"

"Possibly," Muammar said. "There are cobras and vipers in Libya. Also scorpions, but it is likely those are just mice." He considered for a moment. "Of course, mice attract snakes."

"Great," Marc muttered. He got up and moved around to the far side of the fire and scowled at the palm tree.

Moths were attracted to the fire and came spiralling in from the desert, pursued by little bats that swooped and dived past them in silence, snatching insects from the air with ease. The four people watched amazed as the little creatures performed complex aerial acrobatics above them, barely seen against the starry body of the night. A larger insect buzzed in the night, lurching into the light on horny wing-cases just above their heads with two bats in pursuit. The insect sideslipped, evading one bat but falling into the path of the other. Without thinking, Dani put her hand up and the bat shied away, chirruping in alarm, allowing its intended prey to cannon into her hand. She lowered it and looked at the insect in the firelight as it closed its wing-cases and sat quietly on her palm.

"A scarab beetle," Daffyd exclaimed. "I'd call that a sign from heaven, lass."

Dani looked at insect in wonder. "It did come to me, didn't it?"

"Hell of a coincidence anyway," Marc murmured.

Muammar leaned closer and looked at the beetle. "May I ask the significance of this creature? They are common enough in this region."

Dani looked at her friends enquiringly. Marc shrugged and Daffyd murmured, "Up to you, lass."

"It's a long story, Muammar, but we were in Syria on an archaeological expedition when we found a chamber with the account of an Egyptian princess written on the walls. The princess had a nickname--Scarab--and she owned a special scarab ornament that she said came from the gods of ancient Egypt. Well, I found that ornament and I felt a...a connection to the princess."

"Do you have this ornament, Dr Hanser?" Muammar asked. "I would very much like to see it."

"It was stolen from me, and the thief fled into Egypt."

"Ah. That is why you go there--to recover your property. But why do you not enter Egypt openly instead of going to all this trouble?"

"The thief is a powerful man," Daffyd said. "He's closed the borders to her."

"And now," Dani said, softly stroking the hard carapace of the beetle, "As we start on our journey through Egypt's back door, the gods have sent a scarab to me. I choose to look upon it as a sign of their approval."

"I am a Muslim," Muammar said, "though as I have said, not a strict one. However, I cannot accept the existence of other gods but Allah the Merciful and Beneficent. These ancient Egyptian gods were afrit or djinni and they do not look kindly on humans."

"I believe differently, but I do not seek to impose my beliefs on you, Muammar. Let us just agree to differ."

Dani lowered her hand to the sand and tipped the scarab off. It scrabbled off into the gloom and was lost to sight amongst the scrub and leaf litter.

Daffyd eased his back and stretched. "I have a feeling tomorrow is going to be just as cramped, dusty and exhausting as today. I suggest we turn in for the night and make an early start."

"A word of caution," Muammar said as he got to his feet. "Scorpions have a habit of creeping into boots and bedclothes at night, looking for dark, warm places. Be careful and do not put your hands or feet into either without checking there is nothing there."

"If a scorpion comes anywhere near me, it's dead," Marc swore.

"They are God's creatures too. Just be careful."

The night passed without disturbance from either serpents or arachnids, and though everyone shook out their bedding before packing it away and knocked their boots together to disturb possible unwelcome residents, they found nothing. Coffee and toasted bread completed their preparations in the cold dawn, and as the first shaft of sunlight speared the eastern horizon, they set off for Al Jawf.

The road from Ajdabiya ran southeast into the desert and within a mile or two of the village disintegrated into a corrugated dirt track. The suspension on the ancient jeep complained and twanged, shaking their bodies even as a cloud of dust enveloped them. Shafts of morning sunlight threw their shadow out behind them, dazzling Muammar's eyes as he guided their rattling vehicle over the rough surface.

Marc complained bitterly about the dust enveloping them. "I thought dust was supposed to stream away behind us. I'm choking to death here."

"We have a following breeze," Muammar explained. "We can either suffer the dust or shake ourselves to bits trying to outpace the wind."

They opted to maintain their slower speed and suffer the dust, and as the sun climbed into a cloud-free sky, the wind from the northwest dropped and the dust cloud of their passing drifted away behind them. The desert spread out in all directions, patches of rolling dunes interspersed with rocky wastes and the occasional wind-scoured stone outcrop. There were few plants, mostly dry looking scrub or stunted shrubs. They saw few animals--once a boy with a flock of goats, the scavenged carcass of some unidentified animal by the side of the road, and a hawk or two almost motionless in the faded blue above them.

"What a ghastly place," Marc commented. "There's nothing here of any interest."

"I suspect you're wrong there," Daffyd said. While they had been enveloped in the dust cloud he had refrained from smoking, but now he took out his tobacco and rolled a cigarette. He lit up and exhaled a faint blue cloud that whipped away behind them with the dust. "We won't see much while we're travelling, but if we were to stop and sit quietly, I think we'd see quite a bit of animal life."

"Yeah, snakes and scorpions."

"Certainly those, but other things too. Libya has a number of interesting animals. I'm not sure what you'd see around here, but there might be jackals, camels and antelopes--ostriches even."

"And the smaller animals like lizards, hyraxes, small birds, insects and spiders," Dani added.

"What you won't see easily but is here nonetheless, is oil and water," Muammar said. "You'll find oases and wells dotted through the desert, and water seeps where palms and grasses flourish, where animals and especially birds come in their thousands at dawn and dusk. British and American oil companies are drilling wells to bring deposits of oil to the surface. This could mean great things for Libya, though the common people may see little of this wealth. These assets are firmly in the hands of King Idris."

"I take it you're not a supporter of the king," Daffyd said.

Muammar was silent for a while, and then said, "One learns to guard one's tongue in politics, but you are all foreigners and passing through. I think I can safely say that Idris will not last forever."

"Governments come and go," Daffyd said. "Sometimes they are helped on their way."

"Yeah, but what will the next king be like?" Marc asked. "He may be worse than the one you have."

Muammar shook his head. "We will have no king. He will be overthrown by the army and then the people and a council of educated men will rule wisely and democratically for the common good."

"Lots of luck with that," Marc muttered.

The road speared deeper into the desert, and as they progressed on the bone-shaking way, the heat steadily mounted. They drank thirstily from their water bottles and spared a little to dampen cloths and wipe the dust and dirt from their faces. A little after noon, when slim shadows appeared once more, Muammar pulled off the road into the shade of a rocky outcrop and switched off the motor. The sudden silence plunged in upon them, though their bodies still seemed to feel the vibration of their travel. Heat blasted up from sand and rock now that they were motionless, and sweat broke out on their bodies.

Muammar refilled the petrol tank from a spare can, and topped up their water flasks while Daffyd gathered a few dry twigs together to make a small fire. They brewed a pan of tea and broke out a packet of biscuits, sitting around and refreshing themselves. Dani found a passage between the rocks and attended to her personal needs, while the men wandered off in the opposite direction to do the same. On the way back to the jeep, Daffyd laid his hand on Marc's arm, stopping him and pointing off to one side.

"There."

"What?"

"On that rock. A lizard."

"So?"

Daffyd grinned. "Some of the life in this desert. If you take the time to look, you'll see it everywhere."

Marc squinted into the westering sun and briefly scanned the outcrop and surrounding sand. "Nope, can't see anything interesting."

"That's because you're a philistine," Daffyd commented, grinning. "There's more to life than old bones and artefacts."

"Thus speaks my archaeology lecturer who bombards his students with those very things."

Daffyd laughed. "The old bones were living once, and the artefacts were made by living beings. Living beings that had thoughts, people who believed in gods, in love, had babies, got ill and died--people who lived life. They're not just old bones and possessions. They're reminders of one's own mortality, boyo. The past can come alive if you look hard in the right places, but the present is spread out all around you. Learn to enjoy it."

"Enjoy this heat? This dust?" He waved his hand in front of his face. "Flies? Don't tell me you do."

"Not exactly," Daffyd conceded. "But those minor inconveniences don't rob me of a greater enjoyment. Here we are off on an experience of a lifetime. We're in a new country, about to break international law by crossing a border illegally, in pursuit of an undiscovered tomb and a magical artefact--and all you can think of is the heat and the flies. Where's your sense of adventure?"

"Sitting in an air-conditioned hotel sipping on a long cold drink."

"As I said--you're a philistine."

They camped that night a further twenty miles south, though they could not be certain as the speedometer cable broke during the course of the afternoon. Rocky desert surrounded them as dusk fell and the heat of the day drained away, leaving the air crisp and clear. Twigs and dried dung made up the fire that night and everybody was too tired to complain about the evil-smelling smoke. They retired to their tents after a quick meal of spit-roasted lamb, bread and sweet coffee, and fell asleep quickly.

The next few days passed in much the same fashion as the first. Their supplies of water and fuel steadily dropped, but Muammar said he was not worried.

"We can refill both at Al Jawf. There's a small permanent community there and a greater number of itinerants, including my mother's people."

"Who are your mother's people exactly?" Dani asked.

"They are *badawī* or Bedouin as westerners call them."

"Really?" Marc queried. "Honest to God desert dwellers? Camels and tents and such?"

"Indeed. Many of my people have settled in towns and villages but my mother's brother--my uncle--has maintained the old way of life. They should be in or near Al Jawf at this time of year."

"Will we be welcome, though?" Daffyd asked. "I've read that Bedouin are suspicious of strangers."

"That is true," Muammar confirmed. "The *badawī* tend to keep to themselves. We have a saying - *I against my brother, my brothers and I against my cousins, then my cousins and I against strangers.* However, my uncle will welcome me as family and if I vouch for you, he will welcome you too, I am sure."

"Thank you, Muammar," Dani said. "It looks like we were fortunate to find you."

"What about your father?" Marc asked. "Is he Bedouin too?"

Muammar hesitated. "Yes, but of another tribe. He lives in Sabha, far to the west. I lived there with him and went to school there."

"You didn't live with your mother?" Dani hesitated, reading the tension in the young man's shoulders. "I'm sorry, I don't mean to pry," she said.

"There were...reasons. Reasons that are important to *badawī*. I will say no more."

An awkward silence fell which lasted for several minutes until Daffyd lit another cigarette and filled the vehicle with strongly smelling smoke. Marc and Dani's protests lightened the mood and talk resumed on other subjects.

Two days later, the road passed an oasis, where date palms and other vegetation grew in abundance. They looked for an open body of water, thinking of the western concept of an oasis, but there was only a grassy depression. Marc asked about it.

"The water comes closer to the surface here," Muammar explained. "But if any rose above the sands it would quickly evaporate."

The phenomenon was short-lived, and within a mile they were back into sandy desert, where the only hints of water were the lies of darkly dancing mirages.

The journey seemed endless, the thin rutted road stretching out to infinity before and behind, endless vistas of sand and rock meeting their eyes, uncomfortable seats and poor suspension numbing their bodies, and the ever-present heat and dust sapped their strength and their desire to go on.

At last, eight days after leaving Benghazi, Al Jawf came in sight. The collection of houses was unprepossessing and the whole town gave off an air of dusty dejection and sun-baked lassitude. People stopped and stared as the ancient jeep ground its way along the streets to the far side of the town, where the road petered out into the desert. Muammar continued driving carefully over sand and rock until he came to a grove of palm trees, a stone-lipped well, and a patch of lank grass and shrubs.

"We wait here until my uncle's people come," Muammar said.

Dani looked around at the oasis and surrounding desert. "For how long?"

"Who can say? A day, a week? I will ask in the town. Maybe somebody has heard when the tribe is due back."

*   *   *

"Colonel, it is Ali Hafiz again."

"What news do you have for me?"

"The woman, the older man and the young man bought tickets to Rome in Italy. They left word with their colleagues and students that they were going on holiday. I have tracked down the flight they took out of London. It went to Rome."

Sarraj pondered this news while his man waited in silence on the other end of the line. "I must know the truth of it. Go to Rome and find them."

Chapter Seven

A hmed Bashir had been on holiday for a week, enjoying the hospitality of his friend Colonel Michel Sarraj and taking in the sights of Cairo and the associated archaeological wonders of the area. He toured the city itself, wandering through the Khan el-Khalili bazaar, breathing in the rich aromas of the produce and listening to the hubbub of the crowded streets. He nibbled on sweetmeats from street stalls and sipped coffee in small cafés, losing himself for a time in the rich fabric of the ancient city. The al-Azhar university and associated mosque attracted him as it was nearly a thousand years old, a third of the way back to the time of Smenkhkare. More modern universities rated a quick visit too--the Cairo University and the recently completed Ain Shams. Other buildings occupied Bashir's interest also--the Khedivial Opera House and the Cairo Tower, the Borg Al-Qāhira. He stood on the street below the Tower and stared up at its shaft, marvelling at this modern example of technology. The tower was not yet completed, so he could not travel up its six hundred foot length to the observation deck, but he vowed to return in a year or so and see the city laid out below him.

He took a camel ride to the Giza Plateau, and stood staring at the looming mass of the pyramids, the damaged dignity of the Sphinx; the distant views of the Nile River and the bustling city spreading outward. Crossing back over the river, he found a guide to take him to the supposed site of ancient Iunu, where Scarab had communed with her gods, and explored the presumed locality of the city of Zarw, though there was nothing to be seen in the rich farmland of the river delta and the courses of the river did not match the descriptions he had so recently heard.

The lack of recognisable ruins left Bashir depressed, and he contemplated the likelihood of being able to track down the lost tomb of Smenkhkare and Scarab from the vague description given in the account. When Nazim arrived in Egypt with the typed up notebooks and descriptions, he would have another look at the translation and see if they had missed any clue, but in the meantime, he wondered if there was anything else he could do. Perhaps it was worth finding out what the experts knew.

Back in Cairo, he rang his counterpart at the Ministry of Culture in the Egyptian Government and arranged for a private tour of the Museum of Antiquities. The Minister was delighted to help and sent a limousine for Bashir.

The luxurious vehicle entered the city from the south, threading its way along the highway on the eastern bank of the Nile, into el-Tahrir Square and then turning off into Wasim Hasan where the imposing red stone edifice of the Egyptian Museum of Antiquities greeted him. The vehicle pulled up close to the main entrance and the policemen on duty there started forward to move the limousine on, before catching sight of the Ministerial insignia on the windscreen. They turned away, allowing the car to park in the no-stopping zone.

The custodian within the museum was expecting Bashir and was obsequious, bowing repeatedly, and assuring his visitor that the museum staff was totally at his disposal. He called a guide and gave the young man instructions to take Minister Bashir around the exhibits, to show him anything he wished to see, to answer any question.

"I am Rusul, and I am honoured to be your guide, Minister. We have over a hundred halls," the young man said proudly. "We have everything from great statues and stone sarcophagi to mummies and scraps of ancient papyrus, jewellery and furniture. What would you like to see?"

"Eighteenth dynasty," Bashir said. "Anything to do with the Amarnan kings, or Princess Beketaten."

The young man frowned. "Er, I do not know this Princess Beketaten. What dynasty was she?"

"Eighteenth. Just show me what you have."

"Well, the displays with Tuthmosis, Hatshepsut, Amenophis and Tutankhamen are on the first floor. Do you wish to go straight there or will you examine the many fine exhibits of that period that we have on this floor first?"

Bashir thought for a moment, wondering whether he should go straight to the exhibits of Tutankhamen, the only name he recognised from Rusul's list, and then decided he was in no hurry. "Seeing as I'm on the ground floor already..."

They started with the Hall of Statues, moving amongst a scattering of tourists to view great granite and sandstone figures. The persons represented were caught in unnatural-looking poses, with stiff and straight limbs, stone faces staring with blank eyes into infinity. Bashir moved slowly, scanning the statues and searching for any relevance in the ancient carvings.

The Minister stopped before a statue of Amenhotep III and stared up at the scarred and battered stone face. He stared at it for several minutes, paying little attention to Rusul's explanation of just who Amenhotep III was and his importance.

"He is best known as the father of Amenhotep IV, who became the heretic king Akhenaten, but many historians say he was also the greatest king of the Eighteenth Dynasty, and very possibly the wealthiest."

They moved on to view glass-topped cases containing coins of all ages. Modern coins were there, moving back through the ages to pre-Islamic times, to Roman, Greek, Persian and Late Egyptian.

"Money was only invented some fifteen hundred years before the Prophet, peace be unto him," Rusul said. "Before that they used barter, exchanging wheat for meat, lettuces for jewellery, and only later using metals as a form of currency. Eventually, a piece of copper or precious metal would be stamped with its value or cut to size and these became the first coins."

Cases containing scraps of papyrus and shards of pottery followed, but Bashir's interest waned, though Rusul attempted to make it interesting. He described how paper was made from the papyrus reeds, and parchment from the hides of animals, and then talking about the clays used to make the fragments of pots on display.

Bashir stifled a yawn. "Perhaps I could see the other Eighteenth Dynasty exhibits now?" he asked.

"Of course, Minister. Please follow me."

They ascended to the first floor and entered the hall of Tutankhamen. Gilded furniture and tables inlaid with ebony and lapis, ivory and faience greeted Bashir's wide-eyed gaze. Little figurines--human shaped but animal-headed--stared back at him, and his eyes were drawn to the splendid death mask of the young king, molten gold in the warm glow of the spotlights. The face of the boy-king, framed by a gold and blue striped nemes headdress, showed a calm acceptance of his position as pharaoh, his painted eyes fixed upon eternity and the false beard of kingship jutting incongruously from his clean-shaven visage.

Bashir stared at the gold and felt his heart beat faster. Somewhere out there was another tomb as rich as this one had been, and if he found it, none of the artefacts would languish in a museum, being gawked at by tourists. The great wealth would be his.

"Where is the mummy of the king?" he asked.

"It is in storage in the basement," Rusul replied. "Many things were put on display in the museum but other things stayed there, including the mummy in its sarcophagus. One day, we may even return it to the tomb so he can truly rest in peace."

The account of the discovery of Tutankhamen's tomb in the Valley of the Kings in 1922 by Howard Carter was displayed in framed posters on the walls of the hall, together with numerous photographs of the tomb as it was when it had been discovered. Cabinets lined the hall also, containing a mass of artefacts from the tomb, jewellery, toys, baskets and weapons. Bashir wandered along, peering into the glass-topped cabinets, but soon lost interest, returning to the boy-king's golden mask. He stared at it, mesmerised by the blank golden gaze of the long-dead youth. Eventually, he tore himself away and turned to Rusul.

"Where to next?"

"May I suggest the Hall of Akhet-Aten?" Rusul suggested. "The findings at el-Amarna?"

Rusul led the way into the next hall, a chamber dominated by a head-and-shoulders statue of Pharaoh Akhenaten at one end and a glorious representation of the sun's disk at the other. The painted Aten extended its rays downward, each one ending in a little hand, some of which held the ankh, symbol of life. It reminded Bashir of the painting of the Aten in the first chamber back in Syria.

"Impressive," Bashir murmured. "And the king's quite...how do I put it? Deformed?"

The statue of Akhenaten stared back at him, an amused sneer on his full lips, his hooded stone eyes holding a secret. The long face was framed by a Nemes headdress and looked unworldly, almost inhuman. The arms were crossed over the chest and they held the broken remains of crook and flail, symbols of kingship.

"Was he really that odd-looking, or are his features exaggerated for some reason?"

"The king was dolichocephalic," Rusul said. "That is, he had an elongate skull, as did Tutankhamen. Some scholars point to the similarity as proof that Tutankhamen was the son of Akhenaten."

"Or at least a close relative, I suppose. Could Tutankhamen have had other parents? I have heard that he might have been the son of Amenhotep III and one of his daughters."

"It is possible," Rusul admitted. "I am no expert, however."

"What about Princess Beketaten? She was a daughter of Amenhotep III and sister of Akhenaten."

Rusul frowned. "I am not familiar with the name, sir. I believe there were several daughters though..."

"What of King Smenkhkare?"

"I...I'm sorry, sir. I don't know that name either."

"Smenkhkare. He was the king following Akhenaten and preceding Tutankhamen."

Rusul frowned. "I do not know of a pharaoh of that name. Perhaps he was a Vizier or other high official of the court rather than a king?"

"Who in this Museum of Antiquities might know the answer?" Bashir demanded. "I am interested in this specific king."

Rusul licked his lips nervously, apparently fearful of appearing ignorant in front of his superiors. "Er, there is the Director--Jamal Nasrallah. He is on duty today."

"Excellent, take me to see him."

"Yes, Minister. Please follow me."

Rusul took the stairs to the next floor and then up another narrower flight past a sign that read 'Staff Only', arriving in a dim corridor lit by the occasional grimy window. He knocked on a heavy wooden door and opened it immediately, poking his head inside.

"Director Nasrallah, Minister Bashir wishes to speak with you. He has a question I cannot answer."

Footsteps sounded on the carpeted floor of the room and the door was thrown open. A middle-aged man with a carefully trimmed beard stared out at the two men. He straightened his jacket and dipped his head perfunctorily.

"Minister Bashir, you are welcome. Minister ul-Haq at the Ministry of Culture said you might be paying us a visit. Please come in and have a seat. I will do my best to satisfy your curiosity." He waited until Bashir had crossed the threshold before addressing Rusul. "Coffee, at once." He shut the door in the young man's face.

Nasrallah sat down behind his desk and looked across the polished surface to his visitor sitting in one of the two comfortable chairs. "How may I be of assistance?" he asked.

"I wish to know about two persons of the Eighteenth Dynasty. The guide Rusul seemed ignorant of their very existence."

"Regrettable. I shall have a word with his supervisor. Who are the persons concerned?"

"King Smenkhkare and Princess Beketaten."

One of Nasrallah's eyebrows lifted slightly. "Obscure names indeed. No wonder Rusul did not know. I doubt there are more than a dozen people in the Museum who might know."

"But you do?" Bashir asked.

"Yes."

There was a soft tap on the door and Rusul entered, bearing a silver tray with a coffee pot, sugar, and two fine china cups. He placed the tray on the desk, bowed and retreated, closing the door behind him. Director Nasrallah served his guest himself and then settled back to enjoy the strong coffee.

"Pharaoh Smenkhkare is something of an enigma. The name exists in the records, and fits into them at around the time of Akhenaten. You are aware of the heretic Akhenaten?"

Bashir nodded, and Nasrallah continued.

"It is believed that Akhenaten was succeeded by someone called Neferneferuaten, and then by Smenkhkare in the capacity as co-regent, followed by Tutankhamen. However, there are indications that this Neferneferuaten was female--possibly Akhenaten's Queen Nefertiti. Some identify Smenkhkare with this Neferneferuaten. Others say Smenkhkare was a..." Nasrallah pursed his lips. "How to phrase this delicately? That he had an unnatural physical love for the heretic." He shrugged. "Either way, he was a minor figure in Egyptian history."

"Is his tomb known?"

"Not with any certainty. Howard Carter discovered fragments of a box bearing the name of Neferneferuaten close to the site of Tutankhamen's tomb. Then there is the tomb known as KV55 in the Valley of the Kings. Some scholars say it is the tomb of Akhenaten, others that it is the tomb of Smenkhkare--or somebody else." Nasrallah allowed himself a small smile. "Nothing is certain at this juncture. We can only hope that future discoveries will shed light on this obscure part of history."

"I see. Thank you. And Princess Beketaten?"

"She existed, but almost nothing is known of her. She was the youngest daughter of Pharaoh Amenhotep III and his Queen Tiye. That makes her a full sister to Akhenaten."

"That much I know. What else can you tell me?"

"Her name is found twice in inscriptions, both in the tomb of Huya, the Steward of Tiye. She is associated with Tiye in both, but some scholars believe Tiye was her grandmother rather than mother, and that Akhenaten fathered her on a lesser wife called Kiya."

"Is that what you believe?"

Nasrallah stroked his trim beard thoughtfully. "I see no reason to think of her as anything but the child of Amenhotep and Tiye. There is no mention of her after Tiye's death and it is likely she died."

"Is her tomb known?"

"No, Minister Bashir, but that may not be surprising. The tomb of a child would not be a rich one or as well guarded as that of a prominent person. If it was robbed in antiquity, there would be no record of its existence. Also, the bodies of children were often buried with their parents and have no separate identity."

Bashir looked thoughtful and sipped at his cooling coffee, wondering if there was anything else he could usefully ask. The Museum Assistant Director cleared his throat.

"May I ask the reason behind these questions, Minister?"

"Just curiosity. Your museum is such an interesting place it stimulates a spirit of enquiry."

"It is kind of you to say so, but those questions could not arise from a perusal of our exhibits. There is only a hint of Smenkhkare's existence, and none at all of Beketaten's. I am curious as to where you came across their names."

Bashir hesitated again, debating whether to release any details of the account in the Syrian chambers. "In confidence?"

Now it was Nasrallah's turn to hesitate. "Within the limits of my duty as custodian of Egypt's ancient treasures."

"What does that mean?"

"Only that I cannot keep silent if archaeological treasures are endangered."

Bashir refused to meet the Director's eyes, instead wiping the rim of an impeccably clean coffee cup. "That is not the case."

"Then there is no problem," Nasrallah said.

Bashir cleared his throat and hesitated a moment longer. "I came across an Egyptian inscription."

"In Egypt? May I ask where?"

"On a...an artefact discovered in Syria."

"I would very much like to see this artefact. Could that be arranged?"

"It is in, er, private hands."

"A pity, still, there it is. Private collectors hide away much that is useful in the proper study of Egyptology. What did the inscription say?"

"It, er, referred to Smenkhkare and Beketaten."

Nasrallah stared keenly at the Minister. "Just that?"

"That is all that I can remember--the cartouches, you know--they were translated for me. It piqued my interest though, so finding myself in Cairo, I thought I'd see if I could find out anything about them."

"A pity you cannot remember anything else."

Bashir thought of something. "You said the tomb of Smenkhkare was in the Valley of the Kings--a tomb known as KV50, was it?"

"KV55, Minister, and that is only a possibility. Nothing is certain."

"Could his tomb be elsewhere? Not in the Valley of the Kings?"

"There are royal tombs scattered up and down Egypt--Giza, Saqqara, Valley of the Kings, el-Amarna, to name some of the main sites--but most New Kingdom tombs were in the Valley of the Kings."

"New Kingdom?"

"The period we're talking about. Dynasties Eighteen to Twenty. Smenkhkare and Beketaten were associated with the Eighteenth Dynasty."

"Ah, I see. So you think there's no possibility of Smenkhkare's tomb being elsewhere?"

"I think it unlikely--if he was a legitimate king."

"Meaning?"

"If he was a claimant or a pretender to the throne, he might be buried elsewhere."

Bashir thought about the description in the account--the slash of green pointing the way, the notch in the cliffs lining the valley of the Nile. "Perhaps in the Nile Valley itself or in the cliffs?"

"Unlikely. The ancients had a reason for burying their bodies in the desert valleys or on the dry plateau of Giza. It was imperative that the body and the tomb furnishings remain intact. Water would cause them to disintegrate. If we ever do manage to positively identify Smenkhkare's tomb--or even that of your Princess Beketaten--you can be sure it will be in an arid environment."

Bashir nodded thoughtfully. "I must thank you, Director Nasrallah. You have been most informative. You are undoubtedly a busy man, so I won't take up any more of your valuable time." He rose to his feet and reached out to shake the Director's hand.

*   *   *

Director Jamal Nasrallah smiled as he ushered his visitor out but as the door closed his smile slipped and he was frowning by the time he sat down and poured himself another cup of now tepid coffee.

"Now what was that all about?" he murmured.

An obscure Syrian politician was unlikely to be well informed about matters of ancient Egyptian history, so where had he come across the names of Smenkhkare and Beketaten? Was it from an artefact in the hands of some collector, as he said? Or something more sinister? What sort of collector would show a Government Minister such a valuable object that must surely have been looted from a tomb--unless the object had been confiscated--but then it would have been handed back to the Egyptian authorities, would it not?

The names of Smenkhkare and Beketaten were almost unknown outside of academic circles and he had been exaggerating when he said a dozen people within the Museum knew of their existence. He suspected it was far fewer. This was an interesting puzzle indeed.

Nasrallah put through a call to Minister ul-Haq at the Ministry of Culture and after several minutes was put through to him.

"I have just been paid a visit by Under-Minister Bashir from Syria."

"Ah, yes, good. The visit went smoothly?"

"Indeed, Minister, however, he mentioned something that seemed strange."

"Strange, how? Of concern politically? Economically? Security? How?"

"Nothing like that, Minister," Nasrallah hurried to explain. "He had access to specialised knowledge concerning Egyptology and I wondered if..."

"He's probably just interested in the subject. You should be flattered. Now, if there's nothing more, I have a busy schedule today."

"There is one thing more, Minister. Do you know if Minister Bashir made any sort of discovery recently? Or if the Syrian Government arrested any black market dealers in Egyptian artefacts?"

"Nothing that I know of."

Minister ul-Haq cut the connection and Nasrallah returned to pondering the hidden meaning of Bashir's revelation.

Chapter Eight

O
utriders of the Bedouin appeared on the third day. Marc was out in the early dawn light relieving himself behind one of the date palms when he looked up and saw two horsemen watching him from a dune some two hundred yards away. He stared back and the horsemen spurred toward him, their mounts slipping and sliding down the face of the dune. Marc took to his heels, running back into the centre of the oasis, shouting for the others.

Muammar was sitting by the still-warm embers of the previous night's fire, trying to coax a flame from the ashes. He looked up as Marc came running and saw the horsemen beyond him, one levelling a rifle as he rode. Leaping to his feet, he bellowed out a phrase in Arabic that meant nothing to Marc or to Daffyd and Dani who were now emerging from the tents, but evidently did to the horsemen. The man behind the rifle refrained from firing, and both horsemen galloped up to the four people among the date palms and brought their mounts to a halt amid a spray of sand.

The rifleman barked out a demand, and Muammar replied at length, gesturing toward his companions and patting himself on the chest. The other horseman spoke, and Muammar replied again, placatingly. The two Bedouin sat on their horses, robes enveloping them from head to toe, fierce hawk faces staring at the foreigners and rifles pointing in their general direction.

"Who are they?" Dani asked.

"They are my uncle's men, and they are very angry. They say they saw Dr Andrews performing an act of disrespect toward their sheik's property-- relieving himself against a palm tree."

"Jesus, what's all the fuss?" Marc complained. "The tree was probably grateful for the drink."

"I have told you before that when your body seeks relief you must go out into the desert, scoop out a small hole, perform your function, and cover it up again. This is basic hygiene, whereas your action has soiled my uncle's home and perhaps introduced disease."

"The latter is unlikely," Daffyd murmured. "Urine is usually sterile."

"I realise that," Muammar said. "However, these men are largely uneducated and ruled by superstition and archaic beliefs. They have not had the advantage of a western education. What concerns me is that they will report this incident to my uncle and he will withdraw his hospitality before it has been offered. If that happens, you have no way of getting over the Egyptian border."

"Can we make amends?" Dani asked. "Perhaps if we apologised?"

"It couldn't hurt." Muammar addressed the tribesmen once more, eliciting another spate of angry responses from one after the other. Muammar translated when they had finished talking.

"They say that forgiveness is in the hands of the sheik, but for themselves they would wipe out the insult with blood. One of them--the one with the red kūfiyyah,--insists that the offender abase himself. If that happens, he says, he will tell the sheik, my uncle, that the insult was unintentional."

"Then you'll have to do it Marc," Dani said.

"Blowed if I will. Look, Muammar, explain that I'm sorry if I caused offence by peeing on the damn tree, but I'm not about to abase myself--whatever that involves."

"If you do not, this venture of yours is at an end. My uncle will not welcome you into his tents or help you. Your choice will be to either go home to England, or try for Egypt alone--in which case you will die within a day or two. The desert is harsh and unforgiving."

Daffyd looked at Marc. "You're going to have to do it, boyo. For Dani's sake if nothing else. This is her only chance of getting into Egypt and...you know what."

Marc swore and glared at the impassive Bedouin on their stallions. "What do I have to do?" he snarled.

"Lie face down on the ground with your arms by your sides. Repeat word for word what I tell you...and please, Dr Andrews, try and sound repentant. I will translate what you say."

Marc scowled but came forward and lay flat on his face on the sand in front of the two horsemen. When Muammar told him what to say, he repeated each phrase and waited while the young Libyan translated for the tribesmen.

"I, Dr Andrews, a foreigner in your country...acted out of ignorance of your laws and customs...profaning the property of Sheik Ali ibn Hawid ibn al-Qasr of the Harabi Bani Sulaim...and offering up a blood insult..." Muammar saw Marc hesitate at the last phrase. "Say it, Dr Andrews, on your life and as if you mean it. And offering up a blood insult...I do ask forgiveness of Sheik Ali ibn Hawid."

Red Kūfiyyah answered at length, and Muammar replied. The other tribesman shouted out something else and dismounted, striding over to Marc's prostrate body. Marc swivelled his head, trying to watch the man as he approached.

"Keep still, Dr Andrews. Do not offer any resistance."

Daffyd leaned closer to Dani, real concern in his voice. "He's insisting on a blood price. He says the insult is too great for a simple apology...Oh, God..." He broke off as the tribesman's curved dagger came whispering out of its sheath. "Muammar, no!"

Muammar held a hand up toward Daffyd and Dani and spoke urgently. The man snarled a reply and squatted beside Marc. His knife swept down across Marc's forearm and left a thin trail of blood in its wake. The Bedouin rose and strode back to his horse, vaulting into the saddle. The two horsemen turned and spurred their horses away as Marc got shakily to his feet, blood trickling down his arm and dripping from his fingers.

"Blood has been spilt; honour has been satisfied," Muammar murmured.

"Honour be damned. They're just bloody savages," Marc snapped. He clapped his handkerchief over the cut in his arm and pushed past the young Libyan.

Dani ran to get the first aid kit from the jeep. She washed the wound and found it was superficial, the tribesman apparently having deliberately made a shallow cut. The amount of blood made it look worse than it was. Antiseptic cream and a bandage staunched the flow and set the wound on the path to healing.

"What happens now?" Daffyd asked, "when those riders report back to the Sheik?"

"He will be here tomorrow, and we must wait for him to invite us to his tent. This is his well, and these are his date palms. I hope that he will accept that honour has been satisfied and will make us welcome."

"And if not?"

Muammar shrugged. "Then we shall see. Can you make sure your young companion behaves himself?"

"His young companion can hear you," Marc growled, "And is quite capable of answering for himself."

"Then please do so, Dr Andrews. It is very important that you are polite, respectful and suitably deferential. Sheik Ali ibn Hawid is, to all intents and purposes, the absolute ruler of his people. Men live or die by his word."

"I'll be polite to the old savage but I'll be blowed if I'll respect him. It sounds like he's nothing but an outdated feudal tyrant."

Muammar closed his eyes for a moment and sighed. "Then we might as well leave now. Your venture has come to naught before it starts. You have no hope of success without Sheik Ali on your side." He looked up at the position of the sun. "You should pack up and leave before noon. Just follow the road north and you'll survive. I will stay and greet my uncle."

Dani rounded on Marc, eyes flashing. "Damn you, Marc. I'm not giving up on my quest just because you insist on behaving like a child. We're in another country now, subject to different laws, surrounded by different customs and quite frankly, if you can't cope with it, you don't belong here. What's more, I don't want you here if you can't behave like a responsible adult. Take the jeep back to Benghazi and go back to England. I'm prepared to stay out her alone if need be..."

"I'm staying," Daffyd said.

"Thank you, Daffyd. Muammar, will you help just the two of us with your uncle? I can assure you we will do whatever it takes to get on his right side."

"Jeez, Dani..." Marc muttered.

"That will be acceptable, Dr Hanser," Muammar said.

"No way am I going to go home and leave you here," Marc said. "You need me..."

"No we don't, Marc. Not if you're going to act like this. You're a liability, not an asset, and I'd rather you weren't here."

"Oh, God, please Dani, don't send me home. Look, I'll do whatever you want. I'll behave, I'll be polite, and I'll even kiss his damn feet if that's what it takes."

"There you go again. All I need from you is a basic regard for other people. Treat this situation seriously and stop trying to be smart."

Marc grimaced and shrugged. "Okay, I can do serious."

"I mean it, Marc. Ruin this for me and I'll never speak to you again."

More horsemen arrived just before dusk, to prepare the oasis for the arrival of Sheik Ali ibn Hawid. They greeted Muammar warmly and nodded politely at the three foreigners, before scouting out the surrounding territory and checking that everything was as it should be. The tribesmen kept themselves to themselves that night, politely refusing an offer of hospitality from Dani, conveyed by Muammar.

"It is a good thought, Dr Hanser, and I will make the offer on your behalf, but they won't accept it," Muammar had told her. "This is my uncle's oasis and they cannot accept hospitality here unless he grants them permission first."

He made the offer, but as he had predicted, it was turned down. "They thank you though, Dr Hanser, and they will no doubt report your offer of hospitality to the Sheik."

"Is that good?"

Muammar smiled. "Yes."

Sheik Ali ibn Hawid arrived mid-morning, on a richly caparisoned camel, with a dozen armed riders surrounding him. Behind him were heavily laden pack beasts led by numerous women and a herd of camels and goats driven by small boys. Horse riders galloped up as the sheik arrived and swept round the oasis, joining forces with the horsemen who had arrived the previous night. They released a volley into the air from their rifles and uttered ululating cries to greet their chieftain.

Dani was eager to greet the Sheik, but Muammar counselled patience. "You are a supplicant," he said. "You must wait for an invitation to join him in his tent."

They sat in the shade of the palm trees through the long hot day, keeping out of the way of the tribe--the men sitting around cleaning and mending their equipment, women carrying water from the well, cooking, and tending to the tents and their men-folk, and children scampering around playing or standing wide-eyed, staring at the strangers in their midst.

The invitation came that evening. Two robed and armed men came for them and escorted them to the richly ornamented and woven tent of the Sheik. The whole of one side of the tent was drawn up and looking into it, they saw carpets spread out over the sand and piles of coloured cushions. A bearded older man sat crosslegged in the centre of the tent, two hard, cold, hooded eyes staring at them past a sharply hooked nose. The expression on the Sheik's face was one of rapacious lust, and Dani's heart sank as they stepped over the threshold. This was the man who held her future in his hands.

Muammar bowed deeply and spoke in the tribal dialect. The Sheik inclined his head slightly and Muammar went on to introduce the two men and woman with him. Glittering eyes fixed each one of them in turn, and when it came to Marc's turn, the man's upper lip lifted in a snarl to reveal chipped and stained teeth.

Sheik Ali ibn Hawid spoke, and Muammar translated, relief evident in his voice. "My uncle bids you welcome to his tents. He offers everything he has in hospitality. I hasten to add that last bit is not intended literally," Muammar added. "However, you are now under his protection while you are here. He offers food and drink. Please bow to him and utter a few words of thanks--I will translate."

Dani did as Muammar instructed, followed by Daffyd and Marc, each murmuring about how they were glad to be there and thanking the Sheik for his generosity. Muammar seemed to expand on their utterances, but Dani was reasonably certain he was casting them in the best possible light.

"Please sit to his left," Muammar said. "Dr Rhys-Williams closest to him, then Dr Andrews, then Dr Hanser. Be aware, Dr Hanser, that he pays you an enormous compliment by consenting to eat with you. Women usually eat later and in a separate tent."

"Please tell him I am conscious of the honour." Dani went and sat down so the three of them formed a gentle curve on the Sheik's left hand side, Daffyd alongside the Sheik, Marc and Dani facing him slightly. Muammar sat on his uncle's right hand side, and the two armed men squatted on the edge of the carpet, watching the little group.

The sheik clapped his hands and immediately several servants appeared, bearing steaming bowls of food. Two men staggered under the weight of two whole roasted goats on a bed of rice, another bore a platter of round bread and another carried a large bowl of what looked like small charred potatoes. The servant carrying these sliced them with a sharp knife and scattered the pieces over the rice. Everything was placed in front of the Sheik who examined it and nodded his head in acceptance of its quality.

"Eat," Ali ibn Hawid commanded, waving his right hand at the feast. Following Muammar's example, Daffyd, Dani and Marc shifted position until they were all sitting cross-legged around the platters.

"Use your right hands only," Muammar murmured. "Tear off a morsel of meat and fashion a ball of rice around it...no, no, Dr Andrews, your right hand only...observe." He took a piece of goat flesh and expertly rolled rice onto it, added a slice of the charred objects and popped it into his mouth. "Now you." He watched as each of his charges followed his instructions, more or less clumsily and ate. "Make expressions of enjoyment." They did, smiling, nodding and uttering inarticulate sounds of pleasure. Muammar spoke in Arabic and the Sheik beamed, joining his guests in the communal feast.

Dani chewed reflectively, appreciating the flavours of the food. She bit into a slice of the tuber. "What is this?" she asked. "It's delightfully...nutty? Is that the taste? Slightly sweet, perhaps with a hint of...of coconut."

"Desert truffle," Muammar said.

"Truffles!" Marc exclaimed, ripping off a piece of the flat bread. "Aren't they frightfully expensive?"

"*Tirmania* or *Terfezia*," Daffyd commented, picking up a larger piece and examining it. "I can't tell which, but they're not the truffles that cost so much in fancy restaurants in Europe."

"How come you know so much about it?" Dani asked.

"I've travelled a bit, eaten a lot of things--including desert truffles. Muammar, please convey to the Sheik that we appreciate his bountiful hospitality and are forever in his debt."

Muammar did so, and the Sheik nodded, said something, and continued eating. Muammar did not translate his uncle's words and when Marc opened his mouth to ask, Daffyd laid his hand warningly on his friend's arm.

They made inroads into the meal, and as their appetite slackened, the Sheik wiped his hand on a clean cloth and dabbed at his lips before clapping his hands. The servants rushed in and removed the food and distributed clean cloths to the guests.

"The food now passes to the warriors first, and then to the women, children and servants," Muammar said.

The servants issued forth again, bearing a bowl of a dark pulp and a plate of muffin-like cakes. Muammar demonstrated once more, splitting one of the cakes and scooping some of the pulp onto it. "Honeycake and pulped dates," he said, biting into his dessert. The others joined in, the men with gusto and Dani nibbling on a small piece.

"Desserts aren't really my thing," she said with a smile. "But it is delicious."

Servants cleared away once more and brought in a silver coffee pot and small cups. The rich aroma of brewed coffee mixed with freshly ground cardamom filled the air. A servant stayed behind to pour the coffee.

"I had hoped that my uncle might have brewed the coffee himself, in front of us," Muammar murmured. "That would have been a sign of complete acceptance. However, the offering of hospitality may be enough to ensure his assistance."

"Do you think he will help us?" Dani asked.

"We can only ask. I will approach him tomorrow."

"No time like the present," Marc said. "Go on, Muammar, ask him."

"That would be the height of bad manners, Dr Andrews. This dinner is for him to weigh you up, determine if you are honourable men..."

"And woman," Daffyd murmured.

"No. Forgive me, Dr Hanser, but your presence is something of a hindrance, if anything. The Bedouin are fiercely patriarchal, and he has already done you great honour by allowing you to eat with us. He has done this because he knows you are a foreign woman--perhaps the first one he has met--and I have vouched for you. As I was saying, if he judges the rest of you to be honourable men, he may feel inclined to grant a favour, but it won't be until tomorrow at the earliest."

They drank the coffee with every sign of relish, and had their cups refilled. They drank again, draining the small cups, and yet again they were refilled.

"When you've had enough, waggle your cup when they come to refill it," Muammar said. Nobody refused a refill, though they drank the strong, spiced brew more slowly now.

"Conversation is normal during the drinking of coffee," Muammar went on. "If you want to say anything, please do. I will translate."

"Of course," Dani said. "Please thank the Sheik for his hospitality and tell..."

"You misunderstand, Dr Hanser. Your gratitude is assumed. The conversation should turn on events outside the sphere of my uncle's normal experiences. For instance, I have just come from Benghazi, so..." Muammar proceeded to tell his uncle about family matters and also of recent events in Benghazi.

When there was a lull in the conversation, Daffyd mentioned the state of the roads and recounted a couple of amusing incidents that had occurred on their bus journey from Tripoli. The Sheik listened politely, nodding and adding a few comments, but his interest really picked up when Daffyd compared the Libyan transport system with the British one. He started asking questions, Marc and Dani joined in, and the conversation drifted onto life in Britain and the very different experiences they had encountered in that green and gentle land.

One by one, they waggled their coffee cups, and at last the Sheik rose to his feet. Muammar got up quickly and bowed, thanking his uncle for the honour of being accepted into his tent, and Dani followed suit, Daffyd and Marc moments behind her. The two armed men escorted them back to their small tents and left them.

"That went as well as I hoped," Muammar said. "He accepted both Dr Hanser and Dr Andrews, so I anticipate he will grant your request."

"What exactly is our request?" Dani asked. "We came all this way so we could cross the border into Egypt undetected, but how exactly can your uncle help us? We don't have much money to hire camels or anything, even if we knew how to ride them."

"He would not hire camels out to you. Being ignorant of desert ways, you and they would die. You must ask for help to cross to one of the Egyptian towns and let him decide how he will accomplish this. Which town do you need to go to?"

"Hmm. Esna, I suppose, or Edfu. They're both on the Nile."

"That might be difficult, but maybe one of the inland towns? Kharga perhaps?"

"That would work," Dani said. "Do you think he'd help us?"

"We can only wait and see."

"Insha'Allah, in other words," Daffyd murmured.

Muammar nodded. "Indeed, if God wills."

"A useful, if somewhat fatalistic point of view, but we can at least hope," Dani said.

Sheik Ali ibn Hawid granted them an interview the next morning. The Sheik sat on cushions within his tent, but this time at least twenty of the warriors were ranged behind him, armed to the teeth and maintaining impassive countenances.

"They'd slit our throats without compunction," Marc muttered. "All they're waiting for is the nod from the boss."

Daffyd nudged him. "Then for God's sake, keep quiet," he whispered.

Dani stood in front of Sheik Ali and, through the mouth of Muammar, put her request. The Sheik stroked his chin and exchanged a few words with his nephew.

"He asks why you want to go to Egypt this way, and why you cannot travel openly."

"Something of mine was stolen by a powerful man who can close the borders of Egypt to me. I have vowed to recover this thing and prevent this man from desecrating a tomb."

"Which tomb?"

Dani hesitated. "The tomb of one of my ancestors."

Sheik Ali raised an eyebrow. "In Egypt? You are English, are you not?"

"Yes, but my grandmother was Egyptian."

"Muslim?"

"Coptic Christian."

"And this thing that was stolen?"

Dani hesitated again. "A...a family heirloom."

"And where in Egypt do you want to go?"

"Any of the smaller cities along the Nile. Esna, maybe--or Edfu."

"The badawī are people of the desert, not the river."

"Then a desert town?"

Sheik Ali pondered the information.

"You have a powerful enemy, it seems, if he can close the border to you, but borders are nothing to the badawī. We go where we wish and none may gainsay us. Six of my men will travel with you and guide you to the desert town of Kharga, leaving you there. That is my offer to you."

"Thank you, Sheik Ali ibn Hawid. Your generosity overwhelms me."

"Your Arabic is slight, and none of my men speak your English. Muammar al-Hadi, son of my sister, will accompany you as far as Kharga. You will pay him for his time and trouble the sum of one hundred British pounds."

Dani smiled and bowed. "That is most acceptable."

Chapter Nine

❙❙ Colonel, it is I, Ali Hafiz. I am in Benghazi."

"What are you doing there? I told you to go to Rome."

"I did so, Colonel, and found that the three foreigners caught a flight to Tripoli. I followed and found that they journeyed on by bus to Benghazi."

Sarraj thought for a few moments, leaving the other man to wait in silence on the other end of the line. He considered Benghazi and its proximity to the Egyptian border at El Salloum. That must be where they were headed, though they were fools if they thought they could sneak into Egypt that way.

"Follow them to El Salloum," Sarraj said. "I will have them detained there, but I want to know if they do anything..."

"Your pardon, Colonel," Ali Hafiz said, a tremor of fear in his voice as he interrupted. "The foreigners have taken the road south, to Al Jawf. They hired a Jeep."

"Where is Al Jawf?"

"Many miles south, Colonel. In the desert."

"Why are they going there?" Sarraj muttered.

"I don't know..."

"That was not a question," Sarraj snapped. He took a folded map of Egypt out of a drawer in his desk and opened it out, searching the western border for Al Jawf. He could not find it.

"Follow them to Al Jawf," Sarraj instructed. "I want to know immediately if they attempt to cross the border into Egypt."

"There is a problem, Colonel."

"What?"

"I suspect there is no telephone link from Al Jawf. How shall I contact you?"

Sarraj massaged his temples. "Go to the army barracks in Benghazi and ask for..." He leafed through a small book on his desk. "...Lieutenant Fasal ibn Huud. Mention my name and ask for a radio transmitter. He will give you the required frequency and call signs to reach me."

"Yes Colonel."

"Don't fail me in this, Ali Hafiz. I need to know where those foreigners are and what they are doing."

Sarraj terminated the call and leaned back in his chair. He contemplated the problem before him for a few moments, and then pressed the buzzer on his desk. Another few minutes passed and there was a soft tap on his study door. Lieutenant Azib entered and saluted.

"Find me a detailed map of the border between Libya and Egypt."

"There may be one in the library, sir."

"I don't care where it is. Just find it and bring it to me."

Sarraj returned to the stack of papers on his desk, reading through the reports and recommendations from officers above and below him in the local chain of command, and also others that had nothing to do with official channels. He thought of calling for coffee but decided on a cigarette instead, inhaling the harsh smoke and feeling the energy surge within him again. Azib returned with a map and unfolded it on Sarraj's desk. Sarraj pored over it and after a little searching, found the desert township of Al Jawf.

"An exercise for you, Azib. Assume a foreigner intent on entering Egypt illegally has been seen in Al Jawf here..." Sarraj tapped the map. "What is his next move?"

Azib examined the map carefully, noting the few roads, fewer towns, and expanses of unmarked territory. "What does this man have in the way of transport, sir?"

"Unknown. Perhaps a Jeep."

"What else can you tell me about this man, sir?"

"There is no man. This is only an exercise."

"Yes sir. Is this er...hypothetical man...er, is he knowledgeable in the ways of the desert?"

"Assume not."

"Then he will quickly die, sir. The Libyan Desert is deadly. I doubt that a Jeep would be able to negotiate the terrain."

"And if he has knowledge of the desert?" Sarraj asked.

"Then he would travel by camel, sir. His chances of survival would be quite good, particularly if he could engage the help of local tribesmen."

"And his likely destination?"

Lieutenant Azib studied the map. "If he wishes to cross safely into Egypt, then the town of Al Jaghbub is a more logical choice. The Oasis of Siwa is only forty or fifty miles away. However..." Azib went on hurriedly as the Colonel frowned, "...if he is definitely crossing from Al Jawf, then one of the towns near Kharga is likely. Abu Minqar perhaps, or Mut, though they are both many days travel."

"Place a man in each of the towns near there and equip them with radio transmitters. I want to know immediately if a stranger arrives from the desert."

"Yes sir. This er...hypothetical man... Who are they looking for? Can I give them a description?"

"Two Englishmen and an English woman. I doubt there will be any mistaking them."

"They are to be apprehended?"

"No, just observed."

Azib saluted. "Yes sir."

"I shall be most annoyed if, having seen these people, your men lose track of them."

Lieutenant Azib saluted again and withdrew, leaving Sarraj to return to his reports. He got up and locked the door before returning to his desk and removing a thin folder from a locked, steel-lined drawer. Opening the folder, he went over the information inside it once more, though he knew the contents intimately. For two years he had worked on his plans, talking, cajoling, persuading. He had used his position as a full colonel of the Egyptian army to carefully select his men and place them in positions where they would do his cause the most good. He bought some politicians and army officers and blackmailed others. A few he even had removed permanently. And now, at last, he was ready to act, to launch a coup that would wrest power away from Nasser, and usher in a new military dictatorship with Colonel Michel Sarraj as Commander in Chief. All he lacked was money.

For months, Sarraj had contemplated bringing in Soviet Russia as an ally. They had intimated they would be happy to lend funds for such an enterprise, but Sarraj knew the cost was too high. Give the communists a foothold and Egypt would rapidly devolve into a client state. Now there was an alternative--an Egyptian alternative. The undisturbed tomb of an ancient king would provide gold to fund the military revolution. It was going to happen. Just a little bit longer...but he must tread carefully.

Sarraj lit another cigarette and thought about the foreigners that had discovered the account of the tomb in Syria and were even now seemingly determined to find the treasure themselves. *How much did they know?* According to Ahmed Bashir, they had no tangible proof of the tomb's existence and had only fading memories of what the account had actually said. Bashir had the full transcript and could study it carefully, working out the location of untold riches. All the advantages lay with Bashir.

"Why are they coming to Egypt then?" he asked himself. "Is there something Bashir isn't telling me?" He would have to ask him--and observe his face carefully as he answered.

Sarraj's hand hovered over the buzzer, meaning to call Azib to him again, but then decided not to. Bashir was a Minister in the Syrian government and he needed him--for the time being. It would not do to antagonise the man by sending for him like some lackey. He would go to him instead. Sarraj got up and straightened his uniform before setting out to find his guest.

Ahmed Bashir was in the library, sampling the books on offer, removing a volume and dipping into it before replacing it and selecting another one. He looked up as Sarraj entered.

"You have a fine library, Michel."

"It is small, but adequate for my needs."

"You are interested in history, I see."

"There are lessons to be learned in the actions of leaders through the ages. Ahmed, we must talk." Sarraj gestured toward a pair of armchairs. He waited until Bashir had settled himself before speaking.

"How was your talk with Director Nasrallah at the Museum of Antiquities? I trust it was informative?"

"You know about that? How? It is no secret, you understand, but I didn't know myself until it happened."

Sarraj smiled. "Little escapes me."

"Well, as I said, it is no secret. I asked him about certain persons mentioned in the Syrian account--Pharaoh Smenkhkare and Princess Beketaten."

"And what was Nasrallah's reaction?"

Bashir shrugged. "He couldn't help me. Not because he wouldn't, you understand, but because they are relative unknowns."

Sarraj sat silently for a few moments. "How do you intend finding the treasury and tomb?"

"The account contains a description. I hope to use this to find them."

"Tell me what it says."

"Why?" Bashir stared at Sarraj. "We agreed I would search for the tomb and you would provide the financial backing. Are you going back on our agreement?"

"By no means," Sarraj assured him. "I just want to be sure you can actually find it."

"I can."

"So tell me. Reassure me that I am not pouring money and resources into a fruitless exercise."

Bashir hesitated, chewing his bottom lip. "You would not exclude me from the search?"

"Of course not."

"I am a Minister, remember. If I go to the authorities..."

"Ahmed, you are my friend. Let there be no talk of authorities and exclusion. We are in this together and must trust each other. Do you not agree?"

Bashir nodded slowly. "Very well, Michel, as a friend I will share the first part of the account which describes the position of the treasury of King Smenkhkare. It says, 'Three days upriver from Waset, where the cliffs recede from the river, and a line of vegetation points the way to a path up the cliff. A notch guides the setting sun.'" Bashir smiled thinly. "After that, it gets a bit vaguer and more complicated."

"Where is Waset? I don't recognise the name."

"Modern day Luxor."

"Then three days upriver should not be difficult to pinpoint. The cliffs are not near the river at that point...what?"

"Three days upriver," Bashir said. "Is that on foot? Walking day and night, or just by day? By sail perhaps, though with a following wind? Rowing, maybe? How fast? We don't even know if that is exactly three days or approximately three days."

Sarraj swore. "You must have more than this. What aren't you telling me?"

"The original description was of a war galley fleeing upriver from a battle outside Waset. We might be able to work out a speed if we knew the size of the galley and how many oars it boasted."

"Is there any way to find out?"

"Perhaps Director Nasrallah would know what ancient Egyptian galleys were like."

"You saw him yesterday. Did you ask him?"

"No."

Sarraj considered this for a few moments. "It might not matter too much. As long as we can approximate the distance, the other factors will lead us. It has to be a place where the river recedes from the cliffs on the western bank."

"And if the river has changed its course?" Bashir asked. "What then?"

"How can the river change its course?" Sarraj stared at his friend. "Is that likely?"

Bashir shrugged. "Who can say? Rivers do change their courses, meandering back and forth across their river valleys--I have it on good authority. Whether the Nile has done so I couldn't say."

"And the line of vegetation?"

"Plants die. It has been three thousand years."

"The notch? The path up the cliffs?"

"Three thousand years of erosion might have erased all traces."

"Then the task is impossible."

"Difficult, I grant you," Bashir said. "But I would like to examine that stretch of river before I give up on this quest. The rewards surely outweigh a few weeks or months of searching."

Sarraj rose from his chair and started pacing the floor, his face twisted into a deep frown of concentration. "I hadn't thought the problem so difficult when you broached it, Ahmed. Had I known I doubt I would have agreed."

"You're not going to pull out? This tomb could make us both rich."

"It could, but only if we find it. I could still find the money I need from other sources." Sarraj grimaced at the thought of Soviet advisers within his beloved country.

"Don't give up yet, Michel. Give me a month to scout the river before you decide anything. Nazim and I can do that--we don't need any of your men. Just give us a motorboat and we'll get the job done." Bashir saw the hesitation on Sarraj's face. "What have you got to lose?"

"Indeed. Is there something you haven't told me, Ahmed?"

Bashir regarded the military man cautiously. "What do you mean?"

"Do the Englishmen know anything else that might lead them to the tomb more swiftly?"

"Englishmen? Ah, do you mean Dr Hanser and her colleagues? What do they have to do with this? They are back in England."

"Would they know anything that might help them find the tomb? Something you don't have?"

Bashir shook his head. "They couldn't possibly. We all shared the information, and then at the end, I confiscated everything." He thought for a few moments. "Everything. I even had their baggage searched and scrutinised. Nothing they can possibly say to their university authorities would carry any weight. They are harmless."

"Then why are they in Libya, heading for the Egyptian border?"

Bashir leapt to his feet in agitation. "What? What are you talking about?"

"They were seen in Benghazi last week and hired a vehicle and driver to take them to Al Jawf. The woman leader, an older man, presumably Dr Williams and a young man."

"That'll be Dr Andrews--a hothead and a troublemaker." Bashir mopped his brow with a handkerchief and collapsed back into his armchair. "Where's this Al Jawf?"

"In the Libyan desert, quite close to the Egyptian border. I think it is reasonable to assume that they are not holidaying there but intend to cross into Egypt and seek the tomb."

"We...we must...you must stop them."

"My authority does not extend that far. Once they step into Egypt I can arrest them."

"You must make certain of it."

Sarraj regarded the sweating Minister for several minutes. "Why are they coming here?" he asked at length.

"You said it yourself--to find the tomb."

"Yes, but how? They have no written accounts, no artefacts, and no treasure map, because you confiscated all that. They only have their memories of what are very vague directions. What could they possibly achieve? How could they find anything when you, armed with a full description, have doubts about finding it? No. They have something else. What is it, Ahmed? Tell me."

"There's nothing." Bashir frowned and then shook his head. "Dr Hanser was always very good at finding things, but I'm sure that was just..."

"Just what?" Sarraj waited, but Bashir offered nothing more. "What did she have?"

"Nothing, it's ridiculous."

"What were you about to say? How was she good at finding things?"

"I saw her find the third and last chamber when all my scientific equipment could not. I heard stories about her--my men overheard the members of the expedition talking. They said she..." Bashir smiled. "She is experienced in archaeology. She saw clues that others would miss. That's all it was--that, and luck."

Sarraj regarded Bashir coolly. "What did your men overhear?"

"Impossible things, ridiculous things."

"Such as?"

"They said she was descended from the Scarab in the account, and it is true she looked like the paintings of her on the chamber walls, but I'm sure that is just coincidence. They also said she knew exactly where the first two chambers were and pointed them out."

"Did they say how she knew?"

"A scarab told her."

"A scarab?"

"Ridiculous isn't it? If we take that at face value, we either have a talking beetle or...or perhaps there were clues in the inscription. I just thought of that. The woman called Scarab could have told her where the next chambers were hidden."

"And how did she tell her where the first one was? Before they found the written inscription?"

Bashir grimaced. "I don't know." He opened his mouth to say something more and then closed it again as a thought occurred to him. To cover his sudden indecision he yawned and shrugged. "The alternative is to believe the ghost of the woman somehow told her."

Sarraj raised his eyebrows. "You even contemplate such a thing?"

"Of course not. She was a pagan and as such, could not be in paradise with Allah. Therefore she could not do His bidding."

"You believe that?"

"I am a good Muslim."

"Or at least a cautious one, for I have never seen you at prayers."

"Nor I you, Michel."

Sarraj contemplated his friend. "Between you and me, Ahmed, and strictly in private, of course, I have difficulty in believing in the reality of the supernatural."

"You are an unbeliever?"

Sarraj smiled. "No doubt I shall make a full and sincere confession of my faith on my deathbed. But seriously, you don't think this dead princess guided Dr Hanser, do you?"

"It is entirely too fanciful for my taste," Bashir said, "Except that Dr Andrews was heard remarking to one of the other expedition members that the golden scarab had guided her."

"Scarabs are a common enough item in Egyptian tombs."

"Except there was never one associated with this one. In fact, as you know, it was not a tomb, just a series of chambers with a written account adorning the walls. No grave goods, no jewellery, no scarabs--golden or otherwise."

"You are sure they didn't find one and just not reveal it to you?"

"Completely. They, and their belongings, were thoroughly searched and everything related to the find was confiscated. Besides, even if there had been, how would a golden scarab guide them?"

"Perhaps there were instructions on it."

"Fanciful, Michel. Scarabs are small and usually bear no more than the name of the person they are supposed to bless. A short prayer perhaps. To aid Dr Hanser, the scarab would have to say something like 'look on the north wall of the cave fifty paces from the entrance'--and that would just be for the first chamber. There would have to be directions for the other two chambers as well. No, the idea doesn't hold water."

"How then do you explain her talent?"

"Something innate, perhaps. I can't really, without invoking superhuman powers."

"I suppose we could ask her," Sarraj said. "She's on her way into Egypt. I have men out waiting for her even now."

"What makes you think she'd tell you? That would negate her sole advantage."

Colonel Sarraj smiled coldly. "I can be quite persuasive."

Bashir concealed a shudder. "It might be worth a try, but I think I should start looking at the river cliffs south of Luxor anyway. Who knows? Her information may not even be needed."

Sarraj nodded. "I'll have Lieutenant Azib arrange for a small cabin cruiser to be made available. Just for you and your aide?"

"Yes, Nazim is flying in day after tomorrow. We'll fly down to Luxor the day after that."

*   *   *

Bashir took his leave of his friend and went up to his room. Excitement and fear warred within him and he was very afraid that Sarraj had spotted his hesitation. If the military man got wind of Bashir's suspicions, his life would be in danger, his position as a Minister and as a friend of the Colonel notwithstanding. Bashir shut the door of his room and locked it before going to his bed and pulling out the suitcase that lay beneath it. Within the small case lay two of the notebooks that contained the scribbled notes taken down as Dr Hanser had translated the hieroglyphs on the chamber walls. Bashir was not sure, but he hoped very

92

much that the answer to the riddle of how Dr Hanser had found the chambers lay within its stained and creased pages.

He lay on the bed and leafed through the pages, reliving the story of a young woman's battle against the usurpers of her brother's kingdom. Interspersed with the text were sketches of the incredible artistry found on the chamber walls--pictures of lion hunts, spearing hippos in the river lagoons and hunting ducks with bow and arrow in the marshes and reed beds.

"Somewhere here," he muttered. "I've seen it, I remember it--I think-- but I must make sure."

Bashir read through both books without finding the passage he was looking for and threw them both across the room in anger. The leaves of the notebooks fluttered like the wings of the wildfowl brought down in agony by the archer in the Amarnan art.

"God curse it." Bashir forced his anger and frustration down, taking deep breaths to calm himself. "Nazim will be here in a couple of days and he is bringing the rest of the material. The passage I seek lies in one of the other books and I will find it." He smiled. "And when I do, I will have Dr Hanser's secret and then perhaps I will not need Michel's help any more. He can whistle for his gold."

Chapter Ten

D ani's first view of the open desert evoked feelings of wonder mixed with a disturbing sense of familiarity. She knew she had never been there before--or even in any other true desert--but she was definitely experiencing a sense of déjà vu. The land stretched out before her in waves of sand and rock, capped by a pale arch of sky while the disc of the sun--the Aten--fiery and white, poured molten heat down on the little caravan. Dust dried her mouth and she reached out again for her water bottle, sipping at the warm fluid. For some reason, her right eye ached and she pressed her hand against it gingerly, half expecting to find ruin under her fingertips. Her face was whole and untouched, but Dani found it hard to shake the idea that she had been damaged in some way.

Motion dragged her attention away from the desolation around her to the single file of camels heading southeast into the Great Libyan Desert. Immediately ahead of her rode a tribesman of Sheik Ali ibn Hawid, the reins of her camel attached to his saddle and beyond him the swaying bodies of her companions, each atop his own mount and under the control of a tribesman. The sheik had judged their riding abilities before they left, and ordered three men to guide the foreigners until they got used to their mounts. Only Muammar rode free, though his mastery of his beast was not as polished as that of his uncle's men. The young Libyan rode next to the leader of the tribesmen, talking animatedly to him, but everyone else sat in silence, as if cowed by the oppressive weight of limitless sand and sky.

She twisted in her saddle, gripping tightly as the camel's motion threatened to unbalance her, and glanced behind. Another tribesman followed, his hooded, dark eyes fixed unblinkingly on her. The man did not acknowledge her and she turned away again.

"Muammar," she called. "I need to speak with you."

Ahead of her, Muammar glanced behind for a moment, and then resumed his conversation with the tribesman. She heard laughter and anger rose in her.

Marc turned awkwardly in his saddle and called back to her. "What's up, Dani?"

"I just want to talk to Muammar," she said tightly.

Marc called. "Hey, Muammar. Dani wants you."

Muammar turned and stared at Marc for a moment and then said something to the tribesman, evoking another bark of laughter, before wheeling his camel round and ambling back to Dani. He turned his mount to walk alongside hers.

"I have the greatest respect for you, Dr Hanser, but please refrain from giving orders to me. These men are...primitives...and in their society a woman minds her tongue and is deferential to men."

"Is that how you view me too?"

"Of course not, Dr Hanser. I am civilised and recognise that a woman may have a mind as good as my own."

"You are very generous," Dani said dryly.

Muammar flashed a quick smile. "I only ask you to be circumspect in your speech and actions. Now, what was it you required?"

"I don't appreciate being treated as baggage and being led by someone else. I can manage my own camel."

"I understood that none of you had ridden camels before."

Dani hesitated. "Daffyd and Marc haven't, but..." She bit her lip and frowned. "I know I haven't either, but I think I can manage it."

"It's not as easy as it looks."

Dani closed her eyes and breathed deeply, letting her strange feeling of familiarity take hold of her. "I can do it, Muammar."

Muammar pondered and then shrugged. "You are a woman and a foreigner, so they will not expect much of you. You will be in no worse a position when you fail, though you will have to put up with their laughter."

"I won't fail."

"We'll see." He urged his mount alongside that of the man guiding Dani and spoke to him. The man answered and Muammar replied forcefully, after which the tribesman grinned and handed the reins to his Sheik's nephew. Muammar held the reins and waited for Dani's camel to catch up.

"Here you go," he said, handing Dani the leather cords.

The tribesman fell back also, calling to his fellows to watch, and as Dani passed him, flicked the rump of her camel with his quirt. Her camel bellowed and surged forward, Dani clinging desperately to the saddle and fighting to stay on the plunging beast. The tribesmen roared with laughter.

The camel ceased bucking and settled into a straight, rapid rolling gait back in the direction they had come. Dani dragged on the reins but had little effect on the camel's determined desire to return to the oasis at Al Jawf, despite that being close on a hundred miles away. Muammar urged his own mount into motion and rapidly overhauled the fleeing beast. Coming alongside, he leaned across and grabbed the reins, easing both beasts to a walk before turning them back.

"Not as easy as it looks, is it, Dr Hanser?"

Dani flushed with embarrassment. "I'd have been fine if that man had left my camel alone." She sat in silence as Muammar guided them both back to the waiting caravan.

Daffyd and Marc carefully hid any feelings of mirth and only enquired as to whether Dani was alright. The tribesmen made many laughing remarks, luckily unintelligible, as they started the party back onto a south-easterly path. Once again, the three foreigners were led by the tribesmen, and everyone rode in silence, suffering the heat and dust without complaint.

Daffyd was the one who eventually changed their status from children to adults. Two evenings later, when they camped in the shelter of a rocky outcrop, he approached the leader of the tribesmen, Zufir ibn Hawid, with Muammar as translator.

"The desert is a hostile place," Daffyd said.

"Only to strangers," Zufir replied.

"Teach us to know the desert, so we are no longer strangers to it."

Zufir laughed. "It would take a lifetime to teach you the wisdom of the badawī."

"Then guide our feet on the path to wisdom. Teach us how to ride the camels properly. If we could control our own mounts then we would be less trouble."

Zufir stroked his beard thoughtfully and then nodded. "Looking after you is a burden," he conceded.

In the cool of the evening, as the heat of the day dissipated, lessons started. Zufir issued instructions and Muammar translated. He started with basic care of their animals, the proper position in which to sit, and how to make their camel recline for ease of mounting and dismounting. Then followed basic manoeuvring at walking speed, first with tethered camels and then untethered ones, moving up to trotting and pacing. Dani, despite her previous misadventure, proved adept at controlling her mount and Daffyd was almost as good. Marc's mount was recalcitrant though, and refused to cooperate, spilling its rider to the sand more than once, amidst general merriment. Zufir put him on another camel, one of the placid baggage carriers, and Marc soon learned to control it.

They were sore that night, Marc especially, and sat around the campfire wrapped in blankets against the chill of the desert night, sipping mugs of hot, honey-sweetened coffee. The tribesmen talked among themselves and occasionally Muammar translated stories of tribal life which, though almost inconceivable to western experience, still proved to be fascinating. They listened to stories of a harsh existence where ferocity and cruelty were common and kindness seldom occurred. Honour ruled every aspect of Bedouin life, and wrongs were wiped out by blood more often than by peaceable means.

Muammar suggested the three foreigners tell some stories too-- something about their homeland. They responded, much as they had when talking to the Sheik, but enlarged on their tales, more relaxed with these warriors than with the man who ruled them all. Daffyd told tales of the Welsh valleys where he had grown up and of his father and grandfather who had been coal miners. The desert tribesmen had difficulty comprehending a place where rain fell regularly, or why men would willingly go underground to search out dirty stones for a pittance. Coal meant nothing to them, and the idea of working for wages was abhorrent. 'Where is the honour in such an arrangement?' they asked.

Dani told of the cities and what could be found there, including the university at which she worked. Zufir and one of the other men had been to Libyan towns and agreed that such things were found there, but found it hard to believe that women were allowed to attend a university. Dani did not tell them she lectured there, on Muammar's advice, as they would not believe such an outlandish concept. Marc told a story that he had heard from his grandfather, who had fought in Palestine during the Great War.

"He was a Second Lieutenant in the Camel Corps and the officers there used to run him ragged sending him on errands for useless items or giving him the worst jobs possible. They would tell him tall tales of the desert and, being young and inexperienced, he'd believe them all. Some were true, like shaking your boots out because of scorpions, and others were just plain invention, like the sand worm that would crawl into your er, nether anatomy if you sat on the sand. That's why Arabs always squatted, they said."

Muammar translated, and added a few comments of his own, eliciting laughter. "Go on, Dr Andrews."

"One of the tallest tales they told was of bricking the camels. They said that bull camels could be vicious unless they were bricked. He asked what this meant and he was told that you stood behind a male camel with a couple of bricks and slammed them together suddenly, crushing the animal's testicles. After this, the bull camel would be quite docile. 'Good Lord', asked my grandpa, 'Doesn't that hurt?', only to be told, with a perfectly straight face, 'Only if you catch your thumbs between the bricks'."

Daffyd choked and spluttered over his coffee, before coughing and chuckling, whereas Dani just raised an eyebrow and muttered something about 'juvenile humour'. There was silence from the tribesmen for a minute after Muammar translated the joke. Zufir could not see the humour and said so.

"There are better ways of castrating a male camel."

Marc tried to explain the joke, but only got bogged down in details of camel care and double meanings. After several minutes, he shrugged and would have given up, but Zufir made him tell the story again, with Muammar translating after every sentence.

The tribesman listened intently and then said. "I thank you for the story, but I cannot see the point of it. Of course you would hurt your thumbs if you caught them between the bricks."

"My grandfather was concerned that the camel would feel the pain," Marc said, offering one last ditch explanation. "The humour is in the misunderstanding."

"Of course it would hurt the camel. That is why we would not weaken a bull camel by castrating it in such a manner. And why would a man deliberately misunderstand another on such an important subject? A camel is valuable."

"No bloody sense of humour," Marc muttered.

"Actually, they do," Daffyd corrected. "It's just different from ours. Read some of Jack Glubb's writings if you want to understand the Bedouin."

Marc thought for several minutes and then tried again, with Muammar translating.

"A man owned seventeen camels and had three sons. On his death bed he called his sons to him and told the eldest, 'I leave you half my camels'. He told the second son he left him a third of his camels, and the youngest was to receive a ninth part. Then the man died. When the sons came to divide up the camels, they found that you cannot divide seventeen by two, three, or nine."

Zufir nodded his agreement. "The wits of the old man were wandering as death approached."

"Naturally, the sons wished to honour their father's dying wishes, but could not decide on how to do it," Marc went on. "So they consulted a wise man, who told them to borrow a camel from their neighbour and make the division. They did so, and now the herd comprised eighteen camels."

The Bedouin nodded to show they were following the story.

"The eldest son now took half, which was nine camels; the second son took a third, which was six camels, and the youngest took a ninth, which was two camels. Nine plus six plus two equals seventeen, so they gave the extra camel back to their neighbour and everyone was satisfied." Marc grinned broadly as he finished the story, and looked around the faces of his audience for signs of appreciation.

Daffyd snorted and Dani smiled and shook her head.

Zufir accepted the tale at face value. "It is good that the father's wishes were met," he said.

The other Bedouin nodded their agreement, and their conversation turned to other matters.

"They've missed the point of the joke," Marc said. "Should I explain? You see, a half and a third and a ninth don't add up..."

"I would not bother, Dr Andrews," Muammar said.

"As I said," Daffyd added. "Their sense of humour is different from ours. Read Jack Glubb--Glubb Pasha--he lived among the Bedouin."

"I don't think I'll bother."

"Your loss, boyo." Daffyd took out his tobacco and rolled himself a cigarette, leaning back against some of their baggage and staring up into the star-littered sky.

When they set off the next morning, all ten riders controlled their own camels and, after a few hours, Zufir increased the speed of their little group from a plodding walk to a faster paced gait that ate up the miles. Every two or three days, the tribesmen found their way to a small stone-lipped well or dug-out seep covered with a stone slab, and though water was never plentiful, it was enough to keep them alive. Marc complained about the lack of water, saying the first thing he was going to do when they reached the Nile was go for a swim.

"I'd settle for a wash and the chance to do some laundry," Dani said. She plucked at her soiled and stained shirt and slacks and wiped sweat off her brow with one sleeve. "How much longer to Kharga?"

"We've been heading southeast these last few days to take advantage of known water sources," Muammar explained. "There's a major well another half day's ride away, and then we'll swing northeast for about ten days."

They reached the well just after nightfall, and spent the whole of the following day replenishing their water supplies and allowing the camels to drink their fill. Zufir ordered the goat they had carried on one of the pack camels to be slaughtered and prepared, roasting the meat over a bed of coals.

"The next few days will be hard," Zufir explained. "There is little water and you will need your strength. Eat, and rest."

Zufir had not exaggerated the hardship of the next few days as they steadily forged towards Kharga. They travelled slowly, not wanting to push the camels too hard, often starting out each day in the pre-dawn and setting up camp for the night after the first stars sprinkled the eastern sky. The sandy desert became rocky, the camels having to pick their way carefully over a shifting, stony surface, and their pace slowed further. The heat remained though, and the dust, sapping their strength.

Dani thought it was incredibly beautiful, though harsh, and shared her thoughts with Daffyd. "I feel alive out here, as if this is my natural home."

"It is pretty spectacular," Daffyd agreed. "Though a tad stark. I'm glad we've got experts with us. I'd hate to be lost out here."

Dani smiled. "No chance of getting lost. The goddess would show me the way."

"Dani? Are you alright? You know as well as I do that you need the golden scarab, and even then..."

A shadow passed over Dani's face and she sighed. "Yes, of course...I don't know what I was thinking." She was silent for a few minutes. "I've been having daydreams...no, more like memories," she murmured. "Memories of being Scarab out here in the desert."

Daffyd frowned. "Scarab was never out in the western desert."

"Yes I was. When we marched with Smenkhkare from Nubia to Waset. We came the back way to throw Horemheb off the scent."

"That wasn't you, Dani--that was Scarab. I realise you got close to her emotionally while you were translating the account, but keep a grip on reality, for God's sake."

Dani shuddered and her shoulders slumped. "I'll be fine. I just need to...need..."

"What?"

"I need to find the golden scarab."

Two days out from Kharga they entered sandy desert again and they camped near a ravine that split a rocky outcrop, sheltering from a northerly wind that lifted the sand grains, stinging their legs when they walked. They wrapped themselves in blankets and fell asleep, but hours later, in the darkness before the dawn, they were shaken awake. Moonlight glinted on curved daggers as the tribesmen crouched beside each of the foreigners, holding knives to their throats.

Muammar was not under restraint and he immediately confronted Zufir. "What is the meaning of this? These people are under my uncle's protection."

"Sheik Ali is a long way from here," Zufir muttered. "And we are the ones doing all the work for no reward. Is that fair?"

"You are Hawid Badu. Where is your honour?"

Zufir scowled and spat to one side. "We do this for our honour. Now cease your chatter Muammar al-Hadi, or we will treat you like these infidel foreigners."

"What is it you want?" Daffyd asked. Muammar translated.

"Only what is due to us," Zufir said. "You are paying this man..." he indicated Muammar, "...a hundred British pounds to guide you to Kharga, but it is I who do so, not him. I should be the one paid."

"We can discuss this."

"No discussion. You pay."

"We can pay you the same as we are paying Muammar."

"Twice as much. Two hundred British pounds."

Daffyd turned his head gingerly and glanced at Dani. "Have we got that?"

"Yes. It'll leave us very little to survive on, but if we don't get out of this we won't need it anyway."

"All right," Daffyd told Zufir. "Two hundred pounds."

"Each."

"What?"

"Why should I gain at the expense of my brothers? Two hundred pounds each."

"We don't have anything like that much money."

"Search them," Zufir instructed his men.

Their baggage was ransacked and the money counted out.

"Three hundred and twenty pounds only," Zufir cried. He grabbed the loose change and flung the coins into the darkness, the metal clinking and ringing on the rocks. "You owe us another...another thousand pounds."

"We don't have it. You can see that."

"What are we going to do?" asked one of the men.

"Kill them," suggested another.

"Have you lost your senses?" Muammar asked. "What will Sheik Ali say when you return to him with this sorry tale of treachery and deceit?"

"Who will tell him?" Zufir asked. "You, Muammar al-Hadi? What is to stop you sharing their fate?"

"What is going on?" Dani asked. "What are they saying, Muammar?"

"They are angry, Dr Hanser, that you do not have more money." He hesitated. "There is talk of killing you. Me too, if I do not support them."

"What will you do?"

"I don't know."

"The university has money," Dani said hesitantly.

"What do the infidels say?" Zufir demanded.

"They say that their university in England is rich and would pay a ransom--provided they are unharmed."

"A thousand pounds?"

"Yes, but they must be unharmed."

Zufir grinned, his teeth gleaming faintly in the moonlight. "Not a hair on their heads shall be harmed--provided they pay promptly."

The tribesmen discussed the proposition at length and the one who had suggesting killing them--Tahir by name--now raised another point.

"How are we to make our demands? We cannot go to the university in England."

"Of course not," Zufir said. "We must send a letter."

"Can you write in English?"

Zufir grunted. "I cannot write at all. Can you, Tahir?"

Tahir shook his head. "It might be easier to just kill them. Three hundred pounds is a goodly sum."

"We can get a thousand with a little patience. Muammar will write the letter, and we will send it from one of the towns. In a few days or weeks, we will be rich."

Chapter Eleven

Nicholas Evans yawned and looked lackadaisically around the smoke-filled pub. It was brimming with a lunchtime crowd of students and lecturers from Midland University and the noise levels were starting to annoy him. He enjoyed a drink as much as anyone, but he preferred decent conversation while supping his ale, and he knew no one here. His magazine editor had sent him up to Chesterfield of the twisted spire to track down a story but it had come to nothing. The professor in charge of the research project had refused to talk to him, so he was now debating whether to catch a train back to London that afternoon or to spend another night up there. He hated to go back empty handed, but he could not see much mileage in the pub crowd.

Still undecided, he drained his glass and pushed through to the bar for a refill. There was a queue and while he waited he lit up a cigarette and listened idly to the fragments of conversation going on around him. A young bearded man just along from him was chatting up a pretty brunette and she was showing signs that her present resolve was weakening. On the other side, a middle-aged man held forth to a small group of men and women on the realities of life on other planets as evidenced by the rash of UFO reports coming in from all around the world. Nick smiled to himself, retrieved his new glass of beer and edged away through the crowd in search of saner conversations.

His seat had been taken while he was up at the bar, so Nick wandered outside to where a dozen trestle tables were set up on the grass close to the gravel-strewn car park. He found a table occupied by a group of youngsters enjoying the weak sunshine and indicated the vacant end of one of the benches.

"Mind if I sit here? It's a bit crowded inside."

Faces looked up at him warily and then away again. One of the men nodded. "Help yourself."

Nick sat and raised his glass. "Cheers." Then he sat back and surveyed the road absently while keeping his ears tuned to the conversation at the table. Not that there was much, the three young men and two young women said very little, evidently talking about something of which they were all familiar, but that meant nothing to an outsider.

"You think they're connected?"

"Well, don't you?"

"Could be innocent enough. She needed a break."

"So where's she gone?"

"Where do you think?"

"You're guessing. You don't know."

"With the others? What about us?"

"We've got more to lose."

"I really wanted to go dig in Egypt."

"That's out of the question now. And imagine how Dani feels."

"She'll pick up the pieces. We've lost more."

"Rubbish. She could lose tenure."

Nick pricked up his ears. Lecturers did not easily lose tenure at universities. Who was this 'Dani', and what was this about a dig in Egypt? The conversation faded away and glasses were drained.

"Well, that's enough for me," said one of the men. He rose from the bench a tad unsteadily. "Coming?"

One of the other young men got to his feet but the others stayed put. "Doris and I don't have a class for another hour," a young blonde said.

As the two men departed, Nick turned to the remaining youths and smiled. "Look, I'm grateful for a place at your table. Can I buy you all a drink by way of thanks?"

The young man grinned. "I could sink another pint. What about you two? G-and-Ts or wines?"

"White wine, thanks," said the blonde. Her mousy-haired companion that Nick assumed was Doris, nodded and smiled uncertainly.

Nick drained his own glass and got to his feet. "Back in a mo'."

He returned ten minutes later with a tray of drinks and set them down. He lifted his own and said, "Your health."

"And yours." The man and women drank.

The blonde woman held out her hand to Nick. "Thanks for the drinks. I'm Angela, and this is Doris and Al." The others shook hands one after the other, Al offering a hard grip that made Nick wince.

"I'm Nick."

"What do you do, Nick? You're not a local by your accent."

"Freelance journalism."

"Jesus," Al snarled. "Another bloody reporter." He looked sourly at his pint as if contemplating pouring it out on the ground or over the offending reporter, and then thought better of it. He gulped the amber liquid.

"We've had a lot of reporters round the university," Doris said. "We really don't want to talk to another one. Sorry."

Angela smiled. "If you'd said so before, you could have saved yourself the cost of a round of drinks."

Nick laughed. "As I said, they were as thanks for a seat at your table. I'm not a reporter," Nick assured them. "Leastwise, not the sort of gutter reporter who chases scandal and gossip. I came up here to do a scholarly article on research taking place at your university. I take it you are students here?"

"Who do you work for? Which paper?"

"Freelance. Sometimes papers but more often journals and magazines-- whoever's willing to pay me. I'm currently researching a technique by which archaeologists can detect the outlines of medieval foundations from the air." Nick saw a spark of interest in Angela's eyes, and grinned to himself. "It's really amazing what they're discovering these days. I have an interest in history myself, so don't get me started." He laughed. "I expect you're all Arts and Humanities students and I'd bore the hell out of you, so I'll change the subject. What do you think of these flying saucers everyone's talking about inside the pub?"

"Bunch of nutters," Al muttered.

"Don't mind Al," Angela laughed. "What about you? You must have come across many stories of saucers in your line of work."

"Enough to write a book, but that's not really where my interest lies."

"What are you interested in?" Doris asked.

"History."

"What period?"

Nick hesitated, recalling what the youngsters had said about Dani and a dig in Egypt. He decided to take a chance. "Ancient Egypt."

"No kidding?" Doris' eyes opened wide. "That's our field too--well, not really--I mean Al's doing the Palaeolithic and Angela and I are into Neolithic--but we came across an Egyptian tomb in Syria earlier this year and..."

"That's enough, Doris," Al snapped.

Angela put her hand on Doris' as the mousy-haired young woman's eyes filled with tears. "It's alright, Dor. I'm sorry, Nick, but we're not allowed to talk about it."

Nick nodded, trying to look nonchalant, despite his heart starting to race. *An Egyptian tomb in Syria and the finders sworn to secrecy. There's a story here.* "I understand," he said. "I've come across enough academics to know how touchy they get while they're writing up their paper."

"That's not..." Angela stopped and bit her lip. "The university doesn't want us talking to anyone, least of all the papers."

"Then it's just as well I'm not from any paper," Nick chuckled. "But seriously, I respect the er...censorship that's been imposed on you. I remember when I was an undergrad back in the dark ages; the powers that be didn't like us thinking for ourselves either."

Al muttered something and scowled before taking another swallow of his beer.

"That's not really the reason," Angela said. "There was a bit of trouble and...and, well, the university decided it would be better if everything was just forgotten. We're just undergrads, so..." She shrugged.

"Damn, I feel bad now," Nick said. "I've gone and upset you when all I meant to do was thank you for your hospitality and chat about innocuous things. Let me buy another round. It's the least I can do." He hurried off before they could refuse.

The crowd inside had dissipated a little and he was served immediately. He paid for the drinks and bought a couple of packets of potato crisps as well. As the barman handed back his change, he said. "Dreadful business about Dani and her Egyptian tomb, eh? There's talk she might lose tenure."

"Dr Hanser? Heard she got a right bollocking from the VC and professors, but she was only suspended for six months. I doubt they'll do more."

"Well, I'm very glad to hear it. She's a fine academic."

"You know her, do you?" The barman eyed Nick suspiciously.

"I was in one of her classes last year." Nick grinned and pocketed his change. "Thanks."

The three youngsters were still at the table, their heads together, talking. Nick put the drinks down and tossed the crisps onto the table top between them. He ripped a pack open and rummaged for the little twist of blue paper in the bag, sprinkling salt over the snack. "Hope you don't mind a bit of salt. I always find it goes well with beer. Cheers."

"Wine too," Angela said, helping herself to a crisp. "Look, Nick, I'm sorry if we appeared rude, but we really can't talk to reporters...or freelance journalists," she added with a smile. "If you printed anything, we'd get into trouble and Dani might lose her job."

"I quite understand," Nick said quietly, "But you're under a bit of a misapprehension about how these things work. If I was to write an article on the unsubstantiated word of three students, my editor would have my guts for garters." He grinned. "No offence to you chaps, but he'd ask why I hadn't got a quote from the principal character--this Dr Dani Hanser. And I'm hardly likely to get that, am I. She gets back from Syria having made a discovery that sets the archaeological world on its ears, gets a bollocking from her professors for some reason I can't begin to fathom, gets suspended, and disappears." Nick sipped at his beer, his eyes searching the faces of the young women. He had chanced everything on a story that might include bits of the truth. *Dani Hanser. Egyptian tomb in Syria. Suspension and now a disappearance. There's a story here.*

"I'm guessing Dr Hanser has gone to Egypt to search for it," Nick added softly. He hoped they would not ask him what 'it' was--he had no idea.

"I...I didn't think people knew so much," Angela whispered.

"You see?" Al growled. "Those bloody professors threaten us with expulsion if we breathe a word of it and then let the cat out of the bag to any Tom, Dick or Harry who asks around."

"Well, you hear things when you have your ear close to the ground," Nick admitted. "But I daresay a lot of it is just rumour and speculation. Tell you what. How about I mention a few things I've heard and you just indicate whether the rumours are true or not? Just to set the record straight. Then you're keeping your word and not telling anyone anything they didn't already know."

Al snorted and drank half the beer remaining in his tankard. The young women said nothing.

"I heard Dr Hanser discovered an Egyptian tomb in Syria."

"True," Angela said. "Well, sort of."

Nick frowned. "It wasn't Egyptian, or it wasn't in Syria?" His eyes searched for nuances in the blonde's expression. He raised his eyebrows. "It wasn't a tomb? I heard she stole valuable artefacts and that's why she was censured when she returned to England."

"Untrue," Angela said.

"A fucking lie," Al added. "The only thing she found was the golden scarab and..."

"Al. Shush."

"No, I will not fuckin' shush."

"Then temper your language please," Angela said. "You won't offend me, but Doris here is a lady."

Doris smiled and blushed at the same time. "Ange, I'm not..."

"What's this journo joker going to do, huh? Who'd believe him anyway?" Al drained his beer and slammed the tankard onto the table. He belched loudly. "Tell him the truth of it, so at least somebody knows. I'm bloody tired of keeping all this a secret."

"They told us not to," Angela said.

"And why is that? Because they want to hide the truth of the greatest bloody discovery in Egyptology since King Tut."

"The university's not to blame...well, yes they are, but not completely. All they've got to go on is what Bashir said--what he accused Dani of doing."

"Who's Bashir?" Nick asked.

"Under-Minister Ahmed Bashir, of the Syrian Ministry of National History."

"He was the one in charge of your dig? What made you look for Egyptian artefacts in Syria?"

Angela shook her head.

"Tell him," Al growled.

"Are you sure we should be doing this?"

"Yes."

Angela sighed and collected her thoughts. "We didn't go looking for Egyptian things. Dani was in charge and we were looking for evidence of Neanderthal migrations through the Orontes Valley," Angela said. "You know what Neanderthals are?"

"A sub-species of man who died out about thirty thousand years ago."

Angela nodded, and continued.

"We found a chamber carved into the solid rock wall of this cave, all bricked up, and the walls of the chamber were covered in tiny Egyptian hieroglyphs, telling the story of a princess called Beketaten. In the account, she called herself Scarab."

"She's the golden scarab you said Dr Hanser discovered?"

"No. That was something different."

"What was it?"

Angela waved a hand dismissively. "Forget it. The inscription was the important thing. It told the story of someone who lived through the events surrounding the rise and fall of the Aten heresy. You know about the Aten heresy?"

"Remind me."

"I thought you said you were interested in Ancient Egypt," Al said.

"I am. Perhaps it's from a different period."

"The Aten was the god of the sun's disc," Angela went on. "Pharaoh Akhenaten did away with all the other gods in the Egyptian pantheon and elevated the Aten to be his personal god. Then everything fell apart and the succeeding kings restored the old worship of the gods. This princess--Scarab--lived through these times."

"Fascinating," Nick said. *Damn, nobody's going to be interested in this refined stuff. Well, maybe one of the erudite archaeology mags.* "I can't see why this would get everyone upset with Dr Hanser."

Angela looked around at the people left at the outdoor tables before continuing. "One of Scarab's brothers, Smenkhkare by name, had a treasury and a tomb in an out-of-the-way place. The account describes how to find it. Perhaps that of Scarab too."

"This tomb hasn't been discovered yet?"

"If it had, it would be in the history books."

Nick whistled softly. "So it's another undiscovered tomb, like King Tut's?"

"Probably richer."

"And the account tells you where it is?"

"Yes."

"Er, I don't suppose you've got a copy of this account?"

"What? You think we'd just show you?" Al jeered.

"No, we don't," Angela said. "Minister Bashir confiscated everything and threw us out of the country. Now he's putting it about that we discovered a minor tomb and looted it. That's why Dani's in trouble--she can't prove otherwise."

"But this tomb in Egypt actually exists?"

"If the account is accurate."

"But the account still exists?" Nick queried. Angela nodded. "Then why the hell haven't you blown it sky high, held press conferences, and shown this Bashir person for the crook he is?"

"Because we have no proof..."

"And because bloody Bashir is a Syrian government Minister whose word is more believable than that of a handful of academics and students," Al said. "Plus he's spread lies about us looting the place and the fucking university believes him. They suspended Dani, and reprimanded Marc and Daffy."

"So this is why Dr Hanser has gone to Egypt?" Nick asked. "To find this tomb and clear her name? That's a marvellous story. I'd love to write it up."

"You can't print any of it," Doris said, looking alarmed.

"That's true," Angela added. "We gave our word to the university and if they found out we'd said anything, we might get expelled."

"So why did you tell me?"

Al shrugged. "Because somebody should know."

"A journalist can protect his sources..."

"They'd guess," Al said. "You can't say anything."

"Who are Marc and Daffy?" Nick tried to ease the subject away from prohibitions on doing the story. He did not want to have to promise not to publish and then break his promise.

"Daffyd Rhys-Williams, one of our lecturers, and Marc Andrews, a postdoctoral student."

"They were on this...er, expedition to Syria? What do they think? Could I talk to them?"

"They've vanished too."

"Gone to Egypt?" Nick asked. "With Dr Hanser?"

"Who knows?" Al said. "They didn't tell anyone where they were going."

"I heard Rome," Doris said.

Al shrugged. "Whatever."

Nick digested this information for a few minutes, cataloguing the information in his mind. "So all the people who are really in the know have disappeared. Is there anything else you can tell me?"

"I think we've said too much as it is," Angela said. "You can't use it. Promise..."

"Who would believe me?" Nick asked with a wry chuckle. "No, this has been a fascinating tale told over a few convivial drinks, but I can't see an editor agreeing to publish the unsubstantiated words of a few students. I think your secret's safe enough."

Angela looked at her watch. "We've got a lecture." She glanced at Doris and got up, smoothing her skirts. "Thanks for the drinks, Nick. You won't print anything, will you?"

Nick smiled. "I have no desire to see you lovely ladies get into trouble."

Angela smiled uncertainly and hurried off with her friend. Al drained the last of his beer and stifled a belch before staring at the journalist.

"You're going to write the story, aren't you?"

"What would be the point? Nobody would believe me."

"I'm sure you'll find a way." Al rose to his feet unsteadily. "I look forward to reading it."

Nick frowned. "You want me to write it? I thought you were against the idea."

"If you do, you'll drop us all in the proverbial faecal matter, but it'd be worth it to expose that bastard Bashir." Al turned away and walked toward the university, leaving Nick to stare after him.

*   *   *

"I can't see you've got enough to make it stick."

"I tried to talk to the university but the Vice Chancellor's office just said 'No Comment' and the professor of Hanser's department hinted she was deranged."

"Well, there you have it. If you can't back up the students' story, you've got nothing. Now, Nick, I've got this nice little piece you might be interested in, down in Cornwall. Lovely at this time of year and..."

"Dr Rhys-Williams is held in high regard in academic circles," Nick interrupted. "A number of his colleagues are incensed at his reprimand. Now that he's disappeared..."

"You're not going to let this go, are you?"

Nick grinned. "You know me so well, Percy."

"Why involve me?"

"Who else would I involve? You're my agent and I'm sure you can get me a top deal for this story."

"Not as it stands. Now, about this Cornwall piece..."

Nick grinned again. "Did I tell you I contacted a friend in Damascus? It seems that Minister Bashir has taken a leave of absence and gone down to Cairo. Perhaps there's something to this story of an undiscovered tomb after all."

Percy tapped a pencil against his front teeth, frowning. "What do you plan on doing?"

"I thought I might head down to Egypt myself and see what I can find. Can you imagine being in the party that discovered an undisturbed tomb? I could name my price for an exclusive and your ten percent would be one hell of a lot. Interested?"

Chapter Twelve

The Bedouin caravan changed its course to an easterly direction, angling away from the little towns of Abu Minqar, Mut and Kharga, and skirting the oasis of Barqis. Zufir had in mind a small village on the outskirts of the cultivated land of the Nile Valley, not far from the town of Edfu. Here, they would be able to guard their prisoners without disturbance, yet be close enough to a centre of population to send a ransom demand and receive the money when it arrived.

Their prisoners--Dani, Daffyd and Marc--suffered binding of hands and feet and being strapped to the backs of their camels, their reins in the grip of their captors. Muammar was allowed to remain free. None of the tribesmen were prepared to bind the nephew of their Sheik, but they also made it quite clear--in the face of his reluctance to join them openly in their enterprise--that they would brook no interference. Consequently, the young Libyan rode apart from his erstwhile companions and made no effort to influence their condition. At night, he camped with the tribesmen and let one of them feed the captives and see to their needs. After a day or two of keeping to his own company, he relented and assured the men that he would willingly cooperate, writing the ransom note for them.

"I must interrogate the prisoners though," Muammar told Zufir that evening, when the campfire had burned down to embers. "If the university authorities are to give any credence to our demands, they must be certain we actually have them in our hands."

"What will you ask them?"

"I don't know, but they will have to reveal something that only they and the university authorities would know."

"Do so," Zufir said. "But Alif will accompany you."

Muammar shrugged, knowing Zufir did not fully trust him, but also that Alif understood no English.

Marc glared at Muammar when he squatted in front of the captives. "You've got a bloody nerve," he said.

"I'm disappointed," Dani said quietly. "I thought we were your friends."

"As indeed I am, Dr Hanser, but these are my uncle's men and I am in their power as are you." Muammar leaned closer, blocking Alif from seeing Dani's face. "My companion does not understand English, but he is good at interpreting facial expressions. Please maintain your belief in my worthlessness."

"No bloody difficulty there, you bastard," Marc growled.

"What are you saying to them?" Alif demanded.

"I am telling them that we do not wish them harm but require their cooperation." Alif grunted, and Muammar turned back to Dani. "If I had raised a sincere objection, I would be bound alongside you. Instead, I have a measure of freedom."

"To do what?" Daffyd asked.

"I'm working on that. In the meantime, a ransom letter will be sent to your university, demanding a thousand English pounds. Naturally, the university will need to be assured that you are really in their grasp, so you must tell us something that could only come from you."

"Can you get them to free my arms enough to let me have a smoke?" Daffyd asked. "I'm gasping for a fag."

"I think not, Dr Rhys-Williams," Muammar said with a smile. "Anyway, I'm told smoking is bad for you."

"Opinion is divided on that score, but I suppose I'll survive."

"What is he saying?" Alif asked.

"He wants to smoke."

"I will ask Zufir later."

"So," Muammar went on, "may I please have some fact from each of you by which the university will know we truly have you in captivity?"

"Hmm, I'd have to give that some thought," Dani said.

"Not too long, please, Dr Hanser." Muammar sat down on his haunches and leaned back, admiring the scattering of crystal lights scattered over the velvet heavens. He waited.

"I've got something," Daffyd said. "Tell them that on the wall of my room in the university, above my desk, is a print of Joseph Wright of Derby's 'Experiment on a Bird in an Air Pump'."

"That is an art picture? The university will be able to access your room?"

"Yes, and yes."

"What about you, Dr Andrews? Do you have something for me?"

113

"My address is on file at the uni. Have them contact my mother and ask what my aunt Lavinia gave me for Christmas last year. It was a god-awful yellow tie."

"I shall ask about the tie. Thank you. Dr Hanser?"

"Tell them that a Mr Parker from the Foreign Office was at the Vice-Chancellor's meeting that decided to suspend me. I don't imagine his presence is common knowledge."

"Thank you. That should suffice." Muammar rose to his feet and brushed the sand off his trousers. "Is there anything you need? Aside from Dr Rhys-Williams' addiction to tobacco?"

"How about a knife so I can cut my fingernails?" Marc growled.

Muammar smiled but did not answer.

"I'd appreciate a little bit of privacy when I need to relieve myself," Dani said, not meeting anyone's eyes. "It's not as if I'm going to run away. Where would I go?"

Muammar nodded. "I'll see what I can arrange."

The journey through the western desert of Egypt to the edge of the cultivated lands took them a week. Zufir sent two men on ahead to arrange suitable accommodation and nodded his satisfaction at the arrangements they made in the tiny village of Amr ibn El-Aas. For a small sum, the headman of the village rented out two isolated huts some distance from the dirt road that wound toward Edfu. The huts were in the middle of farmland, far enough away from other habitations that there would be no nosy neighbours carrying stories of captive foreigners to the authorities. Each hut, half derelict, had missing boards and a cracked, cobwebbed window. They contained nothing but empty sacks which had once held chemical fertiliser and pesticides, and a rickety bench that ran along one side. Spiders hung in dusty webs, but even the rats and mice common to agricultural areas had deserted the place for more fruitful climes.

The three foreigners were locked into one hut, and the tribesmen, rather than occupy the other, camped beside it. One of them went into the village to secure writing materials, and Muammar bent his head to the task of concocting a ransom note. The first part was easy--the declaration that they held the three foreigners and the demand for money. Zufir had grown greedy and now wanted a thousand pounds for himself and each of his men.

"A thousand for you too if you want it," Zufir said.

Muammar, intent on presenting a united front, rapidly agreed, writing in 'seven thousand English pounds'.

"They are to tell us immediately that they agree to our terms," Zufir went on.

"How are they to do that?"

"What do you mean?"

"Am I to put a return address on the letter so they can send a reply?" Muammar asked. "Then the police will arrive to arrest us. Or should I just put 'care of the headman'? I'm sure he won't give us away for the reward."

"What reward?"

"There is bound to be one offered. Egypt welcomes foreigners for the tourist money they bring into the country. The government is not going to be pleased you have kidnapped some."

"Then what do you suggest?" Zufir demanded.

Muammar considered the problem. "Perhaps..."

"Yes? What?"

"The government should put a notice in the Egyptian Gazette agreeing to the terms and we will then write and tell them where to leave the money."

"Yes, that is good. Write it." Zufir watched as Muammar wrote the letter, hating the fact that he could not read the flowing Arabic phrases. "Say that we will kill our prisoners unless we hear back in a week."

"Give them a month. The message has to go all the way to England, and Egyptian bureaucracy moves slowly."

Muammar continued to write, adding in the identifying information that he had been given. He read it over carefully and considered telling the authorities where they were, but decided that if the police or army stormed the huts, people were likely to be killed. He addressed it to the Minister of the Interior in Cairo.

"Why not to their university? They will be the ones paying."

"Because they are in England. The Egyptian Government must be approached first. They will talk to the English and forward the letter to them."

Zufir shrugged. "Whatever you think. Remember that you stand or fall with us."

"It is enough," he said. "Have one of the men take it into Edfu and post it. He will need to put it in an envelope, address it and put a stamp on it. He will need money for that."

"He can do that in the village."

"The village will not have a post office. Edfu does. Even then it is not a perfect solution. The post office will mark the letter as having come from

Edfu and give the government a clue as to our whereabouts, but there is little we can do about that. Esna might be better, or even Luxor, as they are farther away and bigger."

"Edfu will do. The village is not Edfu." Zufir took the letter and perused the flowing script, unaware that he held the page upside down. He took it to Tahir and gave him detailed instructions.

The little group settled down into a routine. The tribesmen sat around talking and drinking coffee, or took it in turns to graze the camels. Zufir had a man guarding the prisoners at all times, keeping them locked in their dirty, pest-ridden hut, only allowing them out three times a day to relieve themselves, eat and stretch their cramped limbs. Muammar kept himself to himself, thinking. He knew that the government would react, but that their reaction might be too slow to keep the tribesmen satisfied. If the letter was even delivered to the Minister of the Interior, he would want to consult with his colleagues before replying. The chances were good that the letter had got lost somewhere in the labyrinthine convolutions of bureaucracy.

Twice a week, one of the men would go into Edfu and pick up copies of the Gazette, bringing them back for Muammar to read. So far there had been nothing in the way of a reply. If a response did not come soon, Muammar knew, Zufir might give up and kill the prisoners, vanishing back into the desert. Muammar knew he must take a chance, relying on the tribesmen's inability to read.

"There," he exclaimed when the latest batch of papers was delivered to him. "They have replied." He tapped a small news item concerning a car crash in Cairo.

Zufir grabbed the paper and stared at the printed words. "What does it say?" he demanded. "Do they agree?"

Muammar took the paper back and smoothed it out. "The government agrees to pay the money on behalf of the English university..."

Zufir let out an ululating cry of triumph, quickly picked up by the other men. The noise drowned out Muammar's words and he waited patiently for the shouting to die down before continuing.

"They say they will only pay the ransom if the prisoners are alive and in good health."

Zufir grunted. "They are, aren't they?"

"So far."

"Then that is good. Where do we tell them to leave the money?"

"Somewhere in the desert," Muammar said. "You will be able to see them approach and be certain there is no ambush planned. Pick a spot and I will write and tell them."

"Very good, Muammar al-Hadi," Zufir said. "You are good at kidnapping. We must do this again."

Muammar wrote again, explaining within the letter just what he was doing. He instructed the government to take the money to a particular rocky outcrop on the Kharga road and leave it under a certain stone that would be positioned there.

"You can set up the stone ahead of time and keep it in sight. Then you will know when they drop off the money, and can also watch for an ambush," Muammar explained to Zufir. "If you are surprised, you can easily flee into the desert."

"We take the prisoners with us? To exchange when the money has been paid?"

"They might be an encumbrance. Better to leave them here. I will stay and guard them."

"You, Muammar al-Hadi? Why would you seek such a menial part? You will come with me and share in the handover of the money."

Muammar shrugged. "And what if something happens to the prisoners while we are gone? Your men do not understand English. We could return to find them dead."

"What would it matter? We will have the money."

"The government would be most angry. The terms are the money in exchange for live and healthy prisoners. If we broke those terms they would hunt us down."

Zufir laughed. "They could try, but the badawī can vanish into the desert where none can follow."

"Why take the risk? Especially if they suspected we were men of Sheik ibn Hawid. Let me look after the foreigners until you return with the money. Then we can release them unharmed and disappear into the desert."

Zufir stroked his beard and considered his Sheik's nephew, weighing up the man once again. "Very well. You, Alif and Tahir will remain with them."

The new letter was sent, and more days passed until Muammar judged enough time had elapsed. He pointed to another brief article in the latest Gazette.

"They will leave the money in five days' time at the outcrop."

"Then we must leave immediately to be sure they are being honest," Zufir said, his eyes lighting up with anticipation. He took Tahir to one side and spoke to him at length before calling his men to him. They mounted their camels and rode away.

Tahir said little after his companions had left, but insisted on Muammar tending to the needs of the prisoners while he mounted a vigilant guard with his rifle.

"Tell them I will shoot if they cause trouble," Tahir said. "Tell them!" he shouted when Muammar hesitated.

"The others have gone off to pick up the ransom," Muammar told them. "This man has been left in charge and he is not a reasonable man. I ask you to give him no cause for anger."

"How long will they be gone?" Daffyd asked.

"About a week."

"And then we'll be freed? You said the ransom is being paid."

Muammar hesitated, busying himself with checking their bonds. "There is no ransom. It is a story I made up to get the others away."

"What?" Marc exclaimed. "They'll kill us when they get back. You bastard, I'll bet that was your plan all..."

Tahir raised his rifle. "What is he saying? Why is the infidel angry?"

"I told him to behave or else I would keep him tied up and let him soil his clothing."

Tahir laughed and turned to leave the hut. "Hurry up and finish with them. I will brew some coffee."

Muammar waited until the other man left the hut. "Do not think ill of me, Dr Andrews. Were it not for my efforts you would be dead already." He turned and squatted beside Dani. "Please, Dr Hanser, wait an hour and then call out as if in pain. If you are convincing, I may be able to free you all."

Chapter Thirteen

Nazim Manouk, Bashir's aide and secretary, flew into Cairo with a crate containing all the papers and possessions belonging to the British Syrian Expedition. There was no customs inspection and the contents remained locked away. Accompanying Nazim was a Syrian army officer who owed a debt to the Under-Minister and was eager to pay it off. Bashir had put in a phone call to a high-ranking officer in Damascus and had Lieutenant Jamal Al-Din placed on detached duty as a liaison between the Minister and the Egyptian military. Bashir drew Nazim aside in the Cairo airport and explained the matter to him.

"I don't fully trust Colonel Sarraj, and I need someone who understands the military mind. I need someone utterly loyal to me."

"I am loyal, Minister," Nazim murmured.

"Well of course you are, Nazim. Now, have all the baggage sent to this ship at the docks. We sail for Luxor this afternoon." Bashir handed his secretary a slip of paper with the name of a freighter on it.

"Wouldn't it be quicker to fly down to Luxor, sir?"

"I want to get the feel of the river first. This is my first time in Egypt and I want to experience it all. Besides, it may be some days before Sarraj has a launch ready for us."

Later that day, the three men and their stores were aboard a small rusting river freighter called the 'Gamal An Nil' or 'Nile Beauty'. The stores lay in the hold along with other containers making the trip upriver to Luxor, but the accommodation was limited to small cabins with very basic amenities. Nazim and Lieutenant Al-Din accepted them without comment, but Bashir grumbled until the captain of the 'Beauty' suggested he find passage on another vessel if he was not satisfied.

The freighter eased out into the river channel and started churning its slow way south against the current. The muffled thump and rattle of the engines was felt through the rusting iron plates of the decking rather than heard, and after an hour or so their senses tuned it out, allowing them to enjoy the voyage. Cityscape gave way to villages; industrial land became farmland and reed beds, while palms and acacia trees softened the edges of the river. Nazim and Jamal came on deck and stood by the rail, watching the land slide slowly past. Farmers worked their land, ploughing and tilling as their forefathers had done down the centuries, and small boys watched over flocks of sheep, goats and cattle. Fishing boats and other watercraft plied the wide expanse of water, a breeze ruffling the surface and reflections of the bright sun dancing in their wake.

"It is very beautiful," Jamal Al-Din remarked.

"You have been to Egypt before?"

"I have never been out of Syria. I thought my own country beautiful, but this is glorious. I can feel millions of people and thousands of years crowding around me."

Nazim smiled. "I expected an army officer but I have found a romantic."

"Can I not be both?"

They stood and took in the sights in silence for many minutes.

"What exactly are my duties?" Jamal asked.

"What have you been told?" Nazim countered.

"The Minister called in a favour. I was assigned to him and told to obey him as if he was my commanding officer."

"Then do that." After a few minutes, Nazim added, "The Egyptian military is keeping an eye on us and giving us some assistance. Your job will be to liaise with them if necessary and report back to the Minister."

"Report back on what?"

"Anything and everything."

For Bashir, the long trip on the Nile was an opportunity to relax before the stresses of the search engulfed him. He spent the whole of the first full day sitting on the deck of the steamer, staring avidly at the passing scenery. He took breakfast under an awning, and smoked cigarettes and drank strong black coffee while he made notes in a small book. There were certain preparations that needed to be made, but there was little he could accomplish until they docked in Luxor. After breakfast, he put his notebook away and contemplated the scenes slowly drifting past him. He revelled in the sight of cliffs and desert, of farmland and orchard, villages and towns, little fishing dhows and patches of reed bed where birds abounded. He saw swirls in the water and imagined them to be crocodiles; ducks lifted in a thunder of wings from the reed beds and he imagined bronzed archers in loincloths bringing them down with swift arrows; he saw ruins on the banks and imagined them rebuilt and glorious, teeming with priests and nobles. From time to time, Nazim unobtrusively provided him with coffee or, as the sun climbed higher in the sky, with cold drinks and sweet pastries as snacks.

The ship slowed as night approached and though they had lights aboard, in the absence of a pilot familiar with that stretch of the river, they tied up at an overnight dock. The passengers were responsible for their own meals and Nazim bought ingredients from local farmers and fishers and prepared a simple dish of rice and river fish with fresh vegetables on gas burners set up on the afterdeck. After the meal, the three men sat and looked at the darkened river flowing past, at the dim lights of farming households and the brilliant stars littered across a clear sky. Nazim and Jamal murmured quietly to each other, conscious of Bashir's presence and not wanting to disturb him. A few mosquitoes plagued them at first, but these disappeared as the night cooled. Shadows drifted overhead and the muted calls of hunting owls drifted from the fields close to the water. The water rippled and sucked, slipping past the moored freighter, reflecting the starlight.

Bashir retired for the night, but Nazim and Jamal stayed up for a while longer, enjoying a last cigarette and a modicum of companionship. The young army officer flicked his butt over the rail, watching its faint red glow arcing to extinction in the dark water.

"What is it the Minister seeks on this journey deep into Egypt?" Jamal asked. "I ask only that I might serve him efficiently."

Nazim considered the request, wondering whether to ask Bashir for permission or whether to just assume responsibility himself.

"What do you know of Egyptian history?" he asked.

Jamal shrugged. "Almost nothing. I know there were pharaohs who built the pyramids and ruled an empire before the coming of the Prophet, peace be unto him."

Nazim eyed the man sitting beside him. "You are a man of faith?"

"Of course."

"So you believe the gods of the ancient Egyptians to be what, exactly?"

"They are nothing but djinn or afrit," Jamal said.

Nazim nodded in the dark. "I don't suppose it matters what you believe as long as you are loyal." He thought for a few moments. "We found an inscription in Syria that hinted at an undiscovered tomb in Egypt. The Minister has decided, for scientific reasons, to test the veracity of the inscription by looking for the tomb. You have heard of King Tutankhamen?"

"Everyone has heard of him. Why?"

"The tomb we seek is of his brother--another king."

Jamal whistled softly. "Important then."

"Yes." Nazim hesitated, seeking the right words. "It is possible that others--foreigners or even Egyptian military officers may try to cheat the Minister. It will be your job to prevent this."

"A few soldiers would be useful. I am only one man."

"The presence of soldiers might precipitate that very betrayal. Keep your eyes and ears open, Lieutenant Al-Din, and trust no one but me."

Two days later, the steamer passed by the site of El-Amarna on the eastern bank. Bashir stood at the railing and stared avidly at the crescent gouge in the cliffs and the open land filled with rock and sand and very little else. A harsh and washed out light reduced detail, making everything appear flat and unwelcoming. Nazim stood with Bashir, and Jamal close by, though the lieutenant said nothing, being content to just listen.

"There it is, Nazim," Bashir murmured. "The royal City of the Sun, Akhet-Aten."

"It doesn't look like much, Minister. Those piles of rock could be the ruins of palaces and temples, I suppose, but it's hard to tell."

"Do not be fooled by appearances. Much has been discovered there and no doubt much is yet to be discovered. Perhaps when our present enterprise comes to a successful conclusion, we can release the account of the Scarab inscription and scholars can use it to sift through the ruins with greater knowledge."

"Your name will forever be associated with Amarna and its kings."

Bashir looked sharply at Nazim, uncertain whether his secretary was daring to make fun of him. A cormorant dived into the water close by, emerging from the river with a small silvery fish in its bill, and Bashir turned away from Nazim, distracted by the movement.

"It is amazing to think that all the characters we have come across in the inscription--Akhenaten, Smenkhkare, Ay, Tutankhamen, Horemheb-- all walked that land over there, eating, drinking, plotting."

"Not forgetting Scarab herself," Nazim added. "A mysterious figure, Minister. I'm still not sure just what to make of her. Was she as she described herself or did she invent herself? Did she do what she claimed to have done and if so, did she really meet her gods?" He heard Jamal snort derisively behind him and smiled to himself. "It will be interesting to see her face to face at last, gaze upon her golden mummy mask."

The crescent desert field of Amarna fell behind them as the rusty 'Gamal An Nil' steadily forged its way upriver. The cliffs marched close upon the river again, crowding the farmland into thin strips along the water's edge. There were fewer villages here, and fewer fishing boats plying their trade--just cliffs and sunburnt desert, hot breezes and the ever-present hawks circling far above. The presence of mankind was never far away though. Ruins dotted the shore and cliffs, and soon the ramparts of the desert receded once more and the green and fertile land pushed outward from the river, the source of all life in Egypt.

The river curved northeast, then south and southwest to Luxor. Civilisation crowded back, the ancient city known as Waset, Apet, or Thebes, now a bustling modern city replete with all the advances of twentieth century living--traffic, noise, crowds of people, and polluted air and water.

The 'Gamal An Nil' tied up at the docks in the late morning and Lieutenant Al-Din saw to the unloading of their baggage and its transport to the 'Hotel of the Kings' near the Karnak temple. Bashir and Nazim went straight to the hotel, where the Minister lost no time in relaxing in the best room available, while Nazim went in search of Colonel Sarraj's agents in the city. He returned two hours later, hot and grimy but moderately satisfied, and found that Bashir had eaten a meal and was now fast asleep. While he waited to report his findings, he dined with Jamal, and then bathed and changed into clean clothes, before settling down in the hotel lounge to go over the lists he had prepared. Bashir joined him in the lounge in the early afternoon, also refreshed, and ordered coffee for them both.

"Thank God we are back in a civilised city, Nazim," Bashir said, settling into an over-stuffed armchair. "A week of basic living on that boat is about as much as I could take. I feel clean again--rested and ready for discovery."

"There may be more hardship to come, Minister. If the tomb proves to be in the desert, there may be weeks of roughing it in tents."

Bashir waved the idea away dismissively, and poured himself a coffee from the silver pot a servant had placed on the table beside him. "Has Sarraj provided the launch?"

"Yes, Minister. It is fuelled and supplied with food and drink."

"Excellent. We'll start the search tomorrow."

"Have you given consideration to how we identify the place, Minister? The inscription was rather vague."

"We know the region of river it must be in. We'll scout the area and see if anything matches the description."

"Do we know the region of river, Minister?"

"Of course. You have told me yourself--three days upriver from Waset--Luxor."

"Three days by fully laden galley, rowed by weary and injured soldiers. Is that rowing continually for seventy-two hours or only daylight hours?" Nazim grimaced. "The account is vague and I have made some preliminary calculations in the hope of narrowing down our search."

"And?"

"Seventy-two hours with fresh rowers and a light load could take a galley all the way up to modern-day Aswan. That is an enormous stretch of river to search."

Bashir swore. "Are we beaten before we start, then?"

"Perhaps not, Minister. Taking into consideration the state of the men and the load they carried, I think they would get no further than Edfu."

Bashir consulted a map. "That's still a lot of river."

"We know they went upriver for three days. I have calculated the minimum distance they must have travelled as well--Esna. My estimate places what we seek between Esna and Edfu."

"That is much better. Well done, Nazim. It looks like I was right to bring you along after all."

"Your praise warms my heart, Minister."

Bashir looked up sharply, wondering if he detected a faint nuance of sarcasm. After a moment, he dismissed his suspicion. "If we fail to identify the site, we might need to re-examine the inscription. Speaking of which, Nazim, there are numerous references in it to the golden scarab. Remember? And somewhere, something about it being hidden--disguised in some way."

Nazim frowned. "Vaguely, but I didn't pay much attention to the story as such, being more concerned with making sure the recording equipment worked. Is it important?"

"I don't know, but the thought has been running around in my head."

"I could check it for you. The original accounts and translations are in the crate we brought along."

Bashir nodded and sipped his strong coffee. "Do so, when you have the time, but don't shirk your other duties. I dare say it's not important, but I'd like to be certain."

"There is one other thing, Minister," Nazim said after a few moments. "While I was out I heard a rumour that a tomb shaft had just been discovered, carved into the river cliffs a little south of Esna. That is in the region where we expect Scarab's tomb to be."

Bashir spluttered over his coffee, putting the cup down with a clatter and dabbing at his suit with a handkerchief. "They've found it? That's...that's a disaster. Why didn't you tell me immediately?"

Nazim shrugged.

Bashir wiped his hands absently on the coffee-stained handkerchief. "Are you sure?"

"No, Minister. As I said, it's a rumour."

"If it's true, we are finished. Everything will have been for nothing. How do we find out the truth of it?"

"I would imagine the Director of the Luxor Museum would know. Someone in your position should be able to get in to see him at short notice."

"Yes, yes of course." Bashir looked at his watch and leapt to his feet. "I'll go immediately. Make yourself useful while I'm gone, Nazim."

Bashir rushed out of the hotel and took a taxi to the Luxor Museum. He asked for the Director and gave his own name, flashing his diplomatic papers at the flustered receptionist. After a few minutes waiting impatiently by the front desk, a young man arrived and led him along corridors and down stairs to a small office in the basement with the name Dr Hosni Maroun on the door.

A small bespectacled man in a faded tweed suit and bow tie got up from behind a desk to greet his visitor. "Minister Bashir, from the Department of National History in Damascus? You are a long way from home."

"Er, yes. Thank you for seeing me, Dr Maroun. You are the Director of the museum?"

"No. Dr Karim Zewali is currently in Cairo, so I am deputising for him. How may I be of assistance? Is it to do with King Smenkhkare?"

Bashir opened his mouth in astonishment and then closed it with a snap. "How did you know? Has someone been talking?"

Maroun smiled. "You spoke with Director Nasrallah in Cairo concerning this matter. I did not realise it was a confidence." He gestured toward a chair. "Please have a seat, Minister. Yes, we in Egypt are very possessive about our historical artefacts, I suppose because so much of it has been looted in the past."

"I assure you that is not my intention."

"Of course not, but we like to keep tabs on what goes on. Naturally, Director Nasrallah informed me of your interest."

"I understand you have recently discovered a tomb shaft."

"And you wondered whether we had pipped you at the post."

"Pipped me...? Ah, yes, the thought had crossed my mind."

Dr Maroun sat and stared at Bashir for a few moments. "Please do not take offence, Minister Bashir, but excavations within Egypt should be carried out by experts--Egyptian experts of the Department of Antiquities."

"Of course. I would expect nothing less. My own interest in this matter is solely to determine the veracity of an inscription found in Syria-- currently being investigated by Syrian experts of the National History Ministry. I hoped we could work together on this, just as our two countries are joined politically in the great United Arab Republic."

"What was it again you hoped to find?" Maroun asked. "Director Nasrallah spoke to me but I admit to being a little confused. There was talk of Smenkhkare and someone called Scarab, as well as Beketaten, Akhenaten and Tutankhamen."

Bashir grimaced and nodded. "The truth of the matter is, Dr Maroun, the inscription that was found in Syria hints of a tomb in this area, and we are not really sure whose it is, or even of its actual existence."

"Well, Minister Bashir, I believe I can set your mind at rest. It is not the tomb of Pharaoh Smenkhkare."

"You...you have opened it? Who...who was...was in it?"

"The reason I can be certain...or at least moderately certain...is that the body of Smenkhkare was found in KV55, fifty years ago. Like his immediate relatives, that king was laid to rest in the Valley of the Kings, so whoever lies in this tomb of yours, it is not King Smenkhkare."

"I...I see. Then you have not opened the tomb you have found?"

Maroun smiled. "There is no great hurry. If it is a tomb from that period, it has lain there for three thousand years or so. Another few months more won't make any difference. It is far better to move slowly and be certain of doing things properly."

Bashir nodded and sat in silence for a minute. "You said three thousand years. Have you dated the tomb?"

"Not exactly. As you may know, in the absence of a name associated with a tomb, we must rely on circumstantial evidence, such as seals or pottery styles."

"You have found these things in the shaft?"

"A broken seal and some pottery fragments."

"And?"

"See for yourself, Minister." Dr Maroun opened a drawer in his desk and took out a rough disc of baked clay. He laid it carefully on his blotter and passed a magnifying glass to his guest.

Bashir looked and then shook his head. "There are fragments of two royal cartouches. I recognise that much but I cannot read hieroglyphs."

"They say, '...Truth is Re' in one, and 'Amun is...' in the other, or '...maatre Amen...". Almost certainly, the king in those cartouches is Nebmaatre Amenhotep, Amenhotep III, the father of Akhenaten."

Bashir stared at Maroun in surprise. "It is Amenhotep's tomb then?"

"No, that is in the Valley of the Kings."

"Then what...?"

"Seals are used for a great many things. They might indeed be used for royal purposes, but they could also be used to denote the vintage of a particular jar of wine--'in the tenth year of Nebmaatre Amenhotep', for example. The seal would be discarded when the jar was opened and it, along with other rubbish, would be thrown out. Eventually, it might find its way into a vacant shaft."

Maroun carefully transferred the seal back to the safe confines of his desk drawer. "It gives us an approximation of the time period...maybe. You see, the shaft could be older--but probably not too much older--and a fragment of pottery found its way in around the time of Amenhotep. If people still knew of the existence of this shaft a long time after it was dug, then whatever is at the end of it has long since been looted. The shaft has perhaps become just a rubbish dump. We'll know more on that as we excavate. Or it could be younger--but probably not much younger as those fragments would not be around to be used as filler."

"Hmm, I'll take your word for it. You're convinced it has nothing to do with Smenkhkare then?"

Maroun smiled again. "I didn't say that--only that it can't be his tomb."

"So when do you plan to excavate it?"

"In a month or two. There's no real hurry."

"I would have thought the existence of a new tomb shaft would make you excited and eager to start digging."

"It's a shaft sunk into the cliff face, filled with rubble. So far, there's no indication it is a tomb, let alone an occupied one. It could be an unfinished one, a mine entrance, or...or anything. The Museum staff is very busy and this shaft has a low priority."

Bashir considered whether to ask the question that was now uppermost in his mind, or whether to keep his purpose hidden. In the end, he decided he had nothing to lose by asking.

"Would you permit me to see the shaft?"

"For what purpose?"

"It's just possible that we can tell, from the positioning of the shaft, whether it is the tomb we seek."

"And if it is? I cannot permit you to excavate it."

"If it is, then I walk away--go back to Syria. I'll at least have proven that the inscription told a true story." Bashir shrugged in a manner he hoped was convincing. "It'd save me much fruitless searching."

"Let me think on it."

"Can I persuade you in any way?"

Dr Maroun smiled knowingly. "Thank you for your intended generosity, Minister Bashir, but it is not necessary. I'm a simple man with simple needs and my salary is quite sufficient." He got to his feet and extended his hand. "Leave a contact number with my secretary and I'll call you tomorrow."

Bashir fumed as he rode back to the Hotel of the Kings.

Nazim was waiting. "Did you discover anything, Minister?"

"They've discovered a possible tomb shaft that might be the one we seek. If it is, our efforts are for nothing. The Director, Dr Zewali was away in Cairo and I spoke with the Luxor Museum acting deputy, Dr Hosni Maroun...can you believe the son of a whore refused baksheesh? He will tell me tomorrow if we can visit the site; otherwise we have to wait months until they get around to digging it out. Or we can go on looking ourselves in case it is not the tomb, but that might just be a waste of time and money."

Nazim pondered the conundrum. "Perhaps not all is lost, Minister. Director Zewali outranks this Dr Maroun and can countermand his decree. You must see him when he gets back."

"That is a good thought, Nazim. Now I know why I keep you around. I will wait until I hear from Dr Maroun, and if he is uncooperative, I will contact Cairo and speak to Zewali or Director Nasrallah himself."

*   *   *

Dr Maroun phoned just before noon the next day. "I have decided to go and look at the site again, Minister Bashir. You may accompany me if you wish."

"Thank you, doctor. When?"

"In three days' time."

Chapter Fourteen

Nick Evans arrived in Cairo at about the same time as Bashir was arriving in Luxor. The indirect flight from London had been long and arduous, involving many seemingly unnecessary connections and long stops in airports scattered over Europe and the Middle East. His eyes were red-rimmed and his clothes were crumpled, and he knew he needed a bath and a shave. He exited the air-conditioned airport terminal and lurched into the torrid heat of a busy city night. Lugging his suitcase with him, he hailed a taxi and instructed the driver to take him to a certain moderately priced hotel a friend had recommended. The driver stared blankly at him and gabbled something. Nick repeated his instructions, slowly, carefully enunciating the name of the hotel. He was rewarded by a slow dawn of comprehension and another burst of incomprehensible monologue. The taxi moved off and Nick sat back with a sigh of exhausted relief, barely taking in vistas of crowded streets and a seething sea of humanity.

The hotel was in a poorer part of the city away from the areas usually frequented by rich tourists and businessmen, but despite the shabby, faded exterior, the lobby promised an old-world gentility that suited Nick right down to the ground. A young man in a red uniform sporting gold braid and buttons showed him to his room and carried his bag, displaying apparently genuine pleasure when Nick handed him a shilling as gratuity. He closed the door behind the smiling porter and surveyed his room and the small attached bathroom with bleary eyes. It would do. Nick yawned abruptly and reeled with exhaustion. He staggered toward the bed, shrugging off his jacket and tie, letting them fall to the floor. His shoes followed as the bed creaked under his weight, and his head thumped against the pillow. Sleep overcame him before he could remember to switch off the light or draw the curtains.

Nick awoke with the dawn and the muted roar of traffic seeping through his grimy windows. He staggered to the bathroom and relieved himself before pulling the curtains closed, switching off the light, and collapsing back into bed. Another two hours passed and he was hauled back to consciousness by a knock on the hotel room door. He rolled over and regarded the offending door, debating whether to tell the person to go away or just to ignore it. The decision was taken out of his hands. A key rattled in the lock and the door eased open, revealing an Egyptian maid in a starched uniform and with a bundle of towels in her arms.

She smiled at him. "I change towel, yes?"

Nick groaned. "You don't need to. I haven't used the bloody thing."

"Please I change?"

"Go away. Come back later."

The maid shook her head and her smile was replaced by a worried expression. "I change now, yes?"

Nick sighed and shut his eyes. "Go on then." He waved his hand vaguely toward the bathroom and the maid disappeared inside it.

She emerged a few moments later with a frown on her face. "You no need towel. Not use."

"I told you."

"Please?"

"Go away." Nick rolled over and ignored the maid, and a few moments later heard the door close softly. He tried to go back to sleep but it was no use--he was awake now. He lay there for a few minutes more, yawning and cursing, and then got up, stripping off his creased clothing and letting it fall to the floor.

The shower gurgled and spat but quickly settled down to supplying a fierce blast of cold water. Nick stood it as long as he could, lathering soap over his body and through his hair, before rinsing off and stumbling out shivering to his luggage to find his razor. He eased a new blade into the holder and tightened the handle. Plenty of hot water and lather in the basin followed and the smooth strokes of the blade against his bristles soothed him, calming him down. Nick examined himself in the mirror, rubbing his jawline with satisfaction, and then took a light smear of Brylcreem and rubbed it into his sandy-coloured hair before brushing it into a neat quiff. He towelled off and dressed in clean clothes, by which time his stomach was rumbling and he felt a dire need of coffee.

The hotel had no restaurant attached, but there were plenty of small coffeehouses and eateries within a hundred yards or so. He found a clean establishment and enjoyed a cup of coffee and devoured a sticky date and almond pastry. The caffeine and sugar revived him and he started to look forward to the day's activities. A notebook contained a list of his intentions, and he perused the points as he finished off his late breakfast.

Dr Dani Hanser and/or friends--Marc Andrews, Daffyd Rhys-Williams
Syrian Minister Ahmed Bashir
Smenkhkare and/or Scarab

Nick tapped his teeth with his pen and considered how best to investigate each one. *Immigration records or airline arrivals for Dani Hanser, but how the hell do I get those? Bashir? Well, his arrival might be considered newsworthy. The old Egyptians? Cairo museum, I guess.*

He put his pen and notebook back into his jacket pocket and set off to find a friend of a friend, working for the Egyptian Gazette. The man, a grizzled older man in a sweat-stained suit that had once, in its newer days, been white, came down to the lobby in response to Nick's query. He extended his hand cautiously.

"Mr Nicholas Evans, you said your name was--do I know you?"

"Thank you for seeing me, Mr Simmons. We have a mutual friend, Tim Riley at the 'Mail'. He said to look you up."

"It's been a while," Simmons said. "How is Tim? Still married to...what's her name? Jenny?"

"Julia. Yes, and three nippers now."

Simmons laughed. "That'll have put a crick in his love life."

Nick nodded. "He said you might be able to help me."

Simmons regarded Nick solemnly for a few moments, sizing the man up. "That depends."

"Naturally. Can we discuss it over a cup of coffee?"

"I'd invite you up to the newsroom but the brew they have up there would peel paint."

"Then let me buy you a cup at a decent café, Mr Simmons."

"The name's John. Lead on, MacDuff."

They walked down the road to a little café that boasted a shaded garden out back, with tables arranged tastefully in the cool shade of citrus trees. A waiter brought a silver coffee service and poured two cups of strong black coffee, leaving them with sugar, a small jug of iced milk, and sweet cinnamon biscuits.

John Simmons stirred in several spoons of sugar and stirred. He sipped and nodded appreciatively. "Good stuff. Now, what's this help you need?"

Nick tapped a cinnamon biscuit on the plate, shaking loose a few crumbs, as he considered exactly what it was he wanted to ask. "I'm chasing down a story--a possible story--concerning three British scientists who may have discovered something of archaeological importance."

"Really?" John's eyes narrowed. "What discovery?"

"I'll get to that, but I really need to know if these Brits are in Egypt at all. It may just be an unsubstantiated rumour."

"What are their names?"

"Dr Danielle Hanser, Dr Marc Andrews, Dr Daffyd Rhys-Williams."

"Never heard of them."

"You're sure?" Nick couldn't keep the disappointment out of his voice.

"There's a lot of people arriving in Egypt every day, most of them tourists and utterly un-newsworthy. I really have no idea whether they're here or not."

"Any idea how I can find out?"

John shrugged.

Nick glumly dunked his biscuit in his coffee and sucked it. "I feared that might be the case. What about an Ahmed Bashir?"

"Ah, now him I have heard of. He's some government chappie fresh in from Syria. On holiday, I believe. We have someone at the airport that lets us know when politicians or persons of entertainment interest arrive in the country. Is he connected to your three British doctors?"

"Possibly. What can you tell me about him?"

"Under-Minister of National History. Fairly low profile politician from Syria, free of scandal--or at least as far as I know."

"Any idea where he is now?"

John shook his head and nibbled on a cinnamon biscuit. "I've got a friend in the Department of the Interior. He might be able to find out where he is."

"And the British scientists?"

"I can ask. Now, you were about to tell me all about this discovery."

Nick hesitated. "It's only a possibility, and I really need to ask Dr Hanser about it, but it seems there might be an undiscovered tomb in Egypt."

"I thought they'd found them all. Whose is it?"

"Might be two people, or one. Smenkhkare was a name I was given...and Scarab."

"The dung beetle?"

"I'm told it's a name or a title."

"Bloody odd name for a person. Well, I haven't heard of anybody by that name. Or this Smenk chappie either. The best place to ask might be the Department of Antiquities at the museum."

"Thanks, I'll try that. Do you have a contact there?"

John thought for a moment. "Ask for Dr Shubak. As for the other names, I'll ask around and see if anyone's heard of them."

"Thanks, John, I owe you one."

The older man smiled and rubbed the stubble on his chin. "Yes, I rather think you do. You can buy me a gin later."

Nick took a taxi to the Cairo Museum as soon as he left John Simmons at the entrance to the Gazette. He asked at the reception desk for Dr Shubak and within minutes found himself wandering slowly through the exhibit halls in the company of a portly older man.

"Simmons eh? Can't say I know him well, but we've had a few dealings over the years. Look at that." Shubak pointed at a display case. "Magnificent workmanship, isn't it?"

Nick looked at the carved alabaster jar in the display case. "Er, yes, it is."

"Nineteenth Dynasty, reign of Merneptah, son of Ramses the Great." Shubak continued his slow amble and Nick hurried to catch up.

"Dr Shubak, what do you know of a king called Smenkhkare?"

Shubak stopped and turned to look at his visitor. "Smenkhkare, you say? Hmm, let me think...yes, Eighteenth Dynasty...one of the more insignificant kings. Never more than a footnote in history. His tomb is in the Valley of the Kings, I believe."

"His tomb is known?"

"Yes. Valley of the Kings...er, number fifty-five I seem to remember. Don't quote me on that, I could be wrong."

"It was a recent discovery?"

"Oh no, some fifty years ago."

"And you're absolutely certain this tomb is that of Smenkhkare?"

Dr Shubak stroked his neatly trimmed beard pensively. "Well, er, not absolutely certain, I have to admit, but highly likely. May I ask why the interest in such an er...ephemeral monarch?"

"Following up a story, Dr Shubak, but it looks like my story has just evaporated. What about Scarab? Have you heard that name?"

"Ah, now there I can help you," Shubak said. "Follow me."

The rotund Egyptologist led Nick through the hall and into a smaller one where examples of jewellery and ornaments were displayed in glass topped cases, lit by discreet lamps.

"There," he said, with evident pride, "We have one of the finest collections of scarabs anywhere in the world."

Nick's hopes, which had lifted when Shubak said he could help, crashed back to the tiled floor. "Impressive," Nick murmured, "but the Scarab I'm interested in is a person."

"A person, you say? Called Scarab? How unusual. I've never heard of that. Of course, a great many people had 'Khepri' or 'Kheper' as part of their name. Those are the names of the sacred dung beetle that rolled the ball of the sun across the heavens. A delightful story, I've always thought. But a person called just Khepri? I've never come across one."

"Could such a person exist?"

"Anything's possible, I suppose." Shubak gestured toward the other cases in the hall. "Perhaps I could show you some of the other treasures we possess..."

"Is there anyone else in the museum who might know about a person called Scarab?"

"I really think I have as great a knowledge of ancient Egypt as anyone..."

"Who is the head of the museum?"

"Director Nasrallah, but he is in a meeting today. Besides..."

"Ask him if I can talk to him."

"My dear Mr Evans, I cannot just break in on the Director. You will have to come back another day if you want to talk to him."

"Phone him then. Just ask him if he knows about Scarab the person...please Dr Shubak. You're my last hope."

Shubak visibly vacillated, and in the end nodded. "I'll ask, but I'm not going to push him on it. He's a very busy man."

Nick walked back to Reception with Dr Shubak, and listened as the Egyptologist spoke to the director of the museum on the telephone.

"Good morning, Director. Shubak here...yes, I'm sorry to interrupt but I have a journalist here...no, sir, I'm sorry, I wouldn't normally disturb...but he mentioned Smenkhkare and someone called Scarab and...yes, sir, I'll hold." Shubak frowned and covered the mouthpiece with one hand. "Curious. He's in a meeting but his tone changed when I told him the names." He listened to the Director's voice again. "Yes, sir, I'll bring him right up." He replaced the handset and stared at Nick. "He wants to see you--immediately."

Dr Shubak led Nick through the museum corridor. He tapped on Director Nasrallah's door and opened it when told to. "Director, this is Mr Nicholas Evans, the reporter."

"Thank you Shubak. You may safely leave him in my care. Come in, Mr Evans."

Director Nasrallah rose from behind his desk and gestured to a chair close to his desk. "Please be seated, Mr Evans. I am Jamal Nasrallah, Director of the Museum, and this is Dr Karim Zewali of the Luxor Museum."

Nick looked around, having been unaware of anyone else in the room, and spied a short, thin man in spectacles and business suit, standing near the window.

"Good morning Director...Dr Zewali," Nick said. He turned back to face Nasrallah. "Thank you for seeing me. I understand you are busy, so I'll keep it short. I asked Dr Shubak about King Smenkhkare and a person called Scarab, but he couldn't tell me much. He seemed to think you might know more."

"Before I answer, Mr Evans, may I ask where you heard those names? Very few people know much about the first, and even fewer about the second."

"You understand I'm a journalist? I write for a living, and I keep my ears and eyes open for a good story. Well, I follow up on hints and rumours to see if there is anything buried beneath them..."

"You came to the right place if you are looking for buried things, Mr Evans," Zewali said with a smile. "Who do you work for? Who is your editor?"

"I'm freelance. I decide if there's a story worth writing."

"What have you written before, Mr Evans? Anything we might have seen?"

"Possibly. I recently wrote a piece in 'History Today' on the excavations of the Bronze Age civilisation on Dilmun..."

"I've read it," Zewali exclaimed. "It was a well researched and very balanced piece--evocative yet not sensationalist."

Nick grinned with pleasure. "Thank you."

"You see, we are concerned that you are a responsible journalist, Mr Evans," Nasrallah said.

Nick smiled faintly. "Well, I could assure you I am, but you'd just have my word for it."

"I am satisfied," Zewali said.

Nasrallah regarded his companion for a few moments and then grimaced. "Time will tell. Go on, Mr Evans, you were about to tell us where you heard these names."

"Midland University in England sent an archaeological expedition to Syria, in the course of which they discovered a chamber with an account of an undiscovered tomb in Egypt--that of Smenkhkare--and possibly one of Princess Beketaten, sometimes called Scarab. Minister Bashir of Syria threw them out of the country, charging them with scientific improprieties, and has come down to Egypt to find the tomb. I talked to some expedition members in England and they think Bashir intends to loot the tombs if he finds them."

"Smenkhkare's tomb is already known and was probably looted in antiquity," Nasrallah said. "It is in the Valley of the Kings. However, that of Beketaten is unknown. She is a minor personage, barely mentioned by history, but we would very much like to know if her tomb actually exists."

"You say Smenkhkare's tomb has been discovered though? That's certain?"

"There is an element of doubt," Nasrallah conceded, "But it is likely."

"Then that possibly leaves only the tomb of Scarab."

"If it exists."

"Bashir seems to think it does. He believes it rivals King Tut's tomb. I'm told he is in Cairo and presumably looking for it. It's possible he may even come here looking for information."

"He already has," Nasrallah said.

"And again in Luxor," Zewali added. "Bashir spoke to my deputy, Dr Maroun, yesterday afternoon. He is concerned that a shaft found in the cliffs near Esna is the prize he seeks."

"My God. Is it?"

"Who can say? The shaft has not yet been excavated."

"What of the British expedition members? Have they come here too? Dr Hanser, Dr Andrews, and Dr Rhys-Williams."

"I have no knowledge of them."

"Then perhaps they know more than Bashir and don't need to come here." Nick got to his feet. "Thanks for the information, Director...doctor. I'd better get down to Luxor and find this Bashir or the others before they find the tomb."

"How will you do that, Mr Evans?"

"I don't know. Probably just ask awkward questions until someone reveals something of interest." Nick smiled. "I'm a journalist--it's what I do."

"Perhaps we could help you," Nasrallah murmured.

"How? And why would you?"

"You understand the concept of one hand washing the other? There is one thing you could do for us," Zewali said quietly. "If Minister Bashir, or these British scientists for that matter, seeks to despoil an archaeological site in Egypt, we'd appreciate knowing about it. We take a very dim view of foreigners coming into the country and removing its treasures. Quite enough of that happened in colonial days."

Nick sat down again and looked at the two men quizzically. "Why would you trust me to do that? I'm a journalist, remember. I could just get the story and publish."

"You could," Zewali agreed, "But if you're the same man who wrote the Dilmun article, I think you'll want to get at the truth."

"I could still get that and then scarper."

"The Department of Antiquities could help you. You need to get close to Bashir, maybe find these British scientists. We can facilitate matters."

"How? Bashir's not part of your crowd."

"Dr Hosni Maroun is my deputy at Luxor. He has already been approached by Bashir with a request to let him see the shaft. Presumably so he can determine if it's what he seeks. So far, Maroun has not given him an answer, but if I say so, he will let Bashir see the shaft. I could make sure you are in the party that does so. You get close to Bashir and see what you can find out. Quiz him. Ask him what he intends to do. If his intentions are honourable, he will be open with you. If not, I dare say you will be able to tell. Either way, you tell us of his intentions and you also get your story. Interested?"

Nick thought hard. "Sole rights to the story?"

"What do you mean?"

"That I'm the only member of the press allowed to report on this. I get exclusive rights--the backing of the Department of Antiquities."

Zewali looked at Nasrallah. The Director nodded.

"All right, then," Nick said with a grin. "You've hired yourself an investigator."

Chapter Fifteen

Dani's cries were quite convincing, and Alif and Tahir ceased their talking to listen. Muammar also listened, hiding a smile "She says she has a pain in her belly," Muammar said.

"Tell the woman to be quiet," Alif growled. "She disturbs our rest."

"It might be serious. What if she needs medicine?"

"We have none," Tahir said. "Just ignore her."

"Zufir told us to keep them in good health. Do you want to be the one to tell her she died and you did nothing?"

Tahir grumbled but told Alif and Muammar to investigate. They crossed to the hut and entered it, looking down at the three foreigners bound hand and foot. Muammar knelt beside Dani and pretended to examine her while whispering in her ear.

"Keep groaning." He cut the bonds around her wrists with a knife.

"What are you doing?" Alif cried.

"I have seen this before," Muammar said. "It is a weakness many foreign women have. She needs to roll onto her stomach and stretch out her arms." He helped Dani roll over and murmured to her as he did so. "When he comes close, scream and grasp his ankles." To the badawī, he said, "Alif, put your rifle aside and help me."

The tribesman cursed but did as he was told, propping his firearm against the wall of the hut and moving close to Dani's head. As he did so, Dani lunged forward and grabbed his ankles, screaming as she did so. Alif automatically tried to step back, tripped and fell to the ground. Muammar threw himself onto the man and hit him hard on the side of his head, stunning him.

Muammar cursed and rolled off Alif, rubbing his right hand. "That hurt me as much as it did him, the illegitimate son of a camel."

"Stop complaining and free us," Daffyd said. "Your other friend may arrive any moment."

Muammar's knife sawed through the bonds and soon all three were rubbing their wrists and ankles.

"What now?" Dani asked.

"We get out of here before he wakes up or Tahir wonders where we are."

"I say we kill that bugger on the floor and shoot the other one," Marc snarled. "It's no more than they deserve."

"Marc, no," Dani cried.

"Over the top, lad," Daffyd murmured.

"We will do no such thing, Dr Andrews. These men are of my tribe. I will not see them harmed unnecessarily." Muammar went to the door of the hut and peered out. The late afternoon sunlight threw the shadow of the huts straight toward Tahir, who sat under a date palm facing them. The sun would be in the Bedouin's eyes, but they could not rely on that to escape being seen.

"Out the back way."

"What back way?" Marc asked. "There's only one door."

"Then we must make another." Muammar stepped over to the back wall and pressed against the boards, gauging their strength. He found a loose one and pushed. With a squeal of protesting nails, it gave way and clattered to the ground. Another followed, and a third.

Daffyd hissed a warning from his watching position by the door. "I think he heard something. He's standing up...and coming over."

"Quickly then," Muammar said. "It'll have to do." He squeezed through the narrow opening, and then reached back to help Dani through. Marc followed, and then Daffyd. Muammar led them away quickly, but as quietly as possible, keeping the bulk of the hut between them and Tahir.

They heard a shout, and a few moments later a sharp report and a waspish whine as a bullet zipped by in their general vicinity. They stumbled across a ploughed field, crouching low. A drainage ditch appeared at their feet and they jumped down into the muddy bottom of it and, bent double, ran along it as quickly as they could.

"Are we being followed?" Marc gasped.

Daffyd ventured a glance above the lip of the ditch. "I don't see...yes, they're both there and following our trail."

"I should have brought the rifle," Marc said. "Then we could have fought back."

"This way, quickly." Muammar pointed. Together, they bent low and ran, not directly away from the approaching men but angling across their path. Together, the four of them ran for the scrub bordering the fields and hid in a small dry watercourse overgrown with briars and vines. They heard the angry voices of their pursuers approach the scrub, and then fade as they moved away along the edge of the tangled growth.

"What do we do now?"

"We need to get to Edfu," Dani said.

"That's a good idea," Marc agreed. "We'd lose them in a city, even if they bothered to come looking."

Daffyd considered the idea. "Might work, but there are a couple of problems. First, we have to escape two men out there hunting us with guns, and second, we have to find somewhere to hide in the city. I won't go into minor problems like food and shelter and how we pay for those without any money." He saw Dani's expression and smiled reassuringly. "Sorry, Dani, I don't mean to be a wet blanket. It's the best plan we've got, so let's take it one step at a time. Escape first, refine the details later."

"I may be able to help there too," Muammar said. "I have a second cousin, Mohammad ibn Sukrah, in Edfu. We are not close, but if we need help he may aid us."

Tahir and Alif came back, having found no trace of the fugitives and deciding they had overrun them, and were now searching the undergrowth more thoroughly. The two men walked past the dry watercourse and back into the scrub. Marc, Muammar, Dani and Daffyd wriggled out through the vines and briars on the other side and, bending low again, crept away in the opposite direction. After a while, they straightened up and ran.

Half an hour brought them to the edge of the scrub where pastures spread out before them and herds of cattle grazed on lush grass. Beyond the pastures, they could see a village and other fields in the land that sloped down to the distant river. They crouched in the last of the bushes, just outside a rickety boundary fence and considered their next move.

"Is that the village Zufir rented the huts from?" Dani asked.

Muammar nodded. "I think so."

"Then it's probably too dangerous going there."

"I can't see we have much choice," Muammar said. "If we try to reach another village we'll be spotted in the open land."

"We could stay in this scrub," Marc said. "We managed to hide from them before."

"That's true," Daffyd replied. "We sat in an old dry watercourse amidst briars and brambles for half an hour. I don't fancy spending days there; quite apart from the fact we have no food or water. Besides, those Bedouin could stumble over us at any time if they come in this direction."

"What do you think, Muammar?" Dani asked.

"I say we go...now. Tahir and Alif will search a lot more thoroughly than they did before but they still won't take long to get here. We must be across these open fields before they do."

"Sounds like a plan," Daffyd said. "Let's go."

They climbed the swaying fence and walked quickly toward the village. The grass was lush and springy beneath their feet and the numerous cakes and streaks of cow dung attracted swarms of flies that busily investigated the human intruders. A herd of cattle watched them from afar, heads raised, and then as they got closer, trotted over and surrounded them.

Marc stopped and eyed the cattle with distrust. "I really don't like cows," he muttered.

"Don't worry," Dani said with a grin. "They're not cows; they're bulls-- or steers."

"Great."

"Just keep walking," Muammar said. "Do you not have cattle in England?"

"Not personally," Marc grumbled.

Under Muammar's leadership they started forward toward one segment of the ring of cattle, and as they came within twenty or thirty feet, the cattle balked and ran, kicking their hind legs in the air and tossing their heads. After a few tens of yards they turned and stared at the approaching humans again, until proximity drove them away once more. They continued this routine until they came to the far fence where they formed a semicircle and watched the humans climb over into the next field.

There was a dirt road on the far side of the field, stretching away in one direction toward the river, and in the other to a dusty village. They moved in that direction at a brisk walk, and soon found they shared the road with workers coming off the vegetable plots on the other side and villagers moving about their own business. The people were all men and boys who stopped to look at the foreigners with guarded interest.

"Keep walking," Muammar said. "Avoid eye contact and follow my lead."

"Where are all the women?"

"Indoors probably. Maybe fetching water or fuel. This is a male oriented society and women are expected to know their place."

"Shouldn't Dani be walking three paces behind us then?" Marc asked, grinning.

"Please be sensible, Dr Andrews," Muammar said. "Now keep quiet and if anyone addresses us, let me do the talking."

"Er, we have a problem," Dani said. "Look behind us, in the cattle field."

The others turned and saw that the two Bedouin were running across the fields toward them. They were still a few hundred yards away, but would likely catch up within a few minutes.

"What the hell do we do?" Marc asked.

"Run." Muammar turned and sprinted down the road, followed quickly by Marc, Dani and Daffyd. They raced into the village, dust spurting up from their feet and ducked down a side street and then another. Villagers stared at them and one or two called out but Muammar ignored them.

"If we stay in the street, they'll find us," he said. "We'll have to go into one of the houses."

"What? They'll just let us walk in? Or do we break in?"

"Neither. Do you have any money at all? A watch, perhaps? A ring? Quickly."

Dani frowned and unbuttoned the lower part of her shirt, slowly and reluctantly. Marc shook his head, but Daffyd slipped a wristwatch off his wrist. Muammar examined it.

"It'll have to do." He looked around at the houses and walked toward a larger mud brick one. Dani paused with a hand beneath her shirt, waiting to see what would happen.

"Hang on," Marc said. "There are a lot of people around. Won't they just tell them where we are?"

"Maybe, but I'm counting on them not liking armed Bedouin. Anyway, what choice do we have?"

Muammar hammered on the door of the house, and when it was opened by a startled looking man, he started talking fast, gesturing to the three people standing behind him. Then he held out the watch.

The man refused the watch, waving his arms and looking angry, and then he bobbed his head, stepping aside and ushering them into his house. As the door closed behind them, Marc glanced back and glimpsed Alif turn the corner of the street, his rifle at the ready. Moments later, feet pounded past the house. Dani rebuttoned her shirt, and tidied herself.

The man spoke, bowing his head to Dani and limply shaking Daffyd's and Marc's hand, but all they could understand was the word 'effendi'.

Muammar translated. "His name is Aswad ibn Ahud. He welcomes the English Lords and Lady into his humble home. I told him that your boat had tipped over on the river, to explain your bedraggled appearance. He offers hospitality, so please smile and nod your heads politely. Oh, and please remove your shoes."

They hurried to comply, and Marc added a few remarks in his poshest English accent about how grateful they were to be able to be the man's guests. The man plainly did not understand, but beamed and ushered them further into his house, offering them seats on a beautifully patterned rug. He called out and a woman, hurriedly adjusting a scarf over her hair, appeared in a doorway. Aswad spoke and the woman nodded, smiled uncertainly, and disappeared back into what must have been the kitchen. They heard the clatter of dishes.

"You are to be offered coffee and cakes," Muammar said. "The man is evidently fairly well-to-do, so we must be unfailingly polite. Accept the coffee, even if you do no more than sip it, also a cake. It is good manners to accept a second one, but unless you want another, leave a small bite on your plate to indicate you've had enough. Same with the coffee. His wife will continue filling your cup if you drain it. Only use your right hand for eating and drinking--it is the height of bad manners to use your left." He paused in thought. "What else, what else? Ah, yes, very important, especially for you men. By all means smile and compliment his wife on the coffee and cakes, I will translate as needed, but do not make direct eye contact with her. Some Egyptian men are very possessive of their women."

The coffee arrived and the man's wife, introduced as Zera, knelt and poured the steaming black liquid into small cups. They sipped, nodding and smiling, and Marc made appreciative comments, which Muammar translated. Aswad beamed. The cakes were served and eaten, seconds accepted and nibbled. Dani complimented Zera and Muammar conveyed the message. When everyone had eaten and drunk enough, indicated by the dregs of coffee and cake crumbs, Zera cleared away the dishes and left her husband to entertain the guests.

The man spoke briefly and Muammar replied at length. Then he turned to Marc, Daffyd and Dani. "He hopes his humble fare was sufficient for such exalted English Lords and Lady. I replied that you were very appreciative of the excellent hospitality offered and would certainly sing his praises when you returned to Cairo. Please nod and smile again."

Marc nodded and smiled, but also asked. "What do we do about getting away from here? Any moment now, those damn Bedouin are going to find out from someone where we are."

Muammar spoke again, in Arabic, and Aswad listened. He called to Zera and spoke to her. She left and was gone for several minutes during which everyone sat in silence and smiled politely. When Zera returned, she knelt by her husband and whispered in his ear.

Aswad spoke and Muammar translated as he went. "The Bedouin have talked to the headman and demanded to search the village house by house. The headman has refused but the Bedouin are armed and are doing it anyway. The police in Edfu have been sent for, but it may be hours before they arrive--if at all."

"There are only two of them."

"Two is enough. They are armed and the villagers are not."

"How long before they get here?"

Muammar conveyed the question to their host.

"They are two streets away," Aswad said, and Muammar translated. "Why do they seek you?"

"They tried to ransom us for money despite us being hearth guests," Muammar said.

"That is a crime against God and man," Aswad said, horror written upon his face.

"What will you do when the Bedouin come here?"

"What can I do, effendi? I am a man of peace. I cannot stop them entering and finding you."

"Then we must leave--at once."

"That would be best," Aswad quickly agreed. "Where will you go?"

"We will try for Edfu, but we thank you for your hospitality. You have been a gracious host." Muammar rose to his feet and bowed, Marc, Daffyd and Dani following suit.

"Wait," Aswad said. He spoke to Zera again and she nodded her assent and hurried out. She was back in minutes with a young boy in tow. "This is Nassar, the son of my wife's second cousin. He will take you to a place where you may be safe for a while. Go with him."

Nassar took them out the back way and through a series of alleys ahead of the search to the edge of the village. He motioned them to stay hidden while he scouted out the approaches before leading them at a run over the main road and into the vegetable fields. They used a dried up irrigation ditch and ran doubled over for a hundred yards or so, and then took cover behind a stand of poplars.

"Nobody sees us," Nassar boasted. "I lead you to safety."

"You have indeed," Muammar agreed. "But where exactly is this place of safety?"

"Follow and you will see."

Using the poplars as cover should anyone look out from the village across the fields, Nassar trotted away along the rows of onions and lettuce. Men worked in the fields and looked up from their labours as the little party approached.

To each man or group of men, Nassar said, "These people are guests of Aswad ibn Ahud. You have not seen them." Each time the men would nod and go back to their work.

At the far end of the fields was a wooden shed, half derelict. Grass and weeds grew lankly around its edges and the door hung askew from a single hinge.

"Aswad says for you to stay here."

Marc looked around with horror. "Not another bloody shed. How long are we expected to stay here? What do we do for food and drink?'

"We've just eaten," Muammar pointed out. "When it gets dark, I'll go back and try to trade the watch for some supplies. As long as no one saw us getting here, we should be safe enough until we figure out how we're going to reach Edfu."

When the time came, Marc refused to let Muammar go alone. He didn't say so, but Dani suspected his decision had a lot to do with a lack of trust. Muammar just smiled and set out for the village as soon as it got dark, letting Marc follow along as best he could. They stumbled over rows of crops, trampling a few plants, and then tripped on the ruts in the road, but finally made it to the outskirts of the town.

"I'd better go in alone," Muammar said.

"I don't think so."

"I can reasonably pass for a native, but you are obviously a foreigner-- even in the dark--and cannot speak or understand Arabic. You would attract too much attention."

"I'll stay in the shadows."

"And attract attention that way. Please, just stay here. I won't be long."

Marc gave way, though with ill grace, and watched as Muammar drifted into the shadows and disappeared. He paced up and down, stood and stared up at the night sky and listened to the howling of dogs and the chirruping of crickets, getting steadily more bored. The moon rose, casting a silvery gleam over the landscape and scattering inky shadows everywhere. Then, after what seemed like a long time, he heard someone approaching from the direction of the village.

"Muammar? Is that you?"

There was no answer, though the sound of the approaching person grew closer. Marc called again, a trifle nervously, and then stared. The man who emerged into the moonlight was a stranger, and armed.

"Dr Marc Andrews, pray be so kind as to slip your hands into your pockets. We are going for a little walk."

"Who the hell are you?" Marc asked.

"My name is unimportant, but somebody greatly desires to meet you."

"Shit, it's that bugger Bashir, isn't it?"

"Just walk, Dr Andrews, and keep silent."

Marc did so, not really seeing what else he could do. The man, who appeared small and dark in the moonlight, held a big-bored pistol and gave the impression of someone who knew how to use it. They trudged toward the village and soon came across a jeep parked by the side of the road. In the back seat, bound and unconscious, lay Muammar.

"Now, Dr Andrews, where are the others?"

Marc turned to face his captor. "What others?"

The man sighed. "Dr Hanser and Dr Williams. I know you all entered Egypt together."

"Then you should know where they are. I'll be damned if I'll tell you."

"Must I persuade you?"

"Well, you could try, but I'll make damn sure people hear us. I'm guessing you don't want that, so..." Marc grinned, his hands in his pockets, "...fuck you."

"Is that your last word?"

"Yes." Marc added some precise but anatomically impossible instructions.

The man shifted his weight and said, "Look behind you."

Marc started to turn, knowing even as he did so that it was an elementary mistake. Something hit him hard above his right ear and the night sky shattered into pieces. He was unconscious before he collapsed in the dirt of the country road.

Chapter Sixteen

Bashir found time hanging heavy on his hands after Dr Maroun phoned. The museum acting deputy director could not be persuaded to move any faster, so he must perforce wait three days before finding out if the tomb he sought had been discovered already. The Minister spent most of the time in his hotel room reading through the transcripts of the Scarab account, searching for any clues he might have overlooked. He had come across three descriptions of notched cliffs at a distance from the river and a slash of green vegetation pointing the way. It was all rather vague and, at a distance of three thousand years, probably meaningless. Still, it was all he had to go on, so he persevered.

The hotel room was on the fifth floor and faced the river and the western cliffs, so whenever the English type-script and hand-drawn hieroglyphs swam before his eyes, he would stretch and wander across to the balcony. There he had the choice of standing in air-conditioned comfort inside the room, or opening the sliding doors and stepping out onto the tiny balcony. Here he would be assaulted by air so hot it rippled, and pollution billowing up from the snarl of traffic far below. He would cough and his eyes would smart after a few minutes, forcing him back inside, but he kept being drawn outside, his eyes seeking the cliff line beyond the river and farmland. There were notches in the cliff, and every time he saw one he felt a thrill of excitement, though Bashir knew very well that the tomb could not be this close to the city. There was a knock on the hotel room door. Bashir turned back inside and slid the balcony door closed, cutting off heat, stink and noise.

"Come in."

The door opened and Nazim entered. He held a briefcase and a notebook in his hands. "I found it, Minister."

"Found what?"

"The reference to the golden scarab being hidden--disguised if you will."

Bashir gestured toward the paper-strewn table. "Show me."

Nazim opened up the notebook and flipped over several pages before placing it in front of Bashir. "It is in the time when Scarab sought refuge in Zarw at the camp of the Khabiru. She talks to the elder called Jeheshua and argues that..."

"Be quiet and let me read."

Bashir concentrated on the passage scribbled in the notebook, thankful once more that he could read English, even the scrawled cursive of the transcriber.

There...

"Yes." He read the passage slowly. It was Jeheshua talking, one of the Khabiru elders and a friend of Scarab. He said...

"Meryam talked of another gift. One you showed her--a golden scarab beetle."

Scarab smiled gently. "Is that how she described it to you? As a golden beetle?"

"Well, no, she said it was made of stone."

Scarab dug into the folds of her clothing and drew the carving out, placing it on the grass between them. "What do you say?"

Jeheshua leaned closer, his eyebrows knitting together as he scrutinised the object. "This is what you showed Meryam? I can see why she called it a rock." He reached out and then stopped. "May I touch it?" Scarab nodded and he picked it up. "Strange. It is heavier than it looks and although the details of legs and wings are only sketched on, when I rub my finger over it, it feels like they are carved." Jeheshua put it back on the ground and rubbed his hand against his robes. "Did one of your gods give you this or did you find it?"

"It is the gift of Atum the creator."

"And you insist it is made of gold?"

Scarab put her hand over the carving and closed her eyes. *Atum, let him see as I see, if only for a moment.* She opened her eyes and took her hand away.

"Wh...what did you do, child?" Jeheshua asked in a strangled voice. "Is this some magic trick like that of a conjuror in the marketplace?" He stared at the scarab carving, the deep yellow tones gleaming lustrously in the sunshine.

"No trick," Scarab said. "I prayed to Atum to open your eyes."

Jeheshua could not take his eyes off the carved gold insect. "Why? Why hide it like that?"

In the Name of Allah the Merciful and Beneficent, thought Bashir. *Gold? Truly gold? How is that possible?* He started trembling with excitement.

"Nazim. Where is it? Where is the rock Dr Hanser carried?"

Nazim dug into the briefcase, pulling out a small cloth bag. He opened the cords and tipped the bag. A rounded gray-brown stone about the size of an apricot tumbled onto the desk and for several minutes Bashir just stared at it. Then he reached out and touched it gingerly, rubbing his fingers over it gently as the Khabiru elder had done.

It feels like it is carved, but it looks smooth. Could it be? Bashir picked it up, marvelling at the extra weight it seemed to possess, then... *No, I must be mistaken; it does not really feel heavier...only momentarily when I picked it up.*

Bashir replaced it on the desk and stared at it again. *How do I penetrate its disguise? How can I tell if this is truly gold and not rock, despite the evidence of my senses?*

"Nazim, you have read the story and examined the rock. What do you think?"

"I think that Jeheshua had the truth of it when he declared it a magic trick, a common conjurer's illusion. How could it be otherwise, Minister? We can see more clearly than the ancients, after all."

"How so? Explain yourself."

"The ancient Egyptians were pagans," Nazim declared. "Living in times when God had not yet made Himself known to mankind. Of course they believed in all manner of falsehood for djinn and afrit walked the land, posing as gods. Today, we have the Truth of God's Word as revealed by His Prophet, peace be unto him. And we have science, the self-evident information we obtain from our God-given senses. We see a rock because it is a rock, nothing more."

"That makes sense," Bashir admitted. "Then the story of Scarab and Jeheshua..."

"Is just a story, Minister. Probably concocted to show that the gods supported her. It is a measure of how simple people were that this..." Nazim tapped the rock. "...could be used to fool people."

Bashir regarded the gray-brown rock on the table and nudged it with his finger. "A pity," he said. "Scarab performed miracles with the golden scarab in her hands. We could have found the tomb straight away if this rock really was the golden scarab."

"I doubt the golden scarab ever existed, Minister." Nazim paused, his dark eyes taking on a slight twinkle. "You could always test it."

"Test it? How?"

"Can you imagine that the magic of a djinni could ever resist the power of God? Seek Allah's blessing on the rock. Pray out loud for enlightenment. If it is really the legendary golden scarab, God will remove the scales from your eyes and let you see clearly."

Bashir frowned. "If this is an attempt at humour..."

"It was just a thought, Minister. If there is nothing else, I have other duties."

"Yes, yes. Leave me."

"Shall I take the notebook and...ah, rock?"

"Leave them here."

Bashir sat and glowered at the rock for a long time after Nazim left. He wanted very much to believe that somehow he owned the magical golden scarab that would lead him to untold riches, but his common sense and faith told him the idea was ludicrous. The rock was nothing but a rock, though when he picked it up he felt again that momentary heaviness, the brief suspicion that it was made of some heavier substance.

"It is nonsense," he muttered.

Easy enough to prove, he thought. *Invoke Allah's blessing on it.*

Bashir got up and walked to the balcony doors once more. He did not open them but stood looking out through the glass and hearing the muted thrum of the city seep through.

"I am a man of the world," he muttered. "I do not believe in fairy tales."

Yet I am a man of faith. Why is it so hard for me to just invoke Allah's blessing?

"Because you fear to appear a fool, even to yourself."

Or is it that my faith is not strong enough?

"My faith is built on the five pillars of Islam. I make the declaration daily, I pray five times a day, I give alms and I observe Ramadan. I have even been on haj."

So do it. Pray to Allah. You do it every day. Once more will be no great thing.

Abruptly, Bashir turned and strode over to the table, snatching up the rock and holding it in his fist.

"In the name of Allah, the Beneficent, the Merciful. O Allah, hear my prayer and open my eyes so that the falsehood that has been laid upon them might vanish, and I might see this object in my hand as it truly is. O Allah, accept my Supplication. In the name of Allah, the Beneficent, the Merciful."

Bashir closed his eyes, afraid to open his fist and look at the rock.

Where is your faith, Ahmed Bashir? Look, for God has opened your eyes.

He opened his eyes, then his fist, and looked. For a moment, he thought something gleamed and then he saw that it was only a trace of sweat drying on an ordinary gray-brown rock. If it was anything other than a rock, he had not been able to penetrate its disguise. In disgust, he threw it across the room. It bounced soundlessly on the carpet and rolled under the bed.

The telephone rang and Bashir swung round to face it, forgetting the rock. He snatched up the handset and barked, "Yes?"

"Dr Maroun here...from the museum."

"I know who you are," Bashir snapped. "What do you want?"

There was silence on the other end of the line for a few moments. "I thought you were the one who wanted something from me, Mr Bashir," Maroun said mildly. "Am I mistaken?"

"My apologies," Bashir ground out. "I've just had bad news. Never mind that though, please go on. Why have you called?"

"We leave tomorrow for the Esna shaft. I want to say a few words to all concerned before we do so, and I need everyone's full attention, so could you please come and see me at the museum this afternoon at four?"

"Can't you just tell me over the phone?"

"I could, Mr Bashir, but I prefer to do it in person."

"I'm really rather busy."

"I understand. I'll send you a note when we get back telling you what we found."

Bashir fought back his anger, his mind filled with images of Dr Maroun slowly choking between his hands. "I'll be there at four," he growled.

He was, though he left it until the last minute, smiling inwardly as he was shown into a meeting room at the museum where half a dozen people sat around a table. Four of the people were young Egyptian men, obviously students or junior staff, and one was European, middle-aged, florid of complexion with sandy coloured hair. Bashir looked at this man with a touch of interest.

"Very well," Bashir said. "I am here. You may start."

"I'm sure we are grateful, Mr Bashir," Maroun murmured. He got to his feet and stood at the head of the table, looking at each of the men there. "Now, most of you have gone on these little expeditions before, so you scarcely need reminding of the Dos and Don'ts of archaeological work. We will be leaving the docks at eight tomorrow morning, so be on time. I will have no compunction about leaving anyone behind if they're late. The launch belongs to the museum and is small, so we'll be crowded. I must impress on you the absolute authority the captain of the boat has while we are on the water. A request from him is to be obeyed immediately. Safety on the water is essential. Likewise, my authority holds when we are on dry land. I am not a hard task-master but I need you to follow my instructions." Maroun looked around the little group. "Is that clear?" There were a chorus of affirmations and nods.

"The site itself is under the protection of the Department of Antiquities and, in the absence of Directors Nasrallah and Zewali, I have the final authority when it comes to what can and cannot be done. The shaft is marked by a small flag, and when we arrive I will instruct Rusul and Sajjad..." Maroun smiled and gestured toward the two young men sitting opposite Bashir. "...to set out a boundary tape around the shaft. No one is to go inside this boundary for any reason, except with my express permission. Further, nothing is to be removed from the site--not an artefact, nor bone, nor piece of stone--unless I so instruct. So, any questions?"

"Can we take pictures?" asked the florid man.

"Yes, but please ask me first."

"How long will we be at the site?" asked one of the young men sitting beside Bashir.

"Not long. We will not be excavating the site nor doing anything to disturb it. I just want to have a look around, and as one or two of you have asked about this shaft, I thought this was the perfect opportunity."

"How large is the boat?" Bashir asked. "I wish to bring my secretary and my military escort."

"I'm sorry, but that is not possible. The launch takes a maximum of seven persons and as you can see, there are seven of us in this room."

"Who is this man?" Bashir asked. "The young men are obviously just students but this man..." he indicated the florid man, "...does not fit in."

"Under-Minister Ahmed Bashir of the Syrian Ministry of National History--may I present Mr Nicholas Evans, Journalist."

"What is a journalist doing on this investigation? Why wasn't I informed? This is unacceptable."

"I'm sorry you feel that way, Mr Bashir. You are, of course, at liberty to withdraw."

"I want him off the investigation."

Dr Maroun regarded Bashir calmly. "Director Nasrallah has personally given him permission."

"I'm very pleased to meet you, Minister Bashir. Your fame precedes you." Nick rose to his feet and extended a hand across the table. Bashir regarded it with a moue of distaste and then shook it limply.

"Indeed," Nick went on. "As soon as I heard you were going, I insisted on joining this little expedition, and Jamal--Director Nasrallah--kindly obliged me. I've heard so much about you, Minister. I hope we'll find the opportunity to have some serious discussions."

"I very much doubt it, Mr Evans. I'm not in the habit of talking to reporters."

Nick smiled and winked. "I'm sure our mutual friend would like us to talk."

"And who might that be?"

"Dr Danielle Hanser. I believe you've worked with her."

Bashir fought back a flutter of panic. *Who is this man and how much does he know?* "I have met her," he conceded. "I was not impressed."

"No? Well, maybe we'll have an opportunity to discuss your differences of opinion."

"I think we'll leave it there for today," Dr Maroun said. "Please be on the docks by eight o'clock."

Bashir arrived on the docks early, with Nazim and Lieutenant Al-Din in tow, determined to take them if at all possible, but Dr Maroun had spoken the truth--the motor launch was small and the space sufficient only for the designated persons. With ill-grace, he sent his companions back to the hotel and clambered aboard the vessel, claiming the best seat for himself. The others arrived a few minutes later, and after Maroun had spoken to the captain and the sole crewman, he took his seat and they left the Luxor docks on time. Driven by the powerful motor of the launch, the trip took a scant two hours.

There is a point on the river, about six or seven miles past the bend where the Nile turns south again, where the cliffs of the western desert squeeze the farmland and advance almost to the water's edge. Just south of those cliffs, where they recede once more from the life blood of Egypt is the village of El Siteyah and the boat's captain turned the nose of his craft in toward the western bank. He cut the motor until they just made headway against the turbulent current.

"What do you think?" Maroun asked the group as they drifted toward the village wharf. "Does this look like the sort of place the ancients would site a royal tomb?"

"It does not seem dry enough, Dr Maroun," Rusul said. "Moisture would destroy tomb furnishings."

"It may be suitable for a lesser personage though," Sajjad said. "A landowner or merchant might not be able to afford a tomb in a prime position, so might settle for one here."

"Very true," Maroun agreed. "We must keep all these things in mind."

Bashir stared at the cliffs and the farmland, trying to equate the landscape with the descriptions from the account. He had visualised a very different scenario and realised he would have to rethink his ideas. There was no notch visible in the cliffs nor a track or anything that could be interpreted as a line of green.

"Shall we disembark?" Dr Maroun said. "We've a way to go yet and the path is steep in places. I hope you all brought stout walking shoes."

Maroun led his little party through the village and round to the southern side of the cliff outcrop before turning toward the steeply rising land. The road became a path and the path petered out into a vaguely delineated goat track that jinked back and forth across the bare hillside. They soon started sweating and uncorking their water bottles.

"Don't drink too much," Dr Maroun warned. "There's no more water until we get back."

The track steepened and they advanced by clambering from rock to boulder, slipping in the loose dirt, dislodging stones that clattered and bounced down the hill. They helped one another up the steeper courses and rested more often, their faces and clothing soaked with sweat and stained by the dust. Water bottles were used more frequently, and Dr Maroun had occasion to warn them again.

Half way up, they rested on a broad ledge and sat with their backs to the stone and their legs dangling over space while they admired the view. The river had visibly shrunk to a broad ribbon bordered by green farmland, and boats on the water and vehicles on the land were like children's toys.

"I always enjoy this view," Dr Maroun said. "It puts man's efforts in perspective. We're so tiny compared to the limitlessness of sky and land." A hawk circling far above them in the cloudless azure sky called down its agreement--a high-pitched, mocking shrill.

"How'd they ever get a sarcophagus up here, Dr Maroun?" Nick asked. "I'm exhausted and I'm only carrying my notebook and camera."

"Ah. It's not been proven yet that this is a tomb, Mr Evans, but I take your point. There are other cliff tombs and the effort involved in building them and furnishing them for eternity must have been enormous.

Remember that death was the defining point to the life of an ancient Egyptian and a tomb was the most important possession he could have. They thought little of spending a fortune on an eternal resting place, and for it to be secure against tomb robbers it had to be in an out of the way place. What better place than a cliff face?"

"I can appreciate that," Nick said, "But how did they haul a stone sarcophagus up here. It would weigh what? Half a ton?"

"At least," Maroun said. "But the land has changed, and a nobleman could afford to pay hundreds of workers to create a road to the site, destroying it afterward. The stone sarcophagus would be tied to a great wooden sledge and teams of oxen and men would haul it up to the tomb shaft an inch at a time before lowering it into place. A colossal effort but evidently they thought it was worth it." Maroun got to his feet and dusted off his trousers. "Come on then, let us make our final effort. Another hour should see us there."

The shaft, when they came to it, could have been easily missed, were it not for the small marking flag and a tiny tent erected on a square on more or less level ground a hundred yards away. Two men emerged as the small party climbed up to them. They held rifles and looked at them suspiciously, but their faces broke into broad smiles as they recognised Dr Maroun.

"Guards," Maroun explained. "It would be a pity to have the site damaged now when we are so close to exploring it. Come on, it's just up here."

The path steepened again and led up to where a great crack had opened in the rock face. In the narrow, shadowed entrance of the cleft lay a man-made structure, its roughly straight lines standing out against the natural formations around it. A square outline on the rock, hidden by shadow, fell away into a dark, rubble-choked throat.

"There it is," Dr Maroun said proudly. "Magnificent, isn't it?"

"If you say so," Nick said.

"I was sort of expecting more," Bashir added.

"That's the whole point," Maroun said with a smile. "If you have something to hide, you don't want to advertise the fact."

They worked their way closer to the shaft and peered into it. A few feet below the ragged edge, the smooth walls plunged downward and back into the cliff face at a steep angle, only to end in a heap of rubble about eight or ten feet down.

"How deep does the shaft go, do you think?" Bashir asked.

"A bit hard to tell before they've dug it out," Nick murmured.

"Quite right, Mr Evans," Maroun said, "but if similar shafts are anything to go by, it could descend say twenty feet to a stepped gallery that'll run at a gentler angle to a burial chamber. That's a guess, of course. It may be just a tomb that was started and abandoned and there're only a few more feet of shaft below that rubble."

They all stepped back and Maroun had Rusul and Sajjad peg a boundary of tape around the shaft. He sent the other two young men back to the guard's tent to fetch up the ladder, and when it arrived, oversaw the lowering of it into the pit.

"Well, Minister Bashir, do you think this is your tomb?"

Bashir shook his head. "I don't see how anyone can tell at this stage. Can we not persuade you to start your excavations sooner? Or at least dig down a bit deeper and see if this really is a tomb?"

"Quite out of the question, I'm afraid," Maroun said. "I just don't have the work force at the moment. In a month or two maybe..."

"What if I brought a team in and excavated it for you?"

"This shaft is under the aegis of the Department of Antiquities, Minister. Nobody excavates it for us."

"I could lend you the man-power."

Maroun shook his head. "I would only allow trained personnel on site."

"Perhaps we should find Dr Hanser, Minister," Nick suggested, his eyes twinkling. "I hear she is very good at finding things."

Bashir shot him a venomous look and stalked away, leaving the museum staff to start their investigations.

Chapter Seventeen

"They've been gone an awful long time. Do you think anything's happened to them?"

Dani opened her eyes and glanced across at the faint shadow that was Daffyd, sitting with his back to the outside wall of the derelict shed. The star-studded body of the goddess Nut, as Dani liked to think of the night sky, did little to alleviate the blackness of the rural countryside. The hut, and its yawning doorway, was a shadow within shadows, and the ploughed fields and scrub-covered land vague smudges that had to be guessed at rather than discerned. Far to the west loomed the cliffs, black on black, and to the east, toward the river, the sky betrayed just a hint of burnt orange, where the lights of the town of Edfu did their best to hold back the night.

Insects chirruped, whirred and rasped in the undergrowth, the insistent rhythms counterpointed by the occasional croak of a frog and the call of a night bird. Earlier, the high-pitched whistles and clicks of bats had teased their ears as the little flying mammals feasted on the hordes of insects taking wing in the dusk. Mosquitoes had bothered them considerably in the gathering darkness, but their nuisance had abated as the temperature dropped, leaving them to scratch at their welts for a while longer. Cattle lowed in the pastures, and when the gentle breeze veered, brought the familiar stink of ordure.

Dani had made herself comfortable a few feet away from the hut, not trusting the rustle and squeak of its resident wildlife, sitting in a cross-legged pose, closing her eyes and meditating. Now she looked across at Daffyd.

"There's nothing we can do about it."

"We could go and look for them. We know what direction the town lies."

"We wouldn't be able to see where we're going, let alone find them," Dani said. "If we fell and hurt ourselves, we'd be in a right fix."

"So we do nothing?"

Dani sighed. "I didn't say that. But be reasonable, Dafs, we don't speak the language--not very well at least--we can't see a thing, and Muammar may have a very good reason for delaying their return. What if those Bedouin are out there, watching the road to the village?"

"So what do we do?"

"If they're not back by sunrise, we'll head to the village and look for them. It's possible they've sought refuge with Aswad again."

They sat in companionable silence while the stars crept above them in concentric circles.

"I wish those bloody Bedouin hadn't taken my tobacco," Daffyd grumbled. "I'm gasping for a smoke."

"Do you good to go without," Dani replied. "Think of your health, not to mention my comfort."

"Smoking's not that bad for you."

"Come on, Dafs, you're an educated man. You know better."

Daffyd grumbled a bit more but eventually fell silent, closing his eyes and settling back against the crumbling timber of the shed wall.

After a while, Dani unfolded her legs and made herself comfortable in the lea of the hut, with Daffyd a few feet away. Nothing disturbed their rest until the first gray light of the new day. Dani opened her eyes and saw two pairs of sandal-shod feet only a few paces away. She sat up quickly and smiled uncertainly at the two weather-beaten farmers staring down at her. They held mattocks, but she did not think their pose was threatening.

"Hello," she said in what she hoped was Egyptian Arabic. "Friend."

The two men looked at each other, and one of them uttered a string of syllables.

"I wish I understood you," Dani said in English, and then tried again, wrapping her tongue and lips around liquid-sounding Arabic. "Me friend, Aswad, village." She gestured toward the still-sleeping figure of Daffyd. "Him too."

Another utterance, but Dani recognised the name of Aswad in it; smiled and nodded. She got to her feet, stretching away her stiffness and nudged Daffyd with her foot. "Rise and shine, Dafs, we have company."

"Huh?" Daffyd sat up and then leapt to his feet. "Who are they?"

"Local farmers, by the look of it." Dani grinned. "I've tried my fluent classical Arabic on them, but they must speak a different dialect. I think they understood my reference to Aswad though." She addressed the farmers again. "Aswad. Friend."

The farmers nodded. "Aswad." Then, apparently losing interest, they shouldered their mattocks and walked away.

Daffyd yawned and stretched and looked around. "The others not back yet, I take it?"

Dani shook her head. She looked toward the east where shades of rose and gold tinged the sky. "See, here is Khepri of the Dawning Light," she murmured. The disk of the sun rose above the eastern cliffs, the shadows racing toward the river, shortening even as she watched.

Lifting her arms as if to greet the dawn, she started singing, but the words were unlike anything Daffyd had ever heard, and the words evidently had the same effect on Dani, for her eyes widened as she heard herself. The words of the song faltered and died away. She turned to stare at Daffyd, unease written across her face.

"What just happened, Dafs? What did I do?"

"I don't know, love. What was that you were singing? I didn't recognise the tune or the language."

"I think it was..." Dani shook her head. "It just seemed like the right thing to do at the rising of the sun."

"I think we should go look for the others," Daffyd said gently. "The stress of being alone out here, worrying, must be getting you down."

Taking their bearings, Daffyd and Dani set off along the edge of the fields, retracing the steps that had brought them there the previous evening. They came to the road and turned in the direction of the village, nodding and smiling at farmers coming late to the fields. There was no sign of Marc or Muammar, and they became increasingly uneasy as they approached the houses.

"Where are they? Something's happened to them."

"Don't anticipate trouble," Dani said. "Let's try Aswad's house first."

"Do you know how to find it?"

"I think so."

They attracted a lot of attention as they wandered the streets of the village, searching for familiar landmarks. Small boys followed them, chattering and tugging at Dani and Daffyd's clothing, holding their hands out for a coin. They had none to give them but spoke to them anyway, asking for 'Aswad'.

The boys grinned and pointed, then took them by the hand and led them to a door. Aswad answered their knocking and he smiled and invited them in, shooing away the small boys.

"Er, Muammar, Marc--have you seen them? Are they here?" Dani asked.

Aswad screwed up his face. "Effendi?"

"How are we going to find out anything if we can't make ourselves understood? Any ideas, Dafs?"

Daffyd thought for a moment, then spoke his own name, pointing to himself, and then pointed at Dani, speaking her name. Aswad nodded. Daffyd then pointed to a spot just beside him and said "Marc", and then "Muammar".

Aswad stared, his brow furrowing in concentration for a minute before comprehension lit up his face. "Ah, Marc, Muammar." He followed this with a string of syllables and shook his head vigorously.

"I don't think they're here," Dani said.

"Blowed if I know what's happened to them then. Unless the Bedouin captured them." He caught Aswad's attention. "Bedouin? Badawī?"

The man shook his head again.

"Marc, Muammar. Badawī?"

Aswad's denials were vehement.

"What the hell do we do now then?" Daffyd asked. "Do we go looking for them, stay here, or what?"

"We can't stay here," Dani replied. "We can't impose ourselves on Aswad, particularly as we have no idea if Marc and Muammar are coming back. There's a possibility we just missed them and they've gone back to the shed, but if they're not there I think we should go on to Edfu."

"What? Just abandon them? We can't do that."

"I don't like it either, Dafs, but I don't think we have a choice. We came to Egypt to find Scarab's tomb and prevent Bashir getting his hands on it. We can only do that if we continue on. Muammar can speak the language, so they should be alright wherever they are."

"Hardly. They're in the country illegally."

"So are we. If we go to the police, we'll be arrested. The longer we stay here, the more chance there is of the Bedouin coming back or somebody turning us in to the authorities. I really don't think we have a choice."

Daffyd mulled it over. "I don't like it. It feels too much like betrayal..." he lifted a hand as Dani opened her mouth, "...but I can't see we have much of a choice. All right, we try the shed again, and then we head for Edfu." He smiled at Aswad again, bowed and uttered incomprehensible thanks, before pointing to themselves and saying their names, and then

161

indicating the east and saying "Edfu". "Hopefully, he'll get the idea, and then if Marc turns up here, he might tell them where we've gone."

"Good thinking."

Out on the street again, they found the children had dispersed, and made their way out of the village and back to the derelict shed without attracting unwelcome attention. It stood as empty as when they had left at dawn, and there was no trace of their friends having returned while they were away.

"Edfu it is," Dani said.

"What's in Edfu?"

"I don't know, but it's on the river and possibly near where Smenkhkare hid his gold. That was probably between modern-day Esna and Edfu. It's a start."

"You can find the tomb even without the golden scarab?"

"No, but Bashir must be searching for it by now, and he has the scarab. It belongs to me, and I mean to get it back. Then we'll see."

The road to Edfu was long and dusty and they were footsore and weary while still crossing the arid region between the village's fields and the broad swathe of farmland that bordered the river. They pushed on though, into the evening, their throats parched, seeking a place where they could find shelter and water. Fields spread around them now, sensed more than seen in the darkness, flat and almost featureless. The road was unpaved and rutted and curved away beneath their feet, so they followed it by scuffing the road's border, feeling the difference between hard clay and low, dry vegetation. They found sustenance at last, by accident. The road disappeared and they stumbled over ploughed furrows and tangled themselves in vines.

Daffyd tripped and fell headlong, cursing fluently in Welsh. He sat up and investigated the offending obstacle, finding a rough-skinned globe beneath his questing fingers.

"Hello," he said. "What have we got here?" He lifted the object to his face and sniffed. "I think it's a melon."

Dani felt saliva moisten her mouth and she swallowed painfully. "Can you split it?" she whispered.

"Hang on." Daffyd picked at the rind without much effect, thought for a minute, and then slipped his belt off. He scraped the metal buckle against the melon and felt it tear through into the soft and succulently aromatic flesh beneath. "Got it." Digging his fingers into the gap scored in the rind, he ripped the small melon in two and handed half to Dani.

Dani buried her face in the half melon, tearing at the water-laden fruit and gulping down the sweet flesh. She surfaced, gasping, and wiped her mouth.

"God, that's good." She returned to her feast.

For a few minutes, they chomped and slurped their way through the melon, spitting out the pips and scraping the rind clean of every scrap of moist fruit.

Daffyd belched, long and unashamedly. "Damn, I needed that."

"Are there any more?" Dani asked.

"Bound to be. I think we're in a melon field."

There were others, and without much effort they gathered up another four fruit, eating another two on the spot and carrying the others away with them. They retraced their steps to the road and found that they had become diverted onto a farm track in the darkness. The road itself still stretched out toward Edfu and they continued on their way, tired but at least with hunger and thirst assuaged for the time being.

They sheltered in a ditch overnight, huddled together for warmth, and awoke shivering in the cool dawn. Breaking their fast with the last two melons, they left the fleshless skins in the ditch and hurried on at their best pace down the last of the incline from the desert plateau into the rich-soiled fields bordering the river. Traffic increased on the road as they got closer to the river, and they were subjected to much scrutiny. Farmers stared; ox and donkey-carts slowed and the drivers goggled in astonishment at the sight of two dishevelled Europeans walking in the dust and heat.

A small flatbed truck rattled up behind them and slowed. The driver leaned out and accosted them in fragmented but understandable English.

"What for you do? Is English?"

Dani smiled and brushed back her bedraggled hair with both hands. "Yes, we're English. We're going to..."

The driver ignored her and looked at Daffyd. "No talk woman. Where go, effendi?"

"Into Edfu," Daffyd said, with an apologetic glance at Dani. "Can you give us a lift?"

"Lift you?" The man looked puzzled. "You mean ride you in back?"

"Yes."

The man nodded. "You and wife climb up."

"We don't have any money."

The driver waved his hand. "No matter."

Daffyd and Dani climbed onto the back of the truck where three men were sitting amidst sacks of fresh produce, including melons. Dani felt a little guilty in case the melons they had eaten had come from the fields belonging to the truck driver, and found and flicked away a melon seed that had stuck to her shirt. The men made room for the newcomers but, beyond a few inquisitive glances, ignored them.

"Where do we go in Edfu?" Daffyd asked. "We really need to hole up in a hotel or something to consider our options, but I can't see anyone letting us stay for free."

"We might not have to," Dani replied quietly. "The Bedouin took all the money in our bags and pockets, but they missed the belt I was wearing under my shirt. I've got about a hundred pounds in it."

"Bloody hell, lass, you never cease to surprise," Daffyd said with a grin. "That's going to be damned useful."

"I feel a bit guilty actually. I was about to get some out at Aswad's house, and later I should have given some to Muammar to buy food instead of using your watch, but something made me wait."

"Good job you did. I don't suppose you've got a couple of cigarettes tucked away as well?"

"Look upon this enforced abstinence as an opportunity to give up the habit, Dafs."

"You're a hard-hearted wench," Daffyd muttered, but he lay back against the sacks of produce with a contented smile.

The driver dropped them in the farmer's market near the river and after a bit of investigation found a small hostelry overlooking the slow-moving waters, where the owner spoke a little English.

"You are English? Why are you in Edfu?"

Daffyd led the conversation, fearing a repeat of the truck driver's misogyny. He borrowed from Muammar's tale of misfortune back in the village. "We were on a boat and it capsized. We swam to shore and will need two rooms for a few days until we can contact the British Consulate in Cairo."

"I will need to see your passports. It is the law."

"They're at the bottom of the river. We lost everything."

"You have no money?"

"We have some. If you can provide accommodation, we will get fresh documents sent from Cairo."

The owner grumbled, but when Dani produced a few pound notes, his eyes gleamed. "I only have one room," he said.

"We'll take it," Dani said.

"You are married? Man and wife? If not, you cannot have room."

"All our belongings are lost," Daffyd temporised. "Including our documents."

The man grumbled some more, but eventually passed over a brass key in exchange for several pound notes. "Top of the stairs."

Chapter Eighteen

Nazim returned to the hotel with Lieutenant Jamal Al-Din, slightly annoyed that he had not been allowed on board the launch. Since the discovery of the inscription he had continued his secretarial duties but had also become interested in the existence of the Egyptian tomb. He would very much like to have become one of the principals of the search team but Minister Bashir insisted on continuing to treat him as a common servant. It rankled, but he was not sure what he could do about it. Jamal had wanted to talk, suggesting they could go for a cup of coffee, but Nazim pleaded the pressure of work.

"There is so much to do, Jamal. I must take advantage of the Minister's absence to get some real work done."

"Anything I can do?"

"Yes. Sooner or later, we will be following leads on the western shore and desert. We will need a suitable vehicle. See what you can find for hire."

"From whereabouts? Luxor?"

Nazim shrugged. "Who can say? It depends on where we are searching. See what the car hire firms have locally, but also south of here--Esna and Edfu certainly, other towns maybe."

"You want me to go down to these places?"

"Telephone, Jamal. If they have something suitable, put in a tentative booking but don't spend any money. We have a tight budget."

Nazim went to his hotel room and gathered his papers together, going through them again, updating and checking the many issues that revolved around the coming expedition. He used the telephone from time to time, making copious notes in a notebook, and at last stretched and yawned, glancing at his watch.

"Lunch," he murmured, getting to his feet. He moved toward the door and paused, thinking to himself that he really did not feel up to a restaurant and a possible conversation with Jamal who would be sure to search him out. Instead, he crossed to the telephone and ordered room service from the receptionist.

Lunch arrived fifteen minutes later--a dish of *fuul*--mashed fava beans with onion and chopped hard-boiled eggs, a mixed salad and grainy pita bread, along with a large pot of coffee and a sticky almond and sesame cake. Nazim tucked in and felt contentment spread throughout him. He leaned back in his armchair and sipped on his coffee, contemplating what he would do with a free afternoon. Playing the tourist around museums and ruined temples held little interest for him--his mind was too focussed on the problem at hand--how to identify the site of the tomb they sought.

I need to read the accounts again. I might have missed something.

Nazim went up to the Minister's room and let himself in with a duplicate key. Closing the door he looked around the room, noting the disordered state of the Minister's belongings, and then focussed on the notebooks and papers scattered on the desk. He crossed to it and looked down at the mess for a few moments before picking up sheets of paper and loose-leafed notebooks, reading a few words here and there.

Yes, he read the description of the revealing of the talisman. Nazim found himself reading through the description and stopped with a smile. *That is one thing I don't need to do. I must know that passage by heart.*

The power of a djinni or afrit, in the guise of one of the ancient Egyptian gods, had hidden the truth from casual observers, according to the inscription, but he believed that was just nonsense. *The thing was just a stone. How could it be more?*

Nazim looked for the stone on the desk among the scattered papers but could not see it. "What? It's disguised as a sheet of paper now?" He chuckled at the absurdity of the idea, but his mirth faded when he found the empty cloth bag it had been held in.

"He took it with him? Why?"

For a moment, Nazim felt a frisson of fear at the idea that Bashir had prayed to God to reveal the truth of the matter and his prayers had been answered. "Why else would he take it with him?" he muttered. "If it is not a worthless rock..." He shivered and shook himself mentally. "Take hold of yourself, Nazim Manouk. You came for the accounts--take them and leave. Nothing else concerns you."

He gathered up the notebooks and as he picked them up, a slip of paper fluttered to the floor. Nazim bent to pick it up and glimpsed a shape hidden in the shadows beneath the bed. Curious, he got down on hands and knees and lifted the counterpane, allowing a little more light to illuminate the object. It was the apricot-sized piece of sandstone. He picked it up and sat back on his haunches, examining it.

167

I've never really looked at it closely--after all, what else can it be but a lump of rock? Nazim turned the stone over, tracing the bedding lines of the fine sandstone. His fingertips felt tiny corrugations and indentations where his eyes told him the stone surface was smooth and unblemished. *Curious.*

Nazim carried the stone over to the desk, pulled up a chair and switched on the reading lamp, throwing a small pool of yellow light onto the object. He looked at it closely, but could not see any features on the surface, despite the evidence of his fingertips.

So what am I supposed to do? Pray over it? Nazim felt uncomfortable at the thought. Though a Muslim, he paid only lip service to his faith, content to uphold the five pillars except where it was inconvenient. He sometimes contravened Ramadan and had not been on haj, but there was time enough for that in old age. When he finally arrived on his death bed, Nazim intended to make a full and open declaration of his faith, but for now it suited him to be a down-to-earth sceptic. Anything else was rank superstition. *Still...*

Nazim took the object back to his room and sat with it a while, turning it over in his hands, and wondering just why he was so interested in it.

"It is a rock," he said quietly. "Just a rock--fine-grained sandstone from the Orontes Valley in Syria. It cannot be other than it seems...or can it?"

All right, Nazim, let us hypothesise for a moment that it really is the golden scarab of the inscription. How would you prove it?

"If I cannot tell by looking at it, you mean?"

Just so.

Nazim considered the problem at length. "There must be a way."

So find the way, Nazim.

"I have never owned gold," he said slowly, "And therefore I have no expertise with it. However, there are people who work with gold every day. Maybe they could tell."

Who are these people who work with gold?

"Goldsmiths. There must be some in Luxor."

Nazim came to a decision and arose, stuffing the rock into his jacket pocket and grabbing his keys. He made enquiries at the hotel reception, jotting down a few names before catching a taxi into the old city where he visited a number of places. A goldsmith in Khefre Street was his final choice, in part because it was in the poorer part of the city and partly because the smith was old but with eyes that reflected wisdom.

"I seek knowledge rather than gold," Nazim said. "Though I am prepared to pay."

The man nodded sagely. "I am an old man and have seen many things, but my expertise is gold."

"It is that expertise I seek." Nazim put a ten pound note on the dusty counter. The note disappeared into the old man's jacket pocket.

"What do you wish to know?"

"How can I tell if an object is made of gold and not just r...something else?"

The old man took out a pipe and proceeded to pack it with tobacco. "The appearance is the most obvious answer." He struck a match and held the flame over the bowl, sucking to draw the flame into the dried leaf.

"Naturally," Nazim said. "And if the appearance was not enough?"

"An assay would tell you immediately." The tobacco in the pipe bowl glowed red. The old man shook out the match before it burned his fingers and blew out a small cloud of smoke.

"Assay?"

"A small amount of the substance is rigorously tested by fire."

"I do not want the object harmed."

"Ah, you are being offered a curio and want to know if it is pure gold or alloy...or perhaps gold leaf over another metal. It happens, but it is easy to tell the difference."

"How would you do that?"

"Show me the object and I will tell you."

"I, er, do not have it with me," Nazim said, though his hand strayed to his jacket pocket. If the old man noticed the movement he said nothing. "How may I tell the difference?" Nazim went on.

"Gold is heavy--twice as dense as silver and copper and half as dense again as lead. If you would let me touch it, I would tell you instantly if it is gold. Of course, if it has a little silver mixed in that would be harder to tell, but still possible."

"You said 'dense'. What am I to understand by this term--'dense'?" Nazim asked.

"Density is defined as mass per unit volume." The old man chuckled at the look of bafflement on the other man's face.

"You sound like a scientist," Nazim said.

"I have always sought to understand my craft, so I have read widely. Do you know what weight means? And volume?"

"Yes, but not mass."

"Then forget the term and consider weight per unit volume. If you take a single cubic centimetre of various substances, they will weigh different amounts on a pair of scales. Some things are heavy, some light. A cubic centimetre of lead weighs more than a cubic centimetre of wood. You follow? Good. Every cubic centimetre of pure water weighs exactly one gram, and everything else is measured against it. A cubic centimetre of wood weighs less than one gram, so it floats in water. A cubic centimetre of iron weighs nearly eight grams, so it sinks. The same amount of copper weighs nearly nine grams, silver is ten and a half grams, lead is eleven, and gold is a little over nineteen grams."

"What if the object is not exactly one cubic centimetre? The...uh, curio does not have a regular shape."

"Then you must determine its volume. Try immersing it in water--that is, if it will not be harmed by water." The old man stared disapprovingly at his pipe which had gone out while he talked. He struck another match and relit it, puffing vigorously. "I suppose you will now ask me how immersing it helps. Yes, I thought so. The curio will displace the same volume of water as it occupies. You will need a container that measures water accurately--say a measuring cylinder. Put water into it and read the level, drop the curio in, then measure the new level. The difference is the volume in cubic centimetres."

"Ah, I see," Nazim said. "Once I know the volume I can weigh the object and determine what it is made of."

"Exactly," said the old man.

"Thank you. I will apply your methods immediately. Er, where can I find a measuring cylinder? Do you have one?"

"Try the university." The old man turned away.

"One other thing," Nazim said. "What is the density of rock?"

"That depends on the minerals in it. What type of rock?"

"Sandstone."

"Work on a density of three. If we are still talking about a golden artefact you will instantly know the difference if it is gold leaf over stone. Now, do you want to buy anything from my shop?"

"You have already sold me what I need, old man. Thank you."

Nazim left the goldsmith and hailed a taxi, telling the driver to take him to the university. The receptionist there referred him to the Chemistry Department and once there he had to explain his needs to a bored technician.

"We don't sell equipment. You need to go to a scientific supply house."

"Couldn't I borrow a measuring cylinder and scales for a few minutes? I could use them here so they'd never leave the premises."

The technician picked his teeth. "Nah, not allowed."

"Could you ask someone?" Nazim realised the young man was probably stalling in the hopes of getting baksheesh, so he plunked a pound coin down on the bench.

The technician glanced at the coin and slipped it into his pocket. "Wait here, I'll ask the professor." He was back a few minutes later and shook his head, grinning. "The professor says 'no'."

Nazim knew it was no use asking for his money back so he thanked the young man warmly for his trouble, hoping to shame him (unsuccessfully), and went back to the receptionist.

"The technician said to ask you for the addresses of scientific supply houses in Luxor."

"Oh dear, you must have misheard him, there are no supply houses in Luxor. We have to send away to Cairo or overseas when we need anything." The receptionist saw the look on Nazim's face. "You could try the Agricultural Institute out on the Al-Oksor Road, south toward Esna. Ask for Dr Mubarak."

The same taxi was waiting for Nazim outside the university and drove him out of the city onto the Al-Oksor Road, and the Agricultural Institute, where he once more gave his name to a receptionist. Dr Mubarak was in one of the fields near the Institute, so while he was being sent for, Nazim waited in the entrance foyer. He wandered up and down, looking at photographs of the Institute in all its stages and the three directors--two past and one current. Their unsmiling faces seemed to stare down suspiciously at Nazim.

A door opened and a man in a white coat entered, crossing the tiled foyer quickly. "Dr Manouk? I am Dr Mubarak. How may I help you?"

"I am simply Nazim Manouk, doctor. I regret I do not have any qualifications. I was hoping you could help me by letting me use a couple of pieces of your equipment."

"We don't normally cater for members of the public, you understand. Some of our equipment is quite expensive and needs technical training for its proper operation."

"I think I could probably operate it," Nazim said with a smile. "I was told how to by a gentleman in the city."

Mubarak answered with a smile of his own. "I hope you were not after a gas chromatograph. I have been trying to get one for the Institute for nearly two years."

"Nothing so exotic, doctor--whatever that gas chroma thing is. All I need is a measuring cylinder and a scale to weigh something."

"Is that all?" Mubarak looked at his watch. "It's nearly noon. Do you wish to perform Dhuhr prayers? I don't, myself, but I can guide you to a private room if you wish to."

"No, I'll abstain, thank you doctor."

"Then come to my laboratory, and we will find your equipment."

"Even though I'm a member of the public?"

"Perhaps I could make the measurements. Then no one can complain."

Dr Mubarak took Nazim through some double doors and down a long corridor, passing many doors. Through some of the windows set in the doors, Nazim could see laboratories, offices, and what looked like a cafeteria and a library. There were few people in the corridor and they all nodded deferentially to Dr Mubarak and his guest.

"Here we are." Mubarak held open a door and let Nazim precede him into a large laboratory. Benches lined the walls and two more extended down the middle of the room. Glassware and bottles lined shelves above the benches, and the air had a sharp chemical odour to it.

"A measuring cylinder and a laboratory balance, you said? You wouldn't be doing a density measurement, by any chance?"

"Er, yes."

"How big a measuring cylinder did you need?"

"I, er, need to put in an object about...oh, this big." Nazim demonstrated with his fingers. "To find out its volume."

"You have the object with you? May I see it?"

Nazim hesitated and then took the object from his pocket, holding it up for Dr Mubarak to examine.

"It looks like a piece of ordinary sandstone, but I'm guessing there must be something out of the ordinary about it." Mubarak waited a few moments, expectation written large upon his cheerful face and then sighed. "Hmm, yes. I think a five hundred millilitre cylinder will do." He selected a glass cylinder from a shelf and half filled it with water from a tap before carefully adjusting the level to three hundred millilitres from a wash bottle.

"Er, I'm sorry, Dr Mubarak, I should have said. The cylinder needs to measure cubic centimetres, not millilitres."

A smile tugged at Mubarak's lips. "One cubic centimetre is equal to one millilitre. Shall I put your...specimen into the cylinder?"

"May I do it?" Nazim asked. "I...I need to be sure of how to do this...er, just in case there are other samples."

"Of course. I would advise tipping the cylinder and sliding the stone in rather than just dropping it in. You don't want to risk breaking the glass."

Nazim did as he was told, the stone settling to the bottom with a soft 'thunk'. He straightened the cylinder and bent to look at the water level. "The water level is curved," he said in astonishment.

"The curve is called the meniscus. Read the level from the bottom of the curve."

"Three hundred and...thirty...five."

Mubarak had a careful look. "I concur. The stone occupies a volume of thirty-five cubic centimetres. Now we remove the stone and carefully dry it." He tipped the water down a sink and Nazim caught the rock in a towel as it slid out of the cylinder. "Now we weigh it," Mubarak said. He walked over to a balance pan scale and switched it on, taring the pan in readiness for the stone.

"Before we do this," Dr Mubarak said, "May I know the reason? The rock is obviously fine-grained sandstone and with a volume of thirty-five cubic centimetres, it is almost certain its weight will be...oh, around a hundred grams. Why do you seek to calculate the density of an ordinary sedimentary rock?"

"It, er...well, it's a memento..."

"That is scarcely a reason."

Nazim had the grace to look embarrassed. "I would rather not say."

"Well, that is honest at least, but it certainly makes me wonder. Never mind, Mr Manouk, keep hold of your secret if you must. Would you put the rock on the pan, please?"

Nazim reached out and placed the stone in the middle of the balance pan, and it dipped under the weight.

"What...?" Dr Mubarak stared at the electronic readout and closed his eyes, pressing them with thumb and forefinger before looking again. "Ninety-eight point seven grams. Pretty much what I expected, but..."

"But what, Dr Mubarak?"

"For an instant there..." He shook his head. "I had better have this balance checked over. There is obviously something wrong with it if it starts to give a false reading before settling down to the correct one."

"A false reading, Doctor? What was it?"

Dr Mubarak laughed self-consciously. "It's absurd, but I could have sworn it read about six hundred and fifty-something grams. That's obviously impossible though--with a weight like that the density would be..." He took a notepad from his pocket and made some jotted calculations. He shook his head and did them again. "The density would be a shade over nineteen." He laughed. "I don't know what happened to the scales to make it act up like that, but for an instant it read as much as it would if it was solid gold."

"It's gold?"

"No, no, no, that was just a glitch in the measurement, or your fingers pressed down on the pan momentarily. The tare function had obviously not settled down. I'm sorry if I got your hopes up."

Nazim also stared at the smoothly rounded rock on the balance pan. "So now it says ninety-eight grams? It really is sandstone?"

"Many rocks have densities around three or a little less, but it looks like sandstone. May I pick it up?"

Nazim felt an odd mixture of disappointment that the rock was mere sandstone after all, and elation at having brushed against a mystery. He shrugged. "Go ahead."

Mubarak lifted it from the pan and dropped it onto the bench as if it was hot. "Goodness me," he muttered. He reached out and picked it up again, but this time his brow furrowed. "Strange. I could have sworn..."

"What, Dr Mubarak?"

"It slipped from my hand when I took it off the balance. It seemed heavy...but now..." He tossed the rock gently in his hand. "But now it is only what you'd expect of a small pebble." Abruptly, he handed it back to Nazim. "Well, I don't know what you were expecting, Mr Manouk, but there is nothing out of the ordinary here. It is common sandstone, nothing more."

"Thank you, Dr Mubarak." Nazim slipped the stone back into his pocket. "You have been most helpful, but I won't take up more of your time. Goodbye, and thank you again."

"No trouble at all, Mr Manouk. Consider it part of our service to the wider community."

The taxi had gone, so Nazim sat in the foyer while the receptionist phoned for another one. He took out the stone and turned it over in his hands, going over what the scientist had said.

Common sandstone...it is obvious when you look at it...yet for an instant the scales thought it was gold and so did Mubarak. Then when he picked it up...yes, but only the first time...so is it gold or stone? If this really is the golden scarab of the account then it can hide itself by appearing as a stone...but how? By the power of the gods? What gods? There is only one. Why would Allah hide this from me yet reveal it to infidels? It does not make sense.

The taxi arrived and Nazim gave the driver instructions to take him back to his hotel. As the vehicle headed into the city, his thoughts returned to the object in his pocket.

If this is indeed the golden scarab then it will point the way to the tomb--provided I can persuade it to work for me. Nazim smiled, his humour building into a chuckle and then a full-throated bellow of laughter.

The taxi driver swerved and looked back at his passenger in the mirror. "Is everything all right, effendi?"

"Yes, yes." Nazim waved his hand dismissively and as the laughter in him faded, he took out a handkerchief and dabbed at his streaming eyes. *I'm not sharing that little nugget of information with you. You would think me mad. Will I share it with Bashir and Colonel Sarraj, though?* He started chuckling again and clamped down on his mirth. *How do I persuade a rock to work for me?*

* * *

Zufir was exceedingly angry when he rode back into the Bedouin camp after several fruitless days waiting for a ransom drop that never came. He swore vengeance on the infidels that had presumed to dupe him.

"Where are they?" he roared, seeing the empty hut and the shaking men he had left as guards. "What have you done with them?"

"They escaped, Zufir," Tahir muttered. "They were aided by ibn Hawid's nephew."

"What could we do?" Alif added.

"You tell me. What did you do?" Zufir's face contorted into a snarl and his right hand strayed to the handle of his knife.

"We followed them to the village and searched it from top to bottom, but they must have had help, for they disappeared and we could not find them."

"I would have torn the village apart," Zufir declared.

"The police were called and we deemed it wise to withdraw," Tahir said.

"We asked questions though," Alif said. "Foreigners were seen on the road to Edfu."

"You did not think to follow them?"

"If we had, we would not be here to tell you what happened."

"What do we do, Zufir?" asked one of the other men.

"Let me think." Zufir paced and gradually his features softened and took on a cunning look. He reached a decision and whirled, striding toward his mount. "We go to Edfu," he declared. "Those foreigners owe me seven thousand English pounds. I intend to collect it, one way or another."

Chapter Nineteen

T he radio crackled and whined, disbursing staccato bursts of static that evoked oaths of frustration from the sweating operator sitting in the back of a military jeep. The short instruction course--no more than a few minutes really--that he had received at the hands of Lieutenant Fasal ibn Huud in Benghazi, was largely forgotten, and now in the desert heat outside of Esna, he was reduced to twirling knobs at random. Ali Hafiz knew the required frequency and the call signs necessary to make contact, but the instrument was proving recalcitrant. Even tuned as closely to the correct frequency as he could turn the dial, the vacuum tubes and wiring still refused to pick up or transmit messages.

"What is wrong with this damned piece of machinery?" he yelled. "Work, curse you!" Ali Hafiz flipped a switch that he had overlooked and was rewarded with a warble that ascended and descended, ending in an even note. "Now what? Hello, hello. Answer curse you, you piece of camel shit."

"Who is that?"

The Arabic voice that issued tinnily from the receiver sounded angry, and did nothing to calm Ali Hafiz's frazzled nerves.

"And who the hell is that? Get off the line. I'm trying to contact..." Ali Hafiz glanced at the piece of paper in his hand that held the contact details. "HJC17."

"This is HJC17," said the voice. "Who is that? You have called a restricted military frequency. Identify yourself or switch off immediately."

"Go rut with a camel," Ali Hafiz muttered.

"Identify yourself immediately," the voice repeated. "We can track your signal and unauthorised transmissions on this frequency will be dealt with severely."

"This is Ali Hafiz. I want to speak to..." he consulted the paper again. "Iskandar the Great."

"Wait."

There was a pause of several minutes, during which Ali Hafiz calmed down, grateful that the radio was working at last. He jotted down the settings on the dials and the positions of the switches for future reference, but touched nothing.

"Yes? Go ahead, Hafiz."

"Er...you are Iskandar the..."

"Yes. What have you to report?"

Despite the crackle and the tinny voice, Ali Hafiz recognised the voice of Colonel Sarraj and was tempted to sigh with relief. He restrained himself, however, as few people were relieved to be speaking with the Colonel, and he was not one of them.

"I followed the...er, targets into Egypt and captured two of them outside Edfu."

"Only two? Which two?"

"The young man and...and a young Libyan."

"The two most useless ones. Where are the others?"

"I...I don't know, sir. They won't tell me."

"Well, make them tell you. I need the woman in particular."

"Yes, sir."

"I don't need to tell you that I do not look kindly on failure, do I, Ali Hafiz?"

"No, sir."

The radio cut out abruptly and Ali Hafiz flicked the switches off with a sick feeling in his stomach. He sat in the jeep for a few minutes, trying to think what he must do to find out the whereabouts of the English woman. Ali Hafiz had an idea that torture would be involved if his prisoners would not cooperate, but the thought filled him with nausea. A clean kill was infinitely preferable--torture was barbaric, but alas, sometimes necessary.

"Hey!"

Ali Hafiz looked across to where his two prisoners sat in the shade of a rocky outcrop. They were bound hand and foot, and Ali Hafiz would like to have gagged them as well, except when he had tried it with the Englishman to stop his incessant chatter, the prisoner's face became red and congested and his breath came in a snuffling wheeze. The Libyan had said something about the other man's sinuses being blocked--whatever they were--and the alarming wheezing had only stopped when he untied the gag.

"It is no use calling out, Dr Andrews," Ali Hafiz had told him. "There is no one to hear."

"So why gag me?"

"Because you talk too much. Be quiet."

Dr Andrews had shrugged. "Why should I?"

"I will gag you again."

"And risk killing me? If you were going to do that, you'd have done it by now instead of going to all this trouble."

The young man's words had been true, but now that he had spoken to Colonel Sarraj, Ali Hafiz knew that the woman was far more important and that these men were possibly expendable. That was worth knowing. He climbed out of the jeep and crossed to the prisoners, squatting in front of them.

"About time. We're dying of thirst over here."

"Are you ready to tell me where your companions are?"

"No."

"Then I regret I cannot waste water on your comfort."

"Bashir's not going to be pleased if I...we...are in poor shape when you deliver us to him."

"Who is this Bashir?"

"Your boss, who else?"

Ali Hafiz shook his head. "I have never heard of him."

"Then who was that on the radio if you weren't reporting to him?"

"Someone who instructed me to dispose of you and concentrate on finding the woman. You see, Dr Andrews, I now have no need of you if you will not help me. I can offer you either a swift death..." Ali Hafiz drew his pistol, "...or I can just leave you here in the desert to die of thirst."

"There is another choice," Muammar said. "I will tell you where the woman is--but only if you take us with you to find her."

"What the hell are you doing?" Marc demanded. "Shut up."

"These infidels hired me to guide them across the desert," Muammar went on. "They did not pay me enough for me to risk my life. I will guide you to them."

"In exchange for?"

"My life."

Ali Hafiz considered the young Libyan's words. "You will lead me to her?"

"Yes."

"Then I no longer need Dr Andrews." He cocked his pistol.

"You must spare their lives too," Muammar said. "I have eaten their bread and taken their money. It would not be honourable to betray them."

"But you are betraying them by taking me to the woman, aren't you?"

Muammar shrugged. "You want to talk to her, I'll guide you; but I won't help you kill the woman or her companions. Dr Andrews comes with us, unharmed, or we stay here."

"Very well, but if either of you give me any trouble I will kill you both."

Ali Hafiz undid the bonds around their ankles and secured Marc in the back of the jeep, while allowing Muammar to sit up front with him--though with his wrists still bound.

"All right then, where is she?"

"Take us back to where you found us."

"Traitor," Marc growled.

"All the way back there?" Ali Hafiz complained. "That'll take hours."

Sarraj's man ground the gears on the Jeep and sent the vehicle bouncing and lurching back down the rough road that traversed the wilderness of the western desert. The sun beat down on them, especially on Marc lying unprotected in the back, and he swore beneath his breath that he would get even with his captor.

That bastard Muammar too, if I ever get my hands loose.

They reached the main road lying just inland of Esna and turned away from the river, despite the presence of better roads there. Muammar said as much.

"We'd get there sooner on the paved road down to Edfu."

"And there are a lot more people closer to the river. I'm not risking anybody getting curious about a man tied up in the back."

"You could untie his feet and let him sit up at least. He'll choke on the dust lying in the floor well."

Ali Hafiz thought about it for a few miles before pulling over and sitting Marc upright. He loosened the ropes around his ankles but secured his wrists securely to the back of one of the rear seats.

"You see, Dr Andrews? I am a humane person, but I must protect myself as well. That is why I cannot have you attempt something foolish like attacking me from behind."

Marc glowered but said nothing and their journey resumed. The sun set in shades of orange and purple, the glow spreading over the desert vistas and prolonged by the dust in the air. As the last of the light leached from the sky, the vehicle hit a corrugated section of the dirt road and the steering wheel shuddered. Ali Hafiz wrestled with the bucking Jeep, and suddenly, Muammar reached over with his bound hands and tugged violently on the steering wheel. Hafiz yelled out and fought to control the vehicle as it skidded on the dusty road.

The Jeep veered toward the edge of the road and the right wheels hit deep loose sand, digging in. Ali Hafiz and Marc in the back uttered loud cries as the vehicle tipped, skidded and rolled over onto its roof. For a few seconds the engine roared before coughing, catching and spluttering into silence.

"Fuck me, Muammar," Marc muttered from the rear of the upturned Jeep. "Warn me next time you try something like that."

Muammar groaned and shifted. "A warning, by its very nature, would have alerted our captor, Dr Andrews."

"Is he still alive?"

"I don't know. Please wait."

There were more sounds from the front of the vehicle, then a grunt and a faint rhythmic sound.

"What's happening?"

"I have found a knife, Dr Andrews, but I cannot find his gun. Possibly it was thrown out when the vehicle rolled over. I am presently engaged in cutting my bonds...ah, there. Now, our captor is unconscious but without examining him I cannot tell if he is alive. I will pull him from the vehicle and..."

"Fuck him. I'm hanging upside down and my bloody arms are killing me. Get me out of here."

"Of course, Dr Andrews. Please wait a moment longer."

Muammar crawled out of the front and stumbled round to the rear of the Jeep, peering in past a jumble of equipment and torn seating. He found Marc bent double with his arms still bound behind one of the rear seats. The young Englishman was muttering imprecations at all and sundry.

"Are you ready, Dr Andrews?"

"Stop talking and get me out of...whoa! Fuck me!"

The cords parted and Marc tumbled out of his seat into the jumble of debris below him. He pushed his way out of the side of the wrecked vehicle and staggered to his feet, looking around in the dark.

"That you, Muammar?" He raised his fists toward the dimly-seen figure near him. "I haven't forgotten you tried to betray us."

"I rather thought I was saving your life."

Marc considered this point of view. "Yes, well, I suppose there is that," he conceded. He scuffed the dirt of the road with one foot. "What do we do now?"

"I suppose we'd better see how our driver is."

Marc grunted. "That bastard? Leave him and let's get out of here."

"We should make sure he is all right," Muammar replied quietly. "My action injured him; and though he threatened our lives, I don't desire his death." He walked around to the driver's side and knelt in the sand. Ali Hafiz lay in a crumpled heap around the steering wheel and pedals in the foot well, breath rasping noisily from his open mouth. Blood smeared the side of his head where he had evidently knocked it in the crash. Muammar eased the man out of the vehicle gently and, despite not being able to see very well in the darkness, cleaned him up as best he could with his handkerchief. While he ministered to the needs of the injured man, Marc went through his pockets and was rewarded by finding the man's gun in a jacket pocket.

"Excellent. Now the shoe's on the other foot. You know how to use one of these things, Muammar?"

"I have some training with firearms."

"Good. All I know is point and pull the trigger." Marc lined the pistol up at the Jeep and mimicked firing it, making the gun buck realistically. "Pow! Gotcha."

Muammar continued cleaning up Hafiz, and then sat back on his heels. "I think he'll live."

"Who cares? What about us?"

Muammar considered their position. "We're somewhere between Esna and Edfu, I think. Normally, in a situation like this, I'd say we should stay with the vehicle and wait for someone to find us. The road is used, though not regularly and sooner or later another vehicle will come by."

"Sounds like a plan," Marc said. He stretched and uttered a yelp of pain. "Damn it, I think I hurt myself when you decided to crash us." He laid the gun down on the road and gently massaged his ribs.

"Unfortunately, Dr Andrews, we entered Egypt illegally and should we be asked for our papers, will be unable to produce them. We could find ourselves imprisoned."

"So what do we do?"

"We continue on foot south along the road toward Edfu and where we left the others. I doubt they'll still be there, but the city is our best chance of finding them. We know they will head there, and they know we will too." Muammar straightened and took a few steps past the overturned Jeep.

Marc looked into the darkness. "We've got to go out there? I can't see a damn thing."

"The moon will be up soon. There'll be enough light to see the road."

Ali Hafiz let out a groan and started to sit up. Muammar stepped over to him and squatted beside him, putting a hand on his shoulder.

"Take it easy," he said in Arabic. "You hit your head."

"You...you did it," Ali Hafiz mumbled. "You grabbed the wheel." He fumbled urgently in his jacket pocket.

"We took it," Muammar told him. "Marc, give me the gun. I think we need to ask this man a few questions."

"It's right here somewhere." Marc turned quickly and his foot connected with the gun, sending it skittering over the hard road surface. He swore and bent to grab it.

As it did so, Hafiz drew his right leg up and he snatched an additional small pistol from his boot. Muammar threw himself backward as the barrel wavered toward him and muzzle flash temporarily blinded him.

"Run, Marc!" he yelled, scrambling to his feet and ducking behind the vehicle. He saw a figure disappearing into the dark and set off after him as another shot rang out.

The two men pounded down the road until the night swallowed them and then a bit further. Muammar called a halt at last and they stood in the road, panting, while they listened for the sounds of pursuit.

"Have you got the gun, Dr Andrews?"

"Sorry. I kicked it away by accident and then just legged it when the shot went off."

"He had another gun in his boot. I should have checked."

"Bastard." Marc stared nervously into the darkness. "If he's got a gun and we don't, shouldn't we keep going?"

"I don't think he's coming after us."

Marc listened, but could hear no sounds of pursuit. "You called me Marc back there."

"My apologies if I have become overly familiar. The urgency of the situation necessitated a succinct outcry."

"Oh, don't apologise. We've been formally introduced. Please continue to call me Marc."

"Very well--Marc. Judging by the position of the stars we seem to have run north, rather than south toward Edfu. We must go back."

"He's still got a gun--maybe two if he's found the other one."

"I know. We'll have to go around him. I suggest we move westward into the desert a few hundred paces and loop around him before returning to the road."

Marc thought about this for a minute, and though he could not see any real flaw in the plan, felt he had to make a contribution. "Why not eastward?"

"The land is more uneven and rocky to the east," Muammar replied. "I noticed this in the minutes before the crash."

Marc shrugged, unseen in the darkness. "Lead on then."

They left the road and walked westward, Muammar counting out the steps until he reached five hundred and stopped. He turned to the left and set off in a general southerly direction in what he hoped was a course that paralleled the road.

"How far did we run?" Marc asked.

"I don't know. Half a mile perhaps."

"So a thousand paces, then a thousand more to take us past the crash site before we head back to the road?"

"That's about right," Muammar agreed. "We should keep quiet though, sound carries for long distances in the desert at night."

They stumbled on through the darkness, plotting their course by dead reckoning. A couple of times, Muammar stopped and adjusted their course slightly before setting off again. Once, they happened upon a large rocky outcrop and swung around it to the west, estimating when they had worked their way around half of it.

"Are we going in the same direction?" Marc asked.

"I think so."

"I think we should go a little more to our right."

Muammar stopped and looked around. "Maybe." They altered course slightly.

Two thousand paces onward, they turned left and counted out their steps, hoping to find the road after five hundred. They did not, nor after five hundred more.

"Where is the damn thing?" Marc asked querulously.

"We must have overrun it."

"How can we do that? It runs north and south doesn't it? If we headed east we should cross it."

"Maybe there is a bend in the road."

"Or maybe we got turned around and we're not even heading east. Damn it, Muammar, you're an Arab and a Bedouin, can't you tell directions?"

"I am a city Libyan, Marc, though my family are Bedouin. Even so, I could probably navigate at night if I could see the stars. In case you hadn't noticed, it has become overcast."

"So we're lost?"

"Not at all. As soon as the moon rises we can be certain of our direction." Muammar looked around and pointed to some darker shadows in the lee of another rocky outcrop off to one side. "I suggest we rest there until it does."

They made themselves as comfortable as they could, leaning against sun-cracked boulders and excavating out depressions in the sand. The silence of the desert surrounded them, broken only by occasional dry rustlings and the intermittent chirrup of a cricket. Lulled by the silence and giving in to their exhaustion, they dozed and, after a while fell into a deep sleep.

Muammar woke first; his mind still befuddled, and regarded the pale silver light washing the desert sands for a minute before realising the moon was already high in the sky. He shook Marc awake.

Marc yawned and stretched gingerly. "So that's east?" he asked, looking at the crescent moon.

Muammar hesitated. "Well, it rose in the east but it should be swinging round to the south by now. We fell asleep and missed it rising, but I think we can still use it." He got to his feet and brushed the sand off his clothes. "Come on. No time to lose."

Marc rose too and yawned again. "What's the hurry?"

"I want to find the road before daylight. It's going to get very hot out here and we need to try and find someone to take us to Edfu."

* * *

Marc could not believe how hot the sun was. The disc of the sun glowed like a white hot iron ball suspended only feet above him and waves of heat beat up at him from the sand and rock, shimmering the air and seeming to create pools of water in the distance. His boots had tough, thick soles, but his feet felt as if they were naked, stepping gingerly across a summer's road. Figures of men and demons danced and capered mockingly in the distance, but as they drew close the forms resolved into spires and heaps of rock. Nothing moved except the over-heated air and the two humans trudging slowly under a cloudless sky.

He turned and waited for Muammar to catch up, running the tip of a dry tongue over cracked lips. "We've..." he croaked. He shook his head and tried again. "We've got to find water."

"There is no water out here," Muammar whispered.

"Then we're dead."

Muammar still had strength--his body was wiry from his military training but even he looked exhausted. Marc's strength was fading. His reserves were low and his body was overheating. He knew that unless they could find water, shelter and food--in that order--he would die and Muammar would not be far behind him.

He turned back to their unplanned route across the trackless desert. They had wandered in what they thought was the east until the sun rose on their right hand, proving them wrong. They turned toward the rising sun, but had followed it in its course for several hours before realising it was swinging to the south and drawing them off course. It was difficult to follow a straight line on a desert plateau, where one direction looked the same as any other.

Not quite...what's that?

Still in the distance, but just to the right of their present route was a mountain--a hill--a pile of rocks--an outcrop of the underlying strata, revealed where the sand had been blown away. Something gleamed in the sun, shone as if the hill was topped by a glittering crown, and they both stopped to gaze upon it.

"What the hell?" Marc croaked.

"It must...must be the road," Muammar muttered. "The sun is reflecting off a windshield."

"It's on top of a hill."

"It only looks that way. The road must go over a rise. Come on, it's our last chance."

"Oh please God, let it be a road. What about your god, Muammar? Will he save us?" Marc staggered and straightened. "What about the ancient gods--Atum, Geb...who was the one you prayed to for water? Tefnut? Hope they help us..."

They altered course slightly, and another hour or two brought them to a small shattered hill in the last light of the day. By then, Marc and Muammar were supporting each other, staggering with exhaustion, reeling from dehydration and sunstroke.

*   *   *

The loose jumbled rocks that covered the ground had evidently fallen from a central pillar of stone, and that pillar still remained, though truncated. Leaving Marc resting in the shelter of the fallen boulders, Muammar scrambled over the tumbled rocks and onto the solid stone, moving upward carefully in the fading light. Already, the temperature was falling, and he shivered despite the burning heat of his body. About half way up, some hundred or so feet above the desert floor, he emerged onto a broad ledge. Muammar stood and looked around before following it one way until it petered out. He returned and went the other direction, almost immediately coming across a dark patch in the rock wall behind the ledge. On dropping to his hands and knees he found a shallow cave about ten feet across and six deep, ending in rubble. It faced north, so would be shaded from the scorching heat of the day. He smiled wearily.

"It will do," he murmured. "But we still need food and water if we are to survive."

A rock fell, clattering in the stillness, further round the ledge. Muammar froze, his heartbeat loud in his ears as he considered the cause. After a few moments he relaxed--it was either an animal or rock cracking as the temperature dropped. He followed the ledge round to where the ground beneath his feet steepened and became treacherous with loose stones. His feet slid from under him and he put out a hand to steady himself, snatching it away from the rock face and almost falling in his shock. The stone beneath his hand was wet. Muammar touched his face and his lips, tasting the unbelievably sweet dampness on his fingertips, and then he was at the rock, pressing his face close and licking up the thin film that ran down it. He drank until the edge was removed from his thirst and guilt made him remember Marc waiting below.

He had no container to carry water, but he stripped off his shirt and soaked it in the runoff, before carrying it as quickly as he dared over the jumble of rocks to the blackened plain below. He called to Marc and got a weak response.

"I have water. Not much, but there's more if you can get to it."

Marc sucked thirstily on Muammar's shirt, only making a face when the worst of his thirst had been assuaged.

"Salty," he murmured. "And a bit pongy," he added after sucking on the fabric a little longer. "But thank you, Muammar. You say there's more?"

"Yes. Shelter too. It might be a bit difficult climbing up there in the dark though, so perhaps we should wait until tomorrow."

"I'm still bloody thirsty," Marc said. "I'd like to try now. We can take it slowly."

They did, moving step by shuffling step, climbing more by feel than by sight until they climbed beyond the basal boulders and onto the slopes where starlight aided their passage. A breeze picked up, chilling them as heat soaked out of the rock and sand into the star-filled sky. They shivered, teeth chattering, and at last pulled themselves up onto the ledge.

The shallow cave was out of the wind, as was the soak, and they took turns to lick and suck as much water as they could from the meagre but persistent supply.

"Where's the water coming from?" Marc asked. "There has to be a reservoir in the rock somewhere."

"Probably." Muammar sucked up another small mouthful and swallowed. "It would be a waste of energy trying to find it though."

"No, what I meant was, any reservoir up there must be small and can only be replenished by rain--which I gather is pretty scarce out here."

Muammar looked up at the rock face above them. "It is...strange." Then he shrugged. "Ask no questions. Just be thankful."

"Oh, I am, but shouldn't we try storing some?" Marc asked after several minutes. "What if it runs dry?"

"We have no containers, so it's better in our bodies," Muammar replied. "If we don't drink it, it'll run away to waste. Soak up as much as you can."

Exhaustion took over and they staggered back to the cave and huddled together for warmth, taking comfort from each other's presence. After a bit, they slept and only awoke when the sun was already high in the eastern sky. The air was warm again and despite the amount they had drunk the night before, the demand of their bladders was not pressing. Instead, after warming themselves in the sun and working the kinks out of their muscles, they went back to the soak to drink again.

In daylight, the soak was unprepossessing, being little more than a dark patch on the rock wall with a heavy grey-green algal growth beneath the film of water. It oozed out of a crack in the rock a few feet above them and trickled down to the ledge where it gathered in a small pool a foot across and inches deep before apparently soaking into the featureless rock.

Marc looked up at the summit of the hill high above them and frowned. "Where's the water coming from?" he asked. "Springs occur where there's an underground body of water to feed it, or a steady supply of rain. There can't be anything like that here."

"Don't question it," Muammar said, cupping his hand and slurping water from it. "Accept it as a gift from God."

"I'm certainly grateful," Marc said. "Don't get me wrong, but I wonder how long it's going to last."

"However long it lasts, it has saved our lives for the moment."

187

Marc shrugged and yawned. "What's for breakfast? I'd kill for a croissant or even a kipper."

Muammar laughed wryly. "Look around you. Select anything you like from the menu. May I recommend a small helping of slime?"

"There must be something," Marc said.

"Well, despite being a desert, life can exist here, particularly if there is a source of water," Muammar said. "The slime proves it, so all we need to do is look around. I'm sure we can find something to eat."

"What sort of something?" Marc asked cautiously.

"Insects probably. Maybe lizards, small rodents."

"Jesus, you've got to be kidding. I'm not eating those."

"You will if you're hungry enough."

Chapter Twenty

Nick stayed and watched as Dr Maroun and his students investigated the shaft in the side of the cliff. He asked for and was granted permission to take photographs and took a few of the young men engaged in mundane archaeological tasks. Maroun explained what they were doing as they went along.

"We're not here to excavate anything, you understand? However, we can conduct a preliminary examination of the surface--the walls of the shaft and anything that might lie on the top of the rubble filling it. Here, for example..." Dr Maroun pointed to some very faint grooves in the rock wall of the shaft, "...are the marks of what is almost certainly a copper chisel."

"Really?" Nick commented. "I thought copper was a soft metal. Wasn't this the bronze age?"

"Indeed it was, but most of the stone-working tools were made of copper. Bronze was largely reserved for the military. Copper was cheap and easily resharpened."

Nick nodded and made a few notes in a notebook. "Any evidence this is a tomb like Minister Bashir thinks?"

"Not yet. We've found a few fragments of pottery that date from that approximate period..."

"About when exactly?"

"Late eighteenth dynasty, circa 1300 BCE."

"Which makes it just right if it was this Smenkhkare chappie's tomb."

"Indeed, but we know...or rather, we believe...that the king's tomb is in the Valley of the Kings across from Luxor."

"Any way of telling, one way or the other?"

"No, not without a proper excavation. I might have an answer for you in a few months' time."

"No hunches?"

Maroun smiled but said nothing.

"Come on, professor," Nick cajoled. "Off the record."

"Well, based only on an instinct honed over thirty years in the field, I'd say no. I think this started as a tomb entrance for a minor local land-owner but I think it was abandoned early and used as a rubbish tip. Don't quote me on that."

"Wouldn't dream of it, old chap," Nick said with a grin. "I think Bashir will be happy though. It would spoil all his plans if you beat him to the tomb."

Dr Maroun sat back and regarded Nick. "Why did Directors Nasrallah and Zewali ask you to come on this trip? And why would you want to? There's nothing particularly interesting or newsworthy about this discovery--at least not yet."

"I think the real question is why Minister Ahmed Bashir wants to be here."

"And do you know the answer?"

"Possibly."

Maroun laughed. "And you might have an answer for me in a few months--I understand. Any hunch you'd like to share?"

Nick looked down the slope to where Bashir sat, idly tossing pebbles over the cliff edge. "I think the Minister would be sorely tempted if he ever found anything of value, but don't quote me on that."

"Has this anything to do with our Directors' invitation?"

Nick winked and tapped the side of his nose. "Time to earn my keep."

"What do you mean, Mr Evans?"

"Well, I don't ordinarily like to show my hand this early, but the Directors asked me to push the Minister, to needle him, in the hope that he might confirm their suspicions. So, I'll let slip a few things and study his responses. I can usually tell when someone's lying or covering up." Nick got up and moved down the hill to where Bashir sat.

Bashir looked up as Nick approached, but said nothing.

"Fantastic vista, isn't it?" Nick said. "I think if I was a king buried up here, I could sit and look at that view for eternity."

Bashir stared at Nick. "Dr Maroun has found something? This is a tomb after all? A royal tomb?"

"He says he won't know for certain for months, but he thinks not." Nick saw the Minister's shoulders drop as the tension in him eased. "You don't want it to be the tomb, do you?"

"It is immaterial to me."

"Oh, I think it matters very much to you, Minister Bashir."

"What is that supposed to mean?"

190

"Just that you came to Egypt to look for a royal tomb and it would upset you greatly to be beaten to it."

"I don't know where you get these ideas, Mr. Evans, but I came to Egypt on holiday, and when I heard of this find, I thought it might be entertaining to come along and see what Egyptologists did. Dr Maroun was gracious enough to allow me."

"Sounds plausible," Nick said quietly, "Except I know about the Syrian inscription."

"What is this Syrian inscription?"

"I don't have to tell you that it is evidence of an undiscovered Egyptian tomb."

Bashir turned to face Nick. "Mr. Evans, you are a newspaper reporter..."

"Freelance journalist, actually."

"...and I think there must be a dearth of real news if you must resort to these fishing expeditions. I don't know what this Syrian inscription is--if it even exists--and I can assure you I have no connection with it."

"Dr Dani Hanser."

Bashir's eyes flickered. "Who?"

"The leader of the British Midland University team excavating in the Orontes Valley of Syria under the auspices of the National History Ministry, of which you are Under-Minister."

"I have never heard of her. I am a busy man and cannot concern myself with every person who has business with the Ministry."

"The same Dr Hanser who was deported from your country and whom you then complained about officially to her university."

Bashir sighed. "What do you want, Mr. Evans?"

"An exclusive, Minister Bashir. I want to be with you when you discover the tomb, to take the official photographs of the discovery, and to interview you afterward."

Bashir looked away, out over the empty air to the distant river and farmland pressed close to its life-giving waters. A bright speck far above glinted in the azure sky, leaving a rapidly-dissipating contrail in its wake. Nearer at hand, a hawk rode the thermals associated with the cliffs, its thin cry the only sound in the sun-baked silence. After several minutes, he shook his head.

"No."

"Beg pardon?"

"I said 'no', Mr. Evans--not because I am averse to the responsible press, but because I have literally no idea what you are talking about. Yes, I know of Dr Hanser, and yes, I made an official complaint about her, but I would as soon forget her existence. She committed a scientific indiscretion in our country and was punished for it. Let us leave it at that. As far as I am aware, there is no inscription, no tomb, and no story. Now, if you would be so kind as to leave me alone, I will endeavour to enjoy the rest of my holiday."

"She's in Egypt, you know."

"Dr Hanser? I very much doubt that."

"Why would Dr Hanser come to Egypt unless there was some truth to the story?"

"Mr. Evans, you are starting to annoy me."

Nick grinned. "I do seem to have that effect on some people. What do you think, Minister? Is Dr Hanser here to search for your tomb? Did she find out about it in the same place you did--the mysterious Syrian inscription?"

"Enough." Bashir got to his feet and patted the dust from his clothes. "Thank Dr Maroun and tell him that I have decided to make my own way back to Luxor. Good day to you, Mr. Evans."

"Hey, wait. Do you want me to come with you? Keep you company?"

Bashir did not answer, but almost ran down the slope, scrambling and slipping in the loose rock in an apparent effort to escape.

Nick grinned again. "I guess not." Louder, he called after Bashir, "See you later, Minister." He turned and made his way up to Dr Maroun, where he told the museum deputy of Bashir's decision.

"I'm not sure that's a wise move," Maroun said. "How does he think he's going to get back to Luxor? He'll have to find a fisherman willing to take him."

"There was no dissuading him."

"Well, perhaps we can catch up with him at the dock later and offer him a ride home. In the meantime, look what we found in the rubble."

Nick squatted down and examined a small piece of pottery that Maroun held out to him. It was pale and worn with a few scratchings on it that looked nothing like any hieroglyph he had seen.

"What is it? Those aren't hieroglyphs, are they?"

"No, it's hieratic script. Technically, hieroglyphs were only used by priests and in formal inscriptions. Hieratic is the everyday writing of the scribes. This is a fragment that contains the words '...year two of Heqamaat...'." Maroun looked at Nick quizzically. "Mean anything to you?"

"Not a sausage."

"I think it is part of the seal from a wine jar from the reign of Heqamaatre Ramesses, whom we know as Ramses IV, about a hundred and fifty years after the Minister's King Smenkhkare."

"Meaning?"

"We're no closer to identifying the period of this shaft, but it is interesting that in light of the fact that we already have fragments from the time of Amenhotep III and now Ramses IV, it means that for a period of over a hundred and fifty years, people were throwing rubbish into this shaft. Either it was an abandoned shaft, or if it ever was a tomb, it had long since been looted and the body buried elsewhere."

"Unlikely to have been Smenkhkare's tomb then?"

"Highly unlikely."

"That'll please Bashir."

Dr Maroun wound up the work on the site shortly after, instructing the students to take down the tape and tidy everything away. The pottery fragment was packed away carefully in tissue paper for later study. The small group then made their way slowly and carefully down the steep hill face and found themselves back in the heat and relative humidity of the river farmland and village.

Bashir was on the dock, arguing with the captain of the boat. He looked hot and angry and almost snarled when Dr Maroun and his party showed up.

"Can we leave?" Bashir demanded. "I have to get back to Luxor."

"Couldn't find a fisherman?" Nick asked, his eyes twinkling.

Bashir ignored the journalist and climbed aboard the boat, taking a seat in the most shaded part. "Have you got any cold drinks?"

The captain produced a wicker basket dripping water, and took out bottles of Coca-Cola that had been cooling in the river and started opening them. Bashir grabbed one, while Maroun passed one to Nick.

"Nothing alcoholic, my friend."

"No matter. I have good company to lift my spirits." Nick raised his bottle in mock salute to Bashir. "Good news, eh Minister?"

Bashir drained his Coke and stifled a belch, before tossing his empty bottle over the side. "What do you mean?"

"Please return the empties to the basket," Maroun murmured.

"Just that it now looks almost certain that the shaft has nothing to do with your King Smenkhkare."

"Is that true, Dr Maroun?"

"It would appear so, though in science, few things are a certainty."

"So all that gold is still out there--waiting for you."

"Your fables are getting tiresome, Mr. Evans."

Bashir turned away to stare out over the water as the launch forged its way downriver to Luxor. He refused to say anything further, even though Nick continued to probe away at his denials.

*   *   *

The launch tied up at the docks in Luxor in the late afternoon and the passengers disembarked. Leaving Dr Maroun with only a curt word of thanks, and ignoring Nick's grinning goodbyes, Bashir hurried off, taking a taxi back to the hotel. He took his room key from Reception and hurried to his suite, where he found Lieutenant Al-Din hanging around outside in the hallway.

"Good afternoon, Minister. Will there be anything else? There's a re-enactment of a priestly ritual at the Karnack temple this evening and I hoped I could go...with your permission..."

"Anything else? What have you been doing today while I've been risking life and limb?"

"Oh, sir, I was most busy. Secretary Manouk assigned me the job of investigating car hire firms between here and Edfu in the eventuality..."

"Yes, yes. I'm sure you have been busy, but I don't need to know the details. Tell Nazim."

"Yes, sir...about tonight?"

"Go."

Bashir fumbled the key in the lock and pushed the door open. He saw Al-Din waiting and turned. "Was there anything else?"

"Er, no sir. I mean, I just wanted to ask if you wanted me for anything else tonight, before I, er..."

"Tell Nazim I want to see him. In an hour."

"Yes sir. Here?"

Bashir sighed and entered his room, closing the door in the lieutenant's face. He stripped off his clothes and ran the bath full of cool water, allowing himself a long soak before washing his hair and shaving. His moustache was in need of a trim, so he attended to that, carefully clipping away a few hairs and examining the effect critically in the mirror. Satisfied, he dressed in clean clothing and called room service for a pot of coffee. He was standing at the glass doors, looking out at the city with coffee cup in hand, when Nazim arrived.

"Good evening, Minister. Was your trip successful?"

"Depends how you look at it. Deputy Director Maroun now thinks the shaft has nothing to do with Smenkhkare, but that reporter Nicholas Evans evidently knows something. He kept asking questions about my interest in the tomb and about Dr Hanser."

"What did you say?"

"I denied all knowledge of course. What do you think I did?"

Nazim regarded the Minister carefully. "Did he believe you?"

Bashir shrugged. "What do I care? His questions were based on unfounded rumour and supposition. If he knew anything for certain it would be in the papers already."

"If the shaft has proved not to be what we seek, then what is our next course of action, Minister?"

"We must search for it ourselves. We have the description from the account."

"A three thousand year old description."

"If you have no stomach for the search, you may return home, Secretary Manouk. I shall continue, however, for I feel it is my destiny to find this tomb and treasury."

"I did not mean to sound as if I was giving up, Minister, only sounding a word of caution concerning the difficulties of identifying landmarks that may have long vanished."

"I am aware of the difficulties. Now leave me and make sure our launch is ready for us in the morning. I will have dinner and retire early." Bashir waited until Nazim was at the door before asking, "The rock, Nazim. Where is it?"

Nazim turned to face Bashir, his face guileless. "What rock is that, Minister?"

"You know which one--Dr Hanser's rock. It was here on this table."

"I brought it to you before you left for the museum meeting yesterday and you instructed me to leave it with you."

Bashir yawned. "I don't suppose it matters, it is only a rock. Go then." He waved his hand dismissively.

*   *   *

Nick Evans watched Bashir leave the docks, chewing his lip in indecision as to whether to follow him. He decided not to and took his leave of Dr Maroun, returning to his own hotel in the poorer part of Luxor where he bathed and changed into fresh clothes. Sitting on his bed, he thought back over the day's events and contemplated where Minister Bashir's answers left him. With a grimace, he picked up the telephone handset and asked the hotel receptionist to connect him with Director Nasrallah at the Cairo Museum.

There was a long wait, and eventually he was told that the Director had gone home for the day. The museum would not release Nasrallah's home number, so Nick hung up and asked for the Luxor Museum number. A few minutes later, he was connected to Dr Karim Zewali.

"Hello Dr Zewali, sorry to ring you so late, but I thought I'd better report in."

"You should contact Director Nasrallah."

"Yes, I tried him, but he's gone home."

"Perhaps you should call him tomorrow, Mr Evans."

"I will, but I really need to know something tonight."

Zewali paused. "What is it you need to know?"

"I spent the day with Dr Maroun and Minister Bashir at the cliff shaft. I tried to sound out Bashir concerning his plans but he's very cagey, he denies any knowledge of a Syrian inscription or of a tomb in Egypt. He insists he's down here on holiday and is not seeking Smenkhkare's tomb."

"Do you believe him?"

"No, but there's nothing I can prove. Short of catching him red-handed, breaking through a tomb entrance, I don't really see what you can do."

"Well, it was only ever a possibility, Mr Evans. It just might be that Minister Bashir is who he says he is--a politician on holiday in Egypt. Unless you can find out otherwise, I'm afraid there's no story for you here." Zewali paused again. "What is your present relationship with Bashir like?"

Nick laughed. "In a word--tense. You don't often see a man snarl, but I'd swear he's doing that when he sees me. Of course, it could just be indigestion."

"I think you should desist from any further attempts to aggravate him, Mr Evans. He is a visiting politician, after all, from our Syrian partners. If he chose to make a formal complaint and it got out that you were interviewing him at our behest..."

"You want me to stop representing you?"

"It might be best. We thank you for your efforts, but it seems there is nothing going on that is detrimental to Egyptian archaeology."

"You'd have no objection to me continuing to pursue him--on my own time?"

"What you do as an independent journalist is none of our concern," Zewali said carefully. "I would caution you, however, not to break the law in your pursuit of a story."

"Understood, Director Zewali, and thank you."

Nick hung up the phone and frowned, thinking. *Despite what I said, should I just give up on this? Have I got the funds or the time to follow Bashir around in the hope he'll lead me to this hypothetical tomb? Perhaps I should just go home and see if Percy still has that Cornwall assignment for me.* Nick's stomach grumbled. *A meal and a few stiff drinks first, then a good night's kip and I'll decide in the morning.*

Chapter Twenty-One

The room was basic and boasted only a single rickety bed, but Dani and Daffyd made the best of the limitations. They took it in turns to use the bathroom down the hall with its gushing, rust-tinged water, barely heated by a struggling gas heater, and used the non-flushing toilet with its bucket of water standing ready for use. There were no blinds on the window, though the grimy deposits inside and out made it doubtful that anyone could spy on them. Facing in opposite directions, Dani and Daffyd stripped down to their underwear in the twilight and, carefully avoiding looking at each other, climbed into the bed with a blanket strategically placed between them. Sleep overwhelmed them almost immediately, despite feelings of embarrassment at their situation, and when the rays of the sun struggled through the dust-begrimed window, they woke fresh and eager to get to grips with their situation.

They dressed quickly in their grimy clothes and went looking for breakfast. The receptionist at the desk downstairs was not the man who had admitted them the night before and regarded them with suspicion. He said nothing though, so they went out into the streets and looked for a small restaurant. A small table in a corner position suited them nicely, and over a pot of coffee and a parsley-and-onion omelette, they discussed the future.

"First things first--what's our financial situation?" Daffyd asked.

Dani rummaged under her shirt, and after a glance around the almost deserted café to make sure they were unobserved, took out a small wad of low denomination banknotes. She counted it quickly and slipped it back into her money belt.

"Eighty-four pounds."

"And I've got..." Daffyd dug into his jacket pocket and scanned the change in his hand, "...another thirteen shillings and threepence."

"Not too badly off," Dani said with a faint smile. "As long as we don't get carried away, we should be fine."

"Yes, but for how long? Take that excuse for a hotel we're in--four pounds a night means three weeks accommodation, let alone food or anything else. How long is it going to take to find Scarab's tomb?"

"That's not my main concern," Dani replied. "I only want the golden scarab back."

"All right, forget the fact that Bashir will plunder it if he finds it--forget the tomb. How long to find your scarab?"

"I don't know. How can I possibly know?"

"Have you tried asking?"

Dani put down her coffee cup and stared at her companion. "Asking whom? Asking what?"

"The golden scarab, the gods of Egypt, the Nine of Iunu--anyone or anything that might work."

"Don't be silly. If I was Scarab, and if I had the golden scarab in my hand, I might try, but without it I can't ask whoever or whatever to point me at it."

"Have you tried?"

"Of course not."

"Then why don't you? What have you got to lose?"

"I...I'll think about it."

"Next thing then," Daffyd said, apparently of the viewpoint that he had won that argument. "Do we stay in Edfu or go somewhere else?"

"We have to stay here for now. This is the only place Marc and Muammar know we were headed. They'll come here if they can."

Daffyd nodded. "Agreed, but we need to think about our next step, whether or not the others join us. As I said before, we've got money for less than three weeks."

"Is there any way we could get more money? We've both got friends in England--could we ask them to wire us some funds?"

"I'm sure they'd be happy to, but how would we collect the money? We have no identification documents and we're in the country illegally."

Dani grimaced. "Forget that idea then. What else?"

"A bit of shopping. We could do with a change of clothes, towels, hats, a few toiletries..."

"Makeup."

Daffyd smiled. "If you think it necessary..."

"I do."

"...though I think you look most alluring *au natural*."

Dani blushed. "Pyjamas too."

Daffyd almost choked on his coffee. "That wasn't what I meant."

"I know." Dani reached across and brushed Daffyd's hand with her own. "It's sweet of you to say so, but we both know it's not true."

"If you prefer, we could buy a sleeping bag or a blanket, and I could kip down on the floor."

"I'll leave that decision up to you."

They finished their coffee, paid for their meal and went shopping in the bazaars and crowded shops of downtown Edfu. Daffyd purchased a small knapsack and over the course of the morning they added some shirts, skirts and trousers, underwear and socks, cheap shoes, notebooks and pencils, a couple of used paperback novels, towels, some soap, and a few pieces of basic makeup. Dani refused to buy these with Daffyd looking on, so she disappeared into a series of shops seeking out suitable foundation, lipstick and blush. She could not find the right eye shadow, so made do with a neutral brown. She slipped the package into Daffyd's knapsack and stared at him as if daring him to make some comment.

"I didn't say anything," Daffyd protested, but when she turned to look at some silk scarves, he muttered, "Gilding the lily if you ask me."

They walked slowly back to their hotel along the riverbank, taking in views of the river and dozens of boats plying the steadily flowing waters. Within the city limits there was evidence of pollution at the hand of man-- tin cans, glass bottles, paper, and even one or two plastic containers. Daffyd pointed these out to Dani.

"I can live with tin cans, paper and glass if I must," he said. "They'll break down over time, but I hope plastic never becomes cheap enough to be mass produced. The damn stuff will be clogging up the environment for centuries. It doesn't break down."

"It wasn't like this in the old days," Dani said. "I remember days on the river when you could walk for miles and see no trace of men's presence except the odd fishing boat or farmer with his hoe and mattock."

Daffyd cast a quizzical eye over the young woman. "You remember?"

Dani frowned momentarily and then smiled. "Did I say 'remember'? I meant, of course, that I imagine that's how it must have been."

Daffyd offered no comment and they continued along the riverbank, through the city park and back into the streets along the waterfront. They happened upon a shop selling a variety of tobacco products and Daffyd stopped, his nose wrinkling at the aromas of cured and spiced tobacco permeating the surrounding air.

Dani shook her head at his reaction but smiled. "Go on, Dafs, treat yourself to a packet and some papers. We can afford a little luxury. After all, you allowed me this lovely scarf."

Daffyd hesitated, took a step toward the shop and came to a reluctant halt. "No, damn it. I've been without it for days; I can last a little longer."

"Are you sure? I mean, it's fantastic if you want to give up, but is that the reason?"

"No, I'm not sure at all, but while I have the willpower, let's leave it." He turned and stalked off down the street, leaving Dani to hurry after him.

Back at the hotel, they took it in turns to bathe anew with soap and tepid water and this time changed into new, clean clothes. They bundled their old clothes together, and Dani took them to a woman two streets away that the hotel receptionist recommended--a woman who took in laundry for very reasonable rates.

They took tea in a riverside café, and enjoyed some delicious honey cakes with it. As they sipped their drink, Dani said, "I've been thinking. We don't have much time so we need to accelerate the search for the golden scarab."

"Agreed, but how?"

"We know Bashir has it, so we must find him. He's come to Egypt to track down Scarab's tomb and plunder it, and he knows from the inscription that it is somewhere south of old Waset--modern day Luxor--so it's reasonable to assume he'll go to Luxor first. A man of his importance shouldn't be too hard to find even in a big city."

"What about Marc and Muammar? If we head off to Luxor, how are they ever going to find us?"

Dani frowned and stirred her tea unnecessarily, clinking her spoon against the thin china in her agitation. "I don't know, and before you say it, I don't like the idea of abandoning our friends, but really, what choice have we got?"

"Leave that aside for the moment. If Bashir has the golden scarab and we find him in Luxor, what are you going to do? Walk up to him and demand its return?"

"It belongs to me," Dani said, her face set in an obstinate expression.

"You know very well he'll just order your arrest and have you thrown out of the country as an illegal entrant. If he doesn't just kill you."

"So what do you suggest? We sit around in Edfu and do nothing?"

"I didn't say that. Obviously we have to do something, but we need to think it through carefully. We might have only a single chance at its recovery."

"So? What?"

"Let me think a bit." Daffyd dipped his hand in his pocket and withdrew it with a wry grimace. "Habit kicks in. I'm used to rolling myself a fag when I think."

"We can go back to the tobacconist if you want."

Daffyd shook his head. "Let's try it without the weed first." He sat and contemplated the problem and while he did so, Dani ordered another pot of tea and some more pastries--this time sesame and almond paste ones. After ten minutes, Daffyd sighed. "It's no use, lass, my mental faculties just can't discern a way through our difficulties. Perhaps..." He refused to meet Dani's gaze. "Would you think less of me if I went and bought myself some tobacco? I think I need a nicotine boost."

Dani slipped him a pound note and said nothing. Daffyd pocketed it and set off down the street. He returned fifteen minutes later, a cloud of blue smoke trailing him and a contented expression on his face.

"Here," he told Dani, placing the pouch of tobacco on the table, together with the change. "You look after it for me. If I have to ask you each time, I may smoke less. Sorry, lass, but it's the best I can do at the moment."

"Has the nicotine helped?"

"You mean, have I had a wonderful insight that solves all our problems? No. If you mean that I've had an idea, then just possibly." Daffyd sat down and poured himself a cup of the now tepid tea and helped himself to the last pastry. "Do you remember, just after we all escaped from the Bedouin and were discussing where to go, we said Edfu, but that we had no money, no food and no shelter? Well, Muammar told us he had a cousin of a cousin, or the son of a brother's third wife or some such, living in Edfu, who might help us. If we could find this indeterminate and distant relative, we could leave a message with him to tell Muammar we had gone to Luxor."

"I vaguely remember him saying something, but do you even remember his name? We can't go around asking for relatives of Muammar al-Hadi."

"As a matter of fact I do--I think. Definitely Mohammad, like the Prophet, and I think his other name was Sook or Sook-rah. More likely Sook-rah, I'd say because I remember thinking 'How sweet'."

"I don't get it."

"Sook-rah sounds like sucre, the French for sugar."

Dani sighed and shook her head. "I think that nicotine has gone straight to your brain and addled it."

"Well, it was just a thought," Daffyd said, smiling to show he had taken no offence over her remark.

"No, it's a good idea--if this Mohammad Sugar actually exists. How would we go about looking for him?"

"Search me. I'm the ideas half of this relationship, you're the one that acts on it."

"Ah, we're in a relationship now, are we?"

Daffyd grinned. "Well, we did sleep together last night..."

"Literally, I might point out, not euphemistically."

"...And the hotel owner thinks we're married, so you'll just have to make an honest man out of me."

Dani laughed out loud, causing several heads to turn in the café. "Damn it, Dafs, you're good for me. Just when I was starting to feel depressed about the whole affair, you do something to cheer me up."

"Happy to be of service, lass."

They returned to their hotel, picking up their washed and pressed clothing on the way, paying with a few coppers from their diminished funds. The hotel owner was behind the desk once more and glowered at them, demanding to know where their papers were.

"As we told you yesterday, at the bottom of the river. It will take a few days at least for more to arrive from the British Embassy in Cairo."

"You pay more pounds for tonight. In advance."

Dani paid over another fiver, and they repaired to their room. To pass the time until dinner, Daffyd opted to read one of the paperbacks, sitting in an open window to catch the faint breeze off the river, while Dani made notes, trying to recall pertinent bits of information from the inscription written by Scarab. After half an hour, Daffyd, who had turned over some thirty pages without making any sense of them, put his book down.

"We obviously can't go to the police, so we need to go to the mosque."

Dani looked up from her notes. "Why?"

"To find Mohammad Sook-rah."

"They won't let us in if we're not Muslim," Dani objected.

"I don't see why not. Muslims are generally welcoming to non-Muslims as long as they're respectful. Besides, we could just ask to see the imam, the teacher. He should know everyone in his congregation."

"Would he help us though? And while we're at it, do we know enough Arabic to make ourselves understood?"

"Only one way to find out," Daffyd said.

"First thing tomorrow then."

They went out for dinner, using the same café they had used before, this time enjoying a spicy lamb stew with rice and mashed chickpeas, with flat bread and a salad on the side. Dani kept her notebook with her and continued to make notes in between mouthfuls. Daffyd concentrated on eating, but watched Dani's scribbling and attempted to read what she was writing by deciphering the upside-down script.

"What's a green mountain?"

Dani looked up. "What? Oh, you mean this?" She tapped her pencil on the page. "I'm recording what I can remember of the description."

"Why only now? You've had weeks to do this."

"I wouldn't need to if I had the golden scarab." Dani shrugged, and speared a cherry tomato on her fork. "At first I was too discouraged to even think about things..." She popped the tomato in her mouth, chewed and swallowed. "Then I thought I'd get the golden scarab back easily enough. Now I'm not so sure--so I'm writing down what I can remember."

"I don't recall anything about a green mountain," Daffyd said. He reached out and turned the notebook around, scanning the page quickly. "Nor a crystal crown and the Aten's greeting. Where did those phrases come from?"

"The inscription."

"I don't remember them. I recall you translating words describing a green streak of vegetation and a notch in the cliff where the sun shines through as pointers to the tomb, but not these things."

Dani looked down at her plate, a look of embarrassment flooding her features. "That's because I wasn't completely accurate in my translation."

Daffyd's gaze searched Dani's face. "You were lying to us, lass?" he asked quietly.

"Not lying exactly...more misleading."

"But why? Didn't you trust us?"

"You? Of course. The others on the team? Yes. Bashir? Definitely not."

"You couldn't have let us in on the deception?"

"I...I wanted to...but I was told not to."

Daffyd stared at Dani. "Told not to...by whom?"

"A voice inside my head." Dani smiled wryly at Daffyd's expression. "'Hearing voices now', I hear you say. Well, not exactly, but just a very strong impression that I should disguise the tomb description...so I did."

Daffyd considered her words in silence for several minutes, playing with the scraps of food on his plate with his fork as he did so. "You not only rattled off a translation of Egyptian hieroglyphs but managed to fudge a few details as you did so? So fluently none of us suspected for a moment? Why aren't you a professional Egyptologist instead of a lecturer in prehistoric studies if you have these linguistic abilities?"

"That's just it, I don't." Dani nibbled on a piece of flat bread. "I've studied ancient languages a bit, of course, and did a term or two of hieroglyphs, but my ability to translate is limited to working my way slowly through the phrases, nutting out the context as I go."

"That's not the impression you gave in Syria. You just read it off the walls directly--or was it all invention? Did you just make up Scarab's whole life?"

"No. I...I translated what was there, accurately for the most part, but I've no idea how I did it. Look, there's a series of pictographs--lion, hand, feather, sun, bowl, water, etc--my conscious mind wrestles them into a literal translation, but my unconscious mind has already turned them into conversational discourse. My eye sees the pictograph, I disengage my brain, and I utter what my inner voice tells me." Dani smiled, her eyes sad. "Sounds ridiculous, doesn't it?"

"What you uttered was accurate, though? You weren't just spouting any old thing?"

"No. My conscious mind was following along, monitoring my speech, you could say, and it was accurate--far more accurate than if I'd spent hours searching for the context with some linguistics professor."

"That's a hell of a story, lass," Daffyd said slowly.

"And now you know I'm crazy, having just suspected it before--hearing voices, believing in the efficacy of a golden scarab, rattling off a long story that a trained Egyptologist would have difficulty deciphering."

"Not necessarily, lass. I'm no psychologist, but Jung talked about the collective unconscious. Could you just be tapping into that? Somehow?"

"I'm not a psychologist either, but I think he was just referring to the human mind having collective archetypes--like rites of initiation being common to all societies. He didn't mean it as a literal memory gleaned from what other people knew."

"Monopsychism, then. Some writers do say Jung really meant that--that the collective unconscious is the sum total of human experience and somehow you've found a way to tap into that knowledge."

"It might be simpler just to posit that I'm Scarab reincarnated."

"Good God, are you?"

"I've no idea," Dani said. "I don't think so. I certainly don't have any memories of being her, or actually doing the things described in the account."

"That's not exactly the impression I've garnered in the last year, since we discovered the chambers. Even just recently--things like you remembering being in the western desert, or today, when you said you remembered how unspoiled the river used to be."

Dani smiled uncertainly. "I also corrected myself. Those weren't memories--how could they be? My brain, and the neurons within it, wasn't in existence in ancient times."

"That raises questions about what memory is. Is it something that sits in the brain waiting to be recalled, a configuration of neuronal connections, or is it stored elsewhere--in an extraneous energy field for instance--and your brain just acts as a receiver, like a radio, enabling you to access memories that Scarab had thousands of years ago?"

Dani shrugged. "I'm a scientist, Dafs, a materialist--and I have no evidence of anything...of anything supernatural. To believe I'm somehow accessing thoughts somebody had years ago or that I'm somehow the reincarnation of Scarab is ridiculous. Isn't it far more likely I'm just empathising with a troubled young woman?"

"If you say so, lass, but that doesn't explain how you suddenly got so proficient at reading hieroglyphs."

"No, I don't suppose it does, but it's the most reasonable explanation, so I'm sticking with it."

Chapter Twenty-Two

arc and Muammar awoke the next morning stiff and aching from their uncomfortable night on the rocky floor of the rubble-blocked cave. They still suffered the after effects of their trek through the desert, and their bodies cried out for water. The spring still flowed, though sparingly, and they soaked up as much moisture as they could before turning their thoughts toward finding food in the wilderness. Muammar assured Marc that there was life in the desert, things that could be eaten if one was not too particular, but Marc was sceptical.

There was nothing obvious moving around on the ledge, so they descended to the desert floor to search among the boulders, tumbling them aside and chasing down movement in the cooler and more humid undersides of the rocks. They found life--not in any great abundance--but after an hour of fossicking they had a haul of three medium-sized scorpions, a large centipede, and a lizard's tail. The owner of the tail was ensconced beneath a large rock and could not be persuaded to come out.

Muammar laid the corpses out on a flat rock and smiled. "Breakfast is served."

"Don't be disgusting." Marc poked the lizard's tail and it twitched faintly. "It's still alive, for God's sake."

"No, it's not. That's just nerves. So, what would you like? The scorpions are probably the most nutritious but the other titbits may be palatable too."

Marc grimaced, so Muammar picked up one of the scorpions and broke the tail from the body. Clear fluid leaked from the broken end. Muammar dabbed a finger in the fluid and touched it to his tongue.

"Juicy," he said. "But not much of a taste." He held the sting at the end of the tail and put the other end in his mouth, crunching down through the exoskeleton. "Not bad," he mumbled. He swallowed and took another nibble, biting just short of the sting segment and flicking it away as he chewed.

Marc stared at him as he ate, his own stomach growling its complaint of neglect, and then gingerly picked up another of the scorpions. He followed Muammar's example and, closing his eyes, bit down on the tail. A rush of fluid filled his mouth and he gagged, spitting out the fragments in his mouth. "Oh God, that was just awful." He continued to spit, his stomach heaving until he brought himself under control.

"Try again," Muammar said. "We have to have food if we're to survive out here, and this might be the only food we can find."

Marc grimaced and crunched into his scorpion again, disciplining himself to continue even though he almost gagged. He finished his morsel, leaving only the sting and the pincers, which he threw away.

"Good," Muammar said. He finished off his own arachnid and offered the third one to Marc, who refused with a shake of his head. Muammar ate the scorpion and then picked up the centipede. "I've never tried these." Marc shuddered, so Muammar bit into it and immediately spat it out. "Bitter," he explained. Marc refused the lizard tail, so Muammar ate that too, swallowing it in one convulsive gulp. "Now we must hope our stomachs accept this fare."

"I think I'm going for a lie down," Marc said. "Maybe wash my mouth out and try not to think of...of anything."

Muammar continued his exploration of the rubble heap by himself. He found another scorpion and, after killing it, slipped it into his pocket for later. There was little else visible, though after some diligent searching he found a few tough looking threads of ragged vegetation growing near the boulders. He sat on the hot sand and studied the plant, examining the scallops cut out of the leathery leaves and wondering what jaws had made them. Further scouting revealed other plants, also chewed and on one he found the owner of the jaws, a large brown and yellow-spotted grasshopper. The orthopteran stopped eating and looked at Muammar suspiciously with bulging, multi-faceted eyes, sidling around to the far side of the stem as he made a cautious approach. It watched Muammar and as he tried to sneak around the plant, edged nervously round so as to keep the thin stem between them.

Muammar leapt and his hands enveloped the insect. He gave a yelp of pain and opened his hands, whereupon the grasshopper opened flimsy looking wings and soared away. Muammar sucked his thumb where the insect's hind legs had scratched him and started in pursuit. It had landed about ten yards away, but the hot sand was not to its liking, so it whirred back to the shelter of the rocks. He ran after it and threw himself headlong with his hands outstretched, determined to hang on this time, no matter what. The insect raked him again, but Muammar squeezed and one of the hind legs broke off and a wing crumpled. The grasshopper looked at him reproachfully, but he crushed the insect's thorax anyway, killing it.

He pulled the legs and wings off the dead insect and looked at the long tubular body, imagining the nutritious contents. He tucked the body away with the scorpion and went looking for more. Scraggly plants were scattered around the base of the mound, evidently benefitting from the water trickling down, and there were several more grasshoppers of varying sizes. They were hard to catch, but as they seemed reluctant to fly far from the mound--he caught them if he persisted in his pursuit. By the time Muammar started being affected by the heat--somewhere around mid-morning--he had caught eleven.

"I suppose I had better check they are edible," he muttered. "If I am to offer them to Marc." He popped the smallest one in his mouth and chewed. After a few moments he swallowed and considered the taste. "Not bad. I suppose it depends on what they have been eating."

He carried the rest of his haul up to the ledge, first slaking his thirst and then approaching the cave. Marc was asleep but woke up as Muammar shuffled into the cave.

"How are you feeling?"

Marc yawned and shrugged. "I've got a bit of a headache and I still feel sick, but apart from that...just hungry. How'd you get on? Find anything more palatable than bugs?"

Muammar grinned and emptied his pocket, lining up ten grasshopper bodies--some as big as his forefinger--and one small scorpion. "The grasshoppers are all right. I had a small one."

Marc grimaced, but reached out and took a medium-sized one. "What do they taste like?"

"Hard to say exactly, but better than the scorpions."

Marc bit off the end and chewed, eyeing the yellow and grey-purple entrails in the other piece with distaste. He was reluctant to take another bite but forced himself to do so anyway, quickly chewing and swallowing before fighting back the urge to throw up.

"It helps if you don't look at it," Muammar observed. "It's a pity there's no fuel around. I think they'd be a lot nicer cooked."

"How would you start a fire anyway?"

"I thought maybe my watch cover might concentrate the sun's rays enough, but I guess the question's moot without fuel."

Muammar and Marc ate another grasshopper each and dozed, conserving energy, or sat watching the shadows slowly move.

"You know," Muammar said. "This hill has saved our lives, but we'll just die slowly unless we can find another source of food. A few grasshoppers and scorpions won't be enough."

"What do you suggest we do?"

"We have to leave, and soon. If we can't find enough to eat, we'll only get weaker, and nobody knows we're here, so there'll be no rescue."

"In which direction?"

"We have to get to Esna or Edfu or one of the villages, so I'd say we head east to the cliffs and follow them south or north until we find a way down."

"When do we leave?"

"Later tonight. I think the moon will give us enough light to steer by, but I need to be sure of our direction, so I'll study the night sky earlier--see if I can recognise the Pole Star. The last thing we want is to be wandering around in circles. The rising sun tomorrow will confirm the direction once we're on our way."

"Tonight then," Marc agreed. "In the meantime, we'd better catch some more grasshoppers. Maybe if we dry them in the sun they'll taste better."

They found another half dozen small grasshoppers, but they were already apparently exhausting the available food around the hill, confirming their need to leave as soon as possible. Back at the cave in the late afternoon, Marc went in to rest before their coming ordeal.

Muammar went looking for a way up the mound. He had the direction they must take sorted out--more or less--but he still had a faint hope that there might be a source of help closer to hand. The short climb to the summit proved easy once he found the route, for the sides of the mount had collapsed into a steep slope of boulders and rock fragments. A jumble of rocks caught the light, reflecting back the setting sun in a splash of white sparkles. The sight was so unexpected; he dropped to his knees and examined the phenomenon. Thousands of minute mica crystals littered the rock, each one acting like a tiny mirror. He looked up at the peak--now so close--and saw that the jumble of rocks had fallen from its side. Once upon a time, the peak must have flashed with white fire as the sun's rays caught it. *Crowned in glory. That's what we saw--not a headlight on a rise but a reflection...*

Muammar shook his head and hauled himself up the last few yards as the sun dipped and the life went out of the crystals. He stood on the top in the fading light of the day and mapped out their route as best he could, looking for the easiest path over stone and sand.

It's not going to be easy. Normally, I'd say eight hours should bring us to the cliffs and another six moving south to Edfu, or north to Esna...

Rather than dwell on the strenuous task ahead of them, Muammar looked around at the desert, shading his eyes against the low rays of the setting sun. All he saw was a wasteland or rock and sand...

Every way's the same.

...where nothing moved except dust caught in small whirlwinds engendered by the heat of the day. They faded and collapsed even as he watched, the heat draining from the day as the sun dipped below the western horizon and the first stars came out. He knew he should go back down and prepare for the journey ahead, but he lingered, enjoying the deepening chill of the evening. The shadows grew and the landscape lost all colour, becoming tones of grey on black. Light flickered in the southwest, illuminating nothing.

Thunderstorm. We could do with some rain.

The flicker came again but there was no accompanying sound of thunder.

Heat lightning...but that's closer than the horizon...static discharge from dry sand grains rubbing together?

Flick...and for a moment it looked as if two faint columns of light lifted into the clear sky, reflecting off floating dust particles. Muammar stared until spots of light floated in front of him, but the phenomenon was not repeated.

Those were headlights... A road? And close...

Already he was unsure of the right direction so he hurriedly cast about for loose stones and placed them in a more or less straight line from him to where he thought he had seen the lights piercing the night sky. He studied the line thoughtfully and shifted it slightly to the left before taking one last look into the night and starting the climb down to the cave in the gathering darkness.

He was almost at the cave when disaster struck. A stone gave way under his foot, and Muammar lurched and tumbled, falling onto the ledge. Pain flared in his right ankle and he cursed in Arabic. He sat in the darkness and gingerly felt an ankle already swelling, before hauling himself to his foot and limping around to the cave mouth.

"Are we leaving now?" Marc asked. Then, "What's wrong?"

"There's a problem. I fell and hurt my ankle."

"What? Let me see."

It was too dark to see, but by touch alone Marc could tell that Muammar's right ankle was swollen and tender. He eased the boot and sock off and tenderly probed the damage with his fingertips.

"Can you move your toes?"

"Yes, but it hurts."

"Probably not broken then. Sprained or twisted, I'd say. Rest up a couple of days and you'll be fine." Marc was not at all sure of his diagnosis, but tried to keep his friend cheerful.

"We don't have a couple of days," Muammar said.

"You can't walk on that," Marc pointed out.

"We can't just stay here. Nobody knows we're here; we have an uncertain supply of water and only a handful of grasshoppers as food."

"There's no alternative."

"I know but...when I was up there I saw something..." Muammar trailed off into silence, suddenly struck by doubts. "I thought I saw something," he amended.

"What did you see?"

"I saw headlights."

"What?"

"Headlights. I think I saw car headlights."

Marc's worry could be heard in his voice. "Are you all right, Muammar? Not feeling faint or anything?"

Muammar shook his head. "I know, it sounds odd, but I really think I saw the lights of a car. A couple of flashes first, that I thought were lightning, and then two beams stabbing into the air for a second. There's a road out there." He pointed to the southwest.

"What are you saying?"

"I think we should try for the road instead. The cliffs are too far off-- maybe ten miles--and the towns further still. A road may be a lot closer, and if there's one car, there'll be others."

Marc sat down on the ledge with his back to the rock and looked east over the desert. Muammar respected his silence and pulled himself over to sit beside him. After a few minutes, Marc said, "We know the cliffs are over there to the east, but we don't know there's a road in the southwest. What if it wasn't a car you saw, but heat lightning or...or a hallucination. We could wander out there looking for it until we die of thirst and exhaustion."

"But if it is a road there'll be other cars and a car could have us in a town an hour later."

Marc contemplated the darkness, thinking. "You're right. It's worth the risk, but I'll go alone and bring help back."

"The road could be miles away," Muammar cautioned.

"How high is this mound, Muammar?"

"What? Why?"

"How high? From the desert down there to the summit. Estimate it."

"Fifty feet? A hundred? I don't know. What does it matter?"

"I'd have said two hundred feet. If my boy scout days have any relevance, it means that...let's see...square root of two hundred is, er, fourteen...times that by one point three gives us, um, eighteen miles."

"That's a lot further than the cliffs, which we know are there."

"Were the lights at the horizon or closer?"

Muammar tried to picture the desert in his mind's eye. "Closer. Perhaps half way."

"If the lights were halfway to the horizon, then the road could be just eight or nine miles away."

"And if it's not?"

"Then I'll come back and we try for the cliffs tomorrow night when your ankle's a bit rested."

"I don't like it, Marc. I know the desert better than you, so we should go together."

"You'd slow me down. Look, I know it's a gamble, but the presence of a road a few miles away could save both our lives."

Muammar thought it over and reluctantly agreed. "When will you leave?"

"At first light. I'll need daylight to be sure of where I am, and to recognise a road if I find one."

"You'll be walking in the heat. What will you do for water?"

"Drink until I'm sloshing and then..." Marc shrugged. "...I'll just have to do without."

Marc slept through the night and when the first hint of dawn greyed the eastern horizon, he climbed to the top of the mound and took note of hillocks and rock formations in the direction of the line of the rocks Muammar had placed the previous evening. He descended to the ledge once more and drank from the seep until he could hold no more.

"See you soon, Muammar. Take care of yourself while I'm gone. Rest that ankle."

Muammar embraced Marc as the first rays of the new day's sun lit up the east. "May God be with you, Marc. I will see you soon, insha'Allah."

213

Marc set off to the southwest, his shadow angling in front of him and to his right, the sliding outline gradually shortening and swinging further round as the morning progressed. He kept his eyes on the landmarks he had noted earlier, but found it harder to keep his direction true after he passed the first of them. Sweat poured from his body as the heat grew, but he trudged onward, counting his steps as he went.

A pace is a yard; one thousand seven hundred and sixty make a mile, eight miles is...a bit over fourteen thousand.

He counted, registering each hundred on a finger until he had ten and then slipping a pebble in his pocket. After a while a second pebble joined it, and then a third and fourth. When he had five he allowed himself a short break in the narrow shadow of a tall rock before staggering on, trying to ignore his growing thirst.

When twelve pebbles clicked in his pocket, he stopped again and looked around. Behind him, he could still see the mound--or at least he hoped it was the mound. He had not really considered the problem of finding his way back.

Still, the pebbles should help. I will know the distance.

Marc moved slower now, knowing he was in the approximate area where Muammar had seen the headlights. A thirteenth pebble joined the others in his pocket, then a fourteenth, and a little later, a fifteenth.

If that's what they were...be positive man, they were...there's a road...and there'll be cars on it...

He looked up at the sun and saw that it was late morning and the heat had sucked the moisture from his body, leaving a fine rime of salt on his clothes and skin. His mouth was dry and to swallow was painful. Sixteen pebbles jostled in his pocket now and Marc was starting to think Muammar's mind had been playing tricks on him the night before.

He's condemned us both. There's no road...or else I've missed it. Should I go back? Could I even survive the trip back?

Marc trudged on, still counting out his now faltering paces, waves of heat beating up at him from the ground and the taste of dust and failure in his mouth. He stumbled and nearly fell, stumbled again, losing count. He had taken another dozen steps before he thought to look at what had tripped him. Before him, on the stony ground, he saw two more or less parallel depressions, snaking away from northwest to southeast. He stared at them for a full minute before his mind registered what it was seeing.

Ruts. They're bloody ruts and this is the fucking road. Shit, but what a road. Marc's heart sank. *How many cars use it? The car Muammar saw last night might be the only one in a month.*

He started to follow the ruts toward the southeast. After nearly a hundred paces he suddenly thought of something and stopped dead before retracing his steps. He could still see the scuff in the sand where he'd stumbled over the rut, so he collected rocks together and built a small cairn to mark the spot, including a short row to mark the direction he'd come.

Marc started back down the road again, walking purposefully and with as much strength as he could muster. His fingers counted the paces again and pebbles slowly accumulated in another pocket, marking out the slow miles.

The ruts joined another road, a proper one, though unsealed. Again, Marc built a cairn of rocks and a line of stones pointing the way back, before venturing along it. It ran south and started veering southeast, and his spirits rose, for the river, and possibly the city of Edfu lay in that direction.

Then he heard it, an uneven sound, a drone rising and falling behind him and he turned to see a distant plume of dust lifting into the air. It came closer, and the sound grew louder of a vehicle labouring over the rutted surface of the road. A van came in sight, rusted and covered in a patina of red dust, and Marc waved his hands over his head and stepped into the road, waving the driver to stop.

It was only when the van stopped and the bearded face of the man behind the steering wheel looked out through a broken window, that Marc remembered he knew no Arabic.

"Please...need help...water for me and one other. You speak English?"

He could see from the incomprehension in the man's eyes that he did not. He tried again, miming as well as talking. "Me...walk from there..." He pointed to the east. "Two people...one injured...no water...you help me please?"

The man spoke fast, but Marc could not understand a word.

Marc made drinking motions and repeated the word 'water' several times. At last the man nodded, spoke again, and then turned and rummaged around in the van. He pulled out a large glass bottle about half full of water and handed it to Marc.

"Bless you," Marc muttered, lifting the bottle to his lips. He drank in several large swallows, draining about half of the contents before lowering it. "Thank you." He bobbed his head and smiled. The man in the van smiled broadly and, before Marc could react, threw the van into gear and planted his foot on the accelerator.

"Hey, come back!" Marc started after the van, but despite the rutted surface and the decrepit state of the vehicle, it easily drew away from him. He stopped, panting hard and stared after the departing van in its cloud of dust, giving vent to every swear word in his vocabulary and making up a few more on the spot. Then he sank to his knees in the middle of the dirt road and cried with frustration.

At least he left me a bottle of water. He looked at the liquid level. *All right, a quarter bottle. But what do I do now? Keep going in the hope of reaching a major road? Wait for another vehicle? Risk the same thing happening? Why didn't I think of the language problem? Muammar should have come with me--but we wouldn't have got this far.*

Marc sat by the road and waited as long as he dared, but no more vehicles arrived. Noon passed and the sun had started its long descent to the western horizon before he got to his feet and returned the way he had come, hoarding the precious water and the even more precious glass bottle. He found the first cairn of stones and turned onto the double-rutted road and then to the site of the second cairn. Sighting along the line of stones, there was little in the east except low hillocks and stony plains, but he spent a little time sorting out which hillock--which mound--was the one he sought. He decided and set off, again counting his paces and discarding a pebble every time he reached a thousand. Night fell while he still had two pebbles in his pocket, and he could not be certain he was still on track for the mound.

I think I am...I think that's it over there...but what if I'm wrong? If I overshoot, I'll just wander until the water runs out and I die. Then Muammar dies too, waiting for rescue that never comes. Marc continued, discarding first one and then the other pebble. *I must be close.* He stopped in the darkness, listening to the silence.

"Hello!" He listened. "Hello!" Silence again. "Hello! Muammar."

"Marc?" The call came faintly from behind him and to the left. He turned and faced in what he judged was the right direction, putting the bottle down carefully.

He cupped his hands. "Keep calling, so I can follow the sound."

"Marc...this way...Marc...hello...keep coming!"

Marc picked up the almost empty bottle and started forward, stumbling over the rocky surface toward the ever-strengthening sound of Muammar calling him home. At last the mound loomed and he cautiously picked his way up the fallen rock to the ledge and Muammar's arms.

The young man hugged Marc. "Allah be praised you are safe. I was so worried about you."

"And I you. How's your ankle?"

"A little better. The swelling has gone down a bit and I can stand on it--as you can see. Did you find the road? What's that you've got?"

"A bottle. Yes, I found a road--a dirt one--and a car. The car stopped but I couldn't make him understand. I never considered the fact I couldn't speak Arabic. He gave me this bottle of water and drove off before I could stop him."

Muammar groaned. "I didn't think of that. I should have gone."

"You'd never have made it, but we'll both try for the road tomorrow. We can fill the bottle with water and that will help us survive. When we get to the road we wait. There'll be another car--there has to be."

They sat in silent contemplation of their coming task for a little while, and then Muammar cleared his throat. "I will be glad to leave," he said. "I don't want to appear superstitious, Marc, but I think this hill is haunted. I feel as if I am being watched by someone or something that is angered by my presence."

"You felt it too, huh? I didn't want to say anything." Marc shrugged. "Just as well we're leaving then."

In the predawn chill of the next day, they prepared for the trek, drinking as much water as they could, and filling the glass bottle to its brim. Then they climbed carefully down to the desert floor, Muammar leaning on Marc as much as possible, and waited for the dawn to show the necessary landmarks.

They set out as Marc had done the day before, their shadows keeping them company, leading them on their right sides. Marc led, Muammar limping at his heels, carrying the water bottle. They counted the paces again, making a game of it to lighten the mood, and slowly the pebbles collected again in Marc's pocket. Every two thousand paces, he called a halt and allowed them both a sip of water.

Muammar's pace was slow, and by the time he had seven pebbles in his pocket, Marc was supporting the young man, though Muammar limped gamely on, making no complaint. By the time ten pebbles had accumulated, their pace had slowed to a shuffle--and still they stumbled on through the sand and stony desert.

Marc suddenly stopped and pointed at the ground. "We're here."

"At the road?" Muammar asked.

"See?" Marc pointed out the double ruts in the stony desert. They drank again, from a bottle that was now more than three quarters empty and set off along the track to its junction with the dirt and gravel road. They never found Marc's first cairn of stones, having taken a slightly different route to the road, but they did find the second one.

"Edfu's that way, I think."

They rested again, drank more water, and renewed their journey, limping along the rough road. They saw the dust before they heard the noise of the engine, this time coming up from the south, and they waited on the road for the vehicle to arrive.

"I don't believe it," Marc said. "It's the same bloody van that stopped before."

"Well, this time it's going to do more than just stop," Muammar said. "It's going to turn around and take us to Edfu."

He flagged the vehicle down and harangued the driver in fluent, if accented, Arabic. The man argued, protested, and made varied excuses, but eventually he gave in, turning his van around and Marc piled in the back, while Muammar sat up front, engaging the man in conversation, to prevent the driver having second thoughts.

In just over an hour's time, they were in the city centre of Edfu.

* * *

Zufir and his men arrived on the outskirts of Edfu that evening. The small group of Bedouin warriors sat on their camels and regarded the bustling city with its many people, buildings, paved roads and electric lights, with distaste.

"How can people live like this?" one man asked.

"Better we should forget the infidels than subject ourselves to this filth," Alif said.

"What? You will pay me seven thousand English pounds? I thought not." Zufir curled his lip and his men quailed. "Find a place to make camp. Tomorrow we leave one man to guard the camp and the others will spread out through this place. You all know what our cousin Muammar al-Hadi looks like, and you will recall the features of the infidels. Find them."

Chapter Twenty-Three

B ashir was down at the docks in Luxor not long after first light, accompanied by Nazim and Lieutenant Al-Din. The Minister inspected the launch that had been put at his disposal by Colonel Sarraj, talking with the captain and crewman. It was a small launch, with limited accommodation, but it would suffice for a preliminary survey of the river south of Luxor. Bashir ordered his companions aboard and told the captain to cast off.

"I'm sorry, sir, but I have orders to wait."

"Orders? From whom? For how long?"

"From Colonel Sarraj, sir." The captain looked at his watch. "He shouldn't be long."

"Colonel Sarraj is here in Luxor? You've spoken with him?"

"Yes sir. Just last night."

Bashir turned away, dismissing the captain. He climbed back onto the dock and stood looking out over the busy scene of boats loading and unloading. *What is he doing here? Why wouldn't he tell me he was coming?*

He heard footsteps on the wooden boards and turned to see the lithe form of Sarraj striding toward him. The Colonel wore army fatigues without any insignia of rank and walked quickly, averting his face from other people on the docks. Bashir stepped forward to greet him and Sarraj gripped his arm, turning him and pulling him along toward the boat.

"As far as anybody is concerned, I am just Michel and a friend. Your men are discreet?"

"Of course, but why, Michel?"

"I wish my business...our business...to go unnoticed."

Sarraj stepped aboard the launch, followed by Bashir, and the Colonel told the captain to cast off and head south. Within minutes, the propellers bit into the green water and slowly propelled the craft out into the current, the engine note rising as the captain increased power, hurling the launch upriver. Sarraj remained by the captain for several minutes, talking to him, before coming back to join the others.

"Ahmed, introduce me to your companions."

"Nazim Manouk, my private secretary; and Lieutenant Jamal Al-Din. This is...er, Michel..."

"My identity is no secret amongst us, Ahmed. I am Colonel Sarraj. We have a common purpose. You are aware of it?"

Nazim inclined his head in silent affirmation, but Al-Din looked a bit perplexed. Bashir interposed. "The lieutenant is here to offer support and help. He knows nothing of our greater purpose."

"I could have provided all the help you need, Ahmed." Sarraj said reproachfully.

"He is also the son of a friend, and I am doing his father a favour."

Sarraj nodded. "So? Is he to be taken into our confidence?"

"I think we may do so," Bashir said. "Lieutenant Al-Din, it came to the notice of the Ministry in Damascus that an inscription had been discovered. Translated, this inscription purported to show the position of a tomb that we believe has not been discovered. That is why I am in Egypt."

"Forgive me, Minister," Al-Din said, "But shouldn't the local Department of Antiquities be excavating this tomb?"

"Of course, and in time they will. However, at the moment we don't even know if it exists. The Ministry notified the Egyptian authorities at once, but they are understaffed and overworked and could not investigate the inscription. That is why I am here--I volunteered to spend my holidays looking for the tomb. Colonel Sarraj here is along to keep an eye on the whole business for the Department of Antiquities, and offer protection and assistance as needed. Everything is above board."

"Of course, Minister. I never doubted you." Al-Din smiled. "This is a wonderful venture, Minister. Thank you for involving me."

"Well, we can always use an extra pair of eyes."

"I shall be most diligent," Al-Din declared. "The inscription tells you where this tomb lies?"

"More or less," Bashir said.

"How long before we get there?"

"Ah, now that is the big question, Lieutenant," Bashir said. "It seemed fairly straightforward up in Syria when we first discussed the idea, but now we're down here it's looking considerably harder."

"Why is it so hard now you're here?"

"Tell him, Nazim."

"Yes Minister. Jamal, the inscription indicates the tomb is located in a cliff that has a line of green vegetation pointing to it, and from the line you can see a notch in the cliff where the sun shines through. A track leads up from the line of vegetation to a tomb closed by a rock. It seems straightforward, doesn't it?"

"But it's not?"

Nazim pointed out the cabin window to the western bank. "What do you see?"

Al-Din stared across the water. "Cliffs, farmland, trees, villages."

"And what's that? Where the cliff top dips--just there." Nazim pointed.

"It's a notch. Do you think it's the one we're looking for?"

"Can you see a line of green vegetation?"

Al-Din stared at the cliff and scrubland at its base. "No, but maybe the plants have died or been chopped down."

Nazim smiled. "And how would we tell that?"

"I don't know. How?"

"I have no idea. That's why this search is so difficult. Even if that notch there did have a line of green to it, how could we be certain the notch wasn't the result of recent erosion and that it didn't exist in the time of the Amarnan Kings? Three thousand years is a long time. We would have to land and investigate each one in turn, and even then we could not be sure."

Al-Din looked crestfallen. "There could be hundreds of notches. How can we ever find the right one?"

"It's definitely a problem, but maybe not insurmountable." Nazim turned to Bashir. "Minister, you have looked at topographical maps of the Nile Valley. How many possible notches did you find between Edfu and Esna?"

"I cannot remember."

"I counted at least fifty, but less than a hundred."

"That's a lot of notches," Al-Din said. "If we were to investigate only one a day it could take us two or three months."

"There are other considerations," Nazim said. "I noticed a few oddities in the narrative--caution almost, as if the writer was aware her words could be read by men hostile to her." He glanced at Bashir. "May I elaborate, Minister?" When Bashir nodded, he continued. "The first reference to the site we seek came after an account of a battle at ancient Thebes--that's modern-day Luxor. The inscription says it was two days south of the city, conveyed by battle galleys rowing against the current. Later, we are told the tomb is three days south, yet north of the first site. Again, and here is the best description of the tomb, just after the king has died, we are told it is near Behdet--modern day Edfu."

Al-Din considered Nazim's words while Bashir and Sarraj watched him with interest. "Those descriptions do not make sense, Nazim. You say the first site is two days south of Luxor and yet the tomb is three days south of the city, yet a little north of it."

"That is what the inscription says," Nazim said.

"If there is that great a discrepancy, how much reliance can you place on anything in it?" Al-Din queried.

"That remains to be seen," Bashir said.

An hour later, when they had moved past Esna, they came to the first of many possible sites. The captain guided the launch toward the western shore and they all stood on deck and studied the land that lay before them.

A strip of rocky scrubland stretched from the riverside inland for a couple of hundred yards before becoming pasturage. Another half mile further inland, the cliffs towered above them with an apron of overgrown fallen rock spreading out from their base. They landed and the crewman made fast the boat while Bashir led his team into the scrubland. He encouraged them to investigate the ground for signs of former water courses, where vegetation could have grown. They found nothing, and moved inland, examining the cliff face with binoculars, but although a goat track led through the crumbling fallen rock and scrub, it petered out when it met solid rock. Neither was there a cleft in the rock face nor any sign of man's hand, whether ancient or modern.

They trooped back to the launch and moved upriver a bit, to the next site, where a thin wedge of old trees ran inland from near the water's edge. An irregular depression hinted at an old channel and the spirits of all rose at the sight.

"That could be viewed as a strip of green," Al-Din said.

They landed again and followed the strip to where it faded from view a few hundred yards inland. Nazim got down on his knees, digging in the soil in the side of the depression. He got up after a few minutes, moved a few paces and dug again before calling the others over and pointing at his find. "What do you think?"

Bashir grunted. "What am I looking at?"

"Rocks?" Sarraj queried.

"Yes, rounded river boulders only a foot under river silt. The river has been through here within the last hundred years or so."

"I imagine the river has changed its course many times over the centuries," Bashir said. "Is it important?"

"It is if you think that line of trees and old channel are evidence of the line of green."

"Why? Explain your reasoning, Nazim."

"If the river flowed over here in the recent past--and I'm talking no more than a hundred or so years going by the apparent age of the trees-- then this wedge of green and this channel did not exist previously. It's a false trail."

"Are you sure?"

"No, Minister. It could still be an ancient river bed and the trees have been replaced many times over the millennia, but I wouldn't get too excited by just this one sign."

They moved toward the cliffs but it soon became clear that the rocky slopes were devoid of the blemishes they sought, neither cleft nor notch marred the cliff top and no hint of a track scarred the cliff face. Disappointed, they made their way back to the waiting launch.

They moved farther upriver, stopping at intervals to examine a site from the water, landing at a few to investigate a feature more thoroughly. A small town came in sight and they docked at the wharf to refresh themselves at a tiny restaurant before embarking and journeying onward.

"I suppose we are limited to the western cliffs?" Sarraj asked.

"That's what the inscription indicates," Nazim said. "Why do you ask, Colonel?"

Sarraj pointed. "There are many notches in the eastern cliffs."

Bashir stared and after a few moments, swore violently. "Are we wasting our time? Should we be searching that side too?"

"Let us not lose our focus, Minister," Nazim said soothingly. "We saw nothing in the inscription that even hints at deliberate deceit. If the writer says it is on the western shore, then that is a reasonable assumption. Indeed, if we started to think that one part of the description was false, then how could we believe any part of it? We would be better off giving up and going home. As it is, our task is a difficult one--but not impossible."

Sarraj tired of their efforts by early afternoon and requested a return to Luxor. Bashir tended to agree, having decided that the reality of the search was totally different from his concept of what it would be like. Nazim argued for continuing the search, saying that each site examined was one less possibility, and sooner or later they must happen upon the right one.

"I'm sure you're right," Bashir said, yawning, "But I think we've done enough for today. Besides, I've things to do in Luxor."

"I thought the search for the tomb was the most important thing," Nazim protested.

"And so it is, but I don't have to be here for you to carry it out. We'll return home, and you and Lieutenant Al-Din can come out again tomorrow."

They returned to Luxor, arriving in the middle of the afternoon. Bashir and Sarraj went off together, leaving Nazim and Al-Din at a loose end. Nazim intimated there were account books requiring his attention.

"What do I do now?" Al-Din asked. "Are my duties over for the day or have you something you need me to do?"

Nazim sighed. "There are hours more of useful day ahead of us, but little you can do here. We need to be cruising the river and examining potential sites. So no, Jamal Al-Din, I have no more work for you today. What will you do with your time?"

"I have never been to Egypt before. I thought I might do some sight-seeing."

"There is a very good museum in Luxor."

"I thought I might visit the Valley of the Kings or some of the temples. Get some idea of what ancient Egypt was like."

"You'll need a whole day to see the Valley of the Kings," Nazim said. "It's on the western shore, but if you want something you can see properly in an hour or two, I hear the Great Temple of Luxor is worth seeing."

"The Great Temple it is then," Al-Din said with a smile. "Thank you." He turned to leave, and Nazim called after him.

"I don't suppose I could accompany you? All of a sudden, accounting has lost its attraction."

"I'd be delighted," Al-Din said.

They went back to the hotel to change shirts and refresh themselves before catching a taxi to the Avenue that ran between the Luxor Temple and Karnak Temple Complex. The taxi dropped them in the still considerable afternoon heat a half mile from the temple.

"Why so far, Nazim? It's hot out here."

Nazim paid off the driver and pointed. "Look. What do you see?"

Al-Din looked up the length of the Avenue and gasped. A narrow strip of paved stone ran straight as a ruled line toward the temple, lined by broad expanses of coarse gravel on either side. Bordering on the Avenue itself sat, on stone plinths, dozens of carved, human-headed sphinxes. Some were no more than a stone paw or heap of rubble, but others were intact, staring out dispassionately at their fellows across the way.

"Amazing," Al-Din breathed. "One can almost imagine how they must have looked in ancient times. Such a feeling of history - maybe even King Tut walked down here."

"He was more likely borne in a litter or rode in a chariot," Nazim said. "But you're right; it is easy to imagine the ancient glories of Egypt. Of course," he added, "The Avenue would have been very different then. Now don't quote me on this, but I think Queen Hatshepsut and King Amenhotep the Third first put ram-headed sphinxes here--the ram was sacred to the god Amun, whose temple lies at the end. It wasn't until much later though, that the few rams became many."

"But these aren't rams, they're human-headed."

"They have rams-heads toward the Karnak temple, I'm told." Nazim pointed back down the long thoroughfare to where a tall minaret sat opposite the ruined walls of the distant Temple Complex.

They started walking down the long Avenue toward the Luxor temple. As they approached, they saw what appeared to be two high walls in their path, with a cleft between them. To one side a granite obelisk reared taller than the walls and giant stone figures sat in their shade.

"A shadow of its former glory," Nazim murmured.

"Why are the walls so short?" Al-Din asked. "I suppose in the olden days they went all around the temple, but you'd think that if they preserved those bits, they'd keep more."

"I have done some reading on this. Those aren't walls, Jamal, but pylons. A pylon is a gateway, and before it fell into disrepair, it was made up of two tapering towers joined by a cross piece. The actual gateway itself would have been half the height of the towers. I'm told that the form of the pylon is..." Nazim stopped and stared at the structure ahead of them.

"What? Are you all right?"

"Yes...I just had a thought..."

"Do you want to share it?"

Nazim shook his head. "Not yet...no...or rather yes. If I don't, I might forget it. Look, I read that the form of the pylon, the gateway, is that of two low hills between which the sun rises. It mirrors the hieroglyph for the horizon or *akhet*."

"Interesting," Al-Din said, though he shuffled his feet and looked away as he spoke.

"No, that's not the interesting part," Nazim went on. "The Syrian inscription talked about a notch on the cliff top through which the sun guided one to the tomb. We've all been assuming that was a notch in the

225

cliff top, perhaps carved by wind or rain--but what if it's not? What if the notch is really a pylon built on top of the cliff? That could narrow down the search enormously."

"How do you mean?"

"Think, Jamal. There are monuments scattered throughout Egypt--inscriptions, obelisks, temples...and pylons. What if our Scarab woman positioned her tomb in line with an existing pylon, or built one as a guide?"

Al-Din considered the idea. "But wouldn't that lead people to the tomb? The idea was to keep people away, wasn't it--tomb robbers and all that?"

"True, but the ancient Egyptians were a superstitious lot with all their gods and demons. Maybe she thought the presence of a symbolic gateway was a necessary part of the burial process." Nazim grinned. "By Allah the Merciful and Beneficent, I really think this is the answer."

"Do you want to go back and tell the Minister?"

"No hurry. Let's continue with our tour."

As they neared the pylon, the scale of the building impressed itself on their senses. They craned their necks to look up the towering walls, the massive statues of the seated pharaohs at the gateway entrance staring stonily down the great Avenue far above their heads. Nazim said that he thought the statue was of Ramses the Great, but that he was not sure.

Al-Din peered at the worn carved hieroglyphs on the granite plinth. "Doesn't it say who it is?"

"Quite possibly, but I can't read hieroglyphs."

They walked through the gateway into the temple, encountering more statues and huge columns, their carved tops outlined against the blue sky. The passage between the rows of columns was narrow, engendering feelings of inferiority as the weight of stone pressed in around them.

"Guide, effendi?" A dusty-clothed Egyptian smiled ingratiatingly at Nazim and Al-Din. "My name is Ali and I show you the temple--very cheap." He went on to name a price that was exorbitant by any standard.

"No thank you."

The Egyptian immediately halved his price. "You will not find a better guide, effendi. These motherless sons of diseased dogs around here would rob you blind, but I offer you a price to delight your pockets. I know every part of the temple and all its history. I can show you temple writing that is not normally seen by visitors--and can even translate it." He struck himself on the chest and raised his head proudly. "I am educated, effendi, and would be happy to impart my knowledge for a small consideration." The price dropped again.

Al-Din drew Nazim aside. "Why not? It seems like a reasonable price."

Nazim smiled. "You do realise we'll probably be fed a whole lot of stories that have no bearing on the truth?" He shrugged. "Go on then, at least he'll be able to feed his family tonight." He turned back to the waiting Egyptian. "Very well then, Ali. Show us the temple."

"Oh, a thousand blessings on you, effendi, you will not regret it. I will show you everything. Come."

Ali gestured for his clients to follow him and immediately started talking about the structures around them. He claimed that the temple was as old as the earth itself, having been built by Afrit before the Word of Allah was given to a pagan world.

"The very first pharaohs built this entrance way--the same ones that built the great pyramids of Giza. You have seen these pyramids, effendi?"

"You see?" Nazim murmured. "Already he is making up stories. This temple came long after the pyramids."

Ali prattled on, obviously enjoying himself, and Nazim recognised that while he was repeating local legend and embroidering obvious folk tales, some of the information was correct. Nazim was no expert in Egyptian architecture, but he had read books on Egypt and knew the open space within the temple was called the peristyle court. Ali correctly identified it, with its seventy-four columns bearing stylised lotus buds at their crowns. He talked about the shrine to Thutmose III in one corner and the giant colonnade of Amenhotep III beyond the court--seven pairs of fifty-foot columns carved to represent papyrus stems. The huge stone architrave blocks were still in place, and Nazim could imagine them crumbling and plunging to the ground, crushing anyone under them. Ali pointed out the giant statues of Ramses II and told stories of how difficult they had been to erect.

"They were so heavy, effendi, that thousands of men working together could not move them. The king was very angry and the priests prayed very hard to their false gods and a miracle happened. That night, the statues came to life and walked to their places in the temple before turning back into stone. Of course, this power came from Afrit, and not from God, and since the Prophet, peace be unto him, the demons have been powerless and the statues unable to move."

The court of Amenhotep lay beyond the colonnade, and beyond that the serried ranks of the Hypostyle and the sanctuary of the god Amun with walls covered in carvings. There was even an enclosed space with the stone ceilings intact, dedicated to Alexander the Great. The Macedonian ruler had converted part of the temple into a shrine a thousand years after the temple had been built, and the walls of the shrine were decorated with faded paintings and stone reliefs showing Alexander as pharaoh.

One part of the temple took them by surprise. Just inside the entrance was a modern building perched atop of ancient stonework and truncated columns. It was in good repair, whitewashed and painted, with iron railings, a small dome and a slender minaret.

"It's a mosque," Al-Din exclaimed. "What's a mosque doing here?"

"That is an interesting story," Ali replied. "A thousand years ago the faithful built a mosque on a mound of earth at this site, and it was only when the English started to excavate that it was found to have been built on the ruins of the temple. Inside, if you wish to see, there is a grave in which Yousef Ibn Abdel-Raheem, known as Abu Al-Haggag, is buried. The mosque is named after this worthy person."

"What makes him worthy enough to be buried inside the mosque?" Al-Din asked.

"Abu Al-Haggag was a Sufi Sheik, born in Baghdad, but when he came to Luxor, he saw that it needed a mosque. He petitioned the Christian ruler--yes, Egypt was ruled by the Coptic Christians then--a Princess, no less. Abu Haggag asked for land to build a mosque, but the Princess refused, so he asked for only as much land as could be enclosed by a camel's skin. She laughed and agreed. That night, Abu Haggag cut the hide of a camel into a very fine strip, so long that it encompassed a Christian church which stood there. In the morning, the Princess was amazed and angered, but kept her word and gave Abu Haggag the land. Over time, the Princess came to see that Abu Haggag was a holy man and she, herself, converted to Islam."

"A wonderful story, indeed," Al-Din said.

Ali took them to see wall carvings in the open colonnades, but also to see lesser ones in darkened passageways where little sunlight penetrated. The stilted figures of men and animals seem to pause in their eternal actions, half-hidden by the soft shadows, as living men regarded them. The Egyptian pointed to the hieroglyphs associated with each carving.

"See, this one describes an offering by Meny, son of Hotep, a rich merchant of Ta-Senet, who brings cattle and grain as an offering to the priests of Amun; and this one from Lord Amentep offering a hundred jars of fine wine."

"You really can read the hieroglyphs?" Nazim asked.

Ali fidgeted and looked down. "Of course, effendi. I have studied for many years."

Nazim pointed at a series of hieroglyphs enclosed within a cartouche. "What does this one say?"

Ali grimaced and shuffled his feet some more. "That is the offering Lord Amentep makes. It says, 'one hundred jars of fine wine'."

"Thank you, Ali. You have been a most interesting and instructive guide, but the hour grows late and we must leave." Nazim took out his wallet and took out two notes, passing them across to the delighted Egyptian. "Your fee--and a little extra for your fascinating stories."

"Thank you, effendi. May the blessings of Allah be upon thee both."

Nazim and Al-Din left their guide looking for another customer and walked out of the temple and back onto the Avenue with its line of sphinxes.

"I'm surprised you gave him a tip," Al-Din said. "I thought you said he was making up stories."

"He was, but something he said made me recognise the biggest mistake we have been making in our venture to discover Scarab's tomb. I had to reward him for that, even if he was unaware of what he'd done."

"Now you have made me curious," Al-Din said. "What is this great mistake?"

"He translated those hieroglyphs as 'one hundred jars of fine wine' but it couldn't have been that. I know enough about hieroglyphs to know that the figures inside that boundary--the cartouche--represent a royal name. That makes me wonder whether anything the Englishwoman--Dr Hanser-- said was true. We just believed her without suspecting anything was amiss, but perhaps her translation of the Syrian inscription was faulty at best--or even deliberately misleading."

Al-Din whistled. "How can you find out?"

"I have photographs of key passages of the inscription, including the description of how to find the tomb. I will have to show them to an expert at the museum. He will be able to tell me what they really say."

Chapter Twenty-Four

The young woman stood on the balcony of the Nomarch's residence in Behdet, leaning on the stone balustrade and staring out over the night-time city and beyond to where the Great River--Iteru--shimmered in the light of a waxing moon. The night air was cool, and the woman folded her arms across her bare chest, the gold of her arm-bands cold against her breasts, and shivered.

Why am I here? What am I waiting for?

Few lights were visible in the darkened city at this late hour. The cooking fires had long been banked or extinguished and only the rich could afford to keep oil lamps burning through the night. She could make out a fitful glow from the great temple of Heru and from lesser shrines of any of a hundred gods scattered through the darkened streets. Lights burned in the guard posts and in the residence behind her, but they burned dimly, as dimly as moon-washed stars in the body of the goddess Nut and did not blind her. A cry reached her ears and she looked north, pinpointing the wail of an infant in distress. A lamp flickered, butter-yellow, and she imagined the mother, sleepless as she ministered to her child while her husband slept.

A night bird called--an owl perhaps--hunting on silent wings, its keen eyes searching out its prey--a sleeping sparrow in the fronds of the palms or a foraging mouse in the grain warehouses by the river. From the river came a splash and gurgle as some denizen of the waters--fish or crocodile most likely--pursued its own cold purpose.

Why am I here? What has summoned me?

Wood smoke drifted across the balcony, faint and sour, mixing with the subtle undercurrents of massed humanity--the stink of ordure, rank sweat from man and beast, spices, cooked food--from the sleeping city below, and perfumes--rose and lotus--from the Nomarch's wife's bedroom. Incense from the temples beat at her brain and conjured up visions of priests chanting hymns of praise and the silent dark statues of the gods in their sanctuaries.

Why am I here? Who called me to this place?

The woman raised her hands to her face, touching old scars and her fingers brushed her right eye, feeling the hardness under the lid. She opened the eye and felt smooth stone beneath, her mind sensing the cool green-tinged darkness wherein lay the presence of the gods--the Nine of Iunu.

I am here. What do you want of me?

Something flicked past her, arrow-swift in the night sky, piercing the dark body of Nut. A streak of light coursed from the southeast, plunging down across the city, silent as it disappeared into the blackness that lay beyond the walls.

What lies there? The temple of Auset?

Certainty filled her. What she sought was in the temple of Auset. The sign could not be clearer. The goddess had spoken despite her not having the golden scarab in her possession. The young woman felt her heart break anew at the remembered loss and she cried out...

* * *

She sat bolt upright in her lumpy bed, tears in her eyes, and a cry of anguish still ringing in her ears. Near her, in the darkness, she heard scraping noises and she poised herself for battle, her hand scrabbling beneath the head-rest for the dagger that always lay there.

"What the hell's going on?" a male voice queried. "Are you all right?"

"Who is that?"

"Me. Who else would it be?"

"Daffyd?" Dani swung her feet over the side of the bed and sat with her head in her hands. "I...I had a dream...I think. It was...so real."

Daffyd switched the light on and a low-wattage fly-spotted incandescent bulb shone wanly from the ceiling, revealing bedclothes in disarray on the bed and on the floor. Daffyd stood by the door in shorts and a vest, rubbing the sleep out of his eyes.

"Want to talk about it, lass? Sometimes talking about a nightmare makes it seem less real."

"It wasn't a nightmare, or at least I don't think it was."

"You cried out as if your heart was breaking."

Dani nodded. "It was. I realised I didn't have the golden scarab and it tore me apart. It was so real."

"Sounds like a nightmare to me."

"No. At least, not at first. I was there, Daffyd, in ancient Behdet..."

"Where?"

"Behdet. It's the old name for Edfu. I was there on the balcony of the Nomarch's palace, looking out on a sleeping city. It was so real--I could see the lights in the temples, hear the night birds, smell the smoke, feel the chill night air on my bare..." Dani looked down at her pyjama top and smiled. "I was bare-breasted in my dream but I wasn't self-conscious, just a bit chilly."

"We tend to be less inhibited in our dreams."

"It wasn't that. It felt natural because I belonged there. I was wearing what I would normally wear and what I saw, what I heard and smelled and felt were all normal things..."

Daffyd crossed the room and sat down on the bed beside Dani. "What do you mean by normal, lass? As far as I'm aware you've never gone around with your breasts in the breeze in your life."

Dani smiled again, a little uncertainly. "Damn right, at least not as Dani Hanser, but I wasn't me. That sounds stupid I know, but that wasn't Dani standing there on the balcony."

"Scarab?"

Dani nodded. "It couldn't have been me though, could it?"

"Ah lass, who am I to say? If this had happened a year ago, I'd have said it was just a dream, and if you insisted it felt real I'd recommend a good psychiatrist, but after hearing Scarab's story and seeing you interact with the golden scarab..." Daffyd shook his head. "As Shakespeare put it, 'there are more things in heaven and earth than are dreamt of in your philosophy'. Remember what we talked about earlier? The collective unconscious? I'd say we're seeing another example of it here."

"Or as I said, I'm Scarab reincarnated."

"I doubt it lass. All the cases of reincarnation I've read about involved youngsters who remember things but forget them by the time they're seven or eight. I've never heard of an adult suddenly remembering things. No, I'd say it's one of two things--the collective unconscious of the human race, or your mind conjuring up images in a dream state from memories of Scarab's account."

"Scarab was never in the Nomarch's palace in Behdet--at least not in the account--so how did my mind create that?"

"That's true, but there were plenty of descriptions of sights, sounds and smells from other places. You're in Behdet--Edfu--now, so your mind just cobbles together a dream from the descriptions and your experiences today."

Dani chewed her lip, thinking. "You make it sound so reasonable, Dafs, but that wasn't all there was. The gods were there too and..."

"You saw them?" Daffyd shrugged. "They're part of the account as well. Your mind would incorporate them."

"And they showed me where the golden scarab is."

Daffyd stared at Dani. "We know where it is," he said slowly. "Bashir's got it."

"No. It's just north of here, in the temple of Auset. The gods showed me, sending a shooting star to guide me."

"I didn't know there was a temple of Auset--Isis. There's a big temple to Horus, but..."

"Heru, not Horus. And yes, there is one for Auset."

"Even if there is, how can the scarab possibly be there? The last time we saw it, it was in Bashir's possession, in Syria. No doubt he brought it to Egypt, but if it's anywhere it's in Luxor."

"The gods said it was here."

"Dani, you saw a shooting star...no, you dreamed you saw a shooting star and because you are dying to get it back, your mind interpreted it as that. It was a dream, lass, a vivid one, but just your mind striving to make sense of recent events and desires."

"There's one way to find out, Dafs--go there."

"And if it isn't there? It could be a crushing disappointment."

"Ah, but what if it *is* there?"

Dani would say no more on the subject, yawning instead and straightening the bedclothes. She professed herself to be utterly at ease with the thought of going back to sleep and suggested they do so immediately as they had a long day ahead of them.

"At least we can wait in Edfu for Marc and Muammar to arrive. We no longer have to go to Luxor to find the golden scarab."

Daffyd shook his head and switched off the light, shuffling and stumbling in the dark back to his blanket on the floor. He lay awake for a long while, even after Dani's regular breathing told him she was asleep. He waited for her nightmare to resume, but it never did, and eventually he dozed off.

Dani arose early the next morning, a smile on her lips. She disappeared into the bathroom and emerged cleansed and made up, ready for what the day would bring. Daffyd moved more slowly, yawning a lot, but spoke cheerfully enough. They breakfasted lightly and, while the sun was still low in the eastern sky, set off on foot to search for the temple of Auset.

Edfu is a city that runs roughly north-south along the western bank of the Nile, and Dani and Daffyd's little hotel was in the southern part of the sprawling city. As the heat of the day grew, they found themselves tiring, and were only just approaching the city centre.

"This is no use," Daffyd complained. "It'll take us all day just to reach the outskirts, let alone find the temple. We should take a taxi."

"We might be able to afford a bus," Dani countered.

There were buses on the roads and queues at places where people were obviously waiting for something. A bus stopped by one of the queues and people got on and off. The problem was that Dani and Daffyd knew a few phrases of Arabic but could not read it. Deciphering the squiggles showing the destination at the front of each bus was beyond them.

"How do we know which one to get?" Daffyd asked.

"I suppose we'll have to ask. What's the Arabic for 'Which bus must we catch to get to the temple of Auset?'"

Daffyd laughed. "Way too complex. Let's just try 'north'. That's *shamal* I think."

"All right, let me think." Dani concentrated, drawing upon her memory of Arabic phrases. She approached a woman in long flowing robes and headscarf.

"Law samaht...sabah el-khair--Excuse me...good morning."

The woman looked uncomfortable and glanced around for support. Finding none, she mumbled, "Sabah el-khair."

"I'll tell her I can't speak Arabic very well," she said to Daffyd. "La atakhallam 'arabi jayyidan."

"I think that's fairly obvious," Daffyd murmured. "Your pronunciation leaves a bit to be desired."

"If you can do better, please take over." Dani smiled at the woman again, racking her brain for the right words. "We wish to take the bus...el-bus...to the north of the city...shamal Edfu. There is a...a temple of Isis."

The woman shrugged and pointed at a bus passing them on the street and then waved her hands all around, speaking very fast in Arabic. All they could make out were the words 'el-bus' and 'Edfu'.

"I don't think she understood us," Daffyd observed.

"Feel free to exercise your own linguistic abilities," Dani said.

Daffyd tried, more or less repeating what Dani had said and the woman erupted into a torrent of flowing syllables. Passers-by stopped and listened, and added their own gushing contributions.

"I think we're attracting too much attention," Daffyd said. "The last thing we want is a policeman who'd ask for our papers." He tried edging away from the gathering crowd, drawing Dani with him when help arrived unexpectedly.

"You are American?"

Daffyd turned and saw a fit-looking middle-aged man with a bandaged head standing on the edge of the crowd. "English, actually."

"Perhaps I might be of assistance? I can translate."

"Thank you. We want to visit the temple of Auset...of Isis...north of the city and don't know which bus to catch."

"I can help you there." The man turned to the crowd which was dissipating now that someone had happened along who spoke the language of the infidels, and spoke rapidly in Arabic. He listened to the replies and nodded.

"I am told a number five bus will take you to the junction of the roads Nagaa Al Balalees and Al Ghanema. The ruins of the temple you seek are an hour's walk from there, along dirt roads. The bus fare is one shilling each, but the bus will not be here for another hour."

"That long?" Dani asked. "Well, there's no option. Thank you Mr..."

"Hafiz."

"Thank you Mr Hafiz, for all your trouble on our behalf."

"Er, one problem," Daffyd said. "You say bus number five, but the lettering will be in Arabic and we don't read Arabic. How are we going to recognise the right bus?"

Hafiz smiled. He dug into his trouser pocket and, taking out a small battered notebook, tore out a leaf. "You have a pencil?" Dani handed him hers. Hafiz drew on the paper--the Arabic script خمسة--and handed it back with the pencil. "When you see a bus with that on it, you have the right one. If in doubt, ask the driver. Five is khamsa in Arabic." He sounded the kh- sound as if clearing his throat.

"Thank you, Mr Hafiz, we are indebted to you."

"It is a pleasure Miss..." Hafiz cocked his head to one side, regarding Dani with a smile on his lips. "May I be permitted to know your names?"

Daffyd opened his mouth to warn Dani not to give their real names, but too late.

"I'm Dani Hanser; this is Daffyd Rhys-Williams."

"A pleasure to make your acquaintances." Hafiz bowed and turned away, moving a few paces before turning back. "A thought has just occurred to me, Miss Hanser and Mr Rhys-Williams. You are faced with a long wait in the hot sun for your bus. May I offer you the use of my car?"

"That is very kind, Mr Hafiz," Dani said. "But we couldn't possibly impose on you further."

"It would be no imposition, I assure you. I am heading north myself and would be delighted to take you as far as the bus would take you."

"Thank you again, but..."

"It would give me an opportunity to practice my English, so we would both benefit."

"It doesn't sound as if you need the practice," Daffyd said, a faint hint of suspicion in his voice. "You are fluent."

"Thank you," Hafiz said, "But one can always improve. Sometimes the intonation of similar sounding words confuses me."

"In that case, we would be delighted," Dani said.

Hafiz led them to a dusty rental car parked a little way down the street, and held the passenger-side door open for Dani, allowing Daffyd to make his own arrangements. He started the car and pulled out into the traffic, heading north.

"So, you are going to the temple of Isis? Is there a special reason for your visit?"

"Why do you ask?" Daffyd said.

"There are other temples in much better repair in Edfu. The Horus one is quite fine, I believe."

"I have always been attracted to the cult of Isis," Dani said.

Hafiz manoeuvred the car through the city traffic and out onto the roads north of the city, quickly finding the Al Ghanema road and following it to the junction where the bus would have dropped them. A little farther up the road, a rutted dirt track diverged, running into the desert, with a dusty sign in Arabic pointing the way. Hafiz eased the vehicle off the road and made his way slowly down the road, the car bouncing and juddering to the sound of protesting springs.

"You do not have to come this far, Mr Hafiz," Dani said. "You have been most kind bringing us this far. We can complete our journey on foot."

"I wouldn't dream of it. The heat of the day would make a journey like that most...ah, most debilitating--is that a correct English word, Miss Hanser?"

"It is indeed, Mr Hafiz, and thank you."

"Besides, I have lived in this area for many years but have never visited the temple. Perhaps it is I who should thank you for giving me the opportunity."

The road continued on into the desert for a mile or two before ending in a flattened area that obviously served as a car park, though no other vehicles were in sight. Another sign pointed to one side, a curving row of stakes delineating the path to the temple. They got out and followed the stakes, trudging along a path that in places was deep with blown sand. Stone blocks came into view, half buried, and farther along, a truncated column and a fallen one. Another sign stood in their path and Hafiz translated the flowing Arabic script.

"This temple dedicated to Isis was built in the days of Queen Hatshepsut, circa 1460 BCE, and remained as a centre of worship for nearly two thousand years, only falling into disrepair after the Council of Chalcedon, 451 CE, and the taking of control of Egypt by the Coptic Church."

"I had no idea," Daffyd said. "I though Muslims were in control after the Romans."

"That came later, Mr Rhys-Williams."

They walked past the sign and came upon the ruins of the temple, masses of fallen stone and upright columns in rows. The sun beat down on them, making them seek the meagre shade between the standing stones.

"There is not much to see," Hafiz observed.

Dani frowned, looking all around at a desolation of sand and rock, tawny hues covered by a vault of washed out blue and a molten sun high overhead.

"It's not what I thought," she muttered.

"Did you expect to find it lying out in the open, lass? It can't be here. We know B...he has it." Daffyd laid his hand gently on Dani's arm. "It was a dream, lass, nothing more."

"We haven't looked yet."

"Forgive me, Miss Hanser, but what do you seek in such a lonely place?"

"Something lost." Dani shook Daffyd's hand off and walked off in the direction the sanctuary must once have been.

"She has lost something in these ruins?" Hafiz enquired. "You have been here before?"

"No." Daffyd went after Dani, and after a moment, Hafiz followed along.

She heard the chanting and wondered if she was hearing things that could not possibly exist. There was no sign of humans in the vicinity, no sign that anyone had walked into the ruins ahead of them, yet Dani could plainly hear a female voice speaking--singing almost--in an unfamiliar language. She stopped and listened. The words were unintelligible, yet they made sense somehow. Advancing, she saw movement in the shadows within the sanctuary, a robed figure facing eroded sculptures on a sandstone wall, hands aloft as if in supplication, husky voice rising and falling in strange cadences.

Dani waited, watching the woman, interpreting her movements, and realised that the woman was old--very old--her motions shaky and her voice trembled, as if each syllable cost her a great effort. The song cut off abruptly and the woman turned, milky white eyes in a lined and sun-browned face questing for the source of the disturbance. A claw-like hand grasped at the air and the old woman gasped, her head moving from side to side as if attempting to see Dani with blind eyes.

The old woman spoke, and it was Dani's turn to gasp, for although it was not English, Dani understood her. It was not Arabic either, but bore a close resemblance to the hieratic language of ancient Egypt. Only one person had ever spoken like this to her--her grandmother. Dani struggled to remember the words and phrases of the Coptic language, now all but extinct.

"So you have come in answer to the call of the goddess. What is it you seek?"

"Th...that which is lost," Dani stuttered in a mixture of Coptic and English. "The star fell and I...I followed it."

"It is not here."

"No." The cry was ripped from Dani's throat. "Why did it lead me here then?"

"You must seek the organiser."

"What?"

"The man of power is your undying enemy. Ask instead of the organiser."

"Dani, are you all right? You shouldn't wander off like that."

Dani turned and saw Daffyd trudging toward her, Hafiz a few paces behind. "I'm fine, I was just talking to the old woman. She said..."

"What old woman?"

"The old blind woman." Dani half turned toward the sanctuary, stared and looked around wildly. "There was an old woman here just now. Where has she gone?"

"Are you all right, lass? You look a bit...distraught."

"You must have seen her. As you approached. I was talking with her when you called out."

Daffyd frowned. "I didn't see anyone with you. You were just standing there and turned around when I called out."

"That is true, Miss Hanser," Hafiz added. "I was farther back, but you were alone."

"Perhaps you imagined it, lass. You've been under a lot of strain, and after your dream and finding nothing here..."

"The heat can play tricks with the mind, Miss Hanser."

Dani shook her head. "There was an old woman and she spoke to me in Coptic. She told me that the...the thing is not here but that I must..."

"You speak Coptic?" Hafiz asked. "I did not think anyone could any longer."

"My grandmother was an Egyptian Coptic Christian. She taught me a little. Anyway, as I was saying, she told me to seek the...thing elsewhere. She said the man of power was my enemy."

Daffyd snorted. "Well, we all know who that is. I'm sorry, Dani, but that's your own memories speaking."

"Yes, the warning seems superfluous," Dani agreed. "But she was here, nonetheless. If he has the...thing, we must still approach him." She pondered for a moment. "The old woman did say something curious--she said I must ask the organiser, but didn't say what I must ask him. Or her. Or even who the organiser is," she added.

"Organiser?" Daffyd asked. "What does that mean? Organiser of what?"

"That was the word she used."

"In what language?" Hafiz asked.

"In Coptic but my mind translated it into English." Dani paused a moment in thought. "You know, I can't remember the Coptic word she used."

"It doesn't matter," Daffyd said. "We knew what we had to do anyway, before we came out here. We have to get to Luxor somehow and see...you know who."

"He's likely to have us arrested on the spot," Dani said. "Perhaps we should try and see Nazim first and see if he..."

"What is that name?" Hafiz asked.

Dani stared at Hafiz. "You know him? Nazim Manouk?"

"Never heard of him, but the name Nazim, in Arabic, means 'organiser'."

"Bugger me," Daffyd muttered.

"You see?" Dani asked. "How could I know that? The old woman told me to seek the organiser--Nazim--not the man of power, who can only be Bashir..."

Daffyd tried to hush Dani but it was too late. He saw a flicker of something in Hafiz's eyes at the mention of the name and wondered what it meant. "What now then, lass?"

"Luxor. We might be able to get a ferry from Edfu."

"Not from Edfu," Hafiz said. "There is one from Esna, however. As it happens, I have a business appointment in Esna tomorrow, and I would be happy to drive you there."

Daffyd glanced at Dani, concern furrowing his brow at this unexpected turn of events. "That is generous of you, Mr Hafiz..."

"And we'd be happy to accept," Dani finished. "Thank you."

Hafiz smiled and strode away toward the parking lot, Dani and Daffyd following on behind.

"Are you sure that's wise, lass? We hardly know the chap and here he is offering to take us halfway to our goal. I don't altogether trust him--there was a look in his eyes when you mentioned Bashir's name."

"He's just what we need, Dafs. It's about time we had a little bit of luck running our way. And besides, how would a businessman in Edfu have ever heard of a Syrian Minister?"

Chapter Twenty-Five

E arly the next morning, Nazim Manouk sat in his room and leafed through the bundles of photographs taken in the chambers of the Orontes Valley in Syria. The photographs encompassed every piece of artwork on the walls on the three chambers and a good many were of the inscriptions. He was looking for one in particular, and hoped that he had made a mark on it at the time, sufficient to identify it now. The bundle slipped off his lap and cascaded to the floor. He sighed and lowered himself to the carpet, sorting the spilled glossy prints into piles, discarding some and re-examining others.

Ah, is this it?

The print looked like a hundred others, but a scrawled notation on the back read 'tomb'. Nazim put it aside and went through the piles again.

I know there was more than one.

Another photograph bore a red-pencilled exclamation mark on the back, and a third had an India-ink circle drawn roughly over the lines of hieroglyphs. He laid the three prints alongside one another and studied them, comparing them. There were minor differences, but a central portion of the columns was identical. If one was a description of the tomb, as the notation indicated, they all were.

Nazim nodded in satisfaction and slipped the two clearest copies into his notebook, gathering up the other glossy prints and dumping them back into their cardboard box file. He crossed to the chest of drawers and opened the top drawer, feeling under his socks for his hidden treasure. He took out the sandstone rock and, closing his eyes, felt it with his fingertips. Despite his knowledge of its smooth surface, he once more felt the ridges of its carved wing cases, the delicate tracery of wings and antenna. Opening his eyes again, he marvelled at the difference between his visual and tactile senses.

I will crack your disguise. I will learn how to use you.

Nazim returned the rock to its place of safety and picked up his notebook with its precious photographs. He exited his room, and locked the door behind him, deciding to skip breakfast and head straight for the museum. Minister Bashir was already in the lobby and looked surprised to find Nazim up and about.

"Getting an early start on the search?" Bashir said. "I like to see enthusiasm, but where is Al-Din--joining you at the docks, perhaps?"

"He'll be joining me later, Minister."

"In that case, I'll walk down to the docks with you. I feel like a little exercise."

"I would be delighted, sir, but I have to go to the museum first..."

"Eh? Why? Your place is on the launch, scouting out possible sites."

"Indeed, Minister, but our excursion yesterday showed me that our maps are not all they could be. I hope to be able to find better ones in the museum library." Nazim hesitated, wondering if Bashir accepted his story. "It means a lot of poring through files, sir, so I'd be glad of your help."

Bashir grimaced. "Another time, perhaps. But there's another option. Colonel Sarraj has access to army maps. Why don't you just ask him for copies?"

"I would, sir, but it might take several days to get hold of them, whereas the museum is right here."

Bashir grunted. "Well, don't let me keep you."

Nazim hailed a taxi out in the street and a few minutes later was dropped outside the stone-stepped entrance of the Luxor Museum, which was just opening. He went in and found the receptionist yawning at his post.

"I need an expert in hieroglyphs."

"That would be Dr Wodzicki," said the receptionist. "Unfortunately, he is on leave."

"So who might be available today? It is a matter of some urgency."

"There is Dr Zewali, but I'm not sure if he is in yet."

Nazim stood looking at the young man who showed no interest in continuing with his revelation. "Well, could you see if he's in?"

The receptionist looked as if he had just bitten into a lemon. "Just a moment." He picked up the telephone and dialled a number. It rang for several seconds before he replaced the handset. "Dr Zewali is not in yet."

"But he is expected?"

"Yes."

Nazim opened his mouth to ask when, but decided there was no point. "I'll look at the exhibits while I wait," he said.

He spent the next hour wandering around the exhibits, looking at but not really taking in the statues, the jewellery, the papyrus texts and tomb panelling. The information was interesting enough, but his desire to talk to someone about the hieroglyph translation kept him glancing toward the doorway in a constant anticipation of the receptionist coming for him to tell him Dr Zewali had arrived.

A cabinet of carved scarabs distracted him, and he scanned his eyes eagerly over the tiny objects in the hope of finding another golden one. He was disappointed--the majority were of carved wood or stone, some of ivory or bone, and a few of crystal or copper.

A little later, Nazim glanced at his watch and saw that just over an hour had passed. With a snort of annoyance, he cut short his tour and walked back to the reception desk.

"When will Dr Zewali be coming in? Perhaps I can make an appointment."

"He came in half an hour ago," the receptionist said, smirking.

"And you didn't think to tell me?" Nazim controlled his temper and took a deep breath. "Please ask him if he'll see me."

The receptionist took his time in putting a telephone call through to Dr Zewali's office, and spoke in low tones. "A man to see you, Doctor. He wants some hieroglyphs translated." He listened for a moment and turned to face Nazim, a sly expression on his face. "I'll tell him." More time was taken up replacing the handset and straightening his jacket. "Dr Zewali is in a meeting, but if you would care to wait outside his office, he will see you as soon as he can."

"Did he say how long?"

"No. Do you wish to wait?"

Nazim nodded. "Where's his office?"

The receptionist pointed the way and offered terse directions before turning away and ignoring him. Nazim wandered off, taking his time, and eventually came to a corridor and a wood-panelled door inscribed with the name 'Dr Karim Zewali'. He sat down on one of the two upright chairs outside the office and settled down to wait.

An hour later he was still waiting, and seriously considering giving up, when Dr Zewali's door opened and a short, thin man stepped out, a pair of spectacles in his hand. The man rubbed the lenses absently with his handkerchief and stopped abruptly as he realised someone was sitting right by him.

"Hello." The man carefully arranged the glasses back on his face and peered at the sitting man. "Is someone looking after you?"

Nazim stood. "I was waiting to see Dr Zewali. I was told he was in a meeting."

"Eh? No meeting. I'm Karim Zewali. Whatever gave you the notion I was in a meeting?"

"The receptionist."

"You're the man with the hieroglyphs? I told Tahir to send you right up. When you didn't arrive, I thought you must have changed your mind."

"He told me you were busy."

"Hmm, well, probably a misunderstanding. My apologies if you have been inconvenienced." Zewali cocked his head to one side, his eyes twinkling. "You have some hieroglyphs?"

Nazim started to take out his notebook and Zewali stopped him.

"Where are my manners?" Zewali tut-tutted and ushered Nazim into his office and sat him down in an armchair, sitting in another opposite him. "Well, first things first," he said, offering his right hand. "I'm Karim Zewali, Director of the Luxor Museum. You are...?"

"Nazim Manouk." He hesitated a moment. "Forgive me, Director Zewali, but I did not expect anyone so important to help me."

Zewali smiled. "I have some knowledge in this field and, after all, my job is to help members of the public. Now, I know your name, Mr Manouk, but not why you have hieroglyphs in need of translation."

"I am secretary to the Under-Minister of National History in Syria. My employer is here on holiday and I am accompanying him--to facilitate his stay."

"Under-Minister Ahmed Bashir?"

"You know of him?"

"One hears things."

"May I ask what things, Director Zewali?"

Zewali frowned, and sat back in his chair, resting his elbows on the arms and pressing his fingertips together. "How exactly would my expertise with hieroglyphs facilitate his stay in Luxor?"

"My employer is a politician, not a man of learning." Nazim offered the Director a disarming smile. "He has no academic qualification but being an Under-Minister of National History, he likes to think of himself as at least an amateur scientist. Recently, he happened upon an Egyptian inscription. It was translated for him, but we have reason to believe the Minister was misled. I had hoped that someone here at the museum could verify--or not--the inscription."

"You have a copy? An accurate rendition?"

"Better. I have a photograph of the relevant portion." Nazim took out his notebook and slipped one of the photographs from beneath its cover. He passed it to Zewali who glanced at it and put it aside.

"Relevant to what, may I ask?"

Nazim hesitated, ordering the words in his mind before speaking. "There was a passage in the inscription that pertained to a tomb. We were told that the pictographs indicated the whereabouts of the tomb, albeit in very vague terms. My employer seeks, in his amateur fashion, to find this tomb, but this would be impossible if the description has been translated incorrectly and we cannot find a correct interpretation."

"I believe Dr Hosni Maroun, here at the museum, has already made it clear that we cannot countenance any excavation unless authorised by the Department of Antiquities."

"He has, Director, and let me state again that our only desire is to find the tomb using the description we have, purely as an intellectual exercise. Opening and investigating the tomb would be left to the appropriate authorities."

"So, to be clear, why have you come to me?"

"To examine the description."

"And you want me to offer my opinion?"

"If you would be so kind."

Zewali made no move to look at the photograph. "Translation is seldom simple or straightforward, Mr. Manouk. A lot depends on the context, and even when all the symbols have been deciphered, there is still the matter of arranging them into an order that makes sense. I tell you this so you may understand that I can give you no guarantees."

"Should I return at a later date and enquire of Dr Wodzicki? The receptionist said he is the expert in such matters."

Zewali smiled. "Yes, Tahir would tell you that. Well, you may wait until he returns--some eight days' time, I believe--but I doubt his translation will be any more accurate than mine."

"In that case, I would be most happy to hear your opinion of the text."

Zewali picked up the photograph and studied it. After a few minutes, he got up and moved over to his desk, where he sat down and switched on a desk lamp. In the pool of light, he examined the glossy photograph with a large magnifying glass. He copied down symbols on a pad and rearranged them, crossed some out and started again.

"Interesting," Zewali murmured.

"It is?"

"Where did you say this inscription came from?"

"I didn't. Is it necessary to know?"

"Only to judge its provenance, its authenticity. The penmanship is refined, written by someone familiar with the forms and combinations, yet without the shortcuts and omissions one might expect of a seasoned scribe. The style of some of the strokes are Eighteenth Dynasty, and reminiscent of the late Amarnan period."

"You can translate it?"

"Here..." Zewali tapped the photograph. "There are symbols for the Aten, horizon, greeting, green, arrow, mountain, desert, cliff, way--as in road or track, crown, scarab and crystal. Does any of that make sense?"

Nazim shook his head.

"What were you led to believe it said?"

Nazim consulted his notebook. "A streak of green leads to the track up the cliff where the lip is notched." He grimaced. "Nothing like it."

"Don't be hasty," Zewali said. "The elements are there. 'Streak of green' is present as 'arrow' and 'green', cliff is in both, track is there, and your notch could be the horizon through which the Aten rises."

"I wondered whether the notch could be a pylon."

"Quite possibly. It would make more sense than a mere cut in the cliff lip. A pylon built on top as a guide, a marker for what lies beyond in the desert, perhaps."

"Not in the cliff face?"

"The cliff is mentioned, but a number of other things present as symbols are not mentioned in your translation."

"We were misled then."

"Perhaps, though unless the translator was knowledgeable, it would be easy to miss the sense of it. You say this description was part of a larger text?"

"Yes," Nazim said, after a few moments.

"Would it be possible to view the whole thing? Or at least more around this part?" Zewali flicked the photograph with his fingernail.

"Not at the present time." Nazim saw Zewali's disappointment and asked, "Is it important?"

"Possibly. Putting a few words in context could alter the meaning from those same symbols seen alone."

"I will put it to the Minister," Nazim said. "But in the meantime, what would you say the passage means? Using your experience and knowledge?"

Zewali nodded. "Well, let's see..." He pondered his notes and the photograph again. "Aten and his horizon with an arrow, a road and a scarab, a greeting and a mountain of green...no, a green mountain, a crown of crystal, desert and cliff. Putting it together, I get the sense of the Aten's horizon arrow showing the road from the cliff through the desert to greet the green mountain crowned in crystal."

"That makes sense?"

Zewali allowed himself a broad smile. "Think about it, Mr. Manouk. Aten's arrow could be construed as the sun's rays shining through the horizon symbol--the notch or the pylon. This ray, perhaps the dawn ray, illuminates a path through the desert to a green mountain. The crystal crown puzzles me though. I've never come across such a thing. Kings had red and white crowns, war bonnets and headdresses that were styled as crowns, but never a crystal crown." He pondered for a moment. "Perhaps it is not 'crystal' but rather 'glass' or possibly even 'gleam' or 'shine'."

"Where is the green mountain?"

"Another puzzle," Zewali said. "You know, I'm rather enjoying this. It's like a detective story--working with the clues, but this time looking for the dead body instead of the murderer."

"I'm glad it amuses you," Nazim said, "But you must have some idea of the whereabouts of a green mountain. I'd think it would be hard to misplace such a thing."

"As I said, it's a puzzle. I know of a green mountain--Jebel Akhdar--in Oman, and I believe there's another in Libya, but I don't know of one in Egypt."

"And you know of a pylon on the cliff tops?"

"No."

"I thought we were starting to get somewhere."

"Then there's the scarab symbol. Khepri is one of the gods of the sun, like the Aten, so it may be no more than a reinforcement of the part the sun's rays play in identifying the place." Zewali frowned and appeared to be lost in thought for a few moments. "Do you know the significance of the symbol 'scarab', Mr Manouk?"

Nazim hesitated. "Only what you've told me."

"Nothing more? You're sure of that?"

Nazim shook his head.

Zewali looked hard at Nazim for several moments before saying softly, "I don't think you are being completely honest with me."

Nazim said nothing.

"Your employer, Minister Ahmed Bashir, made enquiries in Cairo concerning the tomb of King Smenkhkare, and also of a person called Scarab, seemingly the king's sister. I think this Scarab person may be the scarab symbol in the text, and if this is so, then your purpose here is not simply to follow up the description of the site as an intellectual exercise. Am I right, Mr Manouk?"

"I regret that I cannot confirm this without talking to Minister Bashir first."

"You don't need to. Minister Bashir has already indicated his intentions." Zewali got to his feet and handed the photograph back to Nazim. "I think our business is concluded."

Nazim took back the photograph and frowned. "I...I thought you enjoyed deciphering the puzzle. The solution is as yet incomplete..."

"And it will remain so, Mr Manouk, until such time as Minister Bashir reveals everything he knows about this business. I give you fair warning that while you have as yet contravened no Egyptian laws concerning antiquities, if you attempt to follow up these leads and interfere in any way with a site of archaeological interest, the Department will intervene. Please convey my words to the Minister. Good-day, Mr Manouk."

Nazim left the museum, mildly embarrassed by his rejection, but also elated by what he had found out. He took a taxi down to the wharves and immediately boarded the launch. Al-Din was waiting for him, and hurried to his side as he climbed aboard.

"Is everything all right? Minister Bashir was here only twenty minutes ago, furious that we hadn't left yet."

"Forget him. Are we ready to leave? Then let's do so before he returns."

Al-Din conveyed their readiness to the captain and within minutes they were forging upriver toward the place they had been the day before. Nazim took a bottle of soda from the basket and drank as he watched the riverbanks slide past. He wondered how much to tell Al-Din, and decided it might not be a good idea to reveal what he had learned at the museum just yet.

"We continue our search," he told the lieutenant. "But the western shore only."

*   *   *

Dr Karim Zewali sat at his desk and stared at the symbols he had copied down in his notebook. He made a few small alterations with a pencil, making the corrections while his memory of the photograph was fresh in his mind. Then he wrote out his translation of the symbols underneath--'the Aten's horizon arrow showing the road from the cliff through the desert to greet the green mountain crowned in crystal'.

Not quite right...I've left out the scarab. What else?

He made a few notations, additions, drew an arrow or three, shifted symbols slightly, and wrote it out again--'the rays of the sun through the cliff top horizon show Scarab's green mountain with its glass crown...no, shining crown...in the desert'. Zewali studied the symbols again.

Very close. What am I missing? Something...ahh...

"The sun's rays through the cliff top pylon illuminate the shining crown of Scarab's green mountain in the desert."

My goodness, I'd give anything to see the rest of that inscription. If it is as Bashir and Manouk suspect--an undiscovered tomb--it would be the most exciting discovery since Tutankhamen. And I appear to share the key to its whereabouts.

Zewali placed the notebook in the top drawer of his desk and locked it, pocketing the key. He telephoned the museum switchboard operator, and asked to be connected to Mr Nicholas Evans.

"I'm not sure what hotel he's staying at. Put me through when you find him."

Ten minutes passed, with Zewali drumming the fingers of his hands on the armrests of his chair. His mind was in a turmoil of excitement, while trying to work out how to make the best use of his information.

I'll have to let Nasrallah know, but later, once I've got things moving.

The telephone rang and he picked up the handset. "Yes?"

"Nick Evans here, Dr Zewali. I didn't think I'd hear from you again."

"I'd like to see you."

"I'm on my way down to the train station. I'm catching the eleven o'clock to Cairo."

"Come and see me first."

There was silence on the other end of the line, then, "I've only got forty minutes before it leaves."

"Egyptian trains always run late, Mr Evans. You'll have time."

"What's it about?"

"Bashir's secretary paid me a visit and showed me the part of the inscription that shows where the tomb is located. I believe he and the Minister will attempt to find it and plunder it. I need your help again."

"You know where the tomb is?"

"Yes."

"Then I'm on my way. I'll be there in ten minutes or less."

Chapter Twenty-Six

A li Hafiz no longer had his radio set, having lost it in the crash, but he was resourceful and after an hour or so of telephoning, managed to track down Colonel Sarraj to a hotel in Luxor. Before he rang the number, he went over exactly how he would broach the news of his initial failure to the Colonel, but cast the best light on the future possibilities.

"Good evening, Colonel. It is I, Ali Hafiz."

"What are you doing telephoning me? You were supposed to keep in touch by radio."

"The radio was...ah, rendered inoperable."

"How? No, forget that, I'm not interested. What have you to report?"

"I succeeded in capturing the young Englishman and his Libyan helper. I interrogated them as to the whereabouts of the other two, particularly the woman. After initial resistance, they revealed they were in Edfu."

"That close? Tell me where in Edfu and I will send a squad of soldiers to pick them up."

"No need, Colonel. I met the woman and the older man in Edfu and persuaded them to accompany me to Esna, where we will all take the evening ferry to Luxor. If you meet us at the docks, they will be in your hands by midnight."

"You have done well, Ali Hafiz. Very well. Bring the two young men with you also."

Hafiz hesitated, holding his hand over the mouthpiece as he muttered a quick prayer. "I regret I will not be able to do so, Colonel. After my interrogation...well, the desert is a merciless place and in their weakened state..." *It's likely. I might have died myself if a truck hadn't come along at dawn.*

"A pity," Sarraj said. "I'd like to have interrogated the Libyan myself to establish his motives. Well, never mind, no great loss. You've done well, Ali Hafiz, and I won't forget your service."

The line went dead and Hafiz hung up the telephone, looking thoughtful. He composed his face and went to meet Dani and Daffyd at the park by the river. They had been back to their hotel to collect their meagre possessions and now sat in the shade of a large tamarind tree, watching the boats ply the wide waters of the river.

"My boss says I must go to Luxor tonight, so it looks as though I will enjoy your company a little longer," Hafiz told them.

"If you're sure?" Dani said. "We don't want to hold you up if you're in a hurry."

"I wouldn't dream of it, having given my word. We will drive up to Esna and catch the evening ferry to Luxor. It will be there by midnight."

"There's one thing we have to do before we go anywhere," Daffyd said. "We have to leave a message for Marc and Muammar."

"That's right. They won't know where we've gone otherwise."

"Marc and Muammar?" Hafiz asked.

"Our companions. We were separated, but they knew we were heading to Edfu, so they'll get here when they can..." Daffyd said.

"And if we go to Luxor, we'll have to leave a message to say we've gone," Dani finished.

"You were to meet at a specific place?" Hafiz asked. "You must leave this message there?"

"Not exactly. Our friend Muammar has a cousin in Edfu, called Mohammad ibn Sukrah. We could leave a message with him. When they reach Edfu, it's the only place we all know about."

"Then let us go to this Mohammad ibn Sukrah and leave the message," Hafiz said. "We must leave soon if we are to make the ferry sailing in Esna."

"Well, that's the problem," Daffyd said. "We don't know where he lives."

"So, perhaps you'd better go without us, Mr Hafiz. We can't leave without leaving a message for our friends, and we don't know how long that'll take."

Hafiz frowned. "How were you intending to find him?"

"I thought maybe one of the mosques," Daffyd said. "The imam may know him."

"Do you know enough Arabic to ask? Or to make yourself understood by ibn Sukrah if you find him? If not, perhaps I may be of service again."

"Thank you, Mr Hafiz," Dani said. "Once more we are in your debt."

Hafiz smiled apologetically. "There is one more aspect you might not have considered. As infidels...my apologies, as non-Muslims, you will not be allowed to enter a mosque."

"Really?" Daffyd queried. "I thought that non-Muslims were generally welcomed provided they acted respectfully."

"It is often so, Mr Rhys-Williams," Hafiz said. "However, there has recently been some trouble in Edfu, and many people would look askance at strangers entering their mosques. By Allah's good grace, though, I can act for you in this regard, and talk to both the imam and ibn Sukrah."

Daffyd looked at Dani, raising his eyebrows.

Dani shrugged delicately. "We have no choice," she murmured.

"Will you ask the imam if we can talk to him?" Daffyd asked.

"Of course. I would be happy to translate for you, but if he refuses, what would you like me to say?"

"Well, we only need to know how to find ibn Sukrah," Dani said. "When we find him, you can translate."

"What if he refuses to give me his address? Unless it is my own mosque he may be suspicious."

"Could we leave a note with the imam, to give to ibn Sukrah?"

"Then you have the translation problem again," Hafiz said. "You have said you cannot read Arabic. Can you write it? If not, perhaps I could write it for you if you tell me what to say."

"What if we wrote it in English, and addressed it to Muammar?" Daffyd asked. "Then all ibn Sukrah has to do is give it to his cousin when he shows up. The imam could explain that to him and give him the note without having to divulge his address."

Hafiz smiled. "That will work. Write the letter and I will start trying the mosques."

Dani got to work. She bought a single sheet of paper and an envelope from a small store, and used the pencil in her bag to sketch out a quick letter. 'Dear Muammar and Marc, I hope, if you are reading this, you have made it safely to Edfu. I remembered the name of your cousin, as you see. Now, Daffyd and I have gone to Luxor with a kind gentleman by the name of Hafiz, as it seems that Bashir's secretary, Nazim, has the golden scarab. I'm sorry not to wait for you, but money is running out, so we must make our move while we can. I dare say you two are skint as well, so I'm including twenty pounds. Come to Luxor as quickly as you can. Daffyd or I will be at the entrance of the Luxor museum at opening and closing each day. I can't think of any other way for us all to find each other. Take care, both of you.' She signed it 'from Dani and Daffyd' and sealed it, with twenty pounds from her now-slim money belt, in the envelope which she addressed to Muammar al-Hadi, care of Mohammad ibn Sukrah.

"Here we are, Mr Hafiz. If they make it to Edfu, and to ibn Sukrah, this letter will explain everything."

Ali Hafiz briefly visited two small mosques before offering up the Dhuhr prayers in the third as midday had just passed. He was not an overly religious man, but he had decided that while he was here he might as well spend his time usefully. He was gone some time, raising the hopes of Dani and Daffyd that he had found the imam who knew of ibn Sukrah. In reality, Hafiz, after prayers, had found a quiet corner of the mosque and opened the letter entrusted to him. He slipped the money into his wallet and read the letter, smiling to himself.

Why leave a letter for dead men? On his way out of the mosque, Hafiz crumpled letter and envelope, tossing them casually into a rubbish receptacle.

"Well?" Daffyd asked, as Hafiz got back in the car. "You were in there long enough."

"A measure of success, I feel. The imam knew ibn Sukrah, who is out of town for a day or two. He promised to deliver the letter into his hands the moment he returns."

"To hold for his cousin Muammar's return?" Dani asked. "Ibn Sukrah isn't to open it himself. You made that clear?"

"Indeed I did, Miss Hanser. You need not be concerned. Now, it is after noon, so I suggest we make all speed for the ferry at Esna."

*　　*　　*

The ferry pulled out from the docks to the south of Esna just after nine in the evening, running late like so many Egyptian services, its propeller frothing the water behind it as it eased northward in the current. The captain kept the pace slow as they cruised past the town, cautious because of the number of vessels in the water--everything from small fishing and pleasure craft to freighters and barges belching out black smoke and dribbling runnels of dirty liquid into the wide green Nile waters.

The evening was warm, and Dani and Daffyd made their way up onto the upper deck, finding a secluded seat away from the crowd of other travellers where they could watch the darkened landscape drifting by. They sat in companionable silence for some time, and when they did talk, it was of inconsequential matters, or general affairs, and in low tones, as if unwilling to disturb the quiet of the evening. Ali Hafiz wandered by a couple of times, as if checking up on them, but he would do no more than incline his head or smile, so they paid him no heed.

"I wonder where Marc and Muammar are," Dani said. "I hope they're safe."

"If I know Marc, he's even now on his way to Luxor, having divined our purpose, or having read the letter you left. He's probably on that little fishing boat there..." Daffyd pointed out over the water to a small boat tacking across the river. "It's been following us for a while." He waved, but there was no response from the little craft and after a while it put in to the eastern shore near a village. "Or perhaps not," he murmured.

"Doesn't matter, they'll be all right now, I'm sure. Just soak in that scenery, Dafs. Makes you glad to be alive."

"Oh, I know, old girl. I've always wanted to visit the land of the pharaohs and here I am, courtesy of a bit of Syrian serendipity. What are the chances, eh?"

"I don't think it was chance."

Daffyd smiled. "Determinism? You think all this was fated?"

"I don't know about fate, but I think we're being guided."

"By God?"

Dani laughed lightly. "I think there is more than one possibility. A god or gods is definitely there, but possibilities could also include disembodied spirits, the collective unconscious you like to quote or just our own subconscious."

"You've changed your tune. It wasn't that long ago you decried any attempt to indicate there was more to you than plain Dani Hanser--not that plain could ever describe you."

"I've had time to think, and being on the river is doing something to me. Maybe I'm just being wooed by the romanticism of a Nile cruise but..." Dani lapsed into silence.

Daffyd gave her a few moments before asking, "But what?"

"But that dream I had, the old woman at the temple and...I feel like I've been here before."

"Déjà vu you mean?"

"No, more than that. It's like I'm having a lucid dream. You know what that is, Dafs?"

"I've heard the term."

"More specifically, a wake-initiated lucid dream. That's where a person who is awake slips into a dream state without losing consciousness."

"Daydreaming, you mean? We all do that, old girl."

"No, it's more than that. In a lucid dream you know you're dreaming and you can influence the course of the dream. I do that sometimes, Dafs. I used to a lot when I was a child. My grandmother..."

"The Egyptian one?"

Dani nodded. "She used to say I lived more in the dream world than the waking one."

Daffyd said nothing, but Dani did not seem to notice.

"I'm sort of having one now," she continued.

"What? What do you mean?"

"If I focus, the boat seems much longer...and broader too. There are men pulling on oars and talking. They are subdued, depressed even...as if... as if they've lost a battle..."

"You can see this? Where?"

"All around us." Dani looked down and frowned. "How strange. I'm wearing a kilt and my breasts are bare..." She smiled. "They're larger than mine. I have streaks and spots of blood on me. I've been in a fight."

"Dani, you know all this from the account on the chamber walls. You've read and lived Scarab's life, so of course you know what she did and where she's been. You're describing the account of the flight from Thebes after the big battle with Horemheb. All you can see is just a dream derived from a familiar account. Don't assume it's real."

"It seems real, Dafs. Look, I'm not totally around the twist. I know I'm sitting here with you in the twentieth century, talking to you, seeing the modern-day river craft and towns, but if I concentrate..." Dani fell silent for a few seconds. "...there are no other boats, no towns, just a huge expanse of river and vegetation surrounded by desert cliffs. The sun feels hot on me, I feel tired and my muscles are aching..."

"You see what you expect to see, old girl. This expedition has all been too much for you, coming hard on the heels of your translation. You've been through a lot, had the most precious thing of yours taken away, and your mind is clinging to what it knows...to what it thinks it knows. You need rest, lots of it, to drive these images from your mind."

Dani closed her eyes and sighed. "You think I'm imagining all this? That what I see is a construct of my mind woven from the things I read in the account?"

"I'm afraid so, old girl."

"Not so much of the 'old', Dafs...and you're wrong. I can prove it."

"How?"

She opened her eyes and turned toward the stern of the boat. "There's Huni, one of my brother's soldiers. I read about him in the account, but it never mentioned he had a birthmark. He does, a port wine stain, over his left shoulder. How could I know that unless I could see it?"

"Is there any way of determining whether this Huni had such a mark...or even that he existed?" Daffyd asked gently. "You know the name from the account, and your imagination is filling in the blanks. There's no way you can prove what you see is real."

"You don't believe me."

"It's not a matter of belief or disbelief. You're having this vision, waking dream, lucid dream, hallucination--call it what you will--and I think that in your present state you're unable to distinguish fact from fiction. I doubt if your conscious mind even knows the difference."

Dani smiled wanly. "So when we get to Luxor you'll be calling for the boys in white coats with straitjackets and butterfly nets, will you?"

"And get us both arrested? Nonsense. You're not barmy, just very tired. I think you should take a few days off when we get to Luxor. I'll find Nazim. There's not much we can do anyway, until we get the golden scarab."

"No, I've got the real Scarab instead. I don't think I need the carving any more, Dafs. I think I could see the position of the tomb in one of my dreams."

"Yes, but that's the whole point, old...Dani lass, you'd think you saw it, but there'd be no proof you actually were seeing it. It could just be your imagination filling in blanks again."

Dani was silent for a long time, staring out over the water as the last of the summer twilight drained out of the western sky and stars brightened in the body of the night. At one point she cocked her head on one side, looking so intently at a hatch near her that Daffyd got up to examine it more closely. He could see nothing of any interest, so sat down again, content to give Dani the peace she so obviously needed.

"I can prove it," Dani said suddenly. "I can prove this is more than an illusion. Listen, Kare the ship's master was just talking to me..." She saw Daffyd's expression and pointed at the hatch. "He was kneeling over there. Anyway, he told me about an island we'll be drawing alongside very soon-- round that next bend."

"So?"

256

"So I've never been to Egypt have I? Never taken a Nile cruise? How could I possibly know something like that unless I was getting the information from somebody who'd been there?"

"You've looked at maps of the area," Daffyd pointed out. "I was with you."

"Those maps showed roads and towns, not the river in any detail. It was no more than a heavy blue line running north and south. Did you see any islands or anything depicted?"

Daffyd had to concede he had not.

"So in a few minutes we are going to round that bend in the river and see this island and there's no way I could know of the existence of it unless someone told me. And the only person who has told me is the ship's master from my lucid dream--whom you don't believe exists."

"I didn't exactly say I didn't believe you, lass. It's just that you haven't been able to prove it to me."

"Well, hang onto your hat, Dafs, because in a few minutes I'll make you eat it." Dani got up and walked to the rail, leaning out and looking forward to catch her first glimpse of the promised island. Daffyd came after her, standing close, one arm around her to prevent any act of imbalance tipping her over the side. He kept his eyes on her, his forehead wrinkled in a frown of worry, rather than on the river ahead.

"Any moment now..."

The river curved in a broad sweep, the water dark between village-speckled shores, and Dani leaned out further, her eyes searching.

"Where is it?"

The river straightened again. It remained flat and featureless with no contour breaking its limpid surface. Dani slumped against the rail and Daffyd caught her in his arms, guiding her back to the chairs. He held her close while her shoulders shook and waited in silence for her to gather herself.

"I was so sure it was there. Why would he lie?"

"The ship's master?"

"Yes, Kare. Why would he tell me...Scarab...something like that if it wasn't true?"

Daffyd said nothing, waiting for Dani to draw her own conclusions.

"It was my imagination filling in the blanks again, wasn't it?"

"Afraid so, lass. It is the most likely explanation..." A thought occurred to him. Daffyd closed his eyes and muttered an imprecation under his breath.

"What?"

"I have to be honest--there is another explanation. It's been over three thousand years. An island could have long since vanished in that time."

Dani sat up and looked at the small dark Welshman beside her. She smiled. "Poor Dafs, what it must have cost you to admit that, not wanting to foster what you see as my delusion."

"Ah well, I'd rather be honest with you."

"I appreciate it."

They sat in companionable silence for a while longer, watching the river flowing by, lit now by a rising moon. They each kept their own thoughts to themselves, though Dani's eyes often flicked aft as if watching something unseen.

Dani felt a tremor in Daffyd's arm and turned from her contemplation to the present day. "You're shivering." She looked down at her own jacket and at his thin shirt. "I've been selfish keeping you out in the cold. Go inside, I'll be all right."

"I'll wait a while."

"You don't want to leave me out here alone, do you? Do you think I'll do something stupid?"

"Not really, lass, but you're experiencing something intensely emotional and such things are better shared, if only with an unbelieving codger like myself."

"I can't think of anyone I'd rather share my thoughts and feelings with. But I'm still being selfish keeping you out here. Let's both go in." Dani got to her feet and smiled. "I wonder if the ferry catering runs to a nice hot cup of coffee or soup."

They moved forward to the stairs to the lower deck and Daffyd waited for her, standing aside. Dani turned to look over at the moonlit river as she stepped onto the first step and hesitated, her eyes wide and staring.

"It's there," she murmured. "The tomb is directly west of here."

"You can see it?" Daffyd asked. "It's too dark to see anything."

"It's broad daylight in my dream," Dani said with a smile. "There's already a boat on the shore and my friends are climbing the cliff track to the pylon..." She fell silent. "It's gone."

"The tomb?"

"No, my vision. Scarab's left me."

Daffyd helped Dani down the stairs and along the lower deck to the doors admitting them to the interior of the ferry. Lights and a hubbub of conversation spilled out onto the deck as the doors opened, cutting off abruptly as they closed. Neither of them saw Ali Hafiz emerge from the shadows beneath the stairs.

*   *   *

The ferry pulled into the docks at Luxor a few minutes before midnight, navigation lights guiding the captain in and enabling him to ease alongside the terminal jetty with minimal fuss. Passengers started disembarking, and Dani and Daffyd shuffled along with their few possessions in hand. On the docks they could see the dispersing passengers and a small group of soldiers.

"I wonder what they're doing here," Daffyd murmured. "I think we should avoid them; we don't want to risk being asked for our papers."

As soon as they reached the dock, Daffyd steered Dani away from the soldiers, but Hafiz stopped him. "You cannot leave the docks in that direction. The gates are locked at night. You will have to come this way." He pointed past the soldiers.

"There are other people going in that direction."

"They are locals and will be let through the gates. Come this way."

Hafiz ushered Dani and Daffyd toward the soldiers, stopping in front of the officer. "Colonel Sarraj, these people are the ones you seek."

Dani gasped and stepped back, but the soldiers quickly surrounded them, rifles at the ready. Daffyd glared at Hafiz and then moved closer to Dani, slipping his arm around her protectively.

Sarraj coolly looked them over. "So, Dr Danielle Hanser and Dr Daffyd Rhys-Williams, we meet at last."

"And who the hell are you, boyo?" Daffyd asked.

"I am Colonel Michel Sarraj, and I am here to arrest you."

"On what charges?"

"Entering the country illegally should do for a start."

Chapter Twenty-Seven

Muammar led Marc to one of the parks along the river, where they washed their hair free of desert dust and drank deeply from the water in one of the fountains. Several people passing by stared, but no one accosted them and Muammar started back into the city streets.

"We need to find my second cousin. You remember I mentioned him?"

"You know his address?"

"Not exactly, but I think I can find it."

"You've been to Edfu before?" Marc asked. "I thought you said you hadn't been in Egypt."

"So I did, and no I haven't." Muammar would not say more, just smiled and walked on. He stopped from time to time and spoke with whoever was close by--though always men--short conversations in Arabic, sometimes altering the direction of their travel after doing so. Gradually, they neared the city centre and their path diverged less and less.

"Nearly there, I think." Muammar spoke with another man, this time at length, following the man's gestures as much as his words. Thanking the man, he led Marc up the street and to an unprepossessing door set in a brick wall.

"Here?" Marc asked.

Muammar nodded and knocked. Minutes passed and he knocked again, this time rewarded by the door opening and a bearded face peering out of the gloom.

"Yes?" said the man.

"Are you Mohammad ibn Sukrah?"

The man stared at the two men on his doorstep with suspicion. "Who wants to know?"

"I am Muammar al-Hadi, son of Mostafa al-Hadi and A'isha bint Hawid. I am the son of your mother's sister's daughter. I ask the hospitality of your house for myself and my companion, Dr Marc Andrews."

"Never let it be said that I turned away my cousin. Enter and make this house your home."

Mohammad stood aside to let his guests inside. Following Muammar's lead, Marc removed his shoes and followed the other men into an inside room, where Mohammad and Muammar embraced. Their host gestured to a sofa and waited for them to seat themselves before calling out, "Juman."

A woman appeared from a concealed doorway, and Mohammad ordered coffee for his guests. While the woman busied herself in the kitchen--they could hear the sounds of pots and china being arranged--Mohammad enquired as to the health and welfare of any of the family members associated with Muammar's relations.

All conversation took place in Arabic, and Muammar did not bother translating anything, so Marc's attention wandered. He looked at the wall hangings in a desultory fashion, noted the presence of a large wood-inlaid radio on a small table in one corner, and followed the tracery of a pattern in the rich wool carpet underfoot. Stifling a yawn, he ran his fingers through his beard and crossed his legs, the sole of his foot ending up pointing at their host.

Muammar saw his cousin's outraged expression and turned quickly. "Marc, quickly, uncross your legs," he snapped.

Marc obeyed without thinking, but then asked, "Why?"

"It's very bad manners for the sole of your foot to point at anyone. Apologise and sound as if you mean it. I'll translate."

"It's only my foot, for God's sake," Marc mumbled.

"When will you learn that you're in another country, with people who have different customs and values? Just apologise, please."

"Oh all right, you don't have to go on about it. Mr Mohammad, I'm sorry if I offended you. I didn't mean to."

Muammar quickly translated, adding, "Please excuse the infidel's lack of manners, cousin. I promised his...his elders that I would look after him, but he is a stranger to civilised ways."

"It seems that was a rash promise you made, cousin, but for your sake I will excuse his bad manners."

"Thank you, cousin."

Coffee arrived and Mohammad poured cups of sweet black brew for his guests. They both drank and their cups were refilled. When they finished, Juman appeared again and removed the cups. Mohammad took out a crumpled piece of paper from his gallibaya and smoothed it out.

"Perhaps you can explain this, cousin. It seems to pertain to you and your infidel friend."

Muammar took the piece of paper and read Dani's letter, passing it to Marc when he finished. "This was given to you by a European man and woman?"

"No. Imam Abdel Nour handed it to me this afternoon. He tells me one of the attendants at the Dhuhr prayers in the mosque today was seen to throw it away, and out of curiosity, retrieved it. It is written in English, so neither he, nor I, could read it, but the envelope, from which the paper was obviously removed, bore both your name, cousin, and mine. I know this," Mohammad added, "Because Imam Nour took it to a man who can read English. He was concerned that the person who threw it away may have wanted it back, and sought to identify him. When he found it was addressed to me, he delivered it, with an explanation."

"Did the man who could read English tell you or the imam what was written in the letter?"

"No, and I did not enquire once I knew it was addressed to you. I did not expect to see you, but I held it in case you turned up. Evidently, the letter writer knew of your imminent arrival."

Muammar told Mohammad of the contents of the letter.

"It mentions Hafiz," Marc said. "Is that the same Hafiz, do you think?"

Muammar translated Marc's question for the benefit of his cousin. "I think it likely."

"This Hafiz is an enemy?" Mohammad asked.

"If it is the same man. He tried to kill us."

Muammar hesitated before he went on. "Cousin, was there anything else with this letter. It mentions English pounds--twenty of them."

"The imam told me only of the letter and made no mention of anything else. I hope you do not entertain the notion that Imam Abdel Nour has kept the money." Mohammad's eyes hardened and he glared at Muammar as if to dare him to accuse his own relative of theft.

"Why would any man throw away money?" Muammar asked. "It is obvious that the person who opened the envelope stole the money before throwing the letter away."

"Indeed," Mohammad said. "We must thank Allah, the Merciful and Beneficent that the culprit was seen in the commission of his crime, thus allowing you to take receipt of a letter that was intended for you."

"I will offer up thanks at the earliest opportunity."

"It is close to sunset. Will you join me and my household for Maghrib?"

"I would be honoured."

"What of your companion?"

"He is an unbeliever, though a Person of the Book."

"Then I will show you to a room where you can perform wud'u and don clean garments, for you are travel-stained and unfit to approach God."

Marc was given the opportunity to clean himself up while the Sukrah household--Mohammad, wife Juman, two teenage sons and three small daughters, plus a cook and a manservant--enfolded their relative Muammar and prayed together in the main room. Afterward, as their clothing was in a poor state, Mohammad gave them Egyptian garments to wear--gallibaya and trousers, with skullcaps.

"I presume you will be travelling to Luxor, where perhaps this enemy you mention is lying in wait," Mohammad explained. "In your western attire you would stand out, but dressed as simple fellaheen you will be able to blend in." He allowed himself a small smile. "Even your infidel friend can pass as an ignorant peasant with his sunburnt face and thick beard, as long as he does not open his mouth."

"Thank you, cousin. Your hospitality overwhelms me."

"You are family, Muammar al-Hadi. You will stay for the evening meal before you depart?"

Mohammad embraced his cousin in the doorway in the late evening, pressing a few crumpled notes into his hand as they made their farewells.

"I would not have it said that you left my house without that which was your expectation, cousin. I cannot offer you the full sum that was stolen from you, but this may help."

"May Allah the Merciful and Beneficent shower you with His blessings," Muammar said. "Such generosity should be rewarded. I will repay you double when I can."

Mohammad shook his head. "There is no need, for this offering is Zakāt and brings its own blessing."

Muammar and Marc walked down the darkened street toward the city centre, keeping to the shadows and walking slouched over as befitted their new identities as fellaheen.

"How much did he give us?" Marc asked.

"Six pounds. He was very generous."

"Will that be enough?"

"If we are careful it will get us to Luxor. After that, we must hope that we meet the others."

"How do we get there?"

"Bus and ferry. I doubt there's a bus to Esna before tomorrow morning, but we'll see. Uh, Marc...just in case Ali Hafiz is still looking for us; we must stay in character as ignorant peasants. Keep your head down, your hands in your gallibaya, and don't speak unless we're alone. Let me do all the talking."

Marc shrugged and said nothing.

They found the bus station and found some seating at one end where they could stretch out. Even at this late hour there were several people around, and more drifted in as the hours went by. Most people were farmers, some with produce in wicker baskets, and all were poor. They ignored each other for the most part, sitting and smoking cigarettes, though a few talked, discussing farm prices, and two old men pulled out a battered chess set and started playing. Others gathered round the old men, watching and murmuring comments.

After a few hours, Muammar and Marc got up to stretch their legs and watched the chess players for a time. When they returned to their seats, they found them taken.

"I should have thought of that," Muammar muttered.

He found them a place nearer the middle of the bus station, sandwiched between an old woman and her granddaughter, both women laden with baskets and bags of vegetables, and an old man with a pair of goats. They squeezed between the old people, sitting on the bare ground, Muammar smiling and greeting them politely and Marc saying nothing. The old woman regarded the young men suspiciously and slapped her granddaughter when she gave Muammar a bold look. The old man just grunted and shifted slightly, while the trussed goats stared at Marc. One of them nibbled tentatively at Marc's gallibaya until he tugged it out of reach.

The night became chilly and they huddled together, Marc even allowing the goats to press close, lending their body warmth, while the women kept to themselves, bundled in voluminous robes. Hours passed and in the pre-dawn darkness a motor started up, grumbling and spluttering, echoing around the station and awakening the fitful sleepers. Headlights, weak and yellow, illuminated passengers stiff of limb and yawning, as they prepared to board the bus that crept into the station.

Marc yawned and stretched, scratching beneath his gallibaya. He grimaced and scratched again, before casting a look of disgust at his four-legged sleeping companion. "The damn beast's given me fleas."

The goat owner gave Marc a strange look when he spoke in English but said nothing, and Muammar cautioned him again to remain silent. The young Libyan parted with some of their money and secured two seats at the back of the bus. He bought two cups of sweetened tea and a stale loaf of bread from a young boy hawking his wares near the bus. They stood and chewed on the tough bread, softening it by dunking it in the tea, and drinking the rest of the hot sweet liquid. Marc suggested another cup but Muammar cautioned against it.

"Rest stops are few and far between. The bus won't delay."

"Speaking of which," Marc said. "I could do with a loo break right now."

"Hurry then--behind that shed." Muammar pointed.

The bus driver started the engine while Marc was gone, and Muammar had to remonstrate with him to wait. Voices became raised, but as the driver and a couple of the passengers started to rise from their seats, Marc ran back, gallibaya flapping, and scrambled aboard. With a grind of gears, the bus lurched forward and rumbled out of the bus station in the first light of dawn, turning onto the north road that led to Esna.

The journey was every bit as unpleasant as an earlier bus trip in Libya, though this one lasted only one day. The bus was crowded with people, produce and livestock, it shook and rattled as if on the verge of coming apart, and the open or missing windows admitted copious quantities of dust and waves of heated air. Muammar closed his eyes and went to sleep, but Marc found himself unable to and suffered and scratched for most of the trip.

Shadows from the western cliffs overtook them an hour out of Esna, and the temperature eased, though the stink of bodies and animals stayed with them, overlain with the acrid taste of dust in their mouths. They left the bus in the town centre and, limbs stiff and trailing dust with every step, made their way down to the ferry. After buying the necessary tickets, Muammar had a few shillings left over from the money his cousin had given them. They were famished, so sought out a street vendor in the poorer part of town. A few pence supplied them with a hollowed out crusty loaf filled with a concoction of lentils, beans, onions and chickpeas, and another vendor sold them tin mugs of hot sweet tea.

Marc fell to with a will, not caring what people thought of his manners, digging into the vegetable stew with scooped fingers, biting off chunks of bread and gulping down tea. Muammar followed suit, though a trifle more elegantly--or at least as elegant as one can manage when eating with one's fingers. Marc finished, swallowed the last piece of bread and washed it down with a last mouthful of tea.

"Ah, by God, I needed that." He belched loudly and grinned. "It'll be the other end later after all those beans."

"I will pray not," Muammar murmured. He bought a hand of bananas from a stall and they walked back to the ferry, munching on the sweet fruit.

On board the ferry, they found a place on the upper deck away from other people and hunkered down in the lee of some machinery. The temperature had dropped further as the sun set, so they huddled together for warmth and watched the shore slowly slip past, the vibration of the engines felt through every part of their bodies.

"What's our plan when we get to Luxor?" Marc asked.

"I think we must find our friends first," Muammar replied, "Though we must also contend with the presence of Hafiz."

"I suppose it's the same man? But if so, why was Dani so nice about him in the letter? Why wasn't he marching them off at gunpoint, like us?"

"We cannot be sure it is the same man, but I think it likely. As for his behavior--well, we don't know what he might have said, what threats or persuasion he used. If our experience was anything to go by, he wanted to capture us for someone else, presumably this Minister Bashir who robbed you."

"Yes, but why would he want us?" Marc asked. "We're in Egypt illegally, with no funds or special expertise, and he already has what we want--the golden scarab."

Muammar watched the darkened shoreline and the scattering of lights from the villages they passed for several minutes. At length, he stirred. "I overheard Dr Hanser and Dr Rhys-Williams talking once when we were in the desert with my *badawī* cousins. They talked of being in the desert with someone called Smen-ka-ree and having the golden scarab. I thought it none of my business so walked away, but now you mention this golden scarab also, and it seems that it might be relevant to our present problem. I presume this is the heirloom that was stolen from Dr Hanser. Do you want to tell me about it, Marc?"

"It's complicated."

"We have time."

"Hmm." Marc thought about what he could safely divulge. "Smenkhkare was a pharaoh and he had a sister who called herself Scarab. He was deposed by their uncle Ay and he led an army across the western desert to reclaim his throne, but failed and died. Scarab survived and was loved by the gods of old Egypt. They gave her a...a talisman--a golden scarab--that worked wonders."

"A children's tale, surely?" Muammar said. "A bedtime story."

"One might think so," Marc conceded, "But in Syria, where we discovered a series of chambers in the cliff face with this tale and others from the life of Scarab written upon their walls, Dani also found a carved golden scarab. The same golden scarab. With it, she too worked wonders."

Muammar grinned, his teeth showing white in his bearded face. "Now you are pushing the leg, as you English say. What wonders?"

"I'd never have believed it if I hadn't seen it myself. She could find things with it, for a start. She found the positions of the second and third chambers when even sounding equipment couldn't find them. It could disguise itself too--appearing as a simple rock to Minister Bashir and his secretary Nazim. It was incredible. Bashir would have given his right arm for a precious artefact like that, but he ignored it."

Muammar laughed, a trifle uncertainly, his expression tailing off into a puzzled frown. "These are the people that Dr Hanser believes now hold the golden scarab? These people who only see a rock? Why would they keep something they think is worthless?"

"I don't know, but they confiscated it in Syria along with all our notebooks and photos, so they must believe it is important in some way."

"And if they have discarded it?"

"Then this is all a waste of time," Marc said. "Daffyd and I came along to show our support for Dani, and I suppose she'll know what to do next--either way. That's why we have to find her."

Muammar considered Marc's words. "I understand about the golden scarab, though something that works wonders can only be from Allah, not from non-existent pagan gods; but what about Dr Hanser saying she was in the western desert with this Pharaoh Smen-ka-ree? What is that all about?"

"I don't like to say anything bad about Dani--she's a damn fine lecturer--and sexy as hell, too, but she's also a bit wacky." Marc thought for a moment. "No, that's unfair, but I think she needs a rest, all the same. She got so involved in translating the hieroglyphs on the chamber walls that she came a little unstuck mentally. Sometimes she has difficulty separating her life from that of this Scarab person." He chuckled. "Someone even suggested she was Scarab reincarnated."

"Reincarnation is impossible," Muammar said. "The righteous are in paradise with God and the wicked burn in hell."

"You could be right, but the description of Smenkhkare and Scarab leading an army out of Nubia through the western desert to attack Thebes--olden-day Luxor--was quite vivid, and maybe because of the golden scarab artefact, Dani identifies strongly with Scarab. She slips in and out of a dream world where she is Scarab."

"Then I fear she is in need of a psychiatrist," Muammar said.

"God, I hope not, but the sooner we can get this business wrapped up and get her back to England the better."

"Well, if my cousin was correct and the letter was delivered yesterday, we are only a day behind her and Dr Rhys-Williams. They will be waiting on the museum steps at opening time tomorrow, so we can all plan how we are to get this artefact from Bashir and Nazim."

* * *

Marc and Muammar spent the rest of the night in the portico of the Luxor museum, determined not to miss the arrival of their friends. They did not even step away to find food or a hot drink at dawn for fear of missing them, but nine o'clock rolled round and the doors opened, but there was no sign of Dani or Daffyd. An hour later, they left to find something to eat, though by now all they could afford was bread.

"Something must have held them up," Marc said, searching for crumbs in the folds of his gallibaya. "They'll be there at closing."

There was no sign of them when the museum doors closed, however; nor when they opened next morning. Increasingly desperate, they waited until nearly midday before giving up and spending the last of their pence on day-old bread.

"What do we do now, Marc? You know your friends--what could have happened?"

Marc held up a hand and grimaced. A few moments later he sneezed violently. "Sorry, I think I might have caught a chill. As for Dani and Daffy, if they said they'd be here, they'd be here. They're not, so something has happened to them, and the only thing that is likely to have happened is Bashir."

"How do you mean?"

"They know Nazim has the golden scarab so they've tried to get it back from him. Unsuccessfully. We need to find Bashir and Nazim ourselves."

268

"We also need money for food."

"What do you suggest?"

Muammar considered their options. "You know what these men look like, and I speak Arabic. I think your task today is to find these men by asking at hotels--I can teach you one or two Arabic phrases you can use, and mine is to raise some food money so we can prolong our search. Meet back at the museum at closing?"

*   *   *

Tahir spotted Muammar and the infidel known as Marc as they came out of the door set in the brick wall in a back street in Edfu. The Bedouin remembered the shame of being bested by his cousin when he and the infidels escaped, and ground his teeth in anger. He thought of the sweetness of recapturing these two, but knew that Zufir would kill him if he failed. Better to follow these two in the hopes that they would meet up with the other infidels. Then he could gather his brothers and take them all.

He followed, blending in with the crowds of people on the streets. Muammar and the infidel made their way to the bus station and took seats on a bench, apparently settling in for a long wait. Tahir watched from a distance, certain that the others would arrive to meet them, but by midnight there was no sign of them.

I should return to camp and fetch Zufir and the others. Clearly, they are meeting the other infidels elsewhere.

Tahir left, making his way through the darkened streets toward the place where they had made camp on the outskirts of Edfu. As he moved through unlit alleys, he was set upon by two men intent upon robbing him. With little effort, he left one lying dead in the street and the other whimpering as he nursed a slashed arm. He sheathed his knife and resumed his journey.

Zufir gathered his men at dawn and led them swiftly to the bus station, prepared to overwhelm the passengers and snatch Muammar and the infidel. They were too late, and all the information they could garner from bystanders was that the destination of the bus was Esna.

"We follow," Zufir roared. "And I shall demand extra recompense for all my trouble."

Chapter Twenty-Eight

Nazim Manouk had never thought of himself as particularly imaginative, but he was rapidly changing that opinion of himself. He was also talking to himself, arguing even, and that disturbed him more. The last two nights had become increasingly harrowing as images and sounds invaded his sleep, awakening him from deep sleep, his heart racing. He would sit awake the rest of the night, afraid to close his eyes, and then at dawn drag himself to the nearest café for cups of strong coffee. He found he could doze during daylight hours without fear, but the rest he obtained from these cat naps sufficed merely to give him the semblance of sanity, while below the surface his mind still reeled from the nightly onslaughts.

His demeanour and wan looks invited comment, but he brushed aside Al-Din's concerns muttering that he must have eaten something that disagreed with him, or else had a touch of stomach flu. He withdrew from the Lieutenant, and the Minister as much as possible, keeping up his duties of venturing out on the launch to investigate possible tomb sites though his heart was no longer in the search. Instead, he sent Al-Din ashore to follow up possibilities and spent many hours on board the launch wrestling with the cause of his nightmares. Increasingly, Nazim felt as if his mind was dissociating as his conscience racked him.

Lieutenant Jamal Al-Din often heard Nazim muttering to himself, but not wanting to eavesdrop, paid as little attention as possible. The secretary was obviously worried about something, or was ill and best left alone. He thought Nazim would ask if there was anything he wanted Al-Din to do. The most disturbing aspects of Nazim's condition came from the arguments the man held with himself, and also from the fixation the little man had with a small river stone. Thinking himself unobserved, he would furtively bring it out of his pocket and stare at it, quickly hiding it when anyone approached.

"Obviously disturbed," Al-Din muttered, "But how can I help if he won't confide in me?"

Nazim heard Al-Din muttering and knew he was watching him but felt unable to unburden himself. He waited, staring out at the riverbank with senses attuned, until he was certain the man had moved away.

"He is a spy," Nazim said softly. "I wouldn't be at all surprised if Bashir has told him to look for the scarab."

Don't be a fool, Manouk said after a few moments. *If he suspected that he'd have me searched.* He put his hand in his pocket where the weight of the artefact pulled against the fabric, but then hesitated. *Check to see if he's gone. It never hurts to be careful.*

Nazim got up and crossed to the door of launch cabin, opening it and peering onto the short rear deck. "Nobody there." He returned to his bench seat by the table and pulled the object from his pocket, studying it in the shaft of sunlight from the open window.

"It looks like an ordinary rock to me. Are you sure about this? You wouldn't try and fool me, would you?"

That's the golden scarab--feel the weight.

Nazim weighed the rock in one hand, his expression doubtful. "What do I know about the weight of rocks? It does seem heavy though."

It is. It's made of gold after all.

"If you say so."

I do, Manouk insisted. *And that little thing is going to change my life.*

Nazim considered his words carefully. "How? It weighs what...half a pound? It's worth a couple of hundred British pounds unless the gold price rises. Ten times more as an artefact..." he laughed suddenly, "...but only if people can see it for what it really is."

That thing is a miracle from Allah--and I have it in my possession. With it, I can find the tomb of this Scarab person. They'll never find it, the description is misleading, but this thing, this magic rock, can lead me straight to it.

"Finding it would be nice," Nazim conceded. "But I don't see how I benefit."

Yes, you do. Think about it. What's your skill?

"I'm an organiser."

Precisely. And when I find this tomb, I, Nazim Manouk, will reveal that the golden scarab that masquerades as a stone is the tool that has enabled me to find it; then people will see me as more than a lowly secretary. I will have made the discovery that will make all those self-important sons of whores at the Ministry sit up and take notice of me.

"Shh, shh," Nazim said, waving his hands and looking toward the door. "Don't reveal it before we are ready."

Yes, yes, I am not a fool.

Nazim yawned, suddenly very tired. He slipped the scarab back in his pocket and stretched his arms high above his head, arching his back. "By Allah and the Prophet, I could sleep for a fortnight."

No. Please don't, Manouk begged. *Have some coffee instead.*

Nazim swirled the dark liquid in the cup on the table and sipped at it, grimacing. "Cold," he muttered. "And there's a fly in it." He got up and walked through to the galley, carrying the cup with him.

The crewman in the galley was reading a newspaper and smoking a cigarette when Nazim walked in. The man eyed him warily and nodded, watching as the Syrian tossed the dregs of his cup into the sink and poured a new cupful from the pot on the stove.

"Good coffee, yes?" the crewman said in his village Arabic. "Freshly brewed."

Nazim looked at him suspiciously, wondering if the man had really said something as innocuous as a comment on the coffee. The man's Arabic was hideously accented, not like the dialects he was used to.

Don't you believe it. He asked a question about the scarab. He's Bashir's spy. He knows something.

Nazim shrugged and left the galley, carrying his cup of coffee carefully but quickly to his seat in the cabin. In safety, he drank the strong brew as quickly as he could, not caring if the hot liquid scalded his mouth, welcoming the pain as an added tool to stay awake.

We must keep moving, Manouk said. *Don't give in to sleep. We don't want to see those things again.*

Nazim shivered and looked around the cabin, frowning uneasily. "What...what are they...do you think?"

Nothing--hallucinations--visions sent by djinn. They're not real. We just need to pray to Allah and they will flee.

"I've never seen things like them before. Not even in Damascus in that fever dream. Remember that?"

I'd rather not, thank you, Manouk said, suppressing a shudder. *Look, just think of something else--something pleasant.*

"Like what?"

I don't know. Like the position that will be mine--ours--when the Minister is discredited and the Ministry rewards us. Or the riches that may come to us when we find the tomb. We've always wanted to retire to Jarabulus near the Turkish border-- that house we found near the Euphrates with the large courtyard and the olive grove behind and the fields, green and...

"Green like his skin..."

Be quiet...don't say it.

"Darkness...a feeling as if I'm deep underground in a chamber reeking of spices...a single oil lamp burns and there is...there's movement..."

Silence. I don't want to hear it.

"Neither do I, but it's there every time I close my eyes. He steps into the light of the lamp and looks at me. His skin is green and he's wrapped in linen cloth strips. He has a crown on his head and the crook and flail of a pharaoh. He smells of the grave, of decay and...oh Allah preserve me, his eyes."

Please don't...

"It's haunting us."

Who? What?

"You know."

Manouk shook his head. He stared into the empty coffee cup and drew a shuddering breath. *Osiris. The Egyptian god of the dead. A djinni or afrit--maybe even a shaitan. What does he want with us?*

"Same as the others," Nazim said. He took several deep breaths to calm his thundering heart as panic threatened to grip him.

We can handle them--none of them are real; they are merely dreams.

Nazim laughed, bitterness in his eyes. "Even that red man with the demonic head? The one who stinks of dry sand and bones? The one who makes you think of being lost in a howling chaos for eternity? You can handle him can you?"

Manouk started crying. *What do they want?*

Nazim wiped his eyes and blew his nose loudly on a stained handkerchief. "What do you think they want? What has changed? We have the golden scarab now. They want it back, of course."

But they aren't real. They're only dreams.

"You think so?"

If not dreams then what are they?

"Think about it." Nazim waited a few moments while he thought about it. "The green man in mummy cloths is Osiris, the red chaos is Set, the woman with a chair on her head..."

It's a symbolic throne.

"...a throne then. She's Isis. I can guess that the green man with leaves is Geb and the woman with the starry body is Nut...lions, a hawk...there are nine of them, so I think it's the Nine of Iunu Dr Hanser told us about. The nine ancient gods who gave Scarab the artefact in the first place."

273

You don't believe that. The ancient gods are myths, nothing more than the fearful imaginings of a primitive people, or demons misleading us.

"Well, you can explain that to them next time we see them."

No thank you.

"So what are we going to do?"

What can we do? We only see them when we're asleep, so they must be just dreams. Demons would appear to us awake as well.

Nazim nodded. "And dreams like this are the sign of a guilty conscience."

Manouk shifted uncomfortably in his chair. *My conscience is fine. The golden scarab was given to the original Scarab thousands of years ago. She died, so it belongs to whoever finds it.*

"Dr Hanser found it; Minister Bashir stole it and gave it to us..."

So it's ours.

"...to give back to Dr Hanser."

What are you saying?

"We have to give it back to Dr Hanser. It's the only way to stop the dreams."

By the Prophet--peace be unto him--listen to you. This thing is valuable--not just its intrinsic value, but as a modern day miracle and as a guide to untold riches. We can't just give away what might be our last opportunity for fame and fortune.

Nazim pondered his words. He took the scarab out of his pocket and examined it again, wondering anew how the golden scarab Dr Hanser evidently saw looked just like an ordinary river-polished stone. "You make a persuasive argument," he said at last. "But what do we do about the dreams?"

Manouk hesitated. *They're not so bad.*

"Yes they are."

There are treatments we could try--drugs--we just need something to knock us out.

"I'm not sure I like the idea of not being able to wake up. We'd...we'd be at the mercy of those things."

Manouk laughed mirthlessly. *They're only dreams. And even if they're djinn, then God will protect us--we are faithful, aren't we? They're frightening, but so what? They can't actually harm us, and I'm sure that if we ignore them, they'll go away.*

"You think so?" Nick said uncertainly.

I do think so. When we return to Luxor I'll get some sleeping tablets from the medical supplies and we'll get a good night's rest. You'll see.

"And we keep the scarab?"

And we keep the scarab.

Nazim Manouk put his plan into action as soon as they returned from the cruise investigating possible sites north of Edfu. He dismissed Al-Din and hurried back to the hotel where he removed half a dozen sleeping tablets from the medicine cabinet, making a note to that effect in the log book.

Nazim sat in the hotel lounge with a cup of tea and sweet almond pastries, half-listening to the conversation of others, but paying no real attention as he was debating whether to have an early night and risk the dreams immediately, or stay up and face them later.

Sooner or later, you'll have to face them.

He looked up to see Minister Bashir staring at him. His immediate reaction was one of guilt, convinced that he had somehow heard his thoughts or found out what he had in his pocket. With a struggle, he refrained from putting his hand over the artefact, and managed a weak smile instead.

"Something I can help you with, Minister?" he asked.

"How did you get on today? I expect regular reports, you know."

"We found nothing worth reporting."

"That is for me to decide. You just do your job."

"Yes, Minister."

"Oh, one other thing--that rock I confiscated from Dr Hanser--where is it?"

Nazim hesitated, averting his eyes and wondering if guilt showed on his face. "I brought it to you in your room, Minister. I presume it is still there."

Bashir grunted. "I seem to have mislaid it. Have a look for it, will you?"

"May I ask why, Minister? After all, it is just a rock."

"Colonel Sarraj arrested Dr Hanser and Dr Rhys-Williams at the Luxor docks last night. He is interrogating them and I thought it might be useful to have the rock. If it really is the golden scarab..."

"I did not know they were even in Egypt, Minister. Where are they being held?"

"At the barracks. Why?"

"I will see if I can find the rock. If I do, I can take it to the Colonel."

Bashir nodded. "If you find it, bring it, but only hand it to me. I don't want Sarraj to know of it just yet."

Nazim excused himself and went back to his room, shutting and locking the door behind him. "Just as well no one can see my inner conflict," he muttered. "Do I 'find' the golden scarab or keep it hidden?"

He took the sleeping tablets out and put them on the table, just looking and making no move to take them.

"Is this going to help or make things worse?" he asked himself, but there was no internal debate or comment. There was a little water in the glass by his bed, tepid and with a film of dust clinging to the surface, but he swallowed two of the pills with a gulp of the liquid, considered his options and took two more.

Despite the drug, sleep was a long time coming, though he tried not to fight it. He tidied his bed, changed into his pyjamas, and opened a book he had been reading for the last few months--he was still only a third of the way through the book as he kept getting distracted by work. Now he waited for sleep and tried to lose himself in the plot.

Sleep came upon him unawares, and the first inkling Nazim had that he was no longer awake was the sensation of sand-sprinkled stone beneath his feet. He looked up but saw only darkness with a single oil lamp burning on the other side of the cavern. A feeling of dread gripped him, for he felt the presence of others in the darkness, unknown others who bore him malice. Something moved, a shadow within a greater shadow, and the tiny yellow flame of the oil lamp flickered.

Oh Allah, please let me wake up, Nazim prayed. In his dream he backed away from the unseen presence until his back was against the rough stone wall of the chamber. He ran his hands over the surface, feeling the texture of raw stone and the chisel marks the masons had left when they had carved the tomb from the living rock. Despite his fear, a part of Nazim's mind marvelled at the sensation.

Are dreams usually this vivid? he asked himself. *I...I know this is a dream...nothing but a dream.* The thought gave him a surge of confidence. "Leave me alone," he commanded the unseen presence. "Go away, in the name of Allah and his Prophet."

The lamp flame stilled, but there was otherwise no response. Only utter silence. *The silence of the grave... Stop thinking like that. Has it worked? I can't see anything.* Nazim smiled in triumph. "Oppose the demons in Allah's name and they flee," he murmured. Light, soft and lambent, filled the stone chamber. He screamed.

Standing before him were nine figures--men and women, he thought at first, and then realised the figures were not human. *Not animal either...or...or part...* Nazim saw the green-skinned man wrapped in mummy cloths and recoiled--or would have if his back had not been pressed against the rock wall of the chamber. With him--or it--were a tall woman with a stylised throne on her head, a figure in red with a horrific head, a hawk, a lion and lioness, another green-skinned man sprouting leaves and vines, and a woman whose body was the night sky. He almost missed the ninth figure because it was so ordinary--until he looked full at it. Then he realised that the ordinariness was nothing to do with plainness and everything to do with being human.

The ninth figure was a man, tall and straight, with copper skin and dazzling white kilt. He wore a pectoral of worked gold, armbands of the same precious metal, and the double crown of the Kingdoms of Egypt. His expression was regal, cold and haughty, and Nazim felt his spirit shrivel as the king's gaze swept over him.

"Allah, come to my aid," he cried.

The demons did not flee in terror, but continued to stare coldly at him. He fell to his knees on the hard stone floor and held out his arms in supplication. Words sprang to his lips, words that Nazim would never have contemplated using when awake.

"Mighty Atum, holy Nine of Iunu, spare me."

The Nine regarded him and Nazim felt his soul shrink in upon itself. He cowered like a mouse in the presence of a predator, as if vast stretches of time and space beat about him. Anger buffeted him like enormous vulture wings.

"You have that which is mine," the Atum said. The words compressed the air in the chamber, hammering at his eardrums until he thought they would rupture, though he heard it only as a sibilant whisper.

Nazim felt his bladder loosen and hot liquid course down his thighs. He could only stammer incoherently, his arms still outstretched.

"Why do you delay?" the god asked, his expression stern.

Nazim dug in his pocket--somehow he was still wearing his trousers-- and pulled out the golden scarab. It gleamed warmly in the soft light. He held it out. "Take it. Please."

The anger washed away like a retreating wave and for a moment Nazim beheld the Ennead of Heliopolis in all their glory, and then they too were gone. The light in the chamber lingered a moment longer and now Nazim saw that with the gods gone it was crowded with painted cedar wood panels, with grave furniture, and two sarcophagi side by side. Ivory and gold gleamed and the air hung heavy with the scents of aromatic spices and unguents. As surely as if he read a sign, Nazim knew he was in the tomb of Scarab and her brother Smenkhkare. The light dimmed and then plunged him into a claustrophobic darkness from which he woke screaming.

Nazim lay in his bed, tears trickling down his cheeks, and shook with remembered terror and the utter relief of finding himself back in his own bed. A distant hammering beat upon his consciousness and he heard Jamal Al-Din calling from outside his bedroom.

"Mr Manouk, are you all right? Nazim, answer me."

He gathered his scattered thoughts and framed a reply. "Yes. A nightmare. Nothing more...thank you." Nazim listened and heard a shuffling of feet outside his door. "Good night, Jamal." Footsteps sounded softly in the hallway, a floorboard creaked, and Nazim was alone with his thoughts again.

By the Prophet, what a dreadful dream. He swung his legs over the edge of the bed and became aware of a cold wetness on his pyjamas bottoms and the sheets. *I...I have wet myself...* He stripped off his nightwear and bundled them with his soiled sheets, throwing them into the corner of the room, and then naked, by the light of the lamp that still burned, pulled a chair up to the balcony doors and sat looking out at the darkened city and river. After a while, he calmed enough to revisit the details of his dream.

It results from a guilty conscience. Perhaps it means I should give the scarab back to Dr Hanser. But then again... Nazim took his trousers off the back of the chair and dug in the pocket. He took out the rock and stared at it, realisation flooding into him. *Whether those...things...are gods or demons or dreams, this is not mine. I must return it.*

Nazim sat naked on the chair in his locked room and cried tears of relief at his decision. When, hours later, he drifted off into an exhausted sleep, it was untroubled, and when he awoke the next morning, he knew his course of action.

Chapter Twenty-Nine

Dani and Daffyd had spent an uncomfortable night in one of the cells of the Luxor army barracks. Colonel Sarraj had escorted them there from the docks and locked them in adjoining cells, with an armed guard under orders to watch them at all times. As soon as the colonel left, Daffyd walked across to the bars and called to Dani.

"Are you all right, lass?"

"I'm fine, Dafs." Dani came close to the bars on her own side of the concrete wall and reached out with one hand. Daffyd squeezed her hand gently before the guard barked out an order for them to desist.

Daffyd scowled at the guard and dropped his voice to a whisper. "Who is this Colonel Sarraj anyway? He seems to be army rather than police."

"And how did he know we were in Egypt illegally?"

"While you're at it, who's Hafiz and how did he find that out? I presume he's working for Sarraj, but was he sent specifically to find us or was that pure chance?"

"He must have been sent to find us. Nothing we said could lead him to the conclusion we were illegals."

"So how did he know about us?" Daffyd asked.

"I don't know."

They each contemplated their fate for a while before Dani said, "It can only have been Marc. Marc and Muammar. They've been caught."

"What, and blabbed about us? I don't believe it. The buggers."

"Don't be too hard on them, Dafs. We don't know the circumstances. They might have been threatened or...or worse."

"Think they'll do that with us?"

"What could they possibly want with us? They'll probably just deport us back to England."

"I suppose that wouldn't be so bad."

"Except it doesn't get me my golden scarab." Dani sighed and turned away, pacing the length of her bare cell a couple of times before returning to the bars. "I'm sorry, Dafs. That sounds very self-centred but it was always my purpose and all I've done is lead you into trouble. If you'd stayed at home you'd be safe and..."

"I wouldn't have missed it for the world, lass. Before the Syrian expedition I was just an old stick-in-the-mud lecturer, the butt of student jokes, but you dragged me kicking and screaming into the real world. You've broadened my horizons and...well, all I'm saying is, I'm glad to be here with you."

"Thank you, Dafs," Dani whispered. "It helps having you here."

There was an awkward silence, broken at last by Daffyd shuffling his feet and clearing his throat. "Now if I could only get you and Marc to stop calling me Daffy..."

Dani laughed. "He calls you Daffy--I call you Dafs--and it's a term of endearment on my part. But if you'd rather I didn't..."

"No, I er, sort of like it from you, lass."

The guards turned the lights off in the cell block shortly after and they sought the dubious comfort of their respective pallets. One good thing about the darkness was that they could use the primitive facilities--a battered bucket in one corner--in relative privacy. The mattresses were thin and lumpy and harboured vermin of some sort--they could feel something crawling over them--but the discomfort was not enough to keep Dani awake. After a few words tossed back and forth between the cells, she yawned a 'good night' and went to sleep. Daffyd lay awake a while longer, though a smile creased his face as he tossed and turned, and as the first faint fumbling of the sun's early rays lifted the skirts of the night sky above Luxor, he slept.

The soldiers came for them mid-morning and took them to a windowless room where they sat on hard upright chairs on one side of a small table under the unfriendly gaze of a burly guard. They sat in silence and waited, trying to ignore their pangs of hunger and growing thirst and looking uneasily at a pair of iron rings bolted to the table. At last, the door opened and Colonel Sarraj walked in, accompanied by a young man dressed in the uniform of an Egyptian army lieutenant. The two men sat down and contemplated the prisoners.

Daffyd broke the silence. "I must protest our treatment, Colonel Sarraj. We have not been convicted of any crime yet we are treated outrageously. Why, we haven't even been fed yet, and we're both thirsty."

"That will be remedied, Dr Rhys-Williams, in return for a little cooperation," Sarraj said.

"Why the hell should we cooperate? You have a duty of care."

"This is not England. You are criminals facing charges that attract severe penalties, so it would be in your best interests to cooperate."

"We want to see a solicitor."

"Again, this is not England. That is not going to happen."

"Damn it..."

"What exactly is it that you want, Colonel?" Dani asked.

"Thank you, Dr Hanser." Sarraj consulted a notebook. "Perhaps you could explain something you said last night."

"I don't recall saying anything..."

"On board the ferry. You said, 'It's there. The tomb is directly west of here.' Dr Rhys-Williams then says it is too dark to see anything, to which you reply that there's a boat on shore and men climbing the cliffs to the pylon. What did you mean, Dr Hanser?"

"How did you...ah, your Mr Hafiz?"

"I'm waiting, Dr Hanser."

Dani shrugged. "It was nothing. I'd been dozing on the upper deck and I must have been dreaming. I probably just said something I'd seen in the dream."

"What is the scarab?"

"In what context?" Dani asked. "The sacred scarab of the ancient Egyptians was a symbol of..."

"You said 'the scarab has left me'."

"Probably just something from my dream."

"And the golden scarab?"

Dani shook her head.

Sarraj leaned across and whispered something to the young lieutenant, who got up and left the room. The Colonel then leaned back in his chair and examined his nails, taking out a nail file and trimming one or two. After a few minutes, the door opened and the lieutenant entered, bearing with him a tray with a steaming cup of fragrant coffee and a buttered croissant.

"Ah, just what I need," Sarraj said. "Sometimes my duties keep me so busy I forget to eat." He sipped the coffee, savouring the hot brew, before biting through the thinly-crusted croissant. Butter dripped down his chin, and Sarraj dabbed at it with a clean white handkerchief while he chewed. "Delightful. Now, where were we? Ah yes, the golden scarab."

Daffyd's stomach growled audibly and he glared at Sarraj. "This is a puerile stunt, Colonel. Do you imagine we will crack just because we're hungry and you eat in front of us?"

Sarraj took another bite and sipped his coffee. "Perhaps just a reminder that all I desire is a little cooperation. Answer my questions and we can all enjoy some breakfast. What is the golden scarab?"

"Get stuffed."

Sarraj smiled and finished his croissant and coffee, instructing the lieutenant to place the tray on the ground. He wiped his fingers clean of the last few crumbs and smears of butter and dabbed at the corners of his mouth with his handkerchief.

"The golden scarab is an artefact from the Eighteenth dynasty, supposedly given by the gods of ancient Egypt to a woman called Scarab."

"If you know, then what was all this rigmarole?" Daffyd demanded.

"The golden scarab is mentioned in the Syrian account, but why should it be of concern to you today?"

"Who says it is?"

"One of your students in England. He thinks you have come to Egypt to find it, Dr Hanser--to find it, and a tomb. What do you say to that?"

"I say you can go and..."

"It's all right." Dani put her hand on Daffyd's arm. "I've never made any secret of the fact that there is an undiscovered tomb and that I wanted to come and search for it. My desire is purely scientific though. If you are looking for someone interested in plundering it, then look no further than Ahmed Bashir, Under-Minister of National History in Syria."

"And the golden scarab?" Sarraj persisted.

"I imagine it's one of the precious objects that will be found within the tomb. If it's there it will go a long way toward authenticating the account."

"So you haven't had it in your possession?"

Dani smiled tiredly. "If I had, then where is it? Everything we had in Syria was confiscated when we were deported. Contact Minister Bashir and ask him."

"Ali Hafiz tells me that an old woman instructed you to contact Nazim Manouk. Why?"

"I don't know. She just said to ask the 'organiser'. Your man suggested the name Nazim as meaning 'organiser'. It might be Nazim Manouk, or another Nazim."

"You know Nazim Manouk?"

"Know of him, yes. He's Bashir's secretary."

"What were you to ask him? This Nazim organiser?"

"She didn't say."

Sarraj stared at Dani. "Ali Hafiz says he did not see any old woman."

"I can't help what your man sees or doesn't see."

"How did you enter Egypt?"

Dani debated whether to reveal details and glanced at Daffyd, who shrugged. "We came across the Libyan border."

"A hazardous journey. You were helped?"

"A young Libyan man helped us. He left us here and has no doubt returned to his home."

"I regret not. Ali Hafiz tells me that this man and your colleague Dr Marc Andrews died in the desert."

"Ah, sweet Jesus," Daffyd groaned. "Those poor young lads. Are you sure?"

Dani dabbed at her eyes with the sleeve of her shirt. "How does he know?"

"He was escorting them to Luxor on my instructions. They became violent and crashed the vehicle, escaping into the desert. Ali Hafiz barely made it out alive, and he is certain that they could not survive." Sarraj offered Dani his butter-smeared handkerchief. She accepted, blew her nose and dried her tears. "It appears, Dr Hanser, as if your ill-considered adventure has cost the life of one of your friends already. I beg you not to risk the life of your other friend, Dr Rhys-Williams."

Dani clutched the handkerchief tightly and stared at the colonel. "What do you mean?"

"Just that I must be rigorous in my enquiries, and I would hate to think that ill-considered stubbornness on your part might endanger his health. I will have answers to my questions, Dr Hanser."

"I might remind you that we are British citizens," Daffyd growled. "Even if we have broken the law, you cannot do as you like. There are rules and conventions. When the British Consulate hears..."

"The British Consulate is unaware of your presence in Egypt, Dr Rhys-Williams. They cannot protest what they do not know."

"Surely you are a civilised man," Dani whispered, shocked.

"How little you know me. Shall we start again? But this time you will answer my questions completely and truthfully."

"We already have," Daffyd said.

"We shall see." Sarraj nodded to the burly guard who, with the assistance of the lieutenant, produced two pairs of handcuffs and two short lengths of chain and fastened both Dani and Daffyd securely to the rings bolted to the table. Daffyd tugged on his handcuffs experimentally, rattling the chain through the ringbolt, but could not budge it.

"The table is metal beneath a wood veneer," Sarraj said. "And bolted to the floor. Now, Dr Hanser, let's try again--where is the golden scarab?"

"I told you, it's probably something in Scarab's tomb."

Sarraj held up his left hand, closed his fingers into a fist, and then extended the little finger. At once, the burly guard stepped up behind Daffyd, and before he could react, grabbed his left hand and bent the little finger back.

Daffyd yelled, pain rapidly overtaking the surprise. "Oh, Jesus...you bastard...you've broken my bloody finger...ahh." He jerked away as far as his bonds would let him and tried to protect his finger with his other hand, though the slightest touch sent waves of pain through him.

"I think you'll find it's just dislocated, Dr Rhys-Williams, though still painful. Dislocation has certain advantages in that I can have my man do the same to all ten fingers before moving on to breaking them. I suspect that will hurt much more. Now, Dr Hanser, try again. Where is the golden scarab?"

"Don't hurt him again and I'll tell you," Dani pleaded. "I found the scarab in the mud outside the first chamber in Syria, but it was taken from me by Bashir before we were deported. I don't know where it is now...no, please..." Dani jerked on her chains as Sarraj held up his left ring finger and the burly guard stepped forward again. "It's the truth," she cried out. "No...don't..."

Daffyd yelled incoherently, tears streaming from his eyes as his second finger was bent back with an audible crack. "Oh, bugger me, boyo...that fuckin' hurts."

"What's the point of asking me questions if you don't believe my answers, you bastard?" Dani screamed. "I've told you the truth; it was taken from me by Bashir. He's got it."

"Why did you come to Egypt?"

"To find the scarab and get it back. That's the truth of it."

"You imagined that Minister Bashir would just hand it back? After taking it from you? Such a valuable relic?"

"No...I don't know. But I had to try. It's mine; I found it."

"On a Syrian archaeological site, Dr Hanser. The Syrians acted correctly in confiscating such a precious object."

"He didn't believe it was valuable. He only took it because I had it--wanted it."

"How could he not know? It is called the golden scarab for a reason, isn't it?"

"It looks like a rock...no, wait..." Dani tugged at her chains as Sarraj started to lift his left hand again. "I'm telling the truth."

Sarraj lowered his hand. "Explain."

Dani drew in a ragged breath. "I don't know if I can, but please, hear me out. The account in Syria spoke of a golden scarab that only the woman Scarab and her companions could see. Anybody else saw only a rock. Well, it's the same with the one I found. The expedition members saw a carved golden scarab, but all Bashir could see--and other people--was a rock. I...I can't explain it unless...well, unless the gods are protecting it."

"You try my patience, Dr Hanser. You think you can fob me off with fairy tales?" Sarraj lifted his left hand again and the burly guard moved forward. "I think we'll break a finger this time."

"No!" Dani screamed. "Wait, please, I can prove it..."

"Remind them of the pain that awaits, but do not break the finger."

The guard took Daffyd's left hand and bent his dislocated fingers forward, eliciting a roar of pain from the Welshman and agonised sobs from Dani.

"You were saying, Dr Hanser?"

"I can prove it, but you'll have to get the golden scarab here. If Minister Bashir has it, you'll have to find him and persuade him."

Sarraj sat and looked at Dani, ignoring the muttered imprecations flooding out of Daffyd's mouth. After a minute, he nodded and turned to the lieutenant. "Bring them both--Bashir and Manouk." The man got up and left the room.

"You have them already?" Dani asked. She considered the implications. "You're in it together. You're Bashir's man."

"I am no one's man, Dr Hanser. The Minister and I have an understanding."

They sat in comparative silence for many minutes before Sarraj looked at his watch, got up, and left the room. Despite the presence of the burly guard, Dani and Daffyd felt the tension in the room ease.

"Oh, God, Daffyd, I'm sorry. How's your hand?"

"Feels like I slammed a car door on it," Daffyd said. "I could do with some pain-killers but I daresay I'm not going to get them."

Dani looked over her shoulder at the guard. "He needs medicine, for pain. You get?" The guard ignored her and Dani tried again, dredging her memory for the Arabic words. There was no response and she tried the words for 'water' and 'thirst' with equal result. She sighed and turned back. "Sorry, Daffyd."

285

"You think you could call me Dafs again?" He scraped up a weak smile. "It's not your fault, lass. The bugger was always going to hurt us and better me than you."

"What are we going to do...Dafs?"

"I rather hoped you might have a plan."

"I do, but it involves us being on the other side of that door."

Daffyd grunted, and stared at his swollen, bruised fingers, the pain throbbing up his arm to the point of his jaw. "I've got a plan that involves my hands and Sarraj's neck, but I'm scarcely likely to be able to implement it."

"That's it, Dafs. Positive thinking."

They considered their own thoughts for a few minutes more.

"I hope Bashir confirms what happened and shows Sarraj the rock," Dani said.

"How's that going to help, lass? A rock is a rock, and he's never going to believe it's really the scarab."

"I suppose I'll just have to show them then."

"What? How?"

"Scarab showed Jeheshua when he didn't believe."

"By praying to Atum and the Nine, for God's sake. Those were ancient Egyptian gods, not...you don't really believe in them, do you? That they actually exist?"

"You've seen for yourself how it disguises itself. Does a rock do that by its own power...or is it perhaps just the power of persuasion? Or something else?"

"Put like that..." Daffyd tried to scratch his head with his right hand, but the action dragged the chain through the iron ring on the table and scraped his damaged fingers against the wood veneer. He gasped with the pain, panting until the throbbing died down.

"What if it doesn't work? You...pray...to the gods and nothing happens?"

"Then--as our American cousins so delicately phrase it--we're screwed."

Daffyd grinned. "Dani, lass, I'd never have thought it of you."

Sarraj returned half an hour later, impatiently shepherding Bashir into the cell, with Nazim trailing behind. The Syrian Minister stared at the captives, his lips curling in distaste at Daffyd's bruised and battered hand. He sat in the chair indicated by Sarraj, while Nazim stood near the door, averting his eyes.

"You are a fool, Dr Hanser," Bashir said. "You should have just quietly stayed at home, safe and content. Now you will suffer."

"Nice to see you too," Dani murmured. "I misjudged you."

"How so?"

"I thought you were motivated merely by avarice. Now I see you have a vicious streak and think nothing of murder."

"Murder? I see only injuries sustained while resisting arrest. You will be jailed and deported, nothing more."

"Marc Andrews and our friend Muammar are dead in the desert as a result of your partner's actions. That makes you responsible too."

"Michel? What is this?" Bashir looked at Sarraj in surprise.

Sarraj shrugged. "Accidents happen. They tried to escape and ran off into the desert. My men could not find them so no doubt they died. It is no loss, Ahmed. They were not even officially in the country, so their demise can be laid at no one's door."

"Very true. I am relieved that you are not acting precipitately. Now, why have you dragged me down here? Interrogation is your purview, not mine."

"Dr Hanser is spinning me a tale of some golden scarab that disguises itself as a rock. She claims you will support her in this far-fetched idea."

"I think she is confusing the written account on the chamber walls with reality," Bashir said. "Such a thing was claimed to exist in the times of the pharaohs."

"So there is no truth to it?" Sarraj sighed. "Dr Hanser, it seems we must resume our interrogation."

"Ask him where the rock is," Dani blurted.

"What rock is this, Dr Hanser?"

"You know damn well. The one you took off me in Damascus."

"Ah, that one. Why do you want to know? It is only a rock."

"Give it back to me and I'll prove it is far more."

Bashir glanced at Sarraj. "How would you do that?"

"You've read the transcripts of the account. In the same way Scarab proved it to Elder Jeheshua outside Zarw."

"What is she talking about?" Sarraj asked.

Bashir stared hard at Dani. "You are not the Scarab woman, Dr Hanser. How would you do this?"

"Why should you care as long as it's done? Sarraj wants proof; I'm prepared to furnish it."

"What is she talking about?" Sarraj asked again.

"According to the account, the golden scarab was a talisman of great power that enabled the Scarab woman to find her way in the trackless desert, search out hidden things, conjure up water, even raise the dead. Obvious hyperbole, but she also claimed it could hide itself as a rock. Scarab had the gods demonstrate this power to one of the Hebrew elders. Now Dr Hanser claims to have found the golden scarab but says it is hiding again as a rock. She says she will demonstrate its power, like the Scarab woman did."

"You have the rock?" Sarraj asked. "I would very much like to see it."

"Yes." Bashir beckoned to Nazim. "Where is the rock we confiscated?"

"I gave it to you, Minister. If you recall, I brought it to your hotel room, acting on your instructions, several days ago."

"Then where is it now?"

"I must presume still in your room."

"I don't recall seeing it there. Are you sure?"

Dani leaned closer to Daffyd. "I can feel it," she whispered. "When he stepped closer to the table."

"What are you talking about lass?"

"The golden scarab. I can feel it. I'd know it anywhere and when Nazim the organiser stepped forward, I felt its power."

"Close enough for you to use it?"

"Use? As in...? I don't know."

"Try, lass. We need a bloody miracle."

Dani closed her eyes and concentrated, feeling pulsing warmth emanate from the man near the table. She reached out mentally and stroked the source of the power, tears oozing from the corners of her eyes as she welcomed it back into her life. "Atum, Nine of Iunu, help me. Help us both, I pray. Protect us from harm and help us escape our enemies." She opened her eyes to see Bashir, Nazim and Sarraj staring at her.

"What did you say, Dr Hanser?" Sarraj asked.

"You spoke out loud, lass," Daffyd muttered.

Dani felt a moment's chagrin and then said, "To hell with it. Nine of Iunu--I beg your help." She stood up, her chains rattling. "Come on Dafs, we're out of here."

"Restrain them," Sarraj ordered.

The guard moved forward and grabbed at Daffyd, shoving him back in his seat. He turned to Dani and reached for her. His feet tangled and he tripped and fell onto the table. Sarraj and Bashir fell backward as the wood veneer split under the guard's weight and the metal beneath buckled. The ring bolts sprang free, and both Dani and Daffyd stood with their handcuffed hands and pendant chains swinging free.

"Come on," Dani said, starting toward the door.

Daffyd followed but Sarraj stood in his way. The colonel pulled out a gun and levelled it at first Daffyd, and then Dani.

"Sit down," Sarraj snapped.

Daffyd stepped to the right and the gun swung to follow him. Dani stepped forward, chain swinging and clipped Sarraj on the side of the head. He staggered and loosed a shot, the report deafening in the enclosed space. The bullet whined past Dani and she heard a yell of pain. Glancing to her side she saw Bashir sitting on the floor clutching his left bicep. A grunt swung her attention back to where Daffyd grappled with Sarraj, holding onto his gun arm. A step closer, and Dani brought her ring bolt down hard on the army man's head. He collapsed silently, and Daffyd let him fall to the floor.

Nazim stood by the door whence he had backed as soon as Dani had moved. He now watched her apprehensively, his hands open and in plain sight.

"I mean you no harm, Dr Hanser," Nazim said softly.

"Then stand out of our way and you won't get hurt."

Nazim nodded and moved aside, but Bashir called out to him. "Stop them, you fool. They're unarmed."

Daffyd darted past and looked out into the corridor, both ways. "Which way is out?" he asked.

Dani looked at Nazim. "Where is it?"

"Safe. You want it?"

"Yes."

"Someone's coming," Daffyd called from the corridor. "Several people. Hurry."

Nazim dug in his jacket pocket and pulled out a small object, gold gleaming through his spread fingers. "Here."

Dani swallowed, her eyes fixed on the golden scarab and her hand reached for it. Daffyd burst back into the room and yelled, "We've got to go. Now." Without looking at Nazim he grabbed Dani and yanked her into the corridor just as a soldier came around a corner twenty yards away.

"The scarab!" Dani yelled. "It's back there. I've got to...oh, shit."

A bullet sprayed concrete chips from the wall as it whined past them and they ran, chains dragging and bouncing. Other shots followed, zipping past their heads, ricocheting in the narrow corridor, but none hit them.

They heard shouting and running footsteps, and ducked through a doorway, across an empty room and into another corridor running parallel with the first.

"Which way?" Daffyd asked. "Left or right?"

"I left the scarab back there," Dani moaned. "Nazim was going to give it to me."

"Left it is." Daffyd grabbed Dani's hand and started down the corridor. It met another at right angles and Daffyd guided them to the right this time, finally bursting through another door into a room with a dozen desks at which sat typists and clerks in army uniform. On the far side of the large room were open windows through which a street could be seen, with traffic and pedestrians.

Daffyd ducked back into the corridor, but Dani pushed him into the room. "Bluff it out. Just walk through as if you belonged here." She set off, nodding politely at a young man, ignoring another that addressed her in Arabic. Everyone in the room was looking at them, and one man picked up a telephone and spoke urgently into it.

"Walk faster, lass," Daffyd murmured. He pushed past her to a window and sat on the sill, swinging his legs over.

A man leapt up from his desk and confronted Dani, who pushed him aside, holding her chain loosely, swinging it menacingly. He scowled but just watched as Dani joined Daffyd at the window. Behind them, armed soldiers burst into the room.

"Stop them!"

Daffyd grinned and leapt down to the pavement outside, dragging Dani with him. They scrambled to their feet and ran, dodging through the traffic and into the alleys of the Luxor bazaar.

Chapter Thirty

" " Find them!" Colonel Sarraj howled. "Whatever you have to do, do it. I don't care if you kill them, just get them back."

Soldiers ran to do his bidding, setting the whole barracks on its ear. The building was searched, and quickly news arrived of the fugitives escape through the clerks' room and into the streets where they were swallowed up in the lanes and alleys of Luxor. Soldiers were sent out into the city, but with fresh instructions.

"I want them alive. And put those damn clerks on a charge--they let them escape." Sarraj stamped off to the communications room to contact the police and transport facilities, determined the fugitives would not remain at large for long.

Bashir sat in a chair in the interrogation room, being attended to by an army medic. Sarraj's bullet had pierced his left upper arm and exited without damage to arteries or bone. The medic cleaned the wound out thoroughly and started bandaging it, while Bashir glowered at Nazim.

"Whose side are you on? What were you thinking of, offering Dr Hanser the rock?"

"I assure you I only have your interests at heart, Minister--as always."

"You lied to me. You said I had the rock, whereas you had it all the time."

"I did not lie, Minister. I brought the rock to your room, if you remember. It is reasonable to suppose it is still there. Perhaps under your bed, unless the cleaning woman has removed it."

"But you have it," Bashir said. He lifted his left arm to point but winced and contented himself with nodding in Nazim's direction. "You took it out of your pocket and offered it to Dr Hanser. I saw you."

"This?" Nazim took the rock out and tossed it in his hand before holding it up between forefinger and thumb. "This is just a river rock I found locally."

Bashir frowned and motioned the medic away. He waited until the man had left the room before continuing. "If it is not the rock, why did you offer it to Dr Hanser? What possible interest could she have in it?"

Nazim returned the rock to his jacket pocket. "You examined the rock closely, didn't you, Minister? Did you find any evidence that it was really a golden scarab like the one in the account?"

"No." Bashir decided not to mention his unsuccessful attempts at breaking the stone's disguise through prayer. If it really was a golden scarab, the inefficacy of Allah's name disturbed him. "As far as I'm concerned, it is merely a worthless rock."

"Yet Dr Hanser believes it is more," Nazim said. "Is she, in fact, deluded?"

"Who knows, and with her gone, who cares? You still haven't answered me. Why did you bring that rock and offer it to her?"

"Those are two different questions. You told me earlier the rock was missing, yet if the possibility ever arose that we needed to attract Dr Hanser to us, we would need it--or something that she might believe was it. So I obtained a replica."

"But if she sees it, she will know it's not her rock--her golden scarab."

"And yet she saw it just now, and believed. You forget the power of her delusion, Minister. Such was her need for it that I only had to suggest this was it for her to recognise it."

"Which brings us to why you offered it to her. Did you bring it with that express purpose?"

"How could I, Minister? We were summoned by the Colonel, and while you may have known why, I did not until we arrived here. As to why I offered it--well, Sarraj had shot you, he and the guard had been laid low by two chained prisoners and I--I am not a fighting man. I thought to trick her and perhaps hold onto her until help could arrive, but her companion dragged her away. She believed I had the stone and would have taken it, giving me a chance to grab her."

"Quick thinking, Nazim, yet you risked the only thing we have that she wants."

"It was not the real rock, Minister. Remember? It is lost."

"Ah...yes. And now they are lost too."

Bashir held onto the splintered and buckled table and got shakily to his feet. "I don't know how they managed to break free, but that madman will kill them, Nazim, and I'm starting to think we cannot find the tomb without them. The river search using the vague description in the account is hopeless, yet Dr Hanser came to Egypt to look for her golden scarab. I believe she knows where the tomb is and will beat us all there unless we can stop her." He mused for a few moments. "We need them, Nazim, alive and unharmed. They can guide us to the tomb."

"Our resources are a lot less than those of the Colonel, Minister. He will find them, and it will be up to you to keep them unharmed."

"I cannot be everywhere, and I am injured. Put Lieutenant Al-Din onto it. Let him earn his keep."

Nazim made notes in his notebook, and hesitated, debating whether to share the insights he had gained when talking to Dr Zewali at the museum. The main question he had to answer was whether he could reasonably find the tomb on his own or whether he needed help--he had the knowledge, but Bashir and Sarraj had the resources. He sighed and decided a morsel of information might keep the minister focussed.

"When I was at the museum looking for maps, I found out something that might aid our search."

"Well, go on, Nazim. Don't waste my time."

"While I was waiting for the maps to come out of storage, I read some of the text translations on the wall and noticed..."

"Did you find the maps you were looking for?"

"No, Minister. As I was saying, I noticed that the symbol for 'pylon' is very similar to the one we were led to believe translated as 'notch'. I copied it down carefully and checked with the photographs we took. I believe 'pylon' is a better translation than 'notch'."

"Pylon? Do you mean a power pylon?"

"No, Minister. They did not have electricity in pharaonic times. A pylon is the term given to the gateway of a temple and is made up of two truncated towers with a lower central portion. It looks similar to a notch or valley."

"You have lost me. Why is this of interest?"

"We have been looking for a notch in the cliff top--a notch which may have eroded away over the centuries. A pylon, however..."

"May still be there!" Bashir rounded on his secretary excitedly. "By the Prophet, Nazim, you are proving your worth yet again."

"Thank you, Minister, though it may be too early to judge the worth of my discovery. A building may crumble as easily as a cliff."

"Ahh...well, it's worth looking, I suppose. Traces may remain. We must send word to Sarraj, we'll need his help."

"Another thing Al-Din can do," Nazim said.

Bashir and Nazim made their way out of the kicked ant-nest that was the Luxor army barracks and made their way back to the hotel. Once there,

Bashir retired to his room where, liberally dosed with painkillers, he rested. Nazim went looking for Jamal Al-Din first of all, and gave him his instructions.

"What if he doesn't listen to me?" Al-Din queried. "I mean, he's a colonel and I'm only a..."

"Be persuasive. It is important we keep them alive and unharmed--the woman in particular. Intimate that Minister Bashir would count it a personal favour if he was consulted before any decision was made pertaining to her fate. Remind him that precipitate action may cost us everything, whereas revenge is just as satisfying when delayed. And don't forget to tell him about our discovery. We will need his help on that very soon."

Al-Din looked dubious but agreed to do his best. He hurried off to find the Colonel's search party, while Nazim repaired to the hotel lounge with a pot of coffee and sticky date pastries to consider the events of the morning.

If I did not know it before, I know it now--that rock is the golden scarab. Nazim took it out of his pocket and stared at its rounded contours. *It still looks like sandstone.* He wetted it with a drop of coffee and rubbed, but its disguise remained intact. *I was going to give it to her but I didn't. Why not? I offered it, but as she reached for it I changed my mind. Bashir believed my tale of subterfuge, but I know that was not the reason. I want it. I want the power this thing could give me.* Nazim thought back to the moment of the escape. He had hardly believed what he saw--a small woman overcome a burly guard, the metal table break and release their chains, and an armed man thrown aside. *Was that the power of the scarab? Did she reach out with her mind and take control of it, even though it was hidden in my pocket?*

He recalled the intensity of her stare when she saw the rock--the golden scarab--in his hand. *There was no doubt in her mind--she believed this to be her scarab. How then do I use this knowledge? Could I bargain with her? Offer her the scarab in return for a portion of the tomb's riches?*

Nazim suspected that monetary gain was not uppermost in the Englishwoman's mind. *What then? What does she want? Fame as the discoverer of Scarab's tomb?* It was all very frustrating trying to guess the motives of a foreigner, and a woman as well.

* * *

Colonel Sarraj accepted the presence of Lieutenant Al-Din without comment, and allowed him to follow along as he strode from one checkpoint to another, haranguing the soldiers at his disposal. Men had raced into the alleyways and narrow streets of the Luxor bazaar scant minutes after the foreigners had entered them, but they seemed to have vanished without trace. An English man and woman should have stood out, but the only westerners his men had apprehended had been innocent tourists. He had several officers now engaged in soothing ruffled feelings and apologising for the misguided enthusiasm of some of the men under their command.

"Find them!" Sarraj roared at a local captain. "How hard can it be to find an English man and woman in the bazaar? Start a house to house search."

"Uh, Colonel...we don't have the men for that." The captain quailed at the look in the colonel's eyes and stammered, "The...the police, sir. We c...could borrow s...some men."

"Then why are you still here? Get on with it."

The captain saluted and raced off, shouting orders. Sarraj called another officer to him and ordered him to set up roadblocks around the bazaar. Everyone leaving the area must show their identification and women were to be searched.

"Search women, sir? We can't do that, there would be a riot."

"Not every woman, just Europeans."

"There will still be trouble, sir."

"Just do it."

There was trouble, just as the officer predicted, but it did not come from the handful of European tourists in the bazaar and adjoining streets. They readily produced identification and passed through the roadblocks without incident, but the inhabitants of the area objected to the high-handed methods of police and army as they started the house to house search.

Men of the household remonstrated, the women screamed imprecations and children bawled, attracting crowds who jostled and pushed police lines, shouting and jeering. Reinforcements arrived, but most of those were now needed to control the growing mob, slowing down the speed of the search. Sarraj grew more agitated and ordered every available man into the line, even pulling policemen on point duty away from their duties, which rapidly led to traffic jams throughout the city. By mid-afternoon, there had been numerous incidents, some involving shots being fired in the air--though luckily no one had been injured. The bazaar itself had been closed, shop and stall-holders shutting up shop in the face of growing violence.

Colonel Sarraj pored over a map of the area back in his office at the army barracks, listening to reports coming in from the field, crossing off houses and streets one by one as the inhabitants were sieved and discarded in the search for the fugitives. The telephone rang and, in the absence of a secretary, Sarraj answered it himself.

"Yes? I'm busy; keep it short."

"You'll make time for me, Colonel Sarraj." The silky voice over the wires snapped Sarraj to attention.

"General Gamal. Of course, sir. How may I assist you?"

"I have a report in front of me of rioting in Luxor. What's happening?"

"There is some disturbance, sir, but nothing that can't be contained. An escaped prisoner went to ground in the bazaar and I've instituted a search."

"Who is the prisoner?"

Sarraj paused. "A man and a woman wanted for entering the country illegally."

"Sounds like a police matter to me. Why involve the army?"

"One of my men was attacked by their accomplices. I thought it proper to involve myself."

The general grunted. "Leave it to the police--that's my advice. What are you doing in Luxor anyway? Your regiment is in Cairo."

"I would rather not say over an open line, sir."

The general paused. "I hope you have a very good reason for being away from your station, Colonel."

"I do."

"Very well. You may send me a couriered report explaining your reasons. In the meantime, hand over control of that fiasco in Luxor to the police. Let them carry the blame if the fugitives escape."

Sarraj hung up and pushed the map away from him, thinking about his options. *I can delay a report a week, maybe two or more--and I can invent some plausible reason anyway. Will that be enough time? Relinquishing control to the police need not be a problem. If I don't find the woman in the bazaar, I can have the docks and roads out watched. She'll turn up sooner or later, and even if she doesn't, it may not matter.* He decided to continue searching until sunset and then allow the police to take over.

* * *

Dani and Daffyd ducked behind a curtained stall a few yards into the bazaar and gathered their wits. The stallholder, a silversmith, sensed an opportunity and tried to sell them some of his wares, holding out little coffee pots or plates, jewellery or cups, and jabbered away at them in Arabic. Dani tried to ignore him.

"What now? They're going to be after us in a few seconds."

"I don't know, lass. We're back to being penniless and without anything save what we're wearing. We need to find somewhere to hole up and get these chains off. We're a bit conspicuous with them on."

"How's your hand?"

The chains clinked as Daffyd raised his hand to look at his bruised fingers. "Funnily enough, it doesn't hurt much. The fingers look bad but..." he moved them experimentally and winced, "...the pain isn't nearly as bad as I anticipated."

They heard raised voices and the sound of running booted feet, and slipped away, down a narrow alley, trying to hide their chains from people. They attracted many stares, and a few people called out to them, but the sounds of potential pursuit died away and they found refuge in a crowded market, standing and looking at a stall filled with baskets of produce.

"I think we're in trouble," Dani murmured.

"I wonder if anybody would sell us a bolt cutter." Daffyd said.

"Maybe if we had money." Dani rattled her chains as she examined the linkages, searching in vain for a weakness.

"I wonder if I might be of assistance."

They turned, startled at the English voice, and found themselves looking at a florid-faced man in a wrinkled white suit and homburg. The man smiled and raised his hat, revealing tousled sandy-coloured hair.

"Pardon me for intruding on a private conversation, but I couldn't help hearing you say you were in trouble. I'm only too happy to help a fellow Englishman out--and a lovely lady of course."

"Er...and you are...?"

"Yes, of course...proper introductions...I'm Nicholas Evans. I regret to say I've left my business cards at my hotel, but I daresay you'll take my word for it."

Daffyd nodded. "Of course." He hesitated, wondering whether they could trust the man. Evans was looking at them expectantly, so he cleared his throat and said, "Sorry, yes. My name is Jones, William Jones, and this is my er, wife Marjorie. We er, had a spot of bother with the police--lost our passports, you see--and er, ended up with these." He held up his handcuffs and chain.

"Dear me," Evans said, raising his eyebrows. "That won't do at all. You must be the cause of all the hoo-hah going on a street or two over. You can't just explain the problem to the police?"

"They don't believe us. We need to get these chains off and get to the British Consulate."

Evans smiled and raised his hat again. "Well, I can't leave a lovely lady, and countrymen to boot, in such a fix. May I invite you to my hotel--it's just around the corner? We could have a cup of tea and chat about what to do."

"We don't want to get you into any trouble," Dani said. "Our chains are a little conspicuous."

"Hmm, perhaps some disguise is called for." Evans purchased a few lengths of cheap cotton cloth from a nearby stall and draped it over their hands and arms in such a way as to look as if they were carrying the fabric. "That should suffice, I think."

Evans' hotel was a small, homely establishment a stone's throw from the bazaar and, despite the prevalence of armed patrols starting to close off the streets; they managed to walk past without being challenged. Possibly they were aided by the fact that at that time, the police were looking for a man and a woman, rather than a party of three Europeans. At the hotel, Evans took Dani and Daffyd up to his room--third floor, room eleven-- and ordered a pot of tea and a plate of biscuits to be sent up.

"It would be more comfy down in the hotel lounge, but I think until we can divest you of your, uh, jewellery, we should be more circumspect."

"We're very grateful, Mr, er, Evans," Dani said, "But I don't understand why you're going to such trouble for us. If the police or army catch you, they won't be happy."

"My dear Mrs Jones, didn't I make myself clear? You are countrymen and...er, countrywoman, of mine, in trouble over some silly misunderstanding. If I can help in any way, then I'm delighted to be of service."

There was a knock on the door, and Evans opened it to reveal a porter carrying a tray with tea, three cups, and a plate spilling over with almond and sesame biscuits.

"Ah, capital. On the table if you please, Abdul. Thank you." Evans slipped the porter a coin and showed him out. "Now, Mrs Jones...may I call you Marjorie...would you like to be 'mother' and pour the tea? Help yourselves to biscuits. I'll pop out for a bit and see if I can't find something to use on those chains of yours." Evans tipped his hat and hurried out, closing the door behind him.

Dani shrugged and poured the tea. She almost knocked the pot over with her chains as she picked up her cup, but cradled it in both hands and sipped the hot liquid. Daffyd stirred plenty of sugar into his and wolfed down half a dozen biscuits before sitting back and guzzling his tea.

"Ah, that hits the spot," he said, smacking his lips. He took another biscuit and dunked it, slurping up the soggy mass before it could crumble.

Dani looked pensive as she nibbled on an almond biscuit. "What do you think of this Evans chap? Can we trust him?"

"Not sure about that." Daffyd poured himself another cup, this time with only a little bit of sugar. "He turned up exactly when he was needed, which is a little suspicious. He might be in league with Sarraj or Bashir."

"If he was, he'd have handed us over immediately." Dani refilled her cup and settled back as comfortably as she could. "There's another way of looking at it, Dafs. We escaped because of the golden scarab and it brought us to this man. It channelled the power of the gods..."

"We escaped through pure luck, lass. No need to read anything else into it."

"Nazim had the scarab though--I felt it. I reached out and prayed to Atum and the guard stumbled and fell on the table, breaking it..."

"That was fortuitous, I admit..."

"...and then Sarraj shoots Bashir..."

"Remind me to thank him," Daffyd said with a laugh.

"...and I clobber him with my chains."

"A lucky shot."

"That was the gods helping us, not blind luck. And what about your hand? Dislocated fingers should hurt like billy-o. Do they?"

Daffyd frowned and found he could now move his fingers without pain. Even the bruising and swelling had lessened. "That's odd."

"Just accept the gods were helping us."

Daffyd snorted but did not laugh. "If you say so, lass, but are you really sure Nazim had the scarab?"

"I saw it. He was going to give it to me, but you yanked me away before he could."

"Hmm, so if the scarab is still in Nazim's possession, how did it influence this Evans chap? I thought that you had to have it close for it to work."

"So did I."

"Can you still feel it?" Daffyd asked. "Can you still make it work?"

Dani put her cup down and concentrated, reaching out with her mind, feeling for the familiar texture of the scarab's presence. "It's not there," she said in a stricken voice. "Or rather, it is there, very faintly, but I can't grasp it with my mind."

"Don't stress out over it, lass. It came when you needed it--it'll come again."

Evans returned, brandishing some small metal tools. "This should do the trick." He looked in the pot and dribbled a few sips of cooling stewed tea into a cup and dashed it off with a sigh. "Once we have these chains off you, we'll head out for a bite to eat."

Daffyd picked up the tiny tools and examined them. "What are these?"

Evans winked. "Some people might call them burglar's tools. They all have other uses of course, now...let's see." He seated himself comfortably and picked up the tools, inserting them gently into the lock on one of Dani's handcuffs. The metal clicked and scraped against the mechanism.

"That actually works?"

"Shh." Evans was not looking at the tools, but rather listening to the faint sounds and feeling their resistance against the tiny tumblers of the lock mechanism. "Ahh, there..." One handcuff sprang open and he moved on to the next. He took less time to spring this lock and only minutes more to free Daffyd.

"I could have made a living at this," Evans said with a grin.

"So what is it you actually do?" Daffyd asked, rubbing his wrists where the metal had chafed them.

Evans looked around and slid a slightly battered looking business card out from the pages of a book where it was keeping his place. He slid it across the table. "Nicholas Evans Esquire, freelance journalist, at your service."

Dani looked at Daffyd. "This could be just what we need," she said quietly. "Blow this thing wide open."

Daffyd considered her words. "Go public, you mean? Force them to be honest?"

"As we originally planned in Damascus."

"This sounds rather interesting," Evans commented. "Go public about what, if I might ask?"

"Mr Evans..."

"Nick, please."

"Nick then...I'm afraid we haven't been totally honest with you."

"You mean you're not Welsh?"

Daffyd grinned. "You think I'm putting this accent on, boyo? That's not our secret."

"Our names aren't Marjorie and William Jones, Nick," Dani said. "We're not even married."

"Well, I'm broadminded."

"Nick, I'm trying to tell you something. Will you just shut up and listen?"

Nick said nothing--just smiled.

"My name is Danielle Hanser and this is Daffyd Rhys-Williams..."

"By George!" Nick leapt to his feet, dropping his cup. "The Syrian account? Scarab and Smenkhkare?"

Now it was Daffyd's turn to leap up. "How the devil do you know about that?"

"It's a long story."

"We've got the time."

Nick nodded. "I'll tell you, if you'll tell me your story."

"So you can print it?"

"That's what journalists do, but I'll run the finished article past you first."

"Then, Nick, you have a deal," Dani said. "Now, you said something about getting a meal? I'm famished."

Chapter Thirty-One

Colonel Sarraj handed over the search to the local police at sunset. The bazaar had been closed down and scoured amidst sporadic rioting and violence, and house to house searches conducted in all the neighbouring streets, without result. Another call had been received from General Gamal in Cairo, and the tone of the conversation deteriorated markedly when the general learned that Sarraj was still pursuing the fugitives against his express advice. Gamal made it plain that he would brook no further recalcitrance on the issue, and ordered the colonel to terminate his involvement in the pursuit of the fugitives and fax his report on why he had deserted his regiment to him by the following morning.

Sarraj seethed at this order and cast around for ways of delaying the inevitable. Unless he could find a very good reason for not faxing the report, Gamal might order him back to Cairo, just when the location of the tomb might be within his grasp. Al-Din had hinted at a discovery concerning the tomb, so a week or two might see enough gold in his hands to launch his coup and then it would be Gamal's career in danger. He called Lieutenant Azib to him and posed a question.

"What military threats are imminent in this region?"

"Er, none, sir." Azib looked perplexed and wondered what he could have missed. "None that I know of, sir," he amended.

"Find something."

"Sir?"

"I need a reason to be incommunicado for a few days, but I cannot just invent a reason. If, however, there was an official report of trouble, I could investigate..." Sarraj paused and looked at his aide. "Have that report on my desk within the hour, so I can fax it through to Cairo."

"Yes, sir," Azib saluted and left, his face screwed up with worry.

Fifty minutes later, he laid a manila folder in front of Colonel Sarraj. It contained a single sheet of paper with an outline of an attack made on the Kharga Oasis by armed Bedouin two days before. The commander of the Kharga garrison had, despite suffering the loss of several men and all communications, managed to sneak a message through the hostile forces. What made this attack more than a simple case of clan rivalry was the sighting within the attacking party of a known agent of the Free Officers Movement--a revolutionary organisation within neighbouring Libya. This Movement was opposed to Libya's King Idris, and in light of the friendly relations between their countries, the commander felt some military response was called for.

Sarraj scanned the report and nodded. "Nobody in their right mind would believe this, but it will do. Send it through to General Gamal and tell him I have taken a squad of soldiers out to relieve Kharga. Tell him I will have this report, and the one he asked for, faxed through to him when I return--probably a week or ten days. When you've sent the fax, disable the machine, and have a technician route all calls from General Gamal straight through to my telephone. No one else is to speak to him--it is a matter of State Security."

He sent for Lieutenant Al-Din and quizzed him about the discovery Bashir had made. Al-Din could shed no light on the matter though, saying he had been asked to pass a message on, no more.

"I think you will have to see the Minister, Colonel."

Sarraj thought of sending for Bashir, but decided he did not want him back at the army barracks from whence his prisoners had escaped. He took Al-Din with him and made his way to the hotel. Bashir and his secretary were in the minister's room, poring over maps when Sarraj arrived.

"You've found something?" Sarraj asked, wasting no time on small talk.

"Perhaps. Tell him, Nazim."

"You will recall that the description spoke of a streak of green and a notch in the cliff top as pointers to the tomb?"

"I remember. What of it?"

"It was a mistranslation. The symbol for 'notch' and the one for 'pylon' are similar, so it appears we are really searching for a pylon on the cliff top."

"What is a pylon?"

"A temple gateway--a man-made structure."

"That should be easier to identify."

"Unless it has crumbled into ruins," Nazim said. "There are no existing pylons on the cliff top in the region we've been looking at, but we've identified three places where they once existed." Nazim pointed at the map. "One here, just north of Edfu, used to be a small temple to the goddess Nut, this one a little south of Esna, thought to be dedicated to Min, and a possible site a little north of Esna--a shrine to Khepri."

Sarraj studied the map. "You said before that the region between Esna and Edfu was the most likely place for the tomb. That encompasses the pylons to Nut and Min. the other is outside the area. You agree?"

"That was my thinking," Bashir said.

"Then we should move on this quickly, before the Englishwoman can."

"Dr Hanser? I doubt she's going to be a problem. She's probably in hiding somewhere, afraid to show her face. She is here illegally, with no funds and no backing. What can she possibly do?"

"There is another reason for haste," Sarraj said. "My superior in Cairo is nosing around. We must find the tomb quickly or I will be unable to help you."

Bashir regarded Sarraj coolly. "I daresay we could manage."

"Do not even think of reneging on our deal, Ahmed," Sarraj said softly. "You provide the location, I provide the logistics, remember? Equal shares."

"Of course, Michel. I only meant...I wouldn't dream of cutting you out. We need each other."

"So what's needed now? I want to move on this quickly."

"A team, with jeeps. The regions above the cliffs are generally inaccessible except across the desert. We will need a fully equipped expedition, leaving from either Edfu or Esna, depending on which site you think is most likely."

"Who can say?" Sarraj looked at the map again, noting the presence of roads and the nature of the terrain inland from the maps. "Start at Edfu and work our way north, I think. I'll call the garrison there and tell them to have a squad and a half-track waiting for us in the morning. We'll take the launch up overnight."

"That quickly?"

"If we cannot find it in a week, it may be too late."

*   *   *

Dani and Nick swapped stories in a little café near the bazaar while Daffyd sipped his tea and listened. Nick took copious notes in shorthand and asked many questions. From time to time, he would say something like, "Do you have a photo of this?" or "What do you think is the significance of that?" and even once, "You really believe that's what happened?"

To this last question, Dani replied, "If I had the golden scarab with me, I'd prove it to you."

"Would you, by George? You could do that? It answers to you?"

After Dani and Daffyd had eaten as much as they could, they repaired to Nick's hotel room with fresh pots of tea to finish off the stories and discuss what they meant. Dani sat cross-legged on the bed, while Nick and Daffyd sat in armchairs, the one writing rapidly and the other making comments to enlarge on the tale Dani spun. A while later, as she was finishing up a description of Amarna, Daffyd glanced at his watch.

"It's nearly closing time at the museum, lass," he murmured.

"Is that significant?" Nick asked.

Dani explained how they had become separated from their friends, and how she had left a note for them in Edfu, to look for them at opening and closing times in Luxor. "We should go and meet them, if they're there, but the police are out in force."

"I could go," Nick said. "The coppers don't know me...on the other hand; Your friends don't know me and I don't know what you're friends look like either."

"Hmm, both about middling height, five nine or ten. Marc's got a bushy chestnut beard, hair a bit darker, light complexion, usually smiling, Muammar's clean-shaven or maybe with a thin beard, dark hair. Both were wearing khaki shirts and trousers when we last saw them. I suppose if you're in any doubt, speak English--tell them Dani sent you."

Nick departed for the museum, while Dani and Daffyd took advantage of his absence to use his bathroom--bathing properly and washing their hair for the first time since they left Edfu. They chatted while they cleaned up, saying how good it would be to see Marc and Muammar again and what their plans for the future might be.

"First up--find the tomb," was Daffyd's opinion.

"I hate to leave Luxor now that I know Nazim has it," Dani said.

"We know that Bashir will be heading there, if he can find it. Presumably Nazim and this army fellow will be going too, so the scarab won't be staying in Luxor."

"I really only came to Egypt to retrieve the scarab. I'd be quite happy to leave her tomb in peace, but with Bashir after it, I suppose we have to do something to prevent him."

"So we either follow them to it, or try and beat them to it. Either way, I don't see how we can stop them plundering it."

"We'll think of something, but I'd like to get there before Bashir."

"Unfortunately, we don't have our direction finder scarab."

"I think I can probably find the tomb," Dani said, "Even without the golden scarab. Remember how I said it was west of here when we were on the ferry? I think that's true, so if we can go back there, we can find the starting point of our quest."

"You know where we were on the river?"

"Roughly. Enough to start our search."

The door opened and Nick entered, his face glum.

"No sign of them," he said. "I hung around the entrance, watching everybody leaving. I even asked a couple of people, without success. There were a few people standing around, even a couple of rough-looking fellaheen, but nobody that resembled your chappies."

"Damn," Dani said. "I really hoped they'd be here by now."

"There's no guarantee they've even got the message we left with the imam in Edfu," Daffyd said. "Too many things could go wrong--the imam forgot to send it to Sukrah, Muammar didn't make it to Edfu, they're on their way but ran out of money, had an accident..."

"Or my letter never got to even the imam," Dani concluded. "Hafiz turned us in to the army colonel, so his apparent helpfulness was just an act. Perhaps he just destroyed the letter."

"All of which puts us in a quandary. Do we wait indefinitely for them to turn up, or do we strike out for the tomb immediately?"

"By George," Nick said. "You actually know where the tomb is?" A look of boyish excitement flooded his florid countenance. "I don't suppose I could tag along? I wouldn't be in the way and...and discovering it would be a great climax for your story."

"It could be dangerous," Dani said. "We know Bashir is pretty ruthless, and if he sniffs gold in the tomb, who knows what he might do."

"And there's desert travel involved," Daffyd added. "Have you ever been in the desert? It can be pretty disagreeable."

Nick grinned. "I'm an investigative journalist. I've lived rough from time to time, chasing stories in wild places. And I've faced down bigger villains than Bashir."

"In that case we'd be happy to have you along," Dani said with a smile. "As for when--I hate to leave without Marc, but I think we'll have to. We can't delay if we're to get there ahead of Bashir."

"We could stay another day," Daffyd said. "That would give us another three opportunities to find Marc and Muammar--opening and closing tomorrow, and opening the day after."

"Just our luck, they'd arrive an hour later."

"I say, I've just had an idea," Nick exclaimed. "Look, I know the Director chappie at the museum--Dr Karim Zewali--I could probably persuade him to post a note on the door for your friends. You could tell them where to go next. Sort of like a treasure hunt game, but for real."

Dani considered this idea for a few minutes and then nodded. "Can you get me in to see this Dr Zewali? It's not that I don't trust you, Nick, but I'd like to talk to him myself."

"I think I can do that. I'll recce the place again tomorrow at opening and if your friends don't turn up, I'll make an appointment with Zewali."

They ate that night at another secluded restaurant in one of the quieter streets after Nick checked out the area for police presence. A quick meal later, they were back in Nick's hotel room where they bunked down on the floor--or rather, Daffyd did. Nick graciously gave up his bed to Dani, and slept in the bath. The following morning, they breakfasted early--at yet another café ("no sense in being seen too often at one place," Nick said)-- and then Dani and Daffyd waited impatiently while Nick checked out the museum once more. He was gone longer this time but returned alone.

"Not a sausage, but I got you an appointment with Zewali at eleven o'clock."

"You'd better be careful out there on the streets," Daffyd said. "The police are still out in force."

"A spot of disguise is called for, I think," Nick said. "How do you feel about hijab and veil?"

"I've no objection to that if it'll get me through the city," Dani said, "But I'll need the whole outfit. A hijab with my western clothes would look odd."

"Or you could wear a full burka," Daffyd said. "You could be wearing anything under one of those."

"Let's not go overboard, old chap. A burka is fine for the really straight-laced societies like Saudi Arabia, but a hijab is fine for Egypt. Even a veil isn't necessary, but you'll need it to keep your face hidden."

"Waste of a damn nice face," Daffyd muttered.

Evans went out again, returning half an hour later with an ankle length skirt, a baggy blouse and scarf, and a hijab. He laid them out on the bed with an apology.

"I had to guess at the sizes, but too big is better than too small. You can wrap the scarf around your lower face and with a pair of dark glasses; nobody will be able to recognise you."

"They'll be fine, Nick. Thanks. Keep a tab of what we owe you, we'll pay back every penny."

"Nonsense," Nick cried. "This story will make me a prized commodity. It's a pleasure to be of service."

With half an hour to spare, Nick ushered a muffled Dani out into the streets, bidding her walk ahead of him to the museum.

"The police are looking for a man and woman, so let's not make it easy for them. I'll be behind you, keeping an eye out for the local bill."

"Won't it look odd for a woman to be walking alone?"

"In other Muslim countries maybe; not so much in Egypt. Go on, I'll be right behind you and I'll catch up once we're inside the museum."

They made it to the Luxor museum without incident, even passing close to a pair of policemen who barely spared Dani a glance. Once inside the doors, in the cool, dark atrium, she removed her dark glasses and freed her face from the scarf while Nick approached the clerk behind the desk.

"We can go straight up," Nick said, returning to Dani's side. "I'll introduce you, then you can talk in private if you want."

Zewali admitted them to his office and Nick made the introductions. The director waved them toward chairs and sat behind his desk, regarding Dani with thoughtful eyes.

"So you are Dr Danielle Hanser of Midland University and late of the British expedition to Syria," Zewali stated. "I have heard a lot about you."

Dani smiled nervously. "All good I hope?"

"Very little of it, truth be told, Dr Hanser."

Dani's smile was replaced with a frown. "What have you heard?"

"Minister Ahmed Bashir has spoken of a discovery in Syria that is of great interest to the Department of Antiquities here in Egypt. I made some enquiries and found that the leader of the expedition that found these remarkable chambers had been deported from Syria for despoiling them. Now I find that she is in Egypt, and I am concerned that not content with her depredations in Syria, she is now intent of discovering the tomb alluded to in the inscription, and intends to loot it. What do you have to say, Dr Hanser?"

"I, and my team, were deported from Syria, but on trumped up charges by Minister Bashir. We had found chambers which contained an account revealing the presence of an undiscovered tomb and treasury. We intended to reveal the inscription to the world and institute an open joint search for the tomb, but Bashir confiscated all the evidence and blackened the names of everyone on my team. I believe he has come to Egypt to find the tomb and plunder it. I have come to retrieve an object he stole from me, to expose him, and to prevent him despoiling Egypt's heritage."

"Can you prove any of this?"

"No, but I hope you will watch Bashir. Sooner or later he will seek out the tomb and you will have to act fast to prevent its destruction."

"I can back up some of what she says," Nick said. "I went to Midland University and talked to other members of the expedition, and then to Damascus where I talked to people I know there. They warned me about Minister Bashir. It seems his charge of despoliation was based on his personal word and he offered no evidence. From what I have seen of the man here in Luxor, he is not to be trusted."

Zewali considered the two statements carefully before answering. "Based on my own investigations, and what my colleague Mr Evans says, I'm inclined to believe you, Dr Hanser. Why have you come to see me?"

Dani glanced at Nick, who smiled encouragingly. She took a deep breath and put her future in Zewali's hands. "I'm in the country illegally and what documentation I had was stolen, so I'm limited in what I can do. Two of my companions--Dr Marc Andrews and Muammar al-Hadi--have become separated from us but I have sent word to them that we should meet outside the museum at opening and closing times. Now I have learned that Bashir and his associate Colonel Sarraj are about to set off for the tomb, so I must leave immediately if I'm to get there before them. That means I cannot wait for my friends to turn up. I would like to leave a note at the museum for them, but of course, I need your permission to do so."

"You know where the tomb is?" Zewali asked.

"I think so."

"The sun's rays through the cliff top pylon illuminate the shining crown of Scarab's green mountain in the desert."

Dani went pale. "Where did you read that?" she whispered.

"Bashir's secretary, a Mr Manouk, came to see me. He brought with him photographs of an inscription and wanted to know if the original translation he had was accurate."

"And you told him what it really said?"

"Incompletely. He withheld things from me--for instance, he refused to disclose the significance of the scarab symbol, so I did not disclose what I believe to be the true interpretation. He knows about the pylon though, and the shining crown of the green mountain."

"He could find it with that information."

"As could you, Dr Hanser." Zewali paused, before continuing diffidently. "May I ask how you translated that passage? I found out a bit about you and I know that Egyptology and hieroglyph translation is not your speciality. I would defy anyone to get a true meaning from those symbols without years of study."

"I'm not sure I can give you a satisfactory explanation."

"Please. I'm interested."

"It...it just seemed right."

"Just seemed right? Yet you rattled off a lengthy translation as if you'd been born with an understanding of hieroglyphs?"

Dani smiled nervously. "I don't know what else I can say, Dr Zewali. You say you've looked into my professional life and saw that I don't have the expertise to translate passages fluently, but I did so anyway. So, it's either 'just seemed right' or you posit something else like reincarnation or possession."

Zewali ventured a small smile at her words. "I don't believe in reincarnation, and you don't appear to be possessed of a djinni, Dr Hanser, so I suppose I must accept your rather lame explanation."

"You'll let me leave a note for my friends?"

"Answer me one thing first. You are about to chase off after the tomb alone..."

"I'll be going too," Nick said.

"And a friend of mine," Dani added.

"All right. Three of you go out with the intention of stopping Bashir from looting the tomb. How are you going to stop him? Colonel Sarraj, as a military man, has many men at his disposal, and a reputation as being ruthless. If you balk these men, I fear that you will find yourselves in lonely desert graves. I would not like to have your deaths on my conscience."

"I...I am not without resources."

"I'm sure," Zewali said, "But I would like to add one more resource. Take me with you on this quest for Scarab's tomb. Where you are just an ordinary citizen--and an illegal one, at that--I have an official position and Sarraj would think twice before doing away with me. Furthermore, it is only proper that the Department of Antiquities takes part in any search for ancient artefacts."

Dani considered the offer for a few moments and then nodded. "You would be very welcome, Dr Zewali. Will you then let me leave a note for my companions?"

"Write what you want and leave it at the front desk. I will have a man stand outside for an hour either side of opening and closing, and who will ask anybody who approaches whether they are Dr Andrews or Mr al-Hadi. Will that suffice?"

*   *   *

"They have gone to Luxor," Alif said.

"How?" Zufir was tired and angry, having led his men through a hot day, following the bus north along dusty roads to the town of Esna. The men they looked for had not been at the bus station, and once more the Bedouin leader had sent his men out searching for any sign of them.

"They took the river ferry," Alif reported back. "A man answering the description of our cousin, together with an infidel disguised as a peasant boarded it. It left barely an hour ago."

"Then we must follow," Tahir declared. "When is the next one?"

"Tomorrow at dusk, but who will care for our beasts when we are on this boat?"

"We will not take the ferry," Zufir said. "We rest and eat tonight, and in the morning we ride north until we are opposite this city. Then we shall take a boat across leaving our camels safe on the western shore. I would have them close at hand."

Chapter Thirty-Two

S arraj's expedition--there was no longer any pretence that Bashir was in charge--left the Luxor docks in the early evening, carrying the minimum of equipment. Lieutenant Jamal al-Din was left behind. Bashir could see no use for him and told him so, but Nazim worked to soften the blow to the man's pride.

"Who knows what we may yet need on this expedition," Nazim said. "You look after our interests in Luxor, so be prepared to come to our aid at a moment's notice."

The colonel had radioed ahead to the Edfu garrison to have two half-track vehicles equipped and provisioned for two weeks in the desert and a dozen men on stand-by. Acceleration pinned them in their seats as the launch captain opened up the engines and sent the craft flying upriver with scant regard for the safety of others on the river.

Bashir and Nazim slept in their seats, the former peacefully and the latter once more beset by dreams of terrible beings. Sarraj dozed intermittently, dreaming of the coup now almost within his grasp, or waking to stare hungrily at the dark river stretching out before them. Had the colonel possessed a bit more romance in his soul, he would have appreciated the crystal points of a star-washed heaven reflected in the rippling waters as wavering ribbons of light and the yellow man-made glimmers scattered along both shores as the launch swept past small villages and sleepy towns, past fields and palm groves, past scrub and bare rock.

Hours slipped by like the miles of rippling water. They passed Esna and, as the stars wheeled and faded in the early morning sky, the launch captain cut their speed. The exhaust burbled noisily as he guided the craft in toward the docks at Edfu, where an army officer waited with a handful of soldiers. He shaded his eyes against the dawn light flooding over the river.

"Captain Massri, Colonel." The officer saluted. "I have a vehicle to take your party to headquarters."

"Good. Everything is ready?"

"Yes, Colonel. There is also a message for you from an Ali Hafiz in Luxor. He says..." Massri consulted a piece of paper, "...the woman has been found. He awaits instructions."

Sarraj nodded. "You will place a telephone and a secure line at my disposal immediately."

"As soon as we get back to headquarters, Colonel."

Bashir and Nazim had been standing within earshot. Nazim fussed with the small amount of luggage they had brought but stopped at the mention of the woman. He sidled alongside the Minister and whispered.

"Woman? Does he mean Dr Hanser?"

"How should I know? Or even care. We don't need her any longer."

At the army headquarters, they were greeted by Major Arafa--the commanding officer--who found it hard to restrain his curiosity. He saluted and showed Sarraj into his office while detailing Captain Massri to see to the accommodation of the other personnel.

"What's this about, Colonel?" Arafa asked.

"Nothing to be concerned about, Major. I just need a squad of your men for a week or two. There is no problem, I trust?"

"None sir. Everything is in readiness. Er, may I enquire...?"

"Absolute secrecy, Major." Sarraj made a show of looking around, and lowered his voice. "I don't want it even breathed outside this room as to my destination."

"Of course not, sir. Er, where are you heading?"

"Good man. If asked, even you don't know. Now, you have a secure telephone line?"

The major excused himself and the army receptionist put Sarraj through to Luxor on a secure line.

"You have news for me, Ali Hafiz?"

"Yes sir. Yesterday, while assisting the police in the search for the escapees, I saw the woman, disguised, walk into the Luxor museum, followed by a European man who was not her usual companion."

"Do you know this man?"

"No. He was dressed in a tropical suit and seemed at ease. Knowing that the woman might recognise me, I waited a few minutes before entering the museum. They were not in sight, but I made enquiries, and found that they had an appointment with one Dr Karim Zewali, the Director. They were with him for about an hour before leaving. I followed again and they led me to a small hotel near the bazaar. I watched, and they emerged with her original companion and had a meal at a nearby café, after which they returned to the hotel."

"You have done very well, Ali Hafiz."

"Thank you, sir. What are your instructions?"

Sarraj considered the woman and her companion--companions--and debated whether they were a danger to his expedition, or whether they were of any use. He told Hafiz to hold and bellowed for Major Arafa, telling him to fetch Nazim Manouk to him immediately. While he waited, he had Hafiz recount whatever information he had on police activities, especially whether they were likely to find the fugitives themselves.

"I would have to say it is unlikely," Hafiz said. "Unless they happen upon them by accident while in a café. The police are of the opinion the fugitives have left the city already."

Nazim arrived and Sarraj covered the mouthpiece with one hand. He left the secretary standing. "This description you have of the track to the tomb--how certain are you of its accuracy?"

Nazim hesitated. He knew he had enough information to guide them to the tomb--perhaps--once they found the pylon, but he did not want to reveal that just yet. There was still a chance he might be able to cut both Sarraj and Bashir out, so he temporised.

"I cannot be certain, but I believe the pylon is the start of the track. Once we find that, we might be able to work out the rest."

"How is it that you identified the pylon when this Hanser woman, a supposed expert, could not?"

"There is a strong possibility Dr Hanser misled us in an attempt to safeguard the tomb."

"Why would she...? Never mind. How did you find out she lied?"

"By chance, Colonel. I saw a symbol in the Luxor temple that translated as pylon and I remembered it was the same as one in the Scarab inscription. I consulted a man at the museum who confirmed it and..."

"What was his name?" Sarraj demanded.

"Zewali," Nazim said. "Dr Karim Zewali..." His voice trailed off as he saw a tide of anger sweep across Sarraj's face. "What is wrong, Colonel?"

Sarraj shook his head, mastering his anger. "Dr Hanser escaped into the city, as you know, and I have been looking for her, so far without success. What is your opinion? Do we need Dr Hanser any longer? Can you find the tomb without her? Without this golden scarab she spoke of?"

"The ancients believed in the power of the scarab as a magical object, but we are modern men and know the truth of Allah. I don't think Dr

Hanser knows any more about how to find this tomb than do I. You may as well call off the search, Colonel."

"You are confident you can find the tomb?"

"Yes, providing we can find the starting point--the pylon."

"And Dr Hanser doesn't know where it is?"

Nazim hesitated only an instant. "How could she? By her own admission she has never been to Egypt before."

Sarraj considered Nazim's words for a few minutes, weighing his options. He was surprised to find the telephone mouthpiece still in his hand and spoke into it.

"You are still there?"

"Yes, sir."

He covered the mouthpiece again and dismissed Nazim, before collecting his thoughts. "Ali Hafiz, it seems the woman is surplus to requirements. I want you to silence her and her companions--the Welshman, this new companion she has found, and Dr Zewali, as quickly as possible."

Hafiz was silent for a few moments. "I presume you mean, 'permanently silence', so I must ask whether you desire their demise to be public or hidden. The British are no problem, accidents happen to tourists, but for a prominent person like the museum director, questions could be asked. Will I have the protection of the police?"

"No, you won't, so make sure it looks like an accident."

"May I use other men to help me?"

"I will leave that up to you, Ali Hafiz, but you must ensure their silence afterward. No hint of this can be traced to me."

Sarraj hung up and sat in silence for a while, wondering if he had done the right thing. It hinged on whether Nazim had told the truth about his ability to find the tomb from the description. If he was in any doubt, he would have asked that the search for the woman continue. She was the only other person--except possibly this Zewali person from the museum--who might know more. If that was the case, it was imperative that they be removed from the equation if they could not be bent to his will. He had formed the opinion that the woman would rather die than help him reach the tomb. Sarraj could not take the risk that, with the woman at large, she might beat him to the prize. *I will let no one best me. My destiny is within my grasp at last.*

*   *   *

The expedition left Edfu an hour later, rolling north in two vehicles--a jeep with Sarraj and Bashir as passengers, and a half-track with Nazim and Captain Massri, and ten soldiers in the back. Both vehicles were driven by men experienced in desert conditions. Although Sarraj did not envisage any deep desert travel, it was best to be prepared.

Their route lay along paved roads at first, then onto dirt roads that climbed the escarpment and eventually onto untracked stony desert that swept inland from the crumbling edge of the cliffs. Sarraj consulted the map marked with the approximate positions of the ruins of the known pylons and spoke to the driver of the jeep, pointing out the general direction. Every hour, he would call a halt and they would take compass bearings on known landmarks, plotting their changing position on the map. By mid-afternoon, they were at the first site--or at least where the map indicated it should be.

"I don't see anything," Bashir said. "Are you sure this is the spot?"

"That's what the map says," Sarraj grunted. He got down from the jeep and stretched his legs.

Nazim joined them and scrutinised the map. "On this scale, we could be right on top of it or as much as a quarter of a mile off."

"That's no use to us," Bashir complained. "How do we find it?"

"We know it's a ruined pylon from a small temple to one of the old pagan goddesses, but even if it's a total ruin we should still be able to recognise its traces. Worked stone or mud brick--maybe no more than foundations or a pile of rubble."

"I can't see anything like that."

"Perhaps, Minister, if you were to join us out here, we might be able to find it," Sarraj said.

"I thought that was why we brought the soldiers." Bashir fanned himself with a clipboard. "It's very hot."

"Then the sooner we find it, the sooner we can get out of here."

Sarraj ordered the men down from the half-track and organised them in a line in front of the vehicles. Strung out a few paces apart, they shuffled toward the cliff edge with heads bent, searching the ground for any sign that men had worked the rocks there. When they reached the cliff edge, or as close as was reasonably safe, they moved north a little and wandered inland again, making sure that every square foot of ground was covered. Back and forth they shuffled, slowly working their way north.

Bashir dropped out early, complaining of sore feet and thirst, followed by Sarraj. The rest kept working, stopping every hour for a drink and to reform the line. Colonel Sarraj now sauntered behind the line, snapping out reprimands if he thought a man strayed from a straight line or was paying insufficient attention. Dusk started to fall, and Sarraj saw that they had advanced close to half a mile north of their starting point. It was already getting hard to see, so he ordered the men back to the vehicles.

Nazim marked the spot they had reached in the search and followed the men back to where they were setting up camp. Major Arafa had provided the expedition with tents and cooking stoves, fuel and food, and even a cook, who now prepared a palatable meal from the army rations. They ate and then sat with cups of coffee, cigars and cigarettes, the men apart, talking and joking, while the captain sat with his colonel and his guests, in almost total silence. A stiff breeze blew up, feathering the flames of the fire that heated another pot of coffee and the men brought up rocks to form a low protective wall around the fire.

"I had no idea it would be this difficult," Bashir said, shifting uncomfortably on the rock-strewn sand. "The map says it's here, so why can't we find it?"

Sarraj said nothing, just drew on his cigar and blew a cloud of smoke up into the cold night air. Captain Massri kept silent too, not wanting to enter into any discussion with the Minister, so it was left to Nazim to provide an explanation.

"The map was made some thirty years ago, Minister, and the positions of landmarks depended on the skill of the surveyors with theodolites. Small discrepancies multiply, and when something is a ruin to start with, it is easy to be imprecise. Indeed, if the pylon is no more than a foundation, its position on the map may rely more on guesswork than accurate surveying."

Bashir muttered something that nobody was interested enough to ask about, and silence fell over the little group. They listened to the murmur of voices from where the men sat. A stone fell from the rough wall surrounding the fire and one of the men got up, wrestling the straight-sided stone that had fallen back into the gap. Nazim stared for a moment, then got up and wandered over. He squatted and ran his hands over the block.

"Where did you find this?" he asked. Captain Massri joined Nazim at the other fire, watching him curiously.

The men fell silent and one of them cleared his throat. "Over there." He indicated the direction with a jerk of his thumb.

"Show me."

The soldier looked at Captain Massri and the officer nodded. "Show him, Private Hassani."

Hassani rose to his feet and scooped up a torch, striding out into the darkness with Nazim on his heels. Massri followed, as did a couple of the other soldiers; several torch beams soon wavered in the desert darkness, probing the litter of rocks.

"It was somewhere here," Hassani said, sweeping his torch beam around. "I weren't noticing exactly where; just looking for decent rocks."

Nazim started searching the area, and directed the others to do likewise. They cast back and forth and were soon rewarded with a cry of triumph from Captain Massri.

"I've found something. Is this what we're after?"

Nazim knelt beside a block of sandstone half-buried in the sand and brushed it clean, sweeping the grains away from its sides. Another block lay below it, a third beside the second, with crumbling mortar loosely joining them. Nazim sat back and regarded the blocks with a grin.

"That's just what we're after," he said. "Private Hassani, Captain Massri--I think you've discovered the pylon."

The discovery spurred Bashir into action and, when faced with Sarraj's reluctance to do anything further until morning, cajoled and pleaded until the Colonel agreed to let the men work, provided they volunteered. Surprisingly, nearly half of them did, jokingly talking about digging for buried treasure. They worked with torches and shovels, clearing the sand away from what were slowly revealed as the foundation stones of a small pylon. Nazim carefully sketched the outline, and with the help of a compass, oriented it to the cardinal points. The gap between the two 'towers' was the gate, he explained to Captain Massri, and it pierced the brick wall with an east-west orientation.

"Imagine two truncated pillars with a horizontal crosspiece--rather like the capital 'H' of the western alphabet. The sun would rise within that notch, and if we stand looking west, the rays should illuminate the object of our search," he said. "Providing this is the one we seek," he added.

"It is," Bashir declared. "I feel it in my bones."

"It could just be the entrance pylon to a small temple or shrine," Nazim said. "In which case, the only thing that would be illuminated would be the sanctuary of the god."

The men slept, while Bashir and Nazim kept watch, too excited to sleep. As dawn approached, they woke the others and silently stood in the place where the gate had been, backs to the east and stared impatiently at the dark desert stretching away before them. The sun rose, staining the clouds along the horizon gold and pink. Shadows fled as the light of the sun blazed out along an uneven horizon, flinging the shadows of the waiting men westward through the pylon gate.

"Where is it?" Bashir asked.

"Where's what?" Sarraj said. "What are we looking for?"

"Anything," Nazim murmured. "Everything."

They watched until their shadows shortened, and Bashir uttered a derisive snort, returning to the campsite stamping his feet and beating his arms about his body to ward off the chill of the night air. Sarraj joined him, pouring coffee from the pot sitting in the freshly ignited fire.

"So it's not this one," Sarraj said. "We move on to the next."

"We're not even sure what we're looking for," Bashir grumbled.

Nazim went over to the jeep and pulled out the map, tracing his finger westward from the pylon position, following the contours of the land. Bashir and Sarraj brought their mugs of coffee over and watched him as he worked.

"There was one other thing I noticed in the inscription," Nazim said. "Where Dr Hanser said a 'green streak' which made us all think of vegetation, the account could easily read 'green mountain'. That's what I'm looking for--Jebel Akhdar--but I can't find one."

"I've never heard of one," Sarraj agreed, "But maybe we should ask a local." He called Captain Massri over. "Are any of your men locals? Do they know of a Jebel Akhdar? A green mountain?"

Massri went off to ask and came back a few minutes later. "Sorry, sir. Nobody's heard anything about that. One man says there's a Jebel Shabah in the desert somewhere that has a reputation for being haunted."

"Ghost Mountain?" Sarraj asked. "That's got nothing to do with our quest. Have the men eat, and then pack up. We leave within the hour."

"Leave for where?" Bashir asked.

"North to the next site of course. There's nothing here."

"Shouldn't we investigate this one further? We might be missing something."

Sarraj turned to Nazim. "Well, you seem to be the knowledgeable one--are we missing anything?"

Nazim ignored the venomous look Bashir sent him. "I don't think we are, sir. My understanding of the translation indicates the sun rising through the pylon illuminates the green mountain. Yes, I know..." he hurried on, "...there is no green mountain, but the ancients must have meant something by it. I feel confident that when we look through the right pylon we'll see something unmistakable."

"How did you become so knowledgeable all of a sudden?" Bashir asked, glaring at his secretary. "You were just the note-taker, and now you're translating hieroglyphs and identifying pylons and green mountains. What else are you hiding?"

"Nothing, Minister. I just did a little research, asked a man at the museum about the identity of one or two pictograms, and kept my ears and eyes open."

"You showed strangers the inscription? What were you thinking of?"

"One person, and only a fragment. Where is the harm? We now know about two features we would never have known otherwise."

"I suppose that is so," Bashir grumbled. "But you should consult me about such things."

"You were busy, Minister."

"The man he talked to at the museum was a Dr Zewali," Sarraj said.

"That is correct, Colonel. He seemed to know what he was talking about."

"I'm sure," Serraj said dryly. "This same Zewali has been talking to the woman."

"Dr Hanser? How do you know?"

"I have my own sources of information."

"This is serious," Bashir said.

"Zewali is also connected with the Department of Antiquities and they take a dim view of anyone else getting involved with tombs."

"Will he be a problem? Or Dr Hanser?"

Sarraj smiled. "No. Now, we are wasting time, and it is many miles to the next site."

The two vehicles resumed their slow journey northward along the lip of the western cliffs. As long as the desert remained stony, they had little trouble, though the suspension of the jeep suffered from the bouncing and lurching over and around boulders and steep-sided gullies. The half-track had fewer problems, grinding its way over and through obstacles, though its pace was slow. Then they came to a stretch of soft sand blown by the westerly winds right to the edge of the cliffs. The jeep became bogged down, sinking to its axles. They dug it free and had the half-track haul it out before resuming their slow passage.

A second time the jeep got stuck, and an hour later, again. Sarraj stood on the bonnet and surveyed the low dunes ahead of them before shaking his head.

"We'll have to go around this stretch. There should be solid rock west of us."

They turned aside, making slow progress out of the sand, and once they reached stony desert once more, headed west, skirting the borders of the sand. It cost them a day and a half, but they eventually made it back to the cliff top and continued north. The site of the second pylon lay ahead of them, now no more than a day's travel away.

Chapter Thirty-Three

Ali Hafiz hung up the telephone in the Luxor army barracks, from whence he had contacted Colonel Sarraj. He thanked the switchboard operator and left the barracks, heading for his favourite café, which by chance was in line of sight of the museum. Sarraj had given him a task--not a difficult one, but one that would require some planning. Hafiz had no qualms about killing people; it was sometimes necessary in his line of work. He ordered a cup of coffee and croissants and sat down to think.

He considered his targets. The two doctors from England were known quantities and neither seemed troublesome. The florid-faced Englishman in the stained white suit was an unknown but appeared to be just a middle-aged westerner without any claim to fame, while the museum man was an academic and probably a pushover. Hafiz felt relatively sure he could kill them all by himself. His favoured method of despatch was the gun, but he was equally comfortable with knife, garrotte and explosives. Poison he disdained as being a cowardly form of attack.

Hafiz sipped his coffee and nibbled his buttered croissants, idly watching the people passing on the street. The museum would be opening soon, and a few tourists were already gathering on the steps of the building.

A bomb would be safest. I could set it and be far away when it went off. Except the Colonel requires it to look like an accident. What else then? A shooting is going to look deliberate, so perhaps I could tamper with the brakes of a car...but whose car? The museum director's? How can I guarantee they will all be in it? Further, how can I guarantee that an accident would be fatal?

The museum doors opened and the tourists flocked in, eager for a sight of the exhibits. One of the museum guides came outside and stood on the steps, scanning the surroundings as if looking for someone. Hafiz frowned and shifted his chair slightly so he was sitting deeper in the shadow.

Is he looking for me? No, I am being foolish - how could he possibly know about me? He dismissed the man from his thoughts. *It will have to be the gun then...or knife...but I must make the killings unremarkable. A mugging perhaps? Even a mugging would look suspicious if four people were killed in one incident. Could I induce them to separate? To kill them in pairs, perhaps? Or bring in someone else...*

The museum guide walked across to a man leaning against the museum wall and spoke to him. They exchanged a few words before the guide resumed his watchful position and the man wandered off.

Who is he waiting for? Hafiz considered the people he knew in Luxor--people in his line of work who would be happy to shed a little blood in exchange for a few pounds. *There are one or two. So, how to arrange it? I could just follow them, hoping for an opportunity, but that may never come. I must lure them, but what would bring them to a place of my choosing, unsuspecting?*

The guide approached two fellaheen who stood near the steps and spoke with them at length before turning back to the museum, the men following him inside.

At least he has got what he wanted. As to bait...perhaps their companions who must surely be dead in the desert. The woman thinks she left a letter for them--well, let's say I can make her believe they survived, that the letter was delivered and they came to Luxor. They would come to the museum as instructed. Something niggled at Hafiz's mind, but he thrust it away, following his thoughts. *Why would they not come to the museum? Police presence? They send the woman a message to meet them at the docks...at night. She comes, we are waiting...it is finished.*

Hafiz considered the bare bones of the plan. *It could work, but how would this Mr Marc know where the woman was, if they did not meet outside the museum as arranged? Leave it for now, I will think on it. She comes to the docks...I must find a suitable place--near the warehouses perhaps--with the man, but not the florid man or Zewali. I deal with those two first, and then return to the hotel and kill the others.* He reached a decision, drained the cold dregs of his coffee and dabbed at the croissant crumbs on his plate with a moistened fingertip, before rising and slipping out of the café.

*   *   *

As Hafiz hurried off toward the docks, the two fellaheen came out of the museum, one of them clutching a sheet of paper and, with smiles on their bearded faces, set off in the opposite direction. They worked their way through the streets to a small hotel, where they looked at the sheet of paper again, and then at each other, before entering and climbing to the third floor, and room eleven.

Nick opened the door and his eyebrows lifted slightly as he recognised the peasants he had seen outside the museum. "I think I have some friends of yours inside."

"Marc? Is that you?" Dani called from inside the room. "My God, get in here at once."

Daffyd shouldered past Nick and wrapped Muammar in a fierce embrace, thumping his palms on the man's back. The Libyan looked startled, and then grinned, returning the embrace. Daffyd turned back into the room where Dani and Marc were hugging and slapped his friend on the shoulder.

"We thought you were dead, boyo. That bastard Sarraj hinted as much."

"Tosh, Dafs," Dani chided. "I knew they weren't, whatever he said."

"You got our letter then? I wasn't sure if you would after that snake in the grass Hafiz turned us in. I thought he might have destroyed the letter instead of giving it to the imam."

"He tried to," Muammar said. He went on to explain the fortunate turn of events that had led to the delivery of the letter and their journey to Luxor.

"How have you been living these past few days? If your cousin could only lend you a little money?"

"Hand to bloody mouth," Marc said. "I looked for signs of you and Bashir during the day, while Muammar earned a pittance as a porter to enable us to eat. We slept rough."

"All down to that bugger Hafiz," Daffyd said.

"Indeed, Hafiz has a lot to answer for," Muammar said. "I look forward to our next meeting."

"Ditto that," Marc growled. He turned away and sneezed.

"Are you all right?"

"I'm fine. Just a bit of a cold."

"You just stay clear of Hafiz," Dani said. "With any luck we'll never see him again."

Marc jerked his head toward Nick, who had closed the door and stood watching with an amused smile on his face. "Who's this?" he whispered.

Daffyd made the introductions, and Nick shook hands with Marc and Muammar. "Pleased to meet you," Nick said. "Er, I know it's a bit presumptuous of me, having just been introduced and all that, but would you call me Nick rather than this dreadfully formal Mr Evans? I tend to look over my shoulder expecting to see my father when anyone says 'Mr Evans'. These two delightful people have made me thoroughly welcome and a friend of a friend and all that..."

"Happy to, Nick," Marc said, "Provided you call me Marc. This here is Muammar." They all shook hands again.

"Well, now that that's all out of the way," Dani said. "What do we do next?"

"Are we still heading off today?" Daffyd asked. "Dr Zewali will be expecting to hear from us."

"Heading off?" Marc asked.

"Dani's figured out where the tomb is, so we're heading off to beat Bashir to it."

"And who's Zewali?"

"Director of the museum. He's coming with us as the official part of the group. We're all illegals, remember?"

"Except yours truly," Nick murmured.

"Fine, but can I get some grub first?" Marc said. "I'm bloody famished."

"A bath and clean clothes would be much appreciated too," Muammar added.

They left the two young men to get cleaned up, while Dani and Daffyd went to buy food, and Nick plumbed the bottom of his shrinking wallet to buy some basic clothing. Dressed and cleaned, the two of them sat in Nick's room and ate steadily from the dishes of food brought up from a restaurant, while the others sat around and watched them.

"I 'phoned Zewali," Nick said. "He recommends waiting until tomorrow morning, rather than leaving this afternoon and having to camp on the western bank."

"Good," Marc said indistinctly, dipping a crust of bread in the gravy of a rich lamb stew. "I could do with a good night's kip in a decent bed. Speaking of which..."

"I think I'll have to rent another room," Nick said. "We can't all squeeze in here."

"Can you afford it?" Daffyd asked. "You've been damned generous and we've got no way of paying you back until we get back home."

Nick nodded. "As long as we don't splash out on luxuries. I'll wire my agent for an advance on an article that'll blow his socks off. I'm sure he'll cooperate."

Nick went off to wire his agent while the others spent pleasant hours in the hotel room catching up on the events of the last few days. The young men told of their narrow escape in the desert, first from Hafiz and then from hunger and thirst.

"It's the first time I've eaten bugs, and believe me, it's the last."

"It was a strange rock formation," Muammar said. "We owe it our lives--a water seep where I wouldn't have expected one, a cave, and the rocks at the top full of sparkly bits..."

"Mica, I think," Marc added.

Nick, who had just arrived back, spoke of his surprise at running into Dani and Daffyd in the street. That led to their story and they told of their betrayal by Hafiz and the start of their interrogation by Sarraj and Bashir.

"Who is this Sarraj?" Marc asked.

"An army colonel," Daffyd said, "But why he's interested is anyone's guess."

"I know him," Muammar said. "Or rather, I think I know of him. There is talk within army ranks in Libya of an Egyptian colonel who has his eyes on the Presidential palace. Sarraj's name was mentioned, though nobody is prepared to swear he is the one. Nasser succeeded not so many years ago and he was a colonel too. Now, maybe, there is another one prepared to risk all for a great prize."

Dani went on to describe their escape against all odds from the army barracks. Marc was particularly intrigued that Dani thought Nazim had the golden scarab in his possession.

"I genuinely think he intended to give it back to me," Dani said.

"But why?" Marc asked. "If he viewed it as a worthless rock he wouldn't keep it, and if he knew what it was there's no way he'd be handing it over."

"If he's intent on handing it back, he'll try again," was Nick's opinion. "I hope he does; I'd really like to see this fabulous object I've heard so much about."

Daffyd grinned. "You might see it, but not really see it."

"Stop teasing the man, Dafs."

There came a knock on the hotel door and Nick went to open it. One of the hotel porters handed him a slip of paper. Nick shut the door and turned to the others, a faint crease of puzzlement on his brow as he perused the words on it.

"I say, Dani, do you know of another Marc Andrews in Luxor?"

"No. Why?"

"This is a note from Marc. Did you write it?" Nick held out the piece of paper.

Marc scanned it. "This is bloody nonsense. Listen. 'Dear Dani, we have arrived in Luxor as per your instructions but we are unable to meet you at the museum as arranged because of a police presence. Please meet us tonight at ten o'clock at the warehouse on Al-Obouri Street. Come only with Daffyd. Yours, Mark Andrews.' Honestly, does that sound like me?"

"It does sound a bit formal," Daffyd conceded. "What with the 'Dear' and 'Yours'..."

"Not to mention the 'as per your instructions'," Dani added.

"And why would I sign myself 'Mark Andrews? How many other Marcs do you know? And he miss-spelled it too--with a 'k'."

"So who sent it?"

"Bashir or Sarraj. Trying to recapture us," Dani said.

"I doubt it," Daffyd said. "If they knew we were here, they'd just send the police to come and arrest us. Besides, they told us Marc and Muammar had died in the desert. They'd scarcely use their names as bait, even if they knew it wasn't true."

"Who else then? Who knows about the rendezvous?"

"Hafiz," Daffyd stated. "Us two, and Ali Hafiz. He read the letter we left for them in Edfu and believes them dead in the desert so he thinks he can use their names as bait."

"Indeed, it must be Hafiz," Muammar said. He bared his teeth in a snarl. "I will go in your stead, Dr Hanser, and he will get more than he bargained for."

"I'm going with you," Marc added. "I've got a score to settle too."

"I'd strongly recommend ignoring it," Nick said. "Look, he's an unknown quantity, and from what you said earlier, he's proficient with a gun. Even if you surprised him, all it takes is one stray bullet and one of you is dead or injured. Even if you aren't, the police will get involved and you're illegals. Then your quest is over before it starts." Nick smiled to take away the sting of his words. "Besides, you owe me a bigger story than a waterfront mugging."

"You'll get it," Dani said, returning Nick's smile. "And nobody's going to this meeting. I'm not risking my friends over some silly idea of revenge. He's not worth it."

"Damn it Dani," Marc said. "He tried to kill us and turned you over to Bashir. We can't just let him go."

"We've got more important things to worry about--like our quest. First thing tomorrow morning we're off to stop the others plundering Scarab's tomb. I won't let anything get in the way of that."

"How did he know you were here?" Nick asked quietly.

"What? Who?"

"This Hafiz chappie. How did he know Dani and Daffyd were here at this hotel, in this particular room? He didn't just send a note to every hotel room in the city."

"He's right," Daffyd said. "And that means if we don't go to meet him, the next thing that'll happen is he'll be round here looking for us. Whatever he means to do, he'd rather it was done in a dark, secluded street, but if he can't have that, my guess is he'll settle for this room."

"Then we can't stay here," Dani exclaimed.

"Or we eliminate him," Marc growled.

"Like I said before," Muammar stated.

"I think we've got to do something, lass," Daffyd said. "We're caught in a bit of a cleft stick."

"We could go to another hotel."

"Insufficient funds, old chap," Nick said. "At least, until my agent wires me some readies."

"We could leave anyway, even if we had nowhere to go. If he can't find us, he can't do anything."

"And what if this Hafiz chappie is watching the hotel?" Nick asked.

"If I see him, I'll nobble him," Marc said.

"And if he's hired some thug to watch the hotel? He'll just follow us and report back to Hafiz."

"I'll go and see him--alone," Dani said. "He may not mean us harm. He may have some other motive."

"There's no way you're seeing him alone, lass," Daffyd said. "Besides, he asked for me too."

"And Muammar and I are going as back-up," Marc declared.

"He'll spot you and disappear."

"Unless you go back to being simple fellaheen," Nick said with a grin. "If he never spotted you around the museum, your disguise must be good. He'll never suspect a couple of lounging peasants."

"And what's your role, Nick?"

"Me? I'll be there to cover the story. Lots of action and excitement, don't you know?"

They debated just what they were going to do, how they were going to approach Ali Hafiz and how they were going to get the better of him. Marc pointed out that they had numbers on their side.

"We're four to one--five to one if you count Dani."

"Just you try not counting me," she muttered.

"And if he has accomplices?"

"Then we'll just have to deal with them too."

"He'll have a gun."

Marc shrugged. "We still have to deal with him."

Muammar enquired about the possibility of buying a gun. He explained that his people were usually armed and knew how to use firearms. Even a pistol would lower the odds, he said. Nick explained that even if they had the money to buy one, he had not the faintest idea where to look for it.

They talked about other possibilities--threatening him with a steak knife filched from a café, finding wooden staves or even rocks, a coil of rope to tie him up--but could reach no real conclusions.

"I think we're going to have to play it by ear," Daffyd said. "We can't know what's possible until we see the situation."

"Let's just hope it's not too late by then," Marc muttered.

At eight o'clock, Marc and Muammar changed back into their fellaheen clothes and slipped out of the hotel, trying to look as inconspicuous as possible. They would make their way down to Al-Obouri Street and saunter along its length with Muammar chattering inconsequentially in Arabic. If they spotted Hafiz, they'd attempt to keep him in sight but, on Dani's insistence, promised not to take any overt action until the others turned up.

An hour later, Nick, Dani and Daffyd walked out of the hotel quite openly and turned in the direction of the warehouse. A street or two later, Nick bade them a loud farewell in case they were being watched, and turned down a side street. As soon as he was out of sight, he doubled back and observed Dani and Daffyd walk into Al-Obouri Street.

The street was well-lit at either end, street lights casting bright pools of light over road and pavement, but in the middle, near a number of cliff-sided warehouses, the road disappeared into inky blackness, the darkness alleviated only by the faint orange glow of the surrounding city. Their footsteps sounded loud on the pavement, far louder than the hum of nightlife that leaked through the gaps in the buildings, the sound echoing off the warehouse walls.

"I don't like it," Daffyd murmured. "We're too vulnerable."

They moved away from the buildings, walking in the open road, searching the darkness on either side for any sign of Hafiz, hoping that the first they knew of him would not be the flash from the barrel of a gun.

"Stop right there, Miss Hanser."

Ali Hafiz's voice emanated from a pool of darkness between two warehouses. Dani and Daffyd automatically turned to face their enemy and as they did so, they heard stealthy footsteps behind them. Daffyd turned but men leapt from the darkness and pinioned Daffyd, and a moment later, Dani. A shadow detached itself from the pool of darkness and stepped out into the road.

A match scraped and a tiny flame flared, dimly illuminating the faces of Hafiz and Dani. "Thank you for coming," Ali Hafiz said. "I wondered whether my subterfuge would succeed."

"Why are you doing this?" Dani asked. "How have we harmed you?"

"It is nothing personal, I assure you, but my employer, Colonel Sarraj, wants you dead for reasons of his own. I am only obeying orders."

"Ever the excuse of the weak-willed," Daffyd said.

"Ah, Mr Williams." Hafiz turned toward Daffyd, dropping the match and lighting another one. "I regret to say your fate is tied to that of Miss Hanser."

"I wouldn't have it any other way. You all right, Dani?"

"So solicitous," Hafiz murmured.

"You really don't want to be doing this, boyo."

"Indeed? Why not?"

"Because you don't know who you're dealing with. Why do you think we weren't surprised when you turned up instead of Marc and Muammar? We know they're alive because they were with us when your note arrived."

The match dimmed and died, though not before Daffyd saw the consternation on Hafiz's face. Hafiz fumbled another match out of the box and scraped it into life.

"Well, I have men round there now to take care of that other Englishman and the museum man. Your friends will die with them...as, I'm afraid you must too. Miss Hanser, I wish it could have been otherwise, but I can at least grant you a swift and relatively painless death."

Hafiz shook out the match and lit another one, holding it in his left hand. With his right, he drew out a snub-nosed revolver.

"Are you a man of faith, Mr Hafiz?" Dani asked as the man raised the gun. The man holding her shifted awkwardly to one side to allow him a clear line of fire.

"Yes...ah, I see, you want to pray. Granted, but make it quick."

Dani slumped forward, her guard slackening his grip on her and, as the match in Hafiz's hand sputtered and died, she shook her arm free and slammed her elbow out and up, connecting with her guard's chin. He staggered back, and she kicked out, the toe of her shoe slamming into Hafiz's wrist, the gun falling with a clatter to the ground.

"Get her!" Hafiz yelled, dropping the box of matches. "Kill them both."

Dani turned, and kicked again, this time into the knee of one of the men holding Daffyd. The man uttered a cry of pain and lashed out blindly at her, Daffyd taking advantage of his release to grapple with the other man. They fell to the ground gouging and punching. Dani ducked under the first man's swinging arm and drove her stiffened fingers upward, lancing into his body beneath his ribcage. The man screamed and doubled over. Behind her, in the darkened street, she could hear the sound of running feet and her heart sank, believing more of Hafiz's men were coming to his assistance.

"Marc!" she called. "Where are you? I need you."

"I'm here." Two shadows loomed and cannoned into Hafiz, knocking him backward and the man that Dani had elbowed. Both went down, and Muammar tripped over the elbowed one and fell beside Daffyd who was still struggling with his opponent.

"Dr Rhys-Williams, is that you?" Muammar said breathlessly.

"Of course it's bloody me, boyo. Get this brute off me."

"Er, which one is you?"

"I'm underneath. Hit the bugger. Ow...'

Muammar complied, driving his fist into the man's temple and thumping the half-stunned man's head into the road.

Marc finished off the elbowed man, knocking him senseless and then moved to the doubled-over body of the remaining thug. He cracked his head against the road, and in the ensuing silence gasped out, "Bloody Hell."

"Where is Ali Hafiz?" Muammar asked.

Receding footsteps echoing from the warehouses told of his retreat, and they saw his fleeing figure in the light of a distant streetlight. A figure in faded white moved to intercept him and Hafiz dodged, metal glinting in his hand.

"Nick! Watch out!" Marc yelled, but Dani was already running, racing toward the circling men.

Hafiz swept the knife in his hand toward Nick and Nick batted at the blade with his notebook. He leapt back as Hafiz moved in again, thrusting with the blade. Nick cried out and clutched his arm, dropping his notebook and staggering back, and Hafiz, all thoughts of escape forgotten, moved in for the kill.

"Hafiz!" Dani called, running up behind.

Hafiz swung round, his eyes widening in surprise as he saw a woman running toward him. He grinned as he recognised Dani, dropping into a crouch with his blade held in his left hand, low and to the side.

Dani did not hesitate, closing fast and falling to one side as the knife swept round. She was on her feet in an instant, her eyes never leaving her opponent's face. He slashed again and she danced back, aware from the sound of running feet that her friends were approaching. Hafiz heard them too, and knew he must finish it quickly. He stabbed, feinted, tossed the knife to his right hand and slashed at Dani's belly as she swayed to that side. The blade ripped through her shirt, scoring a shallow cut across her ribcage, the ends of the fabric flapping free.

Dani stepped back, her left hand clutching her bloodied chest and then she stripped off the ripped garment, flinging it to one side as Hafiz moved in. His eyes flicked to follow it--just for an instant--and she stepped through his guard, grasping his right wrist in her left hand and bringing the heel of her right hand sharply up under his nose. She heard the bone crack, the knife clatter to the road surface and felt the tension leave his body as he slumped to the ground. Dani stood over him, breathing hard, as her friends gathered round her.

"How the hell did you do that?" Marc exclaimed.

"I am in awe, Dr Hanser," Muammar said quietly.

"You're hurt?" Dani asked Nick.

"A scratch. And you?" Nick looked away from her shirtless torso.

"The same."

Nick squatted beside Hafiz and felt for the pulse in his neck. "He's still alive, but I think he's got a fractured skull. He's going to need a hospital pretty quickly."

"Leave the bugger to die," Marc growled.

"No," Dani said. "We call an ambulance but make sure we're gone before they get here." She picked up her ripped shirt and draped it around her shoulders, tying the loose ends together to keep it in place.

"And we need to warn Dr Zewali. Remember Hafiz said he'd sent men to kill him."

Nick, Muammar and Marc hurried off to find a telephone, while Dani and Daffyd followed more slowly. Daffyd cast many sidelong looks at his companion, maintaining a respectful silence, until Dani could stand no more.

"What, Dafs? Why are you looking at me like that?"

"I didn't know you were a martial arts expert."

"I'm not. The most I've ever learned to do is kick a man in the shins if he got too familiar."

"Then how did you take down a man with a knife, let alone disarm him of his gun and disable the man holding you? I've never seen anything like it."

Dani was silent for several paces. "Truth be told, Dafs, I don't know. It...it just seemed like the...like the right thing to do. I sort of watched myself do it and...and now I might have killed someone." Dani stopped and turned to look back down the darkened deserted street to the distant body lying under the street light. "Oh God, Dafs, we should go back. I should own up to this."

Sirens sounded faintly from the city, getting louder, and Daffyd tugged at Dani's arm. "Be sensible, old girl. It was self-defence; he meant to kill you--kill us all. The ambulance is on its way and if anything can be done, they'll do it. If you get involved, they'll chuck you out of the country or jail you and then what happens to Scarab's tomb? Bashir wins. You don't want that, do you?"

"No. No, you're right. Scarab comes first." She turned and ran into a side street, with Daffyd on her heels, as a police car, siren wailing, turned into Al-Obouri Street.

*   *   *

"They are in Luxor," declared Tahir. "This very night I saw Muammar al-Hadi in the company of four infidels."

"Four?" Zufir queried.

"Yes. The three we seek and another one. They fought with three men who attacked them on the street."

"They live?"

"Yes. Ah, my brothers, you should have seen how they fought."

"Our cousin acquitted himself well?"

"Moderately, but the woman..." Tahir shook his head. "If I had not seen it with my own eyes I would not have believed it of any woman. She fought like a lioness and killed a man."

"That is hard to believe indeed, brother," Zufir said. "Unless she was armed and the man not?"

"The other way round. He had a knife and she had nothing--yet she prevailed."

The other Bedouin uttered cries of disbelief and outrage.

"Clearly, this infidel woman is worthy of closer examination," Zufir said. "When we recapture them I shall find out the truth of it. In the morning, we take the ferry over the river--all of us--and take them, bringing them back here. Then we shall see what we shall see."

Chapter Thirty-Four

S arraj's men arrived at the presumed site a little south of Esna in the late morning, three days after setting off from the pylon foundations of the temple of Nut. They had no difficulty identifying this pylon as the trunks of the pillars still stood above the desert sands. The ruins of the temple of Min showed only as fragments of foundation and low walls almost submerged by desert sand. The Colonel and Bashir, with Nazim tagging along behind, got out of their vehicles and stood in the ruined gate, gazing westward.

"I don't see anything," Bashir said. "This can't be the right one either."

Sarraj nodded, but turned to Nazim. "What do you think? Is there any evidence that this is the right one?"

"None that I can see."

"Then we move on to the next."

"What? The one north of Esna?" Bashir asked. "That's the least likely. We missed something at the Edfu one; we should return there."

"It may be that we can see nothing because it is the wrong time of day," Nazim said. "We waited for the dawn at the last one."

Sarraj stared at the secretary. "That's because we found it in the middle of the night. We had to wait until morning to see anything." He saw a glint of impatience in the man's eyes and added, "Isn't it?"

"We had to wait until morning to see what we had found," Nazim confirmed. "But that's not all. The whole point of the pylon, the notch in the horizon, is to have the sun rise within it. It seems logical to assume that the rising sun must display some feature that leads the seeker on the next step."

"Such as?" Bashir asked.

"We won't know that until we see it, Minister, but I suspect it has something to do with the green mountain."

"Which we know isn't here."

"Nevertheless," Nazim said. "I feel we should wait and see. We have nothing to lose."

"Except time," Bashir said. "Dr Hanser could even now be on her way to the tomb. We must make sure we beat her to it."

"She knows no more than I do," Nazim declared. "Though if Dr Zewali starts investigating..."

"He won't," Sarraj said smoothly. "Any more than the woman will. I have taken measures."

"What measures?"

"Nothing that you need to be concerned with, Ahmed. We have a bit of time, and we should be certain we have exhausted the possibilities of one site before moving on to the next. Captain Massri?"

The officer hurried across and saluted.

"Have the men set up camp. We wait for dawn."

The night passed as the others had passed. Bashir and the officers kept largely to themselves, and mostly in silence, each lost in their own thoughts. The soldiers were more convivial, joking and laughing, happy to be out in the field but with little in the way of onerous work. They got to sit in the back of the half-track all day, catching up with sleep or smoking, and had, at the most, only light tasks when they stopped. If anything taxed their minds and bodies it was boredom.

Sarraj was conscious of the passing days, but already they had eliminated one of the sites and the dawn would bring a decision on the second. If this one failed, then it could only be the northernmost one--the least likely one. He calculated distances and times, and knew that he was gambling his future on this venture.

Bashir openly fretted at the inactivity, impatient to get his hands on the riches of Smenkhkare's tomb--and Scarab's if it really existed. Descriptions of the king's treasury were alluring and stimulated his greed, but he knew that he would have to move fast to secure it once it was found. The good colonel would prove invaluable, but it was a pity that so much gold must be relinquished to secure his services.

Nazim's thoughts were more cerebral, and he stayed awake longer than the others. Partly this was because of the nature of his thoughts; partly because he feared sleep. The dreams had returned in full force, perhaps exacerbated by the lonely wastes of the desert, but even closing his eyes conjured up visions of the old gods--*demons*--of ancient Egypt. Lions and green men wrapped in grave clothes, animal-headed terrors and the night sky curdling like sour milk, the land splitting and giving forth its dead, all terrified him, but the visions vanished when he opened his eyes. Losing himself in sleep was more dangerous and he gave into it only when exhaustion compelled him.

"It's the golden scarab," he muttered. "What else can it be?" Nazim looked around to see if he was overheard but Sarraj and Bashir were asleep. Captain Massri was awake, but on the far side of the fire, apparently oblivious of Nazim's mutterings.

A chill wind from the desert interior scattered red-gold sparks high into the air where they competed with the cold, white points of fire piercing Nut's body. *Why did I think that?* The breeze brought the aroma of coffee and the sounds of laughter from the soldiers' fire, sounds and smells of a normal human presence and Nazim sighed with longing.

He took the rock out and cradled it in his palm, attempting to look past the fire's glow on sandstone to the rich gleam of gold. For a moment he thought he saw it, and then it became a plain rock again, no different from a million others scattered over the desert around him.

"I should just throw it away, into the darkness. I'd be unable to find it again, even if I wanted to...but then it would be lost to everyone. It isn't mine--I should have given it to Dr Hanser when I had the chance. Then those...things...would leave me alone." He slipped it back in his pocket and scrunched himself a more comfortable position in the rock-strewn sand. *Perhaps we'll beat Dr Hanser to the tomb and I can just leave the scarab there for her to find later. Is the description really enough to find a tomb lost for three thousand years? Are we all deluding ourselves?*

Nazim thought back to his conversation with the museum director. He had said that the inscription might possibly read of Aten's horizon arrow showing the road through the desert from the cliff to greet the green mountain crowned in crystal--or possibly glass, or even gleam or shine.

"Ignore for a moment the absence of a green mountain anywhere in Egypt," Nazim muttered. "He is saying that the sun's rays shining through the pylon show the road to this place which...which is what? Green mountain or mountain of green? Green rock or green vegetation that makes it green? And what of the crystal crown? Does that mean it is made of crystal or glass? Or just shines..." Nazim frowned. "The sun's rays gleam on the top of the green mountain? It doesn't make sense." He thought a while longer, bringing the hieroglyphs to mind and ticking them off mentally against every aspect of Zewali's translation.

"What then, is the scarab? Is it because this is Scarab's tomb, or something else? Scarab's green mountain or...or..." *It cannot have been her tomb, because when the description was first given in the chambers, she was still a young woman with no thought of her own death and burial.*

Nazim considered the symbol for the Aten--the cartouche-enclosed feather, water, half-disc and centred circle--and the scarab symbol itself. "Where is the scarab placed? Is it with the symbols for green and mountain? No, it is near the symbol for the horizon, the notch, the pylon. Scarab's pylon? Why? What is the significance? Scarab, Aten, Re, Khep..." He sat up suddenly. Captain Massri called out in a low voice, concerned, but Nazim ignored him.

"The first pylon was dedicated to Nut, this one to Min, but the third was to Khepri--the sun god Khepri--represented by the sacred scarab. Not the woman called Scarab, but the pylon dedicated to Khepri. This pylon is not the one. We are wasting our time here."

Agitated, Nazim scrambled to his feet, and then stood irresolutely, suddenly unsure of himself. *Do I say anything? Am I certain of my interpretation?* Captain Massri called out, enquiring as to whether anything was wrong.

"Yes...or rather, no. I..." Nazim shook his head and waved the captain back, resuming his own seat. "I just remembered something, but it will keep until morning. Go back to sleep."

His mind working actively, Nazim had little difficulty remaining awake for the remainder of the night, though the time passed slowly. The fires died down, the soldiers' voices quietened and were replaced with sporadic snoring. A night chill enveloped them as the heat of the day fled the arid landscape, but Nazim welcomed the cold as he considered his future course.

What do I do? Does the Minister deserve my continued loyalty or do I betray him? If betrayal, than for whom? Myself, or Dr Hanser. A jackal called, high-pitched and lonely, out in the desert darkness, and something floated overhead on feathered wings, a squeal from some wretched rodent a few moments later suggesting its identity as an owl. *Can I achieve anything on my own? I could keep silent, even at the Khepri pylon, and hope they miss whatever clues are apparent there-- but if I do, can I take advantage of them? Can I possibly gain something from this on my own?* Nazim thought again of the house at Jarabulus on the Euphrates, near the Turkish border-- the house with the large courtyard and the olive grove behind and the green fields. *I would give anything to retire to a property like that, but I need money. Gold from a tomb.* He shut his eyes and saw again the rock tomb with the twin sarcophagi, grave goods, and piled riches. Something moved in the darkness of the tomb and Nazim's eyes flew open. *No. I cannot face that alone.* He wiped the chill sweat from his brow and shuddered. *So, it comes down to helping the Minister or Dr Hanser and hoping that the one who wins will reward me.*

Without knowing it, Nazim drifted off into a dreamless sleep and only woke when Bashir's boot nudged him awake. He stared bleary-eyed at the Minister standing above him, illuminated in the early light, and scrambled to his feet.

"It is already past dawn. We are too late to see the morning rays."

"Sarraj and I looked while you slept. There was nothing."

"You should have woken me. You might have missed..." Nazim shook his head. "No, you are right, Minister. You did not need me."

The rich aroma of coffee and freshly baked flat bread made his mouth water, and he knuckled the sleep out of his eyes as he hurried to break his fast. As he ate and drank, he saw some of the soldiers rolling up their prayer mats from Fajr and felt a rush of guilt that he had forgotten God in his quest for riches.

Yet how can I approach Allah--the Merciful and Beneficent--with the taint of the ancient Egyptian demons on my mind? I must cleanse myself somehow.

"All right, pack and load up," Sarraj called. "Let's get moving." He crossed to the jeep and spread out the map on the bonnet. "Here is the third pylon. A day and a half perhaps. We'll descend into Esna and replenish our water and petrol, stay overnight, and then head up to the cliffs again and find the pylon tomorrow."

Bashir took Nazim aside. "This had better work," he said. "I assured Sarraj that one of these three pylons was the correct one."

"We must wait and see, Minister. There are only three known pylons or ruins on this stretch of cliffs, but perhaps there are others as yet unknown." He hid a smile at Bashir's look of frustration.

Sarraj guided the expedition inland, traversing stony desert until they reached the Edfu-Esna highway. Their speed increased on the main road and they made it to the river town in the mid-afternoon. While Captain Massri saw to the refuelling and resupply, Sarraj and Bashir repaired to a hotel to freshen up after several days roughing it.

Nazim was not invited so found a small hostelry near the army barracks for his ablutions. He was not sure he wanted to hire a bed for the night as he feared to sleep. After a thorough scrub down and change of clothing, he sought out a decent restaurant and enjoyed a good meal in good company--his own. He contemplated attending Maghrib prayers at a local mosque, but still felt tainted by thoughts of the ancient Egyptian gods, so refrained. Instead, he sought out a quiet spot beside the river and enjoyed a cigarette while the cool breeze off the river rustled the palm fronds. It was all very peaceful and Nazim slid into sleep without warning.

"You have that which is mine."

"Eh?" Nazim jerked around and saw a copper-skinned young man...*no, he decided, not young--old, at least in years if not in appearance.* The long stiff beard jutting from the tip of his jaw lent his features a formal, regal look, and his eyes looked as ancient as the universe. It was a few moments before Nazim realised that the man wore a dazzling white kilt, an ornate and colourful pectoral, armbands and a deep blue nemes headdress with gold ends. In his hands, the man bore a shepherd's crook and a solid gold ankh.

"Who are you?"

"You know who I am for you have seen me before. You have that which is mine. There..." The man stared at Nazim's jacket pocket, "...in your uncouth clothing."

"Y...you are Atum."

The man inclined his head in affirmation.

"Why should I give it to you?"

The ancient eyes flashed with anger. "You dare to question the gods?"

The evening was cool but Nazim felt the sweat pouring off him. "M...my god is Allah and M...Mohammed is his Prophet," he declared, feeling his heart tremble inside him.

"I forgive you your disbelief, but you ignore me at your peril. I do not seek to be your god, ignorant man. Return that which is mine, to my servant when she asks it of you, and all will yet be well."

"Your servant? Scarab?"

"Even so."

"But she is dead these three thousand years."

The god Atum opened his mouth and began to laugh. At first, the laughter was deep and booming, but rapidly deteriorated into a harsh braying.

Nazim awoke with a start and stared around him. Two young men--no more than teenagers--were pointing at him and making coarse remarks, interrupting themselves with staccato bursts of mirth. He rose to his feet and hurried off, back to the hostelry, pursued by laughter and ribald comments.

Did that happen, or was it just a dream? Either way, how do I give the golden scarab back to Scarab? Did he mean I should leave it in the tomb when we find it? Or did he mean I should give it to Dr Hanser?

340

Nazim fought against sleep that night, but in the early hours of the morning, after wrestling with his conscience, he came to a decision. He dressed and left his hostel room, searching out a public telephone, and put through a call to the Luxor hotel. The receptionist on duty was quite frosty at first, and determined he was not going to rouse one of his guests at that hour, but was eventually prevailed upon to transfer his call.

"Al-Din." The lieutenant gave a loud yawn. "Who is this please?"

"Nazim Manouk. Are you awake, Jamal? This is important."

"Yes. Yes, I am awake. What is it? What's happened?"

"Listen very carefully. There is a woman in Luxor called Dr Danielle Hanser. You must get a message to her."

"Of course, Nazim. What is her address?"

"I don't know."

There was a pause. "Then how am I to contact her?"

"I don't know...wait, yes. Go to the museum and speak to the Director, Dr Karim Zewali. He knows this woman and may well know where she can be found."

"Very well, as soon as the museum opens. What is the message I am to give her?"

"Tell her...tell her I have what she seeks and I will give it into her hands. Tell her the pylon of Khepri is the one, and that we will be there tomorrow...today. She is to take extreme care because some people will stop at nothing to achieve their ends. Got it? Repeat it back to me."

"Er, you have what she seeks and will give it to her. You will be at the pylon of Khepri tomorrow..."

"Later today."

"...sorry, you will be there later today and for her to take extreme care... uh, Nazim, should we be telling her this? I thought this woman was the...er, the enemy."

"No, we have been misled. It is vital that she gets her hands on what I have. Find her, Jamal. Find her and give her the message."

"Does Minister Bashir know of this?"

"He too is misled. I will take the responsibility for this, Jamal."

Nazim hung up the telephone and returned to his room, his mind at ease for the first time since taking the golden scarab. He slept for five hours, dreamlessly, and awoke refreshed and at peace. Sarraj and Bashir met him at the army barracks and by eight o'clock they were on the road again, winding up the track that climbed the cliffs before turning off to follow the lip northward. The desert here was rocky with firm sand and for an hour they made good time--then the jeep suffered a puncture.

Sarraj swore and ordered the men to set about repairing it, which only took a few minutes. However, a few minutes later, another tyre blew out. This time it took longer to fix as the other spare tyre was itself flat and the inner tube had to be patched and laboriously reinflated using a foot pump. The colonel fretted about the time being lost, and Bashir snarled and snapped at Captain Massri, urging him to berate his men.

"There is no great urgency," Nazim said. "We know where the pylon is and we need the dawn light to verify the next step."

"And what if we have to search for it like we had to for the first one?" Sarraj asked.

"It will not be as difficult," Nazim said. "There is a distinctive outcrop of rock just south of it and another north and west. I believe it will be simple to pinpoint."

"For your sake, I hope you are right."

They reached the southern rocky outcrop at noon and drove slowly thereafter, searching for any sign of the pylon. Time passed and Captain Massri spotted another outcrop to the west.

Nazim studied the map and confirmed this was the second one. "We have passed the pylon," he declared.

Sarraj gave him a black look and turned the vehicles around, travelling south for a while before stopping and ordering the men out to search on foot. The sun had dipped toward the west, lengthening the shadows, when a soldier raised a halloo, waving and pointing to the ground. Sarraj ran over and stood staring, his hands balled into fists by his sides.

"You've found the pylon?" Bashir asked, hurrying over.

"No." Sarraj pointed. "Tyre tracks, heading west."

"They must be ours," Bashir said. "We passed by here an hour or so ago."

"Not travelling west, you fool. Someone else has been here before us."

Bashir looked around at the desert. "It could be anyone," he said. "Why assume anything else?"

Sarraj did not answer, instead striding back to the jeep and taking out a pair of binoculars. He then looked around and clambered up onto the roof of the half-track, focussing the binoculars as he searched the western desert. After a few moments, Captain Massri climbed up beside him and, shading his eyes from the lowering sun, studied the desiccated landscape.

"There, Colonel," he murmured, pointing.

Sarraj altered his line of sight and at length nodded. "It's them."

"Who is it?" Bashir called. "What can you see?"

Sarraj and Massri jumped down, and they examined the map.

"There's nothing out there," Massri murmured.

Sarraj beckoned to the soldiers. "Who knows the area? What's out there?"

One of the men shrugged. "Jebel Shabah."

"Ghost Mountain? Not Green Mountain--Jebel Akhdar?"

"No sir."

"You've seen it? Yourself?"

"No sir. The tale I had was of a ghost guarding something."

"That's where they're heading," Sarraj said.

"Where who is heading?" Bashir complained.

Sarraj scowled at Nazim. "Somehow that woman has got ahead of us, but no matter, we can catch her. Back into the vehicles."

"Should we not find the pylon first?"

"No need. She will lead us to the tomb."

Chapter Thirty-Five

olice swarmed around the residence of Dr Karim Zewali, precluding the possibility of any of the group approaching, with the exception of Nicholas Evans. The police would tell him nothing of what had transpired, and were reluctant to let him in, until he explained that Zewali had sent for him earlier. Messages were passed along and within minutes, Zewali appeared at the front door and welcomed him. He drew him into his study and closed the door firmly in the face of the constable on duty in the house.

"Private business," Zewali said. Turning to Nick he asked after the others.

"They're fine, but what happened here?"

"A man broke in and attempted to assault me."

Nick ran his gaze over the doctor's limbs. "You're unhurt?"

"My manservant came to my rescue, suffering a cut arm in the process. His assailant died." Zewali grunted. "Ex-army--my servant, I mean. He's been taken to hospital."

"I wish we'd known earlier," Nick said. "We were lured to a dark street and attacked by Colonel Sarraj's men. They said you were being targeted too." Nick essayed a tired smile. "No harm done, except to the enemy. The others couldn't come in of course, what with the police presence, but they asked me to ask you whether it's still on for..." He glanced at his watch, "...today."

"Are we still in any danger from Sarraj's men?"

"From the ones who attacked us, no, but if we meet him in the desert, then who knows. I'm sorry, doctor, but better you understand the risks now. If you don't want to come, I'm sure Dani will understand."

"Leaving civilians to protect Egypt's ancient treasures? I'd never forgive myself if they suffered through my cowardice."

Nick looked surprised. "You'll come then?"

"Of course. Now, I have a few things to get ready, so if we can meet at the docks at say, seven in the morning, I'll have the museum launch take us across the river."

Nick re-joined the others in the shadows beyond the reach of police lights and curious bystanders. They went back to their hotel to sleep for what remained of the night, barricaded in a single room, though it was hard to relax knowing that Hafiz's men had been sent to find Nick there and may turn up at any moment.

"I had a word with the front desk," Nick said. "Two men were here earlier but went away when they heard I was out."

"Then they could return anytime," Marc said. "Should we go somewhere else?"

"I think they'll be at a loss now that Hafiz is out of the picture. Besides, they'd now face four men and a woman warrior if they did turn up."

"Even so."

"Well, I'm not losing any sleep over it," Dani said. She stretched out on the bed and fell asleep despite the presence of her companions and the lights being on.

"I'd say she's got the right idea," Daffyd murmured.

"Are you going to sleep?" Nick asked.

"I don't think I could. Has anyone got a pack of cards?"

They sent for coffee and cigarettes, though when faced with the choice Daffyd refused the tobacco, declaring that that was one life choice he had some control over. The hours went slowly, but the four men talked and laughed together, telling stories and imagining what lay ahead of them in the desert. At six, as the dawn light slid greyly round the drawn curtains, the alarm went off, and Dani woke. She looked across at the four unkempt men sitting around the small table, the scattered cards, full ashtrays and empty coffee cups and smiled.

"Been having fun, boys? Is there any coffee left?"

Nick sent down for some more, and croissants, while Dani and the others took turns in the bathroom. A hurried breakfast later, it was time to head for the docks, where they arrived a few minutes after seven to find Zewali and Dr Hosni Maroun waiting by the museum launch.

"Sorry we're late," Nick said cheerfully. "Had a spot of bother cycling four chaps and a girl through a single bathroom. Are we all set to go? Hello Dr Maroun, good to see you again."

"Good morning, Mr Evans," Maroun said. "It appears we are to travel together."

"I asked Dr Maroun to join us," Zewali explained. "His expertise will be invaluable and his position, along with mine, will lend considerable weight to our demand that any archaeological treasures discovered remain under the aegis of the Department."

"I'm not sure that's going to influence this Colonel Sarraj," Daffyd said. "Minister Bashir's an utter rotter, and from what I've seen, Sarraj isn't any better. A detachment of police or his army superior might be more effective."

"I have notified Cairo of his involvement," Zewali said, "and informed the local police of our immediate goal. I doubt he'll try anything."

"I hope you're right," Marc said. "If you're not..." He shrugged.

Dani introduced herself and her companions to Maroun.

"Ah, you are the discoverer of the Syrian inscription. Karim has told me something of what he knows, but I hope we can discuss your findings in more detail. I am intrigued by this character called Scarab. She is Princess Beketaten, I hear..."

"Perhaps we could continue this aboard the launch," Zewali said. "I think we should be making a move."

"Speaking of moving," Marc said. "I gather the tomb is in the desert. How is getting on board a launch going to get us any further than the far shore?"

"The Khepri pylon is on the cliff top, about twenty miles south of here. I have hired two jeeps which are waiting for us on the far side. We will take the road past Madinat Habu and the Valley of the Queens, up onto the desert plateau. A few hours to the pylon and maybe half a day more to Jebel Shabat."

"Shabat? Spirit? Ghost Mountain?" Dani asked. "You're sure that's the place we're after?"

"Not completely," Zewali admitted. "But it answers the description well enough, and it has an evil reputation among the more superstitious peasants. Now, I really must insist lady and gentlemen; please board the launch. We will have ample opportunity to discuss all aspects of our search."

They boarded the launch and the captain prepared to cast off for the short trip across the river, running through his last minute checks. As he was doing so, a man in a military uniform came running across the dock, waving to attract their attention.

"Oh, shit," Marc muttered. "Is Sarraj onto us already?"

"That is not an Egyptian uniform," Muammar said. "Syrian I think."

"Then it's one of bloody Bashir's men," Daffyd said. "Can we cast off before he gets here?"

"Dr Zewali!" the running man called out. "Please wait. I have an urgent message."

"We must wait," Zewali said. "It might be important."

"Perhaps it might be better if our guests remained out of sight," Maroun suggested. "This is a museum vessel, manned by museum staff. Why should it appear otherwise?"

Zewali closed the cabin door behind him and climbed over the gunwale to face the Syrian army officer as he arrived breathless on the dock.

"You are Dr Karim Zewali?"

"I am. You have a message for me?"

"Yes doctor." The man took a deep breath. "My name is Lieutenant Jamal al-Din of the Syrian Army, seconded to the staff of Under-Minister Bashir. His secretary, a Mr Nazim Manouk, asked me to pass a message on to a Dr Danielle Hanser, whom he says you know." Al-Din hesitated. "You do know Dr Hanser?"

"Yes."

"And you know where to find her?"

"It is possible I may know."

"Will you please convey to her a message?" On receiving a nod from Zewali, al-Din concentrated, obviously calling up the message he had been given from his memory. "Tell her I have what she seeks and I will give it into her hands. Tell her the pylon of Khepri is the one, and that we will be there today. She is to take extreme care because some people will stop at nothing to achieve their ends."

"That's it?"

"Yes. Do you want me to repeat it?"

"I have a good memory."

"You'll see that she gets it today? Mr Manouk said the message was urgent."

"I'll see she gets it today."

Al-Din hesitated, as if expecting a more positive response and then shrugged. "I bid you farewell, Dr Zewali." He turned and strode away.

Zewali climbed aboard again and re-entered the cabin. "You heard?" he asked Dani.

Dani wore a big smile. She turned to Daffyd and said, "You see? I knew he wanted to give it back to me. They're going to be at the Khepri pylon and I'll get it back then."

"Didn't you hear the rest of it, lass? You're to take care because some people will stop at nothing. Sarraj already tried to kill us--do you think he's going to allow Nazim to hand you the golden scarab and waltz off to find the tomb? He'll more likely try and finish what Hafiz started."

"He's right," Marc said. Muammar and Nick nodded their agreement.

"Indeed, from what you've told me, that is the most likely outcome, though I doubt he'll try anything while officials of the Department of Antiquities are on hand. There is a difference between evil deeds committed by proxy in the night, and the same deeds carried out in broad daylight in person. I think our best course of action is to find the tomb as quickly as we can and see what we can do to map its location and get the word out. Once the location is official, there's nothing he can do."

"We'll have to move quickly," Nick said. "The message was they'd be there today."

Zewali gave the nod to the captain, the crew member cast off, and the launch motor coughed into life easing them away from the docks. The captain threaded them away, through the numerous other small craft negotiating the river that was the life-blood of Egypt. Muammar and Marc went on deck, wanting to feel the cool breeze on their faces, and watch the far shore draw near. A ferry came toward them, heading for Luxor, and they watched as it approached, close on the port side. People lined the railings of the ferry, men and women both, some laden with produce, others dressed in work clothing, heading off for the day's work.

Muammar stared at the approaching vessel, alarm on his features as the ferry drew alongside. Marc, who had been idly taking in the view, saw his expression and tapped him on the arm.

"What's up?"

"On the ferry there. It's Zufir and the others."

Marc turned to look at the ferry, now receding toward Luxor. "Who's Zufir?"

"The Bedouin who kidnapped us."

"Shit. You're kidding. Did they see us?"

"I think so."

"Why are they here?"

"It seems that Zufir is still determined to get his money and has, somehow, followed us."

Marc blew a raspberry and lifted two fingers in the direction of the ferry. "Well, they're too late. They're in Luxor and by the time they've caught a ferry back, we'll be long gone."

"Let us hope so, though if they have this much determination, who can say what they will do."

The launch pulled into the docks on the western shore, and they readied themselves to disembark. Two jeeps stood waiting, and Zewali went over to meet the drivers and complete the paperwork on the hire vehicles.

Muammar drew Marc aside as they all stood on the dock. "I don't think we should say anything about seeing the Bedouin. If they did not see us, they'll lose our trail in the city. There's no sense alarming anyone unnecessarily."

Marc nodded and sneezed. "Sorry, I think I'm coming down with something."

The two jeeps sped across the narrow floodplain on the western shore, driven by the two men from the museum. Dani and Daffyd rode in the front one, driven by Zewali, and the others followed in the one driven by Dr Hosni Maroun.

"Driving the vehicle yourself?" Daffyd asked. "I thought you'd hire a driver too."

Zewali grinned, slowing as they passed the ruins of a funerary temple dedicated to Amenhotep the Third. "I'm a strong believer in equality. I should be able and willing to perform menial tasks when required. Besides, I don't want to drag innocent rental company drivers into possible danger."

The museum director pointed out the ruined Colossi of Memnon, great seated statues of Amenhotep. "There was a pylon directly behind them," Zewali explained. "We've found some evidence of that, though the temple was plundered for its stonework in antiquity."

"There were three pylons originally," Dani murmured, "Leading onto a long avenue before the Solar Court and the sanctuary. It was a glorious sight in the early morning when the sun's rays shone between the statues, poured through the pylons and illuminated the solar court and sanctuary. The walls were painted in many colours and the sunlight made them glow as if they were made of gold and precious stones. It was truly beautiful."

"I'm sure it must have been," Zewali said, "Though nobody can say for sure whether the temple was painted or gilded." He accelerated away up the road.

"I think you'll find our Dani can," Daffyd muttered.

They came to a fork in the road. Zewali pointed to the left, "Madinat Habu--the temple of Ramses the Third, but we'll go right, toward the

Valley of the Kings and Queens. Does your knowledge of Egypt stretch to the Nineteenth and Twentieth Dynasties, Dr Hanser?"

"No further than Seti, son of Paramessu," she said quietly.

"Well, no matter, the Eighteenth Dynasty is firmly in our sights today."

Te road lay north-eastward, skirting the base of the crumbling cliffs and the two jeeps took it at speed, kicking up great clouds of acrid white dust. This early in the morning, there were few people around and no tourists, though Zewali said there would be many later as the ferries started bringing them over from Luxor.

"That's the real wealth of Egypt--tourism. We need to protect our ancient treasures from the plunderers."

Zewali roared past the entrance to the Valley of the Kings, and about half a mile further on, turned up a rough track that led up onto the cliffs that surrounded the burial valleys of the kings and queens of ancient Egypt. He stopped briefly on the high plateau to allow his passengers to take in the arid desolation spread out beneath them. Incongruously, in the jumble of pale rocks and debris, were laid out rough roads, a car park, and paths delineated by concrete posts and wooden markers.

"Now that's a place I wouldn't mind visiting," Daffyd said. "It must be fascinating. All those tombs of kings and queens over centuries of time. Perhaps when all this is over?"

"You shouldn't disturb the dead," Dani said. "They're buried in these lonely places for a reason. It was quite a frightening experience for a young child."

Zewali raised an eyebrow in surprise. "You've been here before?"

"No." Dani turned and got back in the jeep.

Daffyd just smiled at Zewali's puzzled expression.

The road around the top of the valleys was long and tortuous, having to skirt so many eroded gullies and patches of soft sand, but eventually they reached a section of open desert where few vehicles had travelled before. Their speed increased, both Zewali and Maroun guiding their jeeps skilfully between boulders, jouncing over stretches of pavement rock, shattered gravel and firm sand.

"How far to the pylon?" Daffyd asked.

"A mile or two. We'll be there by noon."

Half an hour later, Zewali slowed and waved Maroun to drive alongside. "Somewhere here, I think," he called out.

Maroun slowed further and looked around carefully before pointing to the southwest. He was right, and a few minutes later they pulled up beside some half-buried foundation stones. Dani and the others got out and stretched cramped limbs, going behind large boulders to relieve themselves. Maroun set about building a small fire and brewing up a pot of coffee.

Marc looked around with a scowl and a complaint. "Sarraj and the others said they'd be here today. Why are we wasting time making coffee? We should go find this tomb before they get here." He sneezed, then took out his handkerchief and blew his nose.

"Don't worry, we'd see them coming a long way off," Zewali said. "We drivers need a break and a cup of coffee."

Dani took a tin mug of coffee and walked over to the ruined pylon, Daffyd tagging along behind quietly, leaving her alone with her thoughts for as long as he could. She stood within the gateway looking west and sipping on her coffee for several minutes before turning away with a sigh.

"What's wrong, lass? Not the right place?"

"No, it's the right place," Dani said. "It's just that things are so different now." She smiled and looked at Daffyd. "Maybe not so very different. I'm here with friends and we're being pursued by an enemy. Let's pray we have as fortunate an outcome."

Back at the jeeps, Nick drained his cup of coffee and ate the last of his biscuits. He tossed the dregs aside and turned to pack his cup away, when he stopped and stared to the southwest.

"I say, chaps, what's that?"

"A dust cloud," Marc said. "One of those desert whirlwinds?"

"It's the dust kicked up by vehicles," Muammar said. "I think the enemy is upon us. What do you think, Dr Zewali?" he called.

"I think you're right. Pack up, we're leaving."

Marc yelled to Dani and Daffyd and pointed. They came running. Maroun tipped the rest of the coffee on the fire and scuffed dirt over it, while everyone piled back into the vehicles.

"Is this the pylon, Dr Hanser?" Zewali asked, starting his vehicle. "We drive due west of here?"

"Yes."

"You don't sound very sure."

Dani nodded. "If I had the golden scarab I could tell immediately, but without it, I can only...should we wait for them? Nazim said he'd give me the scarab."

"He might have, lass, but I'll bet you Bashir and Sarraj won't let him. We need to get out of here and maybe give Nazim a chance later on. So, west of here?"

Dani nodded again. "Yes, west of here."

They set off westward through the trackless desert, their attention divided between the rough country they were passing through and the dust cloud that told of the approach of their enemies. The dust cloud inched around behind them and then disappeared, dissipating in the still afternoon air.

"They must have reached the pylon," Daffyd commented.

"With luck they'll stay there to get a dawn fix before pursuing us," Zewali said. "A day is all we'll need if Jebel Shabah is indeed our goal."

The country became rougher, with great blocks of stone upended in their path, and patches of soft sand that had to be negotiated or driven around, taking them off course. Their forward motion became slower and Dani started to fret as the sun sank toward the horizon.

"We're not going to reach it today," she said.

"Don't worry too much," Zewali said. "We're well ahead of them. They won't stir before first light tomorrow, so we'll get there at least half a day ahead of them."

"Then what?" Daffyd asked.

"Depends on what we find. Let's not get ahead of ourselves."

Maroun tooted the horn of the following jeep and gestured for them to stop. When they did, he drew alongside.

"Marc saw something back there at the pylon."

"What?"

"A flash of light," Marc said. "Like sun glinting off glass." He blew his nose and then stared toward the position of the pylon with the setting sun at his back.

"Or binoculars," Nick added. "I think we've been spotted."

"Doesn't matter," Zewali said. "We're well ahead. We continue on until dusk, and then camp for the night. If we're away at first light we'll get there well ahead of them."

They resumed their journey, travelling westward as fast as the terrain would allow. Marc, Muammar and Nick looked backward, hoping for another glimpse of their enemy's presence, praying that there was no pursuit as yet. When the light became too depleted to drive safely, they turned a little off course, stopping for the night and setting up camp behind a huge tilted slab of rock that they hoped would obscure their camp fire and hide them from their pursuers when the next day dawned.

*   *   *

"It was them, I swear it," Alif said. "Our cousin Muammar and the young infidel."

"Did anyone else see them?" Zufir demanded.

Nobody had, and Zufir paced the boards of the Luxor docks, trying to decide what to do. He looked at the bearded faces of his companions, seeing expressions of trust and fear, mixed in with avarice and frustration.

"What of the other infidels?"

"I did not see them," Alif admitted. "But where two are, the others must also be."

"Perhaps. We look for them first in their hotel, and if they are not there, we take the ferry back to the western shore. I do not know what they seek over there, but we will find them. They have the money that rightfully belongs to us."

Zufir and his men were aboard the noon ferry when it left, heading back across the river.

Chapter Thirty-Six

Sarraj's jeep leapt forward, its tyres superimposing their prints on the vehicles that had gone before. The halftrack followed, its motor roaring as it attempted to keep up with the jeep, but gradually falling behind. After half an hour, as the daylight started dimming, Sarraj ordered a halt while they waited for the halftrack to catch up. When it did, Captain Massri got out to talk with his commander. He pointed out that the light was failing and even with the use of headlights it would soon be difficult to follow the tracks.

"We must camp until dawn, sir, and overtake them tomorrow."

"Not good enough," Sarraj said. "If they get there before us, there's no telling what mischief they might get up to. We drive on."

"Yes sir...but how? We cannot follow if we cannot see the tracks, and if we use headlights, we warn them of our approach."

"Then we must take care. We follow until the light fails utterly."

They drove on, following the intermittent tyre tracks until they could no longer be sure the vague markings in the desert sand were man-made. Sarraj ordered a halt and rummaged in the back of the jeep, pulling out a large wooden box. He pried the lid off and pulled out a contraption that boasted lenses, mirrors and tubes.

"What is that?" Bashir wanted to know.

"A photocathode device," Sarraj said. "It will multiply the light over a hundred times, enabling us to travel in the dark."

"Really? How does it work?"

"I do not care how it works, only that it does." Sarraj passed it to Captain Massri. "I'm told you have used one of these before."

Massri took it and examined it. "I have used night-vision apparatus before, Colonel, but this appears to be a more ancient model. It, er, doesn't appear to use ambient light."

"What does that mean? Can you operate it?"

"More modern devices can use moonlight or perhaps even starlight as the source of illumination, multiplying the available light to enable a person to see where he is going. This particular model has an infrared transmitter instead, so we must supply the light ourselves and pick up what scatters back from the ground."

"Very interesting I'm sure, Captain Massri. Can you operate it?"

"Yes sir. We have a battery dedicated to its use?"

"In the back."

Massri attached the leads, fiddled with switches and dials, and as full darkness fell, announced that he could now see moderately well.

"It's all in shades of green, and the shadows are alternately accentuated and washed out, but I think I can follow the tyre prints."

The captain set out on foot, stumbling along at a slow pace, one hand gripping the bag that held the heavy battery, the other making adjustments to the photocathode clamped by leather straps to his head. Behind him, the jeep crept forward, its lights off, and two soldiers sitting on the bonnet with small torches in hand, guiding the vehicle so as to avoid boulders and potholes. The halftrack followed, with soldiers similarly placed, though the larger vehicle could easily extricate itself from any difficult situation it found itself in.

Massri tripped over a rock and tumbled headlong with a cry. The leads tore free of the battery and he was plunged into darkness. Torches flickered over him and in their light he managed to reconnect the leads and switch on the photocathode again. Nothing happened. He flicked switches and twisted dials, disconnecting and reconnecting wires until he coaxed a flicker of life from the instrument.

They resumed their journey, more carefully. Massri continued to stumble, particularly as he grew tired, but as the night wore on they inched closer to where they estimated their prey must be camped. Twice, Sarraj sent Massri forward to scout with the photocathode without the vehicles following up, and each time he returned saying the tracks continued onward.

"If we get too close, they'll hear us coming," Bashir said.

"I'm aware of that, you fool. Why do you think I send Massri out to scout ahead of the vehicles?"

Midnight passed and weariness overtook them all, but Sarraj drove Captain Massri to continue, knowing there was no one else proficient with the photocathode. An hour later, the captain reported that the tracks were no longer heading west, but had veered to the south. Sarraj immediately ordered a halt and complete silence, while Massri again headed out to scout the vicinity.

"They're there," he whispered, when he returned. "About five hundred yards away, behind a large slab or rock." He slipped the night vision array off his head and massaged his temples. "I'm glad to be finished with that, sir. It's given me an awful headache."

"How many men were there?"

"Seven, sir. I couldn't see enough detail to tell if one of them was a woman. And two vehicles--jeeps, I think."

"Good. We outnumber them and I doubt they are well-armed anyway."

"Do we attack, sir?"

"Not at night. I don't want any of them escaping. Have the men set up a camp. Cold rations only and no talking."

They slept in and around the vehicles, making themselves as comfortable as possible on the hard ground. A chill breeze had them huddling in blankets before dawn, wishing for a fire or the advent of the new day. Sarraj sniffed the breeze and beckoned Massri, bidding him take out two of the men and find them a location near to the other camp where they could keep watch as the dawn arrived. The captain was gone a long time, returning as the first stars started to fade in the eastern sky.

"They are stirring, sir. I think they mean to make an early start."

"We can move in the pre-dawn," Sarraj said. "Get the men up and ready to move. As soon as we can see, we'll surround them on foot."

The soldiers readied themselves, grumbling quietly and stretching limbs that were stiff after an uncomfortable few hours. Sarraj watched the east and waited. The sky lightened and he knew that dawn was not far off, but still he waited, falling back on the words of his faith--that he should wait until the white thread of day could be distinguished from the black thread of night. A few minutes more and he nodded in satisfaction. Five hundred yards to cover, time to ready themselves, and then attack. They would surprise them as the first rays of the sun pierced the horizon and illuminated the desert.

*   *   *

Dani stretched and got to her feet. It was still dark, but the eastern sky had paled, the star-studded body of the goddess Nut fading as the sun god approached. She decided there was time for a cup of coffee before she greeted the dawn, and squatted beside the embers of the fire, adding fuel and fanning the tendrils of smoke until the wood burst into flame.

Behind her, the others started to stir, some disappearing behind rocks to relieve themselves, others digging in the backs of the jeeps to roust out food and water for the coffee. Nick filled the pot with water and added a generous handful of coffee grounds, setting it on the fire. Zewali brought out flat bread and arranged it on flame-stained rocks to warm, while Maroun selected jars of spicy sauces to add to the plain bread.

"Simple fare, but delicious."

Marc unscrewed the top of one the jars and dipped a finger in, hesitantly touching the tip to his tongue. He made a face and tried another one, with similar reaction.

"I don't suppose you've got a pot of marmalade in there?" he asked Maroun. "Toast and marmalade with a nice strong cuppa would go down a treat."

Maroun smiled and rummaged in the box of supplies. "Can't manage marmalade, I'm afraid, but I can manage tahini--that's a sesame paste--with honey. Flat bread and coffee too. Will that do?"

Marc grunted and turned away. "I guess it'll have to. Hey, Dani..." He waved a hand vaguely in her direction, opened his mouth and inhaled in short gasps then suddenly sneezed twice. "Damn this bloody cold." He blew his nose. "How long to find this tomb and get back to the delights of civilisation?"

Dani said nothing--she just stared at the eastern horizon. Daffyd came up behind her and put an arm around her shoulders.

"Are you alright lass? You seem a bit quiet, a bit withdrawn this morning. Are you worried about getting here at last?"

"A tad apprehensive, Dafs." She leaned her head on Daffyd's shoulder for a moment. "I've known Scarab as a living breathing woman for the last year and a bit, and now I'm about to see her sarcophagus and the tomb where she's lain for the past three thousand years."

Daffyd nodded. "I know what you mean. It's like hearing a close friend has suddenly died."

"Look," Dani cried. "Khepri comes."

In the east, the first rays of the rising sun stabbed over the horizon. Dani lifted her arms in a salute and uttered several phrases in a language Daffyd did not understand.

"What are you saying, lass?"

"I...I said, 'Lord Khepri, you raise your beauty in the body of Nut, you light the Two Lands with your splendour'." Dani whirled and faced the west. "There! Oh look, Dafs--it's really there, just as I...she said it would be--the green mountain crowned in glory."

To the west, the rays of the rising sun illuminated a low mound rising no more than a hundred or so feet from the plateau, an unprepossessing mound except for one thing--the sun's rays were reflected back in a coruscating dazzle of light. The others heard Dani's cry and turned, staring into the west as the display flared again before flickering and dying away.

"I say, chaps, what the hell was that?" Nick asked.

"That was the crown of glory," Zewali muttered. He explained the significance to Dr Maroun. Everyone continued staring into the west as if hoping the hill top would flare into life again, but it became just another desert mound under the rising sun. One by one, they turned away, talking quietly amongst themselves.

"Scarab selected the mountain topped with the crown of glory as a suitable resting place for her brother," Dani murmured to Daffyd, "and then later, she was laid to rest there too, by Khu."

"Breakfast's up," Marc called, a few moments later. "Such as it is." He grabbed a large chunk of flat bread and a cup of coffee and wandered off with it. "You eating?" he asked Muammar as the young Libyan passed him.

"My stomach is a little upset," Muammar said. "If you will excuse me, I'll find a private place."

"Don't be long. We'll probably be leaving as soon as we've eaten." He found a handy rock and set about eating his breakfast, tearing off great bits of bread and swallowing them greedily with draughts of coffee.

Dani and Daffyd sat apart, he munching on bread and sauces, she content with a mug of sweetened coffee. Both were still dazed by the sudden revelation of Scarab's green mountain and its fiery crown.

The two archaeologists stood with Nick as he quizzed them about little-known aspects of Eighteenth Dynasty history and just what it would mean if the rest of Scarab's account proved accurate. Both museum officials were excited at the prospect and eager to reach the hill they had so recently seen, clothed in splendour.

"Speaking of which," Zewali said. "We should get moving if we want to get there before Colonel Sarraj." He threw the dregs of his coffee on the ground and turned toward the jeeps, stopping dead as a pistol shot cracked across the desert stillness, echoing off the surrounding slabs of rock. He swung to face the sudden threat.

"Everyone stay where they are."

Sarraj stepped out from behind a boulder, a pistol in his hand, and all around the little group, soldiers joined him, rifles at the ready.

Dani and Daffyd leapt to their feet, and Nick and Dr Maroun turned as Sarraj strolled toward them. Off to the side somewhere, they heard a choking sound but paid it no heed. The danger was here before them, and immediate.

"Dr Hanser, Dr Rhys-Williams, we meet again," Sarraj said. "All of you please raise your hands and offer no resistance while my men search you. If you resist, they have orders to subdue you."

The soldiers came forward and patted down each prisoner, turning out pockets and even probing boots and hats for concealed weapons. They found nothing, and withdrew, though kept their rifles at the ready.

"I protest your actions most strongly," Zewali said. "I am the Director of the Luxor Museum and this is my colleague Dr Hosni Maroun. We are here on museum business and you do not have the authority to..."

"I have the authority," Sarraj cut in. "I have had reports of bandits in the western desert and I am in pursuit of the same. Until I am satisfied as to your innocence, I must presume your guilt."

"That is utter nonsense," Zewali said. "We are museum officials, not bandits."

"Show me your papers."

Zewali and Maroun handed over their identification documents and Sarraj perused them carefully. "They appear to be in order, but it is possible they are forgeries. I will have them examined when we return to Luxor. Who is this man?" He pointed at Nick.

"He is a journalist," Bashir said. "His name..."

"Let him answer for himself," Sarraj snapped.

"As the man said, I'm a journalist. Nicholas Evans, freelance and based in London. And who might you be?"

"Papers?" Sarraj held out his hand, and after a few moments, Nick took them out and handed them across. "They will be returned when I am satisfied you are not aiding the bandits." He smiled and looked across at Dani and Daffyd. "Your papers, please."

"You know damn well we don't have any," Daffyd said.

"Unfortunate. I know you entered Egypt from Libya, illegally. Perhaps you are in league with these bandits from the western desert that I am pursuing."

"That is a ridiculous notion," Zewali said. "These are respected English academics..."

"How do you know that?"

Zewali paused and then grimaced. "They told me."

"Exactly," Sarraj said. "Well, I do not have time to waste on suspected murderers and their accomplices..."

"Where are the others?" Bashir queried.

"What others?"

"Dr Marc Andrews and their Libyan friend."

Sarraj's eyes narrowed as he looked around the camp site. "Where are they?" he demanded of Dani. She refused to answer, and Sarraj gestured toward his soldiers. "Find them."

The soldiers spread out and moments later one of them cried out to come quickly, that a terrible thing had happened. Sarraj and Bashir ran over, followed by their prisoners and the guards who had not been ordered to keep their charges away.

"This man is dead," said one of the soldiers. He looked up from where he knelt beside a man face down in the desert sand.

"Marc!" Dani screamed. She rushed forward, pushing past Bashir and falling to her knees beside the young man. "Marc, what's wrong? Answer me."

Daffyd knelt beside her, an anguished look on his face, and turned the body over. Marc's staring eyes looked out blindly from a cyanotic face, mottled and contorted. Knowing what he would find, Daffyd laid his fingers on the side of Marc's neck, feeling for a pulse. The moments dragged out and Daffyd's shoulders slumped. "Nothing, lass," he murmured. "He's gone."

"No! He can't have. Marc, wake up, damn it. What's wrong?"

"It appears your friend is dead, Dr Hanser," Sarraj said. He bent over and took Marc's limp arm, feeling at the wrist for a moment before letting it drop. "Where is the other man? Look for him. I want him found."

"How?" Dani demanded. "He was fine a few minutes ago. How can he suddenly be dead?"

Daffyd examined Marc's body, tears streaming down his face. "You poor wee boy. What has happened to you? Blue in the face, is it? Choked on something? Ah, what's this?" He gently opened Marc's mouth, reached in with two fingers, and drew out a crust of bread that had lodged at the top of his throat. "Eating too fast, or was startled," he said quietly. "What a damnable way to go."

"Mouth to mouth," Nick said. "It's worth a try."

"I've never done it. Do you know how to do it?"

Nick nodded and knelt across from Daffyd and Dani. "Boy scouts, don't you know." He cleared Marc's tongue out of the way and leaned over, sealing his mouth over Marc's. With his fingers pinching Marc's nostrils, he breathed out gently, took another breath and blew into the dead man's lungs again. Minutes passed as he repeated the procedure, and every now and then he stopped and put his hands on Marc's chest, pushing down to massage the heart. Eventually, Nick leaned back on his heels and shook his head, wiping the sweat and tears from his eyes.

"I'm sorry. He's not responding. There's nothing more I can do. He's gone."

"He's dead?" Dani whispered. "Truly?"

Daffyd put his arm around her shoulders, hugging her to him, comforting her.

"It's my fault," she said, sobbing. "I should have prevented him from coming with me. I as good as killed him."

Chapter Thirty-Seven

S arraj's men returned from a sweep of the area, and Captain Massri reported.

"No sign of the Libyan, sir. We scoured the area out a hundred yards but there was no trace of him."

Sarraj shrugged. "No matter. There's nothing a single unarmed man can do. He's probably just run off. Now, get this man buried and have men bring up our vehicles. The tomb awaits us."

Daffyd drew Dani to her feet as two soldiers pushed in to carry Marc. Two others took shovels out of the halftrack and cast about for a suitable grave site.

"Can't you take him back to Luxor?" Zewali said. "He should at least get a proper burial."

"I can't spare the time or men," Sarraj said. "We either give him a shallow grave here or nothing at all. It's all the same to me."

Nazim had said nothing since Sarraj's men had captured the scientific party. He had stood to one side and watched the unfolding events, as horrified as any when Marc's body was found. Now, as the soldiers started to carry Marc's body away, he decided he had to act.

"Bring him back, Dr Hanser," he called.

Dani's tear-streaked face lifted. "What?"

Sarraj looked round irritably. "I just said we're not taking him back."

"Bring him back," Nazim repeated. "Use the scarab."

"What are you talking about?" Sarraj demanded.

"There is an account of the Scarab woman bringing people back from the dead," Bashir said. "Rank superstition of course, and anyway, she only claimed to be able to do those things by the power of the talisman she owned--the golden scarab."

Sarraj stared at Dani. "Why would this man tell you to use the scarab unless you had it? Yet you were searched..." He turned to a soldier standing nearby. "Search their jeeps and belongings..."

"I don't have it," Dani said. "And even if I did, I wouldn't use it like that." She shuddered. "You know what the account says--the Lord of

Death, Asar himself, will release one of his subjects for an hour. After that, they go back into death. I will not bring back a friend selfishly to face such a fate. Even if I could," she added.

"You're the only person I know that could use the golden scarab," Daffyd said.

"Not you too, Dafs. I don't have it..." Dani looked at Nazim. "Do you have it?"

Nazim reached into his pocket and withdrew a small sandstone rock, holding it up for all to see. "If you want it, it is yours, Dr Hanser. It should never have been taken from you."

"What are you talking about?" Sarraj said again. "That is just an ordinary rock, like a thousand others round here."

Bashir stared at his secretary. "You have it? You told me it was lost."

"And now I have it, and intend to return it to its rightful owner. Take it, Dr Hanser."

"No."

"No?" Now it was Daffyd's turn to stare in amazement. "It's what you came to Egypt for--to reclaim your property."

Dani shook her head. "Of course I want it, but I can't take it. Not now. I...I'm afraid if I take it, I'll use it to bring M...Marc back and..." Tears streamed down her face again. "...and that's just wrong."

"Give it to me," Sarraj demanded.

"No," Nazim said.

"You defy me?" Sarraj gestured. "Bring me that rock."

"Colonel, wait," Bashir interjected. "Don't be misled, this is a delaying tactic. While we argue here about some impossible artefact, and what it might be able to do, who knows what this missing man is doing. He could be summoning help or doing something to the tomb." Bashir pointed to the halftrack which was just arriving, its caterpillar treads grinding over the rocks. "We should leave right away."

Nazim stepped around Sarraj and moved closer to Dani and Daffyd. "Use it Dr Hanser. Bring back your friend."

"Don't tempt me," Dani groaned. "I can feel it call to me."

"Use it, Dr Hanser."

"I told you, no. To use it like that is evil. I won't subject Marc to the horrors of being called back, knowing he must die again after an hour."

"Actually, I think he might be right," Daffyd said. "Wait lass, before you fly off the handle, hear me out." He drew Dani to one side and turned her so she was not looking at Marc's body. The soldiers had carried him to a patch of soft sand and were knee-deep in the hole they had dug. Nazim followed, edging close and listening.

"Think back to the only description we have of Scarab bringing someone back from the dead. It was in the eastern desert when she was pursuing Nakhtmin. She ambushed those soldiers, but her men killed everyone before she could question them..."

"How could I forget? It was horrible. The man came back to life having faced his gods already, wounds gaping and the horror of his situation plastered across his face. Then after an hour he died, knowing his fate. I wouldn't do that to my worst enemy, let alone a friend."

"That's just it, lass. That man died again because the wounds he received in battle were too severe for him to survive without Asar's power. But Marc choked. Nick took the bread out of his throat and now there's nothing to keep him dead. All he needs is for life to be breathed back into him."

Dani sniffed loudly. "Except he's really dead and Nick couldn't revive him even with his own breath."

"But you can. Or rather, Asar can, through the power of the golden scarab."

"I won't deny the power of the gods, but Scarab could do these things--not me."

"How do you know unless you try? You've used it to find things and it disguises itself. Ask Nazim."

"That is true, Dr Hanser. I see only a plain rock."

Dani looked round at Nazim and then at Marc's body. "Even if I did, and it worked, his brain's been without oxygen too long. He'd be brain damaged."

Daffyd smiled. "If you can bring him back from the dead through the power of Asar, you can certainly heal him through the power of Geb. This is Marc we're talking about--our friend. Doesn't he deserve our every effort?"

Dawning hope shone from Dani's eyes. "It...it might be possible."

Nazim held out the rock. "Take it, Dr Hanser. It belongs to you. Use it to save your friend."

Dani hesitated, but then reached out, accepting Nazim's gift. As her fingers touched the rock, there was a flash of gold, hidden as her hand closed around it. She heard a gasp from the men around her and knew that others had caught a glimpse of the golden scarab's true nature. Dani closed her eyes and felt the thrill of power in her hand, but she quashed it, thrust it down, accepting it only as a token of the gods' favour.

She opened her eyes and saw Sarraj and Bashir before her. Their eyes glittered with avarice, and Sarraj held out his hand, demanding she hand it over. Without a word, she stepped between them and ran to where the soldiers were starting to lower Marc's body into the makeshift grave.

"Stop!" she called, and the men let go of the body and stood up, confusion on their faces as they realised they had obeyed the foreign woman without question instead of their commanding officer.

Dani knelt beside the body and bent her head in prayer. Consciously, she was ignorant of the proper words to use as the inscription had been silent on that point, but she framed the request respectfully, calling on Asar to release his subject Marc Andrews into her care as promised to Scarab, beloved of Atum. She prayed to Geb too, the god of living things, asking that any injury Marc had suffered might be healed. For long seconds, nothing happened and then, between one of Dani's heartbeats and the next, Marc drew a shuddering breath and his eyes flew open.

"Aaah...oh, god...what...where...? Dani?" Marc struggled to sit up, the blue colour draining from his face as he drew breath after breath, shuddering as he looked around him.

The soldiers who had been about to bury him leapt back in consternation, fear in their eyes. Behind her, Dani heard exclamations and curses, prayers to Allah and expostulations of wonder, as well as a distinct 'Well done, lass' in a Welsh accent. In herself, she felt joy and relief flooding through her, and hastily offered up thanks to Asar and Geb.

"By George," Nick said. "It's a bloody miracle."

"Extraordinary," Zewali murmured.

"Never seen anything like it," Maroun added.

"What is going on?" Sarraj demanded. "I thought that man was dead."

"He was," Bashir muttered. "And now he is not."

"That's nonsense," Sarraj declared. "When a man is dead, he's dead. If he appears to return to life it only shows he cannot have been dead in the first place. This is nothing more than trickery."

"For what purpose?" Bashir asked.

"You said it yourself," Sarraj said. "To give the man who escaped time to work mischief."

Daffyd, Nick, Zewali and Maroun gathered around Marc who, with Dani's assistance, had risen to his feet. They uttered exclamations of concern and it was Nick who asked what they had all been thinking.

"What was it like to be dead, old chap?"

"Was I dead?" Marc frowned, thinking. "Yes, I suppose I was. I remember eating my breakfast, and then a shot went off near me and I jumped. I couldn't catch my breath...it was...terrifying. And then everything went red and faded out."

"Nothing more?" Nick asked.

"You sound disappointed," Daffyd said. "What were you expecting? Choirs of angels? A bearded white gentleman speaking perfect English?"

Nick smiled wryly. "Well, I've never met anyone who's died before. I'm curious."

"Enough of this nonsense," Sarraj said. "Give me the scarab, Dr Hanser."

Dani ignored the colonel. "How are you feeling, Marc?"

Marc hesitated, as if running his mind over every part of his body. "Actually, I feel fine." He sniffed and drew a deep breath. "Even my cold's disappeared. How did that happen?"

"Dani used the golden scarab," Daffyd said.

"You got it back? That's marvellous. Where did..." Marc's voice trailed off. "What do you mean, Dani used the golden scarab?"

"Remember the gifts that were given to Scarab," Dani said gently. "Tefnut gave water, Nut gave direction, Geb gave healing, Asar..."

Marc went pale. "Asar brought people back to life," he whispered. "But they died again an hour later."

"We don't know that's going to happen."

"You didn't. Please tell me you didn't raise me from the dead for an hour and I've got to go through that all again." Marc clutched at Dani, his eyes pleading. "How could you? It would have been kinder to let me go."

"I'm sorry," Dani whispered.

"There's a good chance it won't happen," Daffyd said, putting his arm around the younger man. "When Scarab did that, the man she revived was stabbed and cut and couldn't have survived anyway, but you only choked. You suffered no lasting injury. We removed the obstruction and Geb has healed you of any ill effect--even your cold--so there's no reason you won't continue to live when the hour's up."

"But you don't know for certain?"

"I'm confident," Daffyd assured him.

"Yeah, but I'm the one who has to die...might have to die. How long have I got?"

Nick looked at his watch. "About forty minutes, give or take."

"Shit, and there's so much I wanted to do--travel, drive fast cars, get married--you didn't know about Jenny did you? Just met her before we left. Lovely girl. I wanted children too...and now I'll never even see her again, or..."

"All very interesting, I'm sure," Sarraj broke in. "But I'm in charge here, and you will do as I say. Get back in the vehicles; we are leaving for the tomb immediately."

Marc drew another shuddering breath and then exhaled, visibly calming himself. "Funnily enough, Colonel, you think you're in charge, but you're not. The Guardian is."

Daffyd raised his eyebrows. "Guardian?"

"Yes, I've just remembered. When I was...when I died, I saw someone. This man approached me and spoke...no, not spoke exactly. It was all very strange and I was trying to work out what had happened. He said...or thought at me...that he was the Guardian."

"Is he here now?" Dani asked.

Marc looked around, saw the soldiers crowded round hanging on every word, his friends with looks of worry or amazement, and the frustration and anger on the faces of Sarraj and Bashir. He shook his head. "No, or if he is, I can't see him."

"What did he look like? Did you recognise him?" Nick asked. "I've researched the Near Death Experience. People often see a close relative."

"Well, it wasn't my uncle Bert," Marc said, a trace of a smile on his lips. "I'd never seen him before, but he told me who he was."

"And?" Daffyd said after a brief pause. "Who was it?"

"Khu."

"What?"

Tears glistened in Dani's eyes. "It was Khu? What's he doing here? He should be at ease in the Field of Reeds, not wandering the desert."

"Who is Khu?" Zewali asked.

"Khu, son of Pa-it, a farmer of Akhet-Re. Companion, friend, lover and husband of Scarab, who was the consecrated king of the Two Lands after the death of her brother Smenkhkare."

"I don't know of any Scarab in the king lists," Maroun said.

"There is a lot in conventional history that is wrong," Dani said.

"And this Khu chappie is still here?" Nick asked. He looked around avidly.

"He offered to guard the tomb while he lived, and the gods extended that after his death. He's been guarding the tomb for over three thousand years."

"Aah, my beloved," Dani whispered.

"There's love for you," Daffyd commented. "Faithful unto death and beyond."

"Er, how is this Khu chappie actually guarding the tomb?" Nick asked. "Should we be concerned? I mean, is he just going to jump out shouting 'Boo!' or...or what?"

"He intimated that those that tried to plunder the tomb had died," Marc said.

"This is all nonsense," Sarraj said loudly. "Take no notice--he's merely trying to frighten you. He has no power; he wasn't raised from the dead; there is no ghost."

"Jebel Shabah--Ghost Mountain," muttered one of the soldiers.

"Be quiet," Sarraj snapped.

"I think we should be cautious, all the same," Bashir interjected. "We could perhaps hang back and send a scout forward to check out the tomb."

Daffyd grinned. "For once, Minister, you're making sense. In fact, let's take it a step further and return to Luxor. You don't want to risk everything by braving the Guardian."

"There is no Guardian," Sarraj shouted. "This is all a ruse. Put these people in the vehicles, Captain Massri. That's an order. We are leaving for the tomb right now and if anyone or anything tries to stop me, I'll kill them."

"I'm not sure you can kill a ghost," Nick observed.

"You won't need to anyway," Marc said. "Khu says he will allow the bearer of Atum's holy scarab and her companions to approach the tomb."

"When did he say that?"

"Just now, but...he's not here. I...it just entered my mind."

"If the bearer of the scarab is safe..."

"Just so. Hand it over, Dr Hanser." Sarraj held his hand out.

"No."

"I will take it by force if I must, but I cannot then guarantee you will be unhurt."

"I'd be careful," Daffyd said. "People who attempt violence on a scarab bearer tend to get hurt. The god Set promised that."

"Utter nonsense."

"Don't say you weren't warned."

"Dr Hanser, the scarab--now."

"The answer's still no."

"Captain Massri, secure that artefact."

Massri snapped out an order to two of his men, who moved forward reluctantly. One reached out for Dani's arm, stumbled and cannoned into his companion, both falling to the ground.

"Ha!" Daffyd crowed, stepping back from the sprawling men. "Set strikes again." Massri frowned and stepped forward himself, and Daffyd held up a hand in warning. "Set protects her. Any action taken rebounds on the evildoer."

The captain hesitated, and Sarraj cursed, drawing his pistol. "Last warning, Dr Hanser. I won't hesitate to use this. I can take the scarab from your dead hands."

Dani smiled. "No."

Sarraj swung his outstretched arm toward Daffyd. "Will you risk your friend?" The pistol swung now toward Marc. "Any of your friends?"

Dani's smile vanished and she hesitated, then "I cannot pass the gift of the gods into the hands of an evildoer. Set will protect him."

Sarraj snorted and pulled the trigger. The pistol cracked loudly and the bullet zipped past Marc and slammed into the halftrack. Sarraj stared and corrected his aim, firing again, and again he missed, the bullet clanging into the vehicle. Smoke trickled from under the bonnet, and soldiers rushed to attend to the stricken halftrack. The Colonel snarled and strode forward, lifting his gun. He tried to club Dani with it, but he uttered a cry of pain and clutched his arm, the gun falling from his hand. Nick grabbed for it, but Massri beat him to it, slipping it into his belt.

Massri helped Sarraj to a rock and sat him down, helping his commander knead away the sudden cramp in his arm. Sarraj pushed him away and got to his feet with an oath.

"Where is my gun? Massri?"

"Perhaps violence is unnecessary, sir," Massri pleaded. "He said the bearer and her companions may approach, so are we not all companions and may approach with her? Dr Hanser, is this not so?"

"Don't ask me," Dani said good-naturedly. "Ask of the Guardian."

"He says all may approach and offer respect," Marc said. "Uhh," he staggered and almost fell, Daffyd supporting him. "I...I feel odd...dizzy."

"The hour is up," Nick said softly.

Marc drew a deep breath and exhaled slowly, then again. He looked around at his friends, his eyes wide and filled with apprehension. "Am I going to die again?"

"I think you'd already be dead if you were going to," Nick murmured. "If the hour is literal."

"I...I feel fine."

"Then give thanks to Geb," Dani said. "He has healed you of that which killed you. You won't die today."

"Don't be too sure of that," Sarraj growled.

Gradually, the realisation that Marc would live swept over them. As the tension eased, Sarraj regained control of his men and he ordered them to prepare to break camp, loading his captives into the jeeps, with two soldiers in each one to guard them. Then he discovered that one of the bullets he had fired had shattered the alternator of the halftrack and there was no spare. Swearing, he ordered his men to set out on foot, and the three jeeps started on their way westward, toward the green mountain and Scarab's tomb.

Chapter Thirty-Eight

The journey over the last few miles should have taken no more than three hours, even allowing for the broken nature of the terrain, but the pace of the soldiers on foot slowed them to a weary trudge through sand and broken rock. At first invisible, lost among half a hundred other elevations, the mound they sought slowly rose to prominence, and by the time the sun sank behind it, they looked up at the green mountain from the jumble of boulders at its base.

"I don't bloody believe it. I've been here before," Marc said.

"You, or Khu speaking through you?" Daffyd asked.

"Well, obviously him, but I have too. When Muammar and I escaped from that bastard Ali Hafiz, we wandered in the desert all day and eventually came to a place where there was water and shelter. It was this place, I'm sure of it. What are the chances of that?"

"Maybe you were guided," Daffyd suggested. "As one of the companions of Dani, the true bearer of the scarab."

Marc shook his head wonderingly. "I felt the presence of Khu even then. Both of us did. It was as if we were being watched."

"I hope you are right when you say there is water here," Captain Massri said. "Our supplies are limited."

"Why do they call it 'green'?" Nick asked. "It's just black and yellowish brown, like the rest of this desert."

"It was green once," Dani said. "The water of the goddess allowed vegetation to clothe it, even when the surrounding desert was dry and barren."

"Nothing left now though."

"Despite there still being water," Marc said. "See the ledge about half way up? That shadow there..." he pointed. "...conceals a shallow cave, and the water seep is round to the left. We found a few straggly plants and grasshoppers. We ate those." He grimaced. "Never again."

Bashir wanted to immediately climb the slope and explore the cave, but Sarraj urged caution.

"My men are tired and it's getting dark. We should wait for the dawn."

They made camp by the boulders at the base of the hill and settled down to wait through the hours of darkness. Sarraj faced the problem of how to secure his prisoners, as most of his men were too exhausted to reliably remain awake. He decided to bind them hand and foot with rope, but Dani pointed out that no one would be permitted to bind her, and if she remained free then her companions would soon be released.

"Just leave us unbound," Dani reasoned. "We came here to find the tomb too. We're not going to run off."

Sarraj reluctantly agreed to leave them unbound, though he insisted one person remain awake and on guard at all times. He even took a turn himself in the early hours of the morning, glowering in the darkness at his peacefully sleeping captives.

Everyone was awake with the dawn and stood transfixed as the rays of the rising sun struck the top of the mound, reflecting a many-faceted dazzle that lasted no more than a few seconds before fading first to a glow and then to nothing more than sunlit rock.

"What causes that?" Nazim mused.

"There must be crystals in the rock," Daffyd said.

"Muammar said it was mica crystals," Marc said.

"A damn good show, whatever the cause," Nick commented. "So what happens now?"

"What happens now is that you stay out of our way as we reconnoitre the hill--especially that cave."

"Need I remind you, Colonel, that if there is the slightest chance of that cave concealing the entrance to a tomb, you must stand down and let the Department of Antiquities take over," Zewali said.

"Indeed," Maroun added. "We have a duty to secure the site against all intrusion."

"Under normal circumstances, that would indeed be the case," Sarraj said, smiling faintly, "However, I have reason to believe that cave is being used by the bandits I am pursuing, which gives me, as the local military commander, the authority to deal with it. I will not endanger any non-military persons by allowing them to interfere with my military duties."

"I am willing to sign a document absolving the army of blame--should that cave indeed hold bandits and I or Dr Maroun were injured."

"I think any bandits would certainly have run off by now with all these soldiers milling about," Nick said.

"I cannot allow you near the cave," Sarraj reiterated.

"Then I insist that Dr Maroun and I examine the cave as soon as your soldiers have ascertained there are no bandits present."

"You are in no position to insist on anything."

Zewali drew himself up. "I am the Director of the Luxor Museum."

"So you say," Sarraj murmured. "However, I cannot be certain of your identity until we return to Luxor, so..."

"This is arrant nonsense," Zewali said. "Mr Manouk here has consulted me at the museum, and Minister Bashir can vouch for Dr Maroun."

Bashir would not meet the archaeologists' eyes. "There is a strong resemblance," he said, "But I cannot swear to it."

"Mr Manouk?"

Nazim shuffled his feet. "I'm sorry, Dr Zewali..."

"You see?" Zewali said triumphantly. "He knows me."

"He is mistaken," Sarraj said. "Furthermore, Mr Manouk has already proven himself unreliable and dishonest. Now, this discussion is at an end. You will all remain down here under guard, or I will have you restrained." He turned and strode away, barking orders to Captain Massri.

"I do not feel like clambering about in the sun," Bashir said, "So I shall keep you company, Dr Hanser, gentlemen."

"Imagine how overjoyed that makes us feel," Daffyd murmured. He went and found a comfortable place to sit, out of the sun, and after a few moments the others joined him. Two soldiers remained on guard by the vehicles, keeping a watchful eye on the civilians. The other men, under the direction of Captain Massri and Colonel Sarraj, quickly worked out the best route up the hill to the ledge. Some continued up to the summit, others ran along the ledge in both directions, seeking out its limits, and one or two, under Sarraj's critical gaze, disappeared into the cave.

"What do you think they'll find?" Daffyd asked.

"The entrance to Scarab's tomb...and Smenkhkare's," Dani replied.

"You're sure? You've used the scarab?"

"I don't need to. It's there, though I dare say the passage is blocked."

They sat and watched the activity of the soldiers for a while. Sarraj emerged from the cave and lit up a cigarette, staring back into the depths as he smoked. The soldiers busied themselves within the cave, staggering out with lumps of rock and pitching them down the slope, raising a small dust cloud that hung in the still, hot air.

"I do hope they are not destroying anything of value," Zewali complained. "You can be sure I will be having words with Sarraj's superiors when we return to Luxor."

"If we return to Luxor," Marc muttered.

Nick looked sidelong at Dani and cleared his throat. "I say, I couldn't have a look at this golden scarab, could I? I've heard so much about it, don't you know?"

Dani took the artefact out of her pocket and held it in the flat of her palm. Any semblance it might have once had for a lump of sandstone was gone, its lithic nature replaced by the rich gleam of pure gold, carved and fashioned into the shape of the sacred scarab beetle.

"By George! No wonder you wanted it back," Nick said. "It's bloody marvellous."

"That's what I think every time I see it," Marc said.

"Amen to that, boyo."

Nazim stared at the object with naked wonder written on his face, while Bashir involuntarily reached out to take it, avarice and envy twisting his features. "Colonel Sarraj wants it," Bashir said, "But I have persuaded him there will be plenty of other valuable artefacts in the tomb."

"You expect us to thank you?" Marc muttered.

"By rights, that artefact is subject to Egyptian laws," Dr Maroun said.

"It wasn't found in Egypt," Daffyd pointed out.

"Even so, it is obviously of Egyptian manufacture."

"It belongs in a museum," Zewali added.

Dani's fingers closed over the golden scarab and she thrust it back in her pocket. "It was given to Scarab and entrusted to me. I could not give it up unless the gods tell me to."

"You surely do not believe these gods are real?" Zewali asked. "We both belong to monotheistic faiths. There is no room for other gods. The ancient Egyptians worshipped forces of nature, not spiritual beings, in ignorance of reality."

"You say that after seeing Marc resurrected and healed?" Daffyd asked.

"I cannot deny the possibilities of a miracle," Zewali replied, "Both our religions recognise the presence of God in everyday life, but it may be something as simple as Marc not really being dead. None of us are medical doctors; perhaps we were mistaken in our diagnosis. Marc was unconscious certainly, maybe even on the borders of mortality, but to return from actual death? I do not wish to offend, Dr Hanser, but as a scientist, the simplest solution is most often correct."

"No offence taken, Dr Zewali," Dani said. "You admit the possibility of a miracle, but if so, by which god? The Muslim Allah is surely the same god as the Jewish Yahweh and the Christian God..." She saw Zewali nod agreement. "...who are worshipped in different ways, so perhaps we could argue that the many gods of Egypt, also worshipped in different ways, were all aspects of the One God. Who is to say that Asar and Geb, Set and Nut, and all the others were not just parts of the Whole, worshipped individually by people not yet ready for a single deity?"

"An interesting argument," Zewali said. "Perhaps we might continue it in more salubrious surroundings after our return to Luxor. I would welcome the opportunity to study the scarab too."

"If we return to Luxor at all," Marc said gloomily. "Do you really think that mad colonel is going to let us live?"

"The scarab can protect us," Dani murmured.

"I wouldn't rely too heavily on it," Daffyd cautioned. "There might be limits to its efficacy. There are six of us...seven if you include Nazim..."

"Thank you, Dr Rhys-Williams."

"...and eight if you include Muammar."

"Where is he anyway?" Marc queried. "I haven't seen him since I...er, woke up. He's alright isn't he?"

"He ran off," Bashir sneered. "First sign of trouble and he ran into the desert. He's probably dead by now."

"Don't you believe it," Daffyd said. "He wouldn't desert his friends. He's probably out there now, looking for a way to help us."

Dani stared toward the east, toward the jumble of stony and sandy desert that lay between the green mountain and the ruined pylon of Khepri. "He's alive," she murmured. "Alive and out there, but not close."

"As long as he's safe," Marc said.

Toward midday, Sarraj returned to the foot of the hill, allowing Captain Massri to bring his men down for a meal and a rest in the heat of the day. Over coffee, the colonel sat with Massri and Bashir, discussing the next move. He allowed the others to listen, though discouraged their participation.

"There is a passageway, a tunnel, reaching back into the hill, rough-hewn and filled with rubble," Massri reported. "We have been able to remove the loose debris, but we have encountered tightly packed blocks that are jammed in. Crowbars will remove it, but because of the confined space, only two men can work at the same time. The work is slow and arduous, as well as hot, so..."

"So I have decided to use explosives," Sarraj finished.

"You can't do that!" Dr Zewali leapt to his feet in agitation. "It would be criminally irresponsible to blow open a tomb with explosives. You could destroy everything you came to find."

"Gold would survive though, wouldn't it?" Bashir asked.

"I'm not even going to acknowledge such a boorish question," Zewali said. "Colonel Sarraj, I appeal to you. Forget such a terrible idea and turn this excavation over to the Department of Antiquities. You could still be hailed as one of the discoverers of an unknown tomb, rather than be vilified as its desecrator."

Sarraj drew on his cigarette with an expression of amusement on his face. "My dear Zewali, or whoever you are, I have no intention of blowing apart a tomb, should there be one. The destruction of valuable objects would be a foolish waste when curios fetch such a high price on the black market. We are merely clearing a tunnel of debris--debris that has no archaeological significance. That is hardly a crime."

"How do you know it lacks significance?" Zewali demanded. "Are you an expert?"

"I am an expert in my own field, and I do not care what you think. I am going to blow open that passage, and if there happens to be a tomb at the end of it, I may let you examine it. Now sit down and cease your irrelevant chatter or I will have you gagged."

"Perhaps Dr Hanser and Dr Zewali could examine the debris excavated from the passage," Bashir suggested. "It would give them something to do--keep them out of mischief--and they may even discover something of interest."

"Amongst the rubble? I doubt it." Sarraj considered the request for a few moments and shrugged. "It is all one to me, as long as they don't bother me."

Zewali and Dani led the others over to the heap of rubble at the base of the hill and started sifting through the blocks. As they had suspected, it was mostly plain sandstone and limestone chunks, but a few of them were roughly trimmed, and Maroun pointed to one that he swore had been fashioned with a copper chisel.

"It is as I thought," Zewali fumed. "That is not just rubble filler. This block was fashioned for a specific purpose. I need to see inside that tunnel."

The soldiers had swarmed up the hill again as the heat leached from the day, and Massri carefully carried what looked like a stick of dynamite into the cave. He emerged after quarter of an hour and made sure everyone moved to a safe distance before detonating it. There was a muffled thump, the rock beneath them trembled and dust and rock fragments blasted out of the cave like an old cannon going off. When the dust settled, the men moved in again with picks and shovels, clearing away the loose debris and tumbling more rocks down the slope.

"Damn philistines," Daffyd muttered.

"Criminals," Zewali muttered. He picked up a rock that had been fashioned at one end, though the explosion had cleaved through the grain leaving fresh, unweathered rock in view. "Where was this rock, I ask you? Was it a fragment of wall? I need to see the rubble in place before they start destroying it."

Massri moved everyone away again, and another explosion shook the late afternoon air, jetting more dust from the cave mouth. More rubble was tipped down the hillside and the scientists moved in to examine it. The nature of the rock changed, becoming fine-grained sandstone and siltstone mixed in with other debris. Daffyd picked up a crumbling piece and studied it in the fading light.

"There's some vegetable matter in this piece," he exclaimed.

Dani peered over his shoulder. "You're right, Dafs. It looks like straw."

Zewali almost snatched the piece from Daffyd. "It's mud brick," he howled. "Those idiots have smashed right through into the tomb." He turned and started scrambling up the slope down which fragments of debris were still tumbling.

Dani climbed after him, with her friends on her heels, shouting to Massri to halt operations. The captain appeared in the cave mouth with Sarraj just behind him. Sarraj took one look at the irate archaeologist and pulled his gun out.

"That's far enough, Zewali. The rest of you too."

Zewali was breathing hard after the climb. He waved the piece of brick at Sarraj and spoke as forcefully as he could. "You unmitigated fool. I'll have your commission for this when I've finished with you. You've blasted into the tomb, destroying who knows how many priceless objects. This is a piece of mud brick--part of the wall that sealed off the tomb. Your actions are criminal, Colonel, and I will be bringing the full weight of the law down on you."

Massri attempted to cool the scientist down, watching his gun-wielding commander nervously from the corner of his eye. "Come now, Dr Zewali. It is premature to be laying blame when we don't know the effect of the latest blast. We'll let the dust settle and examine the tunnel most carefully before attempting any more explosions. In the meantime, why don't we all descend to camp and..."

"I insist on inspecting the tunnel," Zewali declared. "Dr Maroun and I will conduct a thorough examination and only then..."

Sarraj lifted his gun and pulled the trigger, loosing off a shot above their heads. The report shattered the still air and everybody stared up at the figures around the cave mouth. "The next shot goes into your chest," the colonel snarled. "I am in charge here and I will not be dictated to. You are my prisoners, not my colleagues."

"Of course, Colonel," Dani said quietly, "But may I ask you to consider a very important point? You are attempting to break into an undiscovered tomb which you hope is filled with treasure, but you are taking a sledgehammer approach when a gentle one is called for. Daffyd, Marc and I are trained archaeologists and Dr Zewali and Dr Maroun are experts in ancient Egyptian tombs. Doesn't it make sense to use every asset at your disposal? Let us examine the shaft for you. It's possible you won't need any more explosive." She looked at the jumping muscle in Sarraj's jaw and paused, willing him to calm down. "It is your choice, Colonel Sarraj. Nobody is trying to make you do anything. I'm only offering advice."

Dr Maroun nodded his agreement. "Nothing is gained by letting emotion rule us. Surely we can reason out a proper response to whatever lies in that shaft. It is in no one's interest to destroy valuable artefacts."

Sarraj allowed himself to be talked around, and everybody went down to the camp, leaving two soldiers on guard at the cave mouth. Dusk fell swiftly, and with it the temperature, the heat vanishing from the air and rocks, leaving them shivering until fires could be built up and hot food prepared. When everyone had eaten and food and coffee taken up to the guards on the ledge, Sarraj came across to where the scientists sat, with Massri, Bashir and Nazim in attendance.

"I have decided to let you examine the tunnel in the morning."

"All of us?" Dani asked.

"Why not? You may regard yourselves as acting in an advisory capacity."

"Does this mean you accept I am director of the museum?" Zewali asked.

"Let's just say I am giving you the benefit of the doubt for now," Sarraj said. "I still intend to investigate your credentials when we return to Luxor."

The military men walked off, Bashir in attendance, but Nazim remained behind for a few moments. He looked nervously in the direction of the colonel and lowered his voice.

"Please be careful, Dr Hanser. Colonel Sarraj is not to be trusted."

"Has he said something?"

"Not in my hearing, but the Minister seeks the tomb solely for the gold and Sarraj is his friend. I believe his motive is the same. Unscrupulous men are dangerous men."

When Nazim departed, Dani discussed what he had said with the others. None of them were particularly surprised at his disclosures and regarded both Bashir and Sarraj with intense suspicion. Zewali shrugged and went to sleep, advising everyone to do likewise.

"There's no point discussing anything as we know nothing about what's up there. We'll find out in the morning."

Dani and Daffyd remained awake; shivering in their blankets near the fire as the residual heat of the day vanished, plunging the area around the green mountain into a frigid calm.

"I knew it got cold in the desert at n...night," Daffyd said, his teeth on the verge of chattering, "But I didn't think it got this bad. Look, you can even...even see my breath."

The noise of the camp died down. They heard the challenge and reply as the guards at the cave were relieved, and then the camp settled down to sleep. After a time, Dani and Daffyd dozed, leaning against one another. The cold air was very still and the sounds of the desert were magnified, bringing them awake as rocks cracked in the cold or soldiers groaned or snored in their sleep. Normal desert sounds were absent, the scrabbling of scorpions and mice across rocks, or the soft susurration of an owl's wings. Once, they heard the distant screech of a hunting owl, but nothing came near the green mountain and its encamped men.

In the early hours of the morning, a scream brought the camp awake. People sat upright or stood, clutching rifles, unsure whether the sound had beaten upon their collective eardrums or was merely the product of some nightmare plaguing twenty people at once. The scream came again a few moments later, and people shouted or cried out at the shock of it. Everyone was up on their feet, Captain Massri shouting for lights as the men babbled, talking excitedly, and trying to pinpoint the source of the cry.

"What the hell was that?" Marc asked.

"A jackal, maybe," Daffyd said. "Or an owl."

"That was a human being," Zewali stated. "*In extremis.*"

"Where? Who?" Nick asked.

Nobody answered him, and the scream was not repeated. They waited, the minutes slipping past, waiting for something to happen, and when nothing did, they slowly relaxed.

"I say," Nick murmured. "Have you noticed how it's got warmer?"

"Odd," Daffyd said. "I'd expect it to get colder toward dawn. Maybe the wind has changed direction."

"What wind?" Marc asked.

The men settled back into an uneasy sleep, but were shocked awake again just before dawn when two men climbed the hill to relieve the guard on the cave.

Chapter Thirty-Nine

"Captain! Captain! They are dead. Come quickly."

The shout brought everyone awake again and sent Sarraj and Massri scrambling up the hill with the remaining half dozen soldiers on their heels, any semblance of military discipline vanishing in the grey light. Bashir and Nazim, left alone in their camp, moved across to where the scientists stood, seeking comfort in the face of the shocking revelation.

"It's Muammar," Marc murmured. "I'm sure of it. I knew he wouldn't leave us in the lurch."

"If it is, I'm disturbed that he could kill two men in cold blood," Dani said.

"We don't know what's happened," Daffyd said. "I suggest we don't speculate until we know more."

They did not have long to wait. As the eastern sky flushed pink in anticipation of the new day, Sarraj came down the hill and strode across to them. Behind him, Massri had organised the soldiers, having them bring the two bodies into the camp.

"What happened, Colonel?" Zewali asked.

"Two of my men are dead, and I must assume it is one of you. Or else the man who ran away."

"How did they die?" Daffyd asked.

"That has not been determined," Sarraj said. "You are all confined to the camp. If you attempt to leave it, for any reason, I will have you shot."

A little later, as the sun rose, Captain Massri came to see them, his face troubled. "The guards apparently died of heart failure," he said. "However, two men dying together within moments of each other is highly unusual. There is not a mark upon them, though their faces are contorted as if in great pain."

"Or fright?" Dani asked.

"Possibly. What do you know?"

"When Marc returned from the borders of death, he spoke of a Guardian. If a spirit guards the tomb, how will he guard it, not being physical?"

"By frightening them."

Dani nodded. "Some men would flee a terror while others, under orders to remain at their posts, took the only way out they could." She looked across to where Sarraj was deep in conversation with Bashir. "What will you do now, Captain? More to the point, what will Colonel Sarraj do?"

"If it were up to me, I would leave this place," Massri said. "I believe the Colonel will stay however. He seems driven to find this tomb."

"Yes, he intends to plunder it of its treasures," Zewali said. "Naturally, when he does this he can leave no witnesses behind to accuse him of his crimes. What will you do then, Captain Massri?"

The troubled look on the captain's face deepened. "I cannot believe Colonel Sarraj could do such a thing. He is not a criminal."

"He already is," Dani said. "He tortured Dr Rhys-Williams to extract information from him and now he employs explosives to blow open a tomb in direct contravention of Egyptian laws."

"And he knows that if we are allowed to return to Luxor, we will report his infractions to his superiors and the Minister of Antiquities," Zewali added. "Those threats are nullified if we do not return, so I repeat, what will you do then, Captain Massri? Will our lives be on your conscience too?"

"I must think on this."

"Don't take too long, boyo," Daffyd murmured.

Sarraj sent armed men back into the cave, though the soldiers' reluctance was obvious. They found nothing and returned quickly, glad to be out in the sunshine again. He stamped across to Dani and Zewali again, and ordered them up to the cave.

"All of us, I trust?" Dani said.

Sarraj scowled. "If you must, though I fail to see what use a reporter can be."

Nick sniffed, but kept his eyes averted, not wanting to provoke the colonel into refusing him permission.

They climbed to the ledge and thence to the cave entrance. Daylight seeped inward a dozen paces before fading out over the remains of the debris loosened the evening before. The scientists examined the cave walls with interest, looking for signs that the rock had been worked in the ancient past. Massri and three soldiers joined them, armed with torches, and Dani and Zewali, with Daffyd just behind, were the first to enter the shaft that lay at the rear of the cave. Their feet crunched on the gravel and grit that littered the floor, and the torch beams flicked and flashed over the walls, probing the dust-polluted air. Thin intermittent streams of dust fell from thin jagged cracks in the roof of the shaft, adding to the air burden.

Dani touched Zewali's arm and pointed with her torch beam. "There."

At the limit of their vision, the shaft ended in a pile of rubble, and through the gaps in the piled rock, they could see serried ranks of mud bricks and stones.

"My God." Zewali advanced cautiously and shone his torch on the bricks, running his fingertips over the surface. He moved one of the rocks and it released a small landslide, raising another cloud of dust into the air. Coughing, he waited for the debris to subside before studying the wall again.

"There's a cartouche," he said, excitement growing in his voice. "Vigorous is the Soul of Re, Holy of Forms. I don't believe it, that's the nomen of Smenkhkare-Djeserkheperu. It can't be his tomb though; he's in the Valley of the Kings--KV55."

"Isn't that the tomb that Queen Tiye's supposed to be buried in?" Dani asked.

Zewali nodded. "It's not exactly decorated like a royal tomb."

"The male buried there is probably another son of Amenhotep by a slave girl. I can't remember his name but he died of the plague around the same time as Tiye."

"How do you know that?" Daffyd asked. "I'm sure that wasn't in the account."

"I don't know. I just do."

Zewali gave her an odd look and turned his attention back to the wall. "Whether Smenkhkare is in KV55 or not, this must be a tomb sealed in his reign, which is why it has his cartouche."

Dani pointed to another seal, half obscured by dust. She lightly brushed it off. "Here's another."

Zewali looked over her shoulder, his eyes screwing up in puzzlement as he read. "It's a royal cartouche. Beautiful of Forms--Neferkheperu and Scarab joined to the Atum--Khnumt-Atum Scarab. I've never come across any name like that. I'd swear it's not a king, probably female--maybe a consort?"

"Have you forgotten what this whole quest is about, Karim? It's a search for the tomb of Scarab, otherwise known as Beketaten, daughter of

Amenhotep the Great, and sister of Akhenaten, Smenkhkare and Tutankhamen. She was also pharaoh in her own right, being crowned after the death of Smenkhkare by Aanen, the Hem-Netjer of Amun."

"How could you possibly know that?"

"She told me." Dani laughed at the expression on Zewali's face. "The inscription in Syria, Karim. It was quite detailed."

"I have to read it."

"That's not in my power to grant, but what are we going to do with this?" She touched the brickwork tenderly.

"There's no question of that. It will have to be guarded and excavated properly. This could be a major discovery."

"And Sarraj?"

Zewali grimaced. "He must be made to see reason. The use of explosives on this shaft was criminal. It could have destroyed a national treasure."

"Well I doubt he'll use explosives any more. Pick and shovel will be enough." Dani drew the museum director aside. "Karim, there's nothing we can do to prevent Sarraj and Bashir entering the tomb. All we can do is be on hand and try to stop any wilful destruction or theft of artefacts. These things can be recovered." She did not voice her suspicion that they might not long survive the plundering of the tomb.

"There's nothing we can do?"

"Sarraj is in control, but perhaps the Guardian can stop him."

"Guardian...? You don't really believe in that, do you?"

"Those two soldiers died of something, and Marc saw a Guardian during his Near Death Experience."

"Suggestibility? Hallucination induced by an oxygen-starved brain? I don't rule it out, you understand, but relying on a ghost? I don't say it can't happen, but I think we'll need something more substantial to protect this tomb."

They exited the shaft, brushing off the dust that had covered them, and spitting to clear the grit from their mouths. Sarraj demanded to know what they had found and punched the air in triumph when told they had possibly found the walled-up entrance of a tomb. Zewali pleaded with him to step back even now from any desecration, but the Colonel refused.

"I am prepared to be generous, however. You may have the honour of opening the tomb." When Zewali shook his head, Sarraj smiled and added, "Or I can have my men just flatten it."

"I will do it," Dani said, "And Dr Zewali can watch me, but first, your men must clear all the debris from in front of the wall."

Captain Massri took charge, coaxing his reluctant men to enter what they all now believed was a haunted cave on Jebel Shabah--Ghost Mountain. After the deaths of two of their comrades, the soldiers were becoming increasingly recalcitrant, bordering on mutinous when ordered to carry out duties in the cave. Leading by example and exhorting his men to put their faith in Allah, Massri and his men slowly demolished the last of the rubble and pitched it down the slope.

Marc shaded his eyes and stared up at the slopes above the cave mouth, frowning as a few loose pebbles slid downward, clattering onto the ledge near them. Nick came and stood beside him, following his gaze.

"What do you see?" he asked. "This Guardian chappie of yours?"

"No, but something disturbed the rocks up there. I can't see anything though."

"Probably just natural erosion. It's a hot day after that frigid night and those rocks expand and contract. I wouldn't worry about it."

"Who's worried? It's Muammar, I'm concerned about. He had enough worries without being lost in the desert."

"I'm sure he's fine."

"Guys," Dani called, from near the cave mouth. "Do you want to come and see? They've cleared the wall."

Everyone showed interest in gazing upon the exposed wall before they broke through, but the room in the shaft was limited, so Zewali and Dani took it in turns to escort two or three others to the mud brick surface and explain what they were seeing. They pointed out the royal cartouches and translated them to each group of visitors, moving on to age-worn inscriptions scraped into limestone blocks incorporated in the wall.

"They're mostly prayers for the repose of the occupants," Zewali explained. "There are two sets..."

"No curses?" Bashir asked.

"The ancient Egyptians didn't write curses on tombs," Zewali said. "Only prayers. As I was saying, these prayers were apparently inscribed on two different occasions. See here where this inscription exhorting the Ennead of Heliopolis..."

"Who?" Nick asked. "I've never heard of a god called Ennead."

"The Ennead is a group of nine gods--Atum, Shu, Tefnut, and so on. To continue, this prayer partly overlays another dedicated to the god Amun, implying two separate burials some years apart."

Zewali ran his fingertips over the wall, brushing away the dust. "These are the seals of the officiating priests--the High Priest or Hem-Netjer of Atum and this one of Amun. I can't make out the name of the Atum priest--as you can see, the rubble has chipped it away, but the Amun priest is...is Nn."

"Strange name," Bashir commented.

"No vowels in the written language," Dr Maroun murmured. "Speakers of the day would be familiar with the names and supply vowels as needed. For instance, the god Amun was represented as Mn and could equally have been Amen or Amon. This priest Nn could be Enen or Anen or..."

"Aanen," Dani said. "Brother of Ay and uncle of Scarab."

"Enough of this prevarication," Sarraj declared. "Open the tomb, Dr Hanser." He moved everyone back, but allowed Daffyd to stand alongside Dani in the confined space to lend his strength should it be needed.

Daffyd looked at Dani's pale face with concern. "Are you all right, lass? It can't be easy for you."

"It's not, but I can't think what else to do. If I don't do it, Sarraj will and he'll be heavy-handed."

"Is it really going to matter in the long run? If he lets us go, the contents of the tomb are still going to disappear into the hands of private collectors. Everything will be lost."

"It matters, Dafs. Don't ask me how or why, but it's important I'm the first one in there."

"Why the delay, Dr Hanser?" Sarraj called. "If you have lost your nerve I'll have my men knock it down."

"I'm just checking the best place to enter," she replied. "Somewhere we won't cause too much damage." Dani sighed and pointed. "There, I think, Dafs, but please be careful." She stepped back, allowing the Welshman room to move.

Daffyd swung a pick in the cramped passage, the point glancing off the wall in a puff of dust. Again he swung, harder this time, and the point dug into the sun-hardened mud brick, gouging out a chunk. He kept up a steady battering at the wall, limiting his blows to a few bricks around the first one, making the dust fly and a shattered fragments drizzle onto the floor of the shaft. Then the pick sank in several inches and stuck. Daffyd waggled it experimentally.

"I think it's gone through." He tugged the handle sideways and the metal head ripped out, revealing a small dark hole in the wall.

Dani shone her torch through the hole, the beam almost solid in the thick dust, but shook her head. "I can't see a thing. You'll have to enlarge it."

Daffyd resumed his efforts, sweat staining his shirt and dripping in his eyes, in the close, hot atmosphere of the tunnel. The hole widened slowly, brick fragments now dropping inside the chamber beyond as often as not. At last he stood back, panting as he leaned on the handle of the pick.

Dani moved forward and knelt in the dust, shining her torch into the chamber. Stale air, sealed inside for three thousand years, wafted over her, and as the dust slowly thinned and settled, she could start to make out details of the tomb's interior.

"What can you see?" Nick called, his voice reverberating in the narrow shaft.

For a few moments, Dani considered saying something memorable, like Howard Carter when he first peered into Tutankhamen's tomb saying 'Wonderful things!', but decided this was a more solemn moment. It almost felt as if she was peering into her own tomb, and the thought dampened her excitement.

"Not much...wait, yes, I can see two long objects on the ground toward the back of the chamber. It's not a big chamber...there's some debris and...you'll have to see for yourself."

The others started forward, eager to see inside, but Sarraj and Bashir pushed them back and shouldered Daffyd aside. They knelt and peered into the chamber, the beams from their own torches probing the dusty darkness beyond.

"I can't see anything," Sarraj complained. "Break down more of the wall. I'm not going to crawl through that."

The two men moved back and Daffyd applied himself again, Marc coming up to lend a hand as the older man tired. Eventually, they punched a hole through that would allow even Bashir, the most portly of them, to enter, having to duck only slightly. While the hole was being enlarged, Sarraj had sent down for two kerosene lanterns, and these now cast a strong yellow glow over the walls of the shaft, adding a hydrocarbon stink to the acrid dust.

When Sarraj and Bashir entered the chamber, each bearing a lantern, they found Dani and Daffyd already there, shining the weak beams of their torches around. The glow of the lanterns threw back the shadows and all four people stared at the contents of the tomb, not at all expecting what they saw.

"I thought it would be more like King Tut's tomb," Daffyd murmured. "You know, full of grave goods, statues, furniture, with a gold-plated shrine and stone sarcophagus, painted walls and such. Not this."

"You forget, Dafs," Dani said. "Both burials were conducted in secret. They couldn't transport all the things a king would need in the afterlife, let alone heavy coffins. Remember the account? A wooden coffin, cedar panels inscribed with prayers, a few personal items."

"Where's the gold?" Sarraj rasped. "Ahmed, you told me there would be gold--lots of it. Have I wasted my time?"

"Yes, Dr Hanser. Where is the treasury of Smenkhkare? You said it would be here."

"That's what the account said." Dani looked around the small chamber and stepped across to some mounds of debris along one wall. She bent and sifted through the dirt, pulling aside strands of rotted fibre and fragments of wood.

"Here. Here's your treasure." She lifted out a finger-length roughly fashioned bar of gold and held it up. The metal gleamed in the lantern light, untarnished, sullied only by a patina of dust. She rubbed it and the metal glowed richly.

Sarraj gasped and strode past her, plunging his fingers into the mounded debris, scattering it as he drew out bar after bar of gold. Some he slipped into his pockets, others he stacked neatly on the floor. Bashir joined him and found piles of yellowed ivory in short curved lengths. He smiled as he ran his hands over the smooth surfaces.

"Hippopotamus tusks," Dani said. "And jewels over there."

Necklaces and pectorals, armbands and anklets lay spilled over the stone floor, all manner of precious stones and gold ornaments, many now lying loose as the cords connecting them had decayed, but still undisturbed in their patterns--turquoise and lapis, zircon and faience, amid a scattering of more precious stones--uncut rubies and diamonds held by gold and silver thread.

"Didn't I tell you?" Bashir crowed. "There are hundreds of gold bars and almost as many ivory. We're rich."

"Remember our agreement," Sarraj said. "I get the gold and ivory, you get the artefacts." He looked around the chamber with a smug look on his face. "I don't see many artefacts, unless you count the necklaces, and most of those are made of paste and semi-precious stones."

"There must be more here," Bashir said, scowling. "Whoever heard of a tomb without gold statues and such?" He started rummaging at the back of the chamber, near the long objects. "What are these?" he nudged one with his foot.

"My goodness," Daffyd said, shining his torch over them. "They're wooden coffins. You can still see the painted features on them."

Dani stood looking down at the mortal remains of what must have been Scarab and her brother Smenkhkare. "Leave them in peace," she pleaded. "You don't need to disturb them."

Bashir licked his lips, his eyes gleaming with avarice. "I hear they put jewels and gold artefacts in the mummy wrappings. They'd be worth a fortune."

"No, Minister. Please. Have some decency."

"Come, Dr Hanser, you wouldn't deny me..."

A series of reports interrupted him and all heads turned toward the entrance. Voices cried out distantly, mixed with closer shouts and more shooting.

"Those are gunshots," Sarraj said. "What are those fools shooting at?" He ran out of the chamber, Dani and Daffyd on his heels.

Chapter Forty

The camp was a scene from bedlam. Soldiers were hunkered down behind rocks and jeeps, firing their rifles at a largely unseen enemy that sniped at them from several directions. Already one soldier lay dead and one or two more bore wounds. Captain Massri crouched within the cave mouth, and as Sarraj emerged from the chamber, turned a shocked face to his commander.

"They came out of nowhere, sir."

"Who's our enemy?"

"I don't know, sir. I got a glimpse of robed men, so it might be those bandits we were after."

"That was a fiction, you fool," Sarraj snarled. He stared out at the surrounding terrain, noting positions where a puff of smoke betrayed a shooter, where a rifle protruded from cover or a head garbed in keffiya ducked quickly behind a rock. "I see four, maybe five." He pointed. "Get down to the jeep and organise the men there. Circle round that large rock and onto that other one. See? If you can do that, you'll make those positions there and there..." he pointed again, "...untenable. Go!"

Massri ran from the cave mouth and scrambled down the hillside. By the time he was halfway down, the attackers had spotted him and bullets were whining off rocks and kicking up dust near him. He dived behind a rock, gathered himself and sprinted for the cover of the jeep. A bullet knocked one leg from under him as he reached the jeep and he stumbled and fell, dragging himself under cover.

Sarraj, meanwhile, took advantage of the diversion to slide and run down the steep slope toward a rock behind which two of his men sheltered. He made it unscathed and immediately led his men out in sprinting probes toward the jumble of rocks from which the enemy were firing.

The scientists watched from the cover of the cave, and Nick positioned himself near the entrance, sticking his head out frequently to follow the course of the battle, ducking back in to write copious notes in his notebook. "By George, this is going to make an interesting story--a quest for buried treasure, fugitives, ghosts, and now a gun battle. Who are they? Any ideas?"

"Bandits," Marc stated. "Sure to be."

"Sarraj told Massri that was a made up story," Dr Maroun said. "He said so just now."

"Those may have been, but there's bound to be more than one group of bandits in the western desert."

"They're pretty audacious attacking an army squad," Daffyd said. "It's not as if anyone knows there's treasure here."

"There's not much we can do to help, though to tell the truth, I'm not sure which group I want to help," Zewali said. "So I'm going to take advantage of Sarraj's absence to examine the tomb for myself. Coming, Maroun?"

The two museum archaeologists disappeared back into the cave. Nick watched them go, torn between the excitement of the shooting, and his desire to see the object of their search. After a few seconds, he gave in and ran back into the cave.

"You not going back to check on them?" Daffyd asked Dani.

"I think I can trust Karim not to disturb anything," she replied.

"Yeah, but what about Bashir?" Marc asked. "He's still back there." He saw Nazim standing deeper in the cave. "What about you? You're not with your master?"

"He is no longer my master, Dr Andrews," Nazim said. "I intend to retire from his service as soon as I can."

"Good for you."

"Thank you, Dr Hanser, though I do not doubt he will make life difficult for me."

Massri and his men had worked his way to the slab of rock and were now pouring fire down on the bandits, who also found themselves under attack from Sarraj as he worked his way round. The bandits fell back and as they ran for new cover, a shot caught one of them and spun him around. He recovered and threw himself behind a rock, though blood had soaked his sleeve.

"Did that man look familiar?" Dani asked.

Daffyd shook his head, and Marc muttered, "They all look the same to me. Why? Who do you think it was?"

"I thought it was one of the Bedouin tribesmen who brought us into Egypt."

"Great," Marc groaned. "If Sarraj wins, he shoots us; if the Bedouin win, they hold us for ransom and then shoot us."

"How did they know where we were?" Dani asked. "We didn't exactly leave a trail to follow."

"If it is indeed them," Daffyd murmured. "Look!"

Sarraj had over-reached himself in his attempt to harry and pursue the retreating foe. A burst of gunfire from an unexpected direction cut down his two men and sent him scrambling back to the rocks, bullets whining off the boulders near him. Massri worked round further with the remaining five men, but now with them bunched in one place, he came under fire from at least three different positions.

"If it is them, the odds are nearly even now," Marc said. "There were six Bedouin and ten soldiers--two died of fright and now three have been shot. That's seven left including Massri and Sarraj."

Zewali rejoined them at the cave mouth. "That is an incredible find, Dr Hanser," he said. "Very basic furnishings, and the prayers and inscriptions are cut down to a minimum, but there is much in the way of valuable things. I fear too much is transportable, and Sarraj will plunder it. I hope we can persuade him to leave the coffins intact. I'd very much like to take them back to the museum for proper study."

"You could just leave them to rest in peace."

"It would be hard to guard this site, and inconvenient to travel all the way out here to study the remains."

"Where's Bashir?" Daffyd asked.

"He shows a lot of interest in the coffins," Zewali said. "I left Maroun to keep an eye on him."

Down below, amid the jumble of rocks, one of the attackers called out in Arabic. A few moments later, Sarraj replied.

"What are they saying?" Marc asked, as a further burst of Arabic was hurled back and forth.

"The bandit tells Sarraj that he is surrounded and should surrender," Zewali translated. "Sarraj replies that he...well, suffice it to say he is quite crude in his suggestion." Zewali listened, and translated as best he could.

"Hand over the infidels...the foreigners..."

"It *is* the Bedouin," Dani said. "They followed us somehow."

"Why do you want them?" Sarraj shouted back.

"Our business is not your business. Hand them over and you may withdraw in safety--upon my word."

Sarraj laughed. "Of what worth is the word of a bandit?"

"I am not a bandit," shrieked the man. "I am badawī, Zufir ibn Walid of the family of ibn Hawid. My honour is not to be questioned, you son of a diseased camel."

The conversation disintegrated into a flurry of invective and insult, and a few minutes later shots were once more being exchanged.

"You know these people who attack us?" Zewali asked.

Daffyd explained the situation. "They probably want to ransom us as before, but it's also possible they're now motivated by feelings of revenge. We sort of rubbed their noses in the dirt by escaping so easily."

"I was going to suggest you made your way into the desert to meet up with them as a way of escaping Sarraj, but that might not be wise. You might be safer here, at least for now."

"Dani's safe enough as long as she has the golden scarab, and she might be able to protect one or two more, but..." Daffyd glanced at Dani. "I know, lass, you think you can protect us all, but it's a big ask."

"How exactly does Dr Hanser intend to protect you, or even just her?" Zewali asked.

"The god Set promised Scarab that evil would be turned back on the one offering it," Daffyd said. "It appears that Dani can command the same protection."

"Not command," Dani said quickly. "I can only ask and the god answers my prayer if he so desires."

Zewali shook his head. "Forgive me, Dr Hanser, but a belief like this could be a very dangerous delusion. Please do not rely upon this supposed protection."

"You saw it when Sarraj tried to shoot Marc and missed at point blank range. It's another aspect of the same power that brought him back to life."

"You know my views on that," Zewali said. "However, I think this is neither the time nor the place to debate such things. We should be looking for a credible way of extricating ourselves from this situation."

Footsteps crunched in the debris on the cave floor, as Nick came up behind them. "I heard you discussing ways of escape. What about this Guardian chappie? He's already killed two soldiers--would he remove a few more for us?"

"I'm not sure he did it for us," Dani said. "In his eyes, we're probably all trespassers."

"Oh, come on, Dani," Marc said. "It's Khu. Can you imagine him acting against the legitimate bearer of the golden scarab?"

"Perhaps not."

The gunfire became sporadic and died away, and everyone's attention turned to the situation below. The Bedouin were still hidden among the boulders, their presence only revealed by glimpses of keffiya or robes, but the watchers from the cave could see Sarraj gathering his men for an assault. Massri was evidently wounded in the leg, so he lay behind a jeep ready to give covering fire. The men broke cover, sprinting across an open space and disappearing among the boulders, from which erupted shouts and screams. Gunfire broke out again, a short eruption of sound that fell away as first one, and then three other Bedouin stepped out into the open. One raced across to the jeep and kicked away Massri's rifle, dropping to his knees beside the prostrate man, curved knife held to the captain's throat.

Sarraj emerged from behind the rocks, pushed along by another Bedouin. A man in khaki stepped out, helping the sixth Bedouin, who had been wounded. He helped his wounded comrade to a seat by a jeep and turned to face the hill, cupping his hands around his mouth.

"Ho, Marc! Are you there? Dani, Daffyd, Nick. Come out. You are among friends once more."

"It's Muammar," Marc yelled. He raced down the slope, barely keeping his footing, and grabbed the young Libyan, hugging him unashamedly. "You bugger. I thought you were dead."

"I told you I'd seen them on the ferry," Muammar said. "I headed back to find them and bring them to your rescue."

"Our rescue? Really?"

"Well, sort of..."

The others from the cave followed more sedately, and greeted Muammar warmly. Daffyd looked askance at Zufir and the other Bedouin, and moved to stand beside Dani as if to protect her. Zufir spoke, and Muammar translated.

"You owe me a ransom," he said, a wolfish grin creasing his bearded face. "I am minded to double it for all the trouble you have given us. My brother Tahir has spilled blood and you must pay him."

Dani nodded. "And so I shall. That man there..." She nodded in the direction of Sarraj, "...has gold in his pockets. It is yours as a reward for your service on behalf of Sheik ibn Hawid. It will cover the ransom and the blood price on your brother Tahir."

Zufir swung round and stared at Sarraj. "Search him."

A Bedouin grabbed the colonel and dug through his pockets, hauling out a dozen finger-length gold bars. He threw them down on the sand and let out an ululating cry of joy and triumph.

Sarraj moved, his hand snaking inside his jacket. He stepped forward, a pistol suddenly in his hand and fired into the Bedouin's back, striding forward even as the man started falling and, pushing Daffyd to one side, took hold of Dani. One arm swept around her neck and the other pressed the barrel of the pistol to her right temple.

"Have no doubt;" Sarraj said coldly, "I will kill Dr Hanser if anyone tries to stop us leaving."

"You won't kill me," Dani said calmly. "It would not be in your interests to try."

"You forget I am the military authority here. No one will question me should an unfortunate accident occur."

"Alif, Abu," Zufir rapped out. "Aim at the army man. If he kills the woman, shoot him dead. If he does not release her in a minute, shoot him dead anyway."

The two Bedouin raised their rifles obediently, but Alif said, "If we shoot him, we may hit the woman also."

"It is a price that must be paid," Zufir replied. "I will have vengeance for my brother Tahir's wound and for the life of my brother Abdul who now lies dead at this man's hand."

"Surrender," Dani said, "And I'll protect you."

"You? Protect me?" Sarraj uttered a bitter laugh. He started shuffling toward the jeep, and the two Bedouin moved with him, maintaining their aim. "Stay back."

Sarraj bumped his hip on the jeep and stumbled, recovering himself quickly, but Dani dropped to her knees, wrenching herself free of Sarraj's grasp and elbowing him sharply in the groin as she fell. The two Bedouin fired their rifles, missing him as the colonel doubled over in pain. He held onto his gun though, and shot the Bedouin kneeling beside Massri, thrusting him out of the way and scrambling behind the jeep. Rifle bullets slammed into the vehicle, narrowly missing Dani.

She waved back Daffyd who started across to help her, and called out to Sarraj again. "Surrender, Colonel. Please. It's not too late."

"Too late for you, bitch." Sarraj lifted his gun and took aim at Dani, ignoring the bullets that hissed past him.

"Shoot him, you imbeciles," Zufir yelled.

Sarraj's hand trembled, and an agonised expression gripped his sweating face. "H...help me. Allah, I call on you..."

Abruptly, Colonel Sarraj brought the gun to his own head and pulled the trigger. His head jerked sideways in a shower of blood and bone fragments, and an instant later, a rifle bullet caught him in the chest and another in the shoulder, flinging his lifeless body backward onto the hot sand.

Daffyd rushed to Dani's side and held her, wiping away spatters of blood with his handkerchief, the others close behind.

"Set's breath," Daffyd murmured. "That was a close one. It was the scarab wasn't it?"

Dani offered up a shaky smile. "You know, I quite forgot to ask him, but perhaps he was listening from earlier."

Captain Massri, the sole survivor of Sarraj's squad, got shakily to his feet, holding onto the jeep for support. He limped across to the group around Dani, putting them between him and Zufir, who had now turned to his fallen comrades.

"I...I surrender to you, D...Dr Hanser," Massri stuttered. He offered up his pistol and Marc grabbed it, stuffing it into his belt.

Zewali went over to where the colonel's body lay and squatted beside it, looking down dispassionately at the ruin of the man's head. "He died with Allah's name on his lips," he said. "Perhaps God will have mercy on him."

Zufir's men were swarming over the corpses of the soldiers, stripping them of items of clothing, their boots, rifles and wallets. The Bedouin leader saw Dani watching him and grinned fiercely.

"We take what is our due, infidel, and leave you your lives."

"Leave us the jeeps too," she said. "We will need them to return to Luxor."

Zufir nodded. "You have more gold?"

Dani patted her pockets. "No."

"If the gold had been yours I would have left you some, but it belonged to that piece of offal, so it is mine now."

"Then go in peace, Zufir ibn Walid. You have been rewarded for your trouble."

The Bedouin gathered together their spoils and loaded their two dead comrades and the wounded Tahir onto their camels and departed, heading westward. Daffyd organised a burial party and they searched out the fallen soldiers, carrying them into camp and laid them out while Massri identified them and made notes. They dug a mass grave in the lee of the hill, covering the soldiers with sand and rocks, and erecting a small cairn of rocks as a marker. Sarraj they buried separately as Captain Massri did not want his men associated in death with such a wicked man.

"He might have died with God's Name on his lips," the Captain said, "But Iblis had already claimed his black soul. I do not want the fires of hell touching the souls of my men."

"Speaking of black-hearted bastards," Marc said. "Where's Bashir?"

Chapter Forty-One

Ahmed Bashir had been making an inventory of the contents of the chamber. He had freed the gold bars from the rotted detritus of the boxes and bags they had once been held in, and stacked them neatly to one side. The hippopotamus ivory made another less neat stack, and he noted down how many of each there were, estimating the value of each pile.

"It's not right," he commented. "I get the artefacts, while Michel gets the bullion. There must be a million pounds worth here, but only a handful of necklaces. Is that fair?"

Dr Hosni Maroun, his arms folded, regarded the Minister with distaste. "You are both thieves and will not get away with this."

"I am not a thief," Bashir said hotly. "This treasure is mine by right of discovery. I was the one in charge of the expedition in Syria that discovered the inscription. It was by my efforts that we found the tomb, so of course I must have a share of its contents."

Bashir gently teased the necklaces and pectorals away from the overlying debris, collecting up loose beads and wrapping them in twists of paper torn from a notebook. Then he started searching through the rest of the chamber. He gazed at the faded paint on the cedar wood panels and nodded.

"I know collectors who would pay handsomely for these."

A decayed box in a corner yielded statues, tiny figurines of men and women carved from wood or lapis, a few with gold leaf, and more fashioned from faience.

"Not of any intrinsic value, but better than nothing, I suppose. I don't know why they couldn't be solid gold though."

"That wasn't the point of them," Maroun said. "Don't you know anything about the things you loot? Those are shabti figures and represent servants that were there to do the bidding of the deceased. They're very common."

"Where are the gold statues, the scarabs and things like that?" Bashir complained. His gaze roamed the chamber and stopped at the coffins. He crossed to them and stood looking at them with hunger on his face.

"Dr Hanser appealed to my decency just now, and I listened to her. I abstained from opening them. Yet there is little else in the tomb, and unless I open the coffins, Sarraj will walk away a rich man and I will remain poor."

"You are trying to justify your actions," Maroun said. "It will not work. Your actions are despicable."

"You think I care what you say? You are nothing to me. If I choose to open them I will." Bashir brought one of the kerosene lanterns over and held it high, looking over the pitted and cracked coffin with the faded, painted features of a king of Egypt and of a royal, though indisputably female person.

"I should open them, if only to check that the mummies are in good condition."

"If you do, you will put them at risk," Maroun said. "Sarcophagi should only be opened where trained archaeologists can control the conditions. Plundering of a mummy's wrappings has resulted in much destruction."

"I'm not going to plunder, just to look."

Maroun snorted. Bashir knelt beside the coffin of Smenkhkare and examined it by the light of the lantern. He ran his hands around it, seeking the join between base and lid, tugging at it futilely. He took a penknife from his pocket and worked the blade into the hairline crack, twisting it. The blade tore through the decaying wood and then, all of a sudden, the lid creaked and lifted a fraction.

Bashir gave a grin of triumph and slid the blade along a few inches, twisting and tugging with his other hand. He was rewarded by another groan of yielding wood, and the lid lifted a little more.

"Enough, I beg you," Maroun said. "You are damaging priceless artefacts."

Bashir ignored the archaeologist. He got to his feet and stooped over the coffin, dug his fingertips into the narrow crack and heaved upward. The lid came free, clattering on the floor of the chamber and stale, musty, dust-laden air still smelling faintly of spices and resins after three thousand years gusted over him, making him cough. The mummy of the king lay in repose, swaddled with brown and black-stained cloths. Vaguely, through the coverings, Bashir could make out the corpse's arms crossed over his chest, and the thin, eviscerated body, but the face made him gasp. Covering the head and shoulders of the mummy was the golden mask of a young man, his features clear and calm, the sightless eyes staring into infinity. The gold glowed warmly in the lantern light and Bashir fell to his knees again, tentatively reaching out to touch the cool metal.

"That is an artefact," the Minister said, "And as such, it belongs to me. It is worth a fortune."

"It belongs to the people of Egypt," Dr Maroun said.

Bashir took hold of each side of the mask with his hands and pulled. The whole mummy rose slightly in its wooden sarcophagus, but the mask did not separate from the body. He tried again, with a similar lack of success.

"Why won't it come free?" Bashir asked in frustration.

"Gums and resins used in the bandages have stuck face and mask together. Please cease your efforts. You could do irreparable damage to the mummy--even bend the mask."

"That wouldn't do," Bashir declared. "It would lower the price I could get for it." He thought for a few minutes, staring down at the peaceful golden features. "I might have to remove the head and apply heat to melt the gums."

Maroun gasped in horror and stepped forward as if to contest Bashir's possession of the mummy, but the Minister laughed and slashed the air with his penknife blade, sending the archaeologist reeling back.

"I'll leave it for now," Bashir said. "Let's see whether the woman has a similar mask. She was the king's sister, after all."

Maroun turned and ran from the chamber, followed by Bashir's laughter. He fled along the passage and into the outer cave, emerging onto the ledge and staring down blankly at the ravaged camp site and the people standing around.

"Come quickly," Maroun cried. "Bashir is desecrating the coffins."

Hard on the heels of his cry, a shriek of terror poured from the tomb, magnified by the throat of the passage, and echoed out over the desert.

Marc and Muammar were closest to the hill and ran for the slope, climbing upward, but Nick and Daffyd were close behind, leaving the others to follow on.

"It's the Guardian," Marc yelled. "It's got Bashir." He reached the ledge and pulled Captain Massri's gun from his belt, brandishing it as he and Muammar brushed Maroun aside and disappeared into the cave.

"Wait," Dani called. "Dafs, stop him! As far as the Guardian is concerned, Marc is just another invader."

"Marc!" Daffyd shouted. "Marc, wait!" He dashed into the cave after his friends. Nick followed more circumspectly, allowing Dani, Nazim and Zewali to catch up with him as they reached the remains of the tomb entrance. The temperature of the air dropped precipitately as they crossed the threshold, their breath showing white in the suddenly frigid air.

Dani looked in and saw only the backs of Daffyd, Marc and Muammar. They blocked her sight of the chamber except for a scattering of gold bars and ivory at their feet. Beyond them, shadows danced on the walls and ceiling of the chamber as two figures swayed back and forth. She pushed between Marc and Daffyd, gently pressing down the muzzle of the pistol in Marc's hand.

"That won't do any good now," she whispered.

In front of her, close by the open coffin of Smenkhkare, stood Bashir, neck stretched upward, his face congested and eyes bulging. The tips of his shoes scrabbled for purchase on the dusty floor of the chamber and his hands plucked at his neck where a shadow moved. Dani gasped out loud and the shadow moved again. She saw a gleam of eyes as something tenebrous turned and regarded her with cold hostility.

Bashir collapsed gasping to the floor of the chamber as the Guardian released him and moved toward Dani, a swirl of shadow hinting at a human presence rather than a definite figure, the eyes the only recognisable part. Daffyd stepped in front of Dani, arms outstretched protectively, but the Guardian never hesitated, picking up the Welshman and throwing him aside. Muammar thrust himself forward, muttering a prayer to Allah, but Marc yelled out, "No, Khu!"

The Guardian halted, its form swaying slightly as if in a non-existent breeze and turned its attention to the young man.

"Khu, remember me? You came to me when...when I died. We mean you no harm--we mean Scarab no harm. This is Dr Hanser--Dani--a...a learned woman...a scribe."

The shadow's attention swayed toward Dani again and she felt a cold intelligence scrutinise her.

"She is the bearer of the golden scarab," Marc said. "It answers her call, just as it did for Scarab."

He gasped as the chill presence rushed past him and expanded, filling the air around Dani. The temperature dropped still further and the being solidified, its formless body becoming head and cloaked body, skeletal hands and staring eyes, an expression of anger somehow conveyed by the forward thrust of its visage.

"Sh...show it...show him the s...scarab," Marc stuttered.

Dani fumbled it from her pocket and held it up. The gold gleamed in the shadowed air and the figure of the Guardian drew back, hesitating, its attention fixed on the artefact. It reached out a hand and Dani felt a brief stroking touch of bone on her fingers. Dani uttered a cry and collapsed, the golden scarab falling free from her grasp. Daffyd and Marc fell to their knees beside her, the former cradling her head, the latter taking her hand in his. The others pressed close, though their teeth chattered in the numbing cold, and the presence of the Guardian filled their hearts with dread.

"Oh my God," Nick cried. "What's that?"

Lifting like a swirl of smoke, something oozed from Dani's body, pouring up into the cold air and taking form.

"Allah protect us," Zewali muttered, "It is a spirit--another spirit."

"Is it the ghost of Dr Hanser?" Muammar asked, his face screwing up in an anguished presentiment of grief. "Has the Guardian killed her too?"

"I can feel a pulse," Marc said. He stared wide-eyed at the figure forming above them. "It looks like her though..."

"But not her," Daffyd added. "The hair is different and...and the dress is...is a dress. Dani's wearing slacks."

Nick frowned. "A ghost can have a hair style? Or wear a dress? How does that work?"

"It's not me," Dani whispered.

"Dani? You're alive. Thank God." Daffyd hugged Dani and kissed her forehead.

"It's not me," she repeated. "It's Scarab."

"It has the form of a New Kingdom lady as depicted on tomb walls," Zewali confirmed, "Though we are told that djinn and afrit can assume any shape."

"It's not a djinni. It's Scarab."

"What the hell is she doing here?" Marc wondered. "Was she inside you? Possessing you? Or was she actually you?"

"I don't think so," Dani said. "I'm still me, but..." she fell silent for a few moments, staring up at the spectral body of a woman floating in the air. "I used to...sort of feel her sometimes, even before we found the account, though I didn't know who or what it was. I don't know how to describe it, but that feeling's not there anymore."

The woman stood facing the Guardian, and as the seconds passed, the image of the one known as Khu changed. It became less skeletal, seeming to flesh out, to take on earthly substance and almost youth. The two spectres appeared to stare at one another for several minutes while their human audience watched in wonder and a little trepidation. One Guardian had proved formidable enough; who knew what two would do.

Scarab turned to face Dani, a gentle smile on her face--and then she abruptly disappeared.

"What?" Marc cried out. "Where's she gone?"

"I am here," Dani said. Her voice was normal and recognisable; being formed by her own lungs, mouth and vocal cords, but the content of what she said was not of Dani.

"I thank you for reuniting me with my beloved. For a long time I was unaware of his fate...of his service to me beyond death. That has finished, and you will see us no more."

Dani looked around the small rock tomb. "Take not what you want, but what you need, and leave this place undisturbed."

Dani staggered and would have fallen but for Daffyd's strong arms around her. "She's gone," she whispered in a stricken voice. "Gone for good. I can't feel her anywhere."

"The Guardian's gone too," Nick said. "When you staggered, he winked out like he'd been switched off."

"What do you think she meant; take what you need?" Marc asked.

Nobody answered. The air in the tomb was warming already, and people trembled with the release of pent up emotion, still trying to get to grips with what they had seen. Dani stumbled across to where the golden scarab lay on the floor of the chamber and slipped it into her pocket again. Ahmed Bashir, lying near the coffins, groaned--Nazim and Zewali went to him, knelt and examined him.

"He needs medical care," Zewali said. "I wouldn't advise moving him until we can get a stretcher."

"I think there is one in one of the jeeps," Nazim said. "I will go and get it." He walked past the others who were looking at the damage Bashir had done to Smenkhkare's coffin, and hesitated beside the jumbled pile of gold bars.

"Take what you need, not what you want," he muttered. He did a quick calculation and scooped up a handful, stuffing them into his trouser pockets. More went into his jacket pockets, bulging the fabric and weighing it down. "What I want is to live in luxury, but what I need is a deposit so I can retire to that house at Jarabulus near the Turkish border. I must not be greedy." He nodded, and then continued on his way out of the tomb.

Marc had seen Nazim's actions. "Cheeky bugger," he murmured, and then grinned. "Well, why not? Scarab said he could, and only he knows what he needs." He sauntered across and slipped four gold bars into his own pockets.

Daffyd and Nick had wrestled the lid back onto Smenkhkare's coffin, and were looking for a way to secure it, when Zewali told them not to bother.

"It'll take us a day to get back to Luxor, a day to prepare and another back here. Three days aren't going to matter too much. We can pile rubble in the entrance to deter jackals or casual visitors, though I doubt there will be any out here."

Dani pulled Daffyd aside. "Scarab said to leave it undisturbed. I can't allow Zewali to plunder it--even in the name of science."

"I could have a word with him. He may see reason."

"No. He needs to be unable to get here again." Dani pulled out the golden scarab again and closed her eyes. She muttered a prayer, of which Daffyd could only distinguish the names of the gods Geb, Set, and Nebt-Het.

"What was that all about?"

"I don't know exactly, but it seemed right to ask the gods of the earth, of the desert and of protection, for assistance. How they'll do it, or even if they will, remains to be seen. Now that Scarab's gone, the golden scarab may be no more than a piece of jewellery."

Nazim returned with the stretcher, accompanied by Dr Maroun, and together they helped Bashir, now conscious but groggy, from the chamber, carrying him on the stretcher over the rubble to the cave entrance. Others joined in here, and they slowly lowered him down the hill side to the camp below.

Signs of devastation and death were everywhere, though at least the bodies had been decently buried. Marc and Muammar started to tidy up, but Dani called them back.

"We're not going to be here long enough to bother. Just make sure the jeeps are functional."

Bashir sat up awkwardly on his stretcher, fingering his bruised neck. He looked around fearfully as if expecting to be attacked again. "What was that thing?" he rasped.

"The Guardian of the tomb," Daffyd told him. "Khu by all accounts."

"The farm boy? I never liked him."

"Well, he's gone now. Vanished with Scarab."

Bashir struggled to his feet. "Gone? He's not coming back?" He looked around at the shattered camp site. "Where is Colonel Sarraj?"

"Dead, along with all his men except Captain Massri."

"How?"

"Desert Bedouin attacked us." Daffyd decided he could not be bothered explaining the situation. "They've gone too."

"And Nazim?"

"He's alive, but he tells me he has left your employ."

"If he hadn't I would fire him. I cannot abide disloyalty."

Daffyd snorted derisively. "I can't say I blame him...what the hell?"

The ground shook; a mild trembling that stopped all conversation in an instant. In the silence they could hear the clatter of falling stones around them.

"Earthquake?" Nick asked. "I didn't think Egypt got them."

"Occasionally," Zewali said. "Mostly centred in the Red Sea or Gulf of Aqaba. The Gulf is part of the Afro-Syrian Rift, you know."

"Must have been a big one if we could feel it here," Nick commented.

"Is there any reason to hang around?" Marc asked. "This whole place reeks of death and violence. We've found what we came for, Dani's got her golden scarab back and we proved the truth of the inscription. I say we head back to Luxor and then on to England's green and pleasant land."

"We need to seal up the tomb again," Zewali said. "We cannot just leave it open, even for a few days."

"It won't take long," Maroun added. "My word, though, I'm excited at the prospect of examining it properly."

"What about the gold and ivory?" Nick asked. "We could take that with us. I mean, the bars aren't artefacts or anything, and some have already gone..."

"What? Where?" Zewali looked shocked.

Marc looked away as if suddenly struck by the beauty of the desert, and Nazim pushed his small knapsack a little further under his seat in the jeep.

"The Bedouin, remember?" Nick continued. "They took the gold bars that Sarraj brought out." He caught Marc's eye and winked. Marc blushed and looked down at his feet.

"By rights, I should have a share of that gold," Bashir said. "I have spent much money financing this whole expedition."

"Forget it," Daffyd said. "You'll be facing charges, not profiting from your actions."

The earth shook again, harder than before, and Zewali stumbled and fell. Maroun went to his assistance, while the others clutched hold of some support to remain upright. For a minute, everyone stood stock still, holding their collective breaths, waiting for the ground to resume its shaky dance. When it didn't, they breathed again.

"Where's Bashir?" Daffyd asked.

Nazim pointed. "He's on the hill."

Bashir scrambled up the slope, and as Marc and Muammar took off after him, entered the cave and disappeared from view.

"Take care," Zewali yelled after them. "The tremor may have weakened the rock..."

A roar like an express train drowned out his words and the desert around the green mountain turned into a dancing jumble of sand and rock, throwing everyone to the ground. Slabs of stone rose and fell, and the vibrating sand grains fell away around Sarraj's grave, the dead colonel's grisly, shattered head rising above the surface. The hill itself groaned, shaking violently and a great gout of dust and rock fragments vomited out of the cave. Marc and Muammar rolled amidst fresh debris to the bottom of the slope, but scrambled free as the tremor died away.

In the silence that followed, everyone got to their feet and stared at the ruin of the hill. After a few minutes, Marc and Muammar tried again, cautiously picking their way through the rubble to the cave mouth. They peered inside before turning and calling down to the others.

"It's chockers," Marc called. "It looks like the roof has collapsed."

"Any sign of Bashir?"

"Not a sausage."

The others joined Marc and Muammar on the shattered ledge and peered through the dusty air at the rubble choking the shaft that led to the tomb. Dust still fell from the roof, and the rock pile groaned and shifted as the whole mass settled.

"I suppose we'd better see if we can dig him out," Dani said.

"You're joking?" Marc replied. "He'll be as flat as a pancake under that lot."

"And if he's not under it? What if the chamber's intact and he's trapped in there? We can't just leave him."

"Why not? He'd have done the same to us." Marc saw Dani's expression and sighed. "Yeah, I know. We dig him out."

They started a chain, one or two at the edge of the rubble, passing chunks of rock or boulders back, throwing the freed debris down the slope. It was finicky work, prising loose rocks that tended to support others, leading to small collapses every few minutes. Despite this, the work continued and they advanced a few feet into the shaft.

When they stopped for a break, Zewali brought one of the kerosene lanterns and inspected the roof of the shaft. He pointed to several cracks and to thin intermittent curtains of sand and dust that fell from them.

"It's too dangerous," Zewali said. "The roof could collapse at any time."

"You're saying we should just abandon him?" Daffyd asked.

"I don't like it, but yes. We need to return to Luxor and get help. Get some equipment that can hold the roof up while we dig him out."

"That will take at least three days," Muammar said. "Even if he is uninjured, he will die of thirst in that time."

"We have to keep trying to dig him out," Dani said.

They resumed their labours, working even more slowly and carefully now, and gradually worked their way back another two feet. Daffyd, taking a turn at the rubble face, felt his fingers slip on something smooth when he bent to pick up a rock. He stared at the brown leather surface of a boot, almost obscured by a layer of dust and grit.

"I've found him," he said quietly.

Zewali joined him and knelt in the dirt. Working cautiously, he tugged the boot off and felt the left foot beneath it.

"It's cool." He pressed a finger hard into the flesh and saw the indentation whiten--and stay white. "I think he's dead."

Daffyd sat back on his haunches and looked at the rubble-choked shaft with one bare foot sticking out of it. "The question is, do we continue to risk our lives digging out a body, or do we leave him?"

"Are you absolutely sure he's dead?" Dani asked.

"Um...ninety per cent. He's under all that rock."

"I think we have to be sure."

"I was afraid you were going to say that."

Daffyd motioned Zewali back and kept hauling out rocks, concentrating on the area where Bashir's body lay. The bootless foot led to a trousered leg, though blood had soaked the ripped and frayed fabric. Just past the knee the material was ripped clean away and Daffyd could see a deep wound in the flesh. Blood had gushed at this point, congealing into a sticky mess with the dust, but no more blood was coming from the wound. As he moved forward to examine the wound more closely, his shoulder brushed the fallen rocks. They settled, spilling a gush of loose gravel and dirt, and the whole pile groaned ominously.

"There's a deep wound in his thigh, but there's no blood coming out of it now."

"That means his heart has stopped," Zewali said. "The man is dead."

"Come out of there, Dafs," Dani said. "Slowly and carefully. There's nothing more you can do for him."

Daffyd shuffled backward, taking great care not to touch the walls, step at a time, and as he reached the place where the rubble wall had stood before they started clearing it, there was another earth tremor. A small one--scarcely more than a vibration in the stone of the green mountain, but the unstable rubble collapsed, burying Bashir's body once more and driving his rescuers back with a cloud of fresh dust and debris. They gathered on the ledge outside the cave, coughing and brushing the dirt out of their hair and clothes.

"That's it," Zewali said. "Minister Bashir is dead. We must leave his body here for now, but we will return in a few days with the equipment we need to excavate the tomb properly. We can give him a decent burial then."

"You are determined to open the tomb again?" Dani asked.

"Of course. The tomb of King Smenkhkare and his sister Beketaten will become as famous as that of their brother Tutankhamen." Zewali smiled at her expression, mistaking her thoughts. "Do not worry. I will see that you get the full credit for the discovery--all of you."

Chapter Forty-Two

I t was late in the day by the time they came down from the green mountain. Before they left for Luxor, they reburied Sarraj, and made sure the other bodies were secure from scavengers beneath the hot sand. One of the jeeps had taken a few stray bullets through the vitals, so it was left behind after stripping it of everything useful, from tyres to spark plugs, and draining the petrol, oil and water.

Dani walked apart from the others while they busied themselves getting ready and faced the site of the tomb of her distant ancestress. She held the golden scarab in her hands, but it seemed lifeless, as if the power that had energised it had drained away. *It didn't work. Maybe in ancient times an earthquake would have been enough, but modern man has machines that can dig this out. The power of the gods is not enough.* She felt depressed and drained, and turned to leave.

Nobody spoke much as they drove eastward, the nine survivors filling the remaining two vehicles, each person lost in their own thoughts. Captain Massri and Daffyd drove the two jeeps carefully back along the trail, arriving at the ruined Khepri pylon at dusk. They camped for the night, eking out the last of the stores and fuel to create a plain but hot meal. Exhausted, emotionally and physically, they retired early.

The earthquake struck just before midnight, shocking them awake as a deep-seated rumbling rocked the desert. It went on longer than the previous tremors, and then died away completely. No one could get back to sleep afterward, so they sat around the camp fire, drinking coffee, and discussing what the future held.

"How are we going to explain all this?" Daffyd asked.

"All what, exactly?"

"Everything." Daffyd sighed. "Where do I start? Colonel Sarraj and ten men are killed by Bedouin in the desert, Syrian Minister Bashir dies, buried by falling rubble in the shaft of a tomb, four of us are in Egypt illegally, but it's our information that leads to the discovery of the previously unknown tomb. Anyone care to add anything?"

"That about covers it, I think," Marc agreed. "We're going to need a good story."

"Why do we need a story?" Zewali asked. "We just tell the truth of it."

"Which is what exactly?"

"That Dr Hanser and Minister Bashir both came to me with descriptions of a tomb. We went looking for it, found it, and plan on returning to excavate it properly."

Daffyd nodded. "That covers you nicely, but what about us? How do we explain how we came into Egypt, and why would we blow our cover by coming to you? The authorities will prosecute us when they catch us-- either jail us or deport us..."

"Probably both," Marc said.

"And I will face the same fate," Muammar said. "The Libyan Army may even regard me as a deserter."

"And Colonel Sarraj," Nick added. "What's his involvement in this? The army in Luxor now has records of Sarraj interrogating Dani and Daffyd, plus we have police records of an attack on your household by thugs whom they'll likely track back Ali Hafiz and thence to Sarraj. They'll probably want to know your involvement."

"That's true, Dr Zewali," Maroun said. "Minister Bashir is on record of having dealings with the museum in Luxor and with Director Nasrallah in Cairo. He also is connected to Dr Hanser and her team, being responsible for preventing them entry to Egypt--yet here they are."

"And the Minister is a close friend of Colonel Sarraj," Nazim said. "They plotted together to find and plunder the tomb..."

"It would serve no useful purpose to make that known," Zewali said.

"That depends," Daffyd said. "Bashir and Sarraj are painted as criminals, yet they have close dealings with the Director of the Luxor Museum. I imagine questions would be asked."

"Oh indeed," Nick grinned. "Newspapers would have a field day. Corruption in high places, and all that."

"Are you threatening me?" Zewali asked tightly.

"Not at all, Karim," Dani said. "We just need an explanation we can all agree upon that doesn't disadvantage anyone."

They sat and considered the problem.

"Let me just voice a few thoughts," Nazim said. "First, there is no one more knowledgeable than Dr Hanser where the Syrian inscription is concerned. Minister Bashir is on record as having had her and her team deported from Syria and has gone to great lengths to neutralise any possible interference by her..."

"This is all old hat," Marc grumbled. "What's this got to do with anything?"

"I am coming to that, Dr Andrews. Now, where was I? Ah, yes...Minister Bashir comes to Egypt to find the tomb, engaging the help of his powerful friend Colonel Sarraj. The Minister enquires of the Department of Antiquities, both in Cairo and Luxor, and finds that the descriptions given in the account are insufficient to allow him to find the tomb. Sarraj has his agents kidnap Dr Hanser and her friends from Libya..."

"What were they doing in Libya?" Maroun asked. "It is rather fortuitous."

"I'd been suspended from the university," Dani said. "I went on holiday and I'd never been to Libya."

"Neither had Marc and I, so we accompanied her. All very straightforward. We hired Muammar to show us the desert, and in Al Jawf we..."

"They were abducted," Nazim continued. "Brought into Egypt and forced to lead Sarraj and Bashir to the tomb. You are in Egypt illegally, but no blame can attach to you. You were brought in against your will."

"That might work," Daffyd said. "Provided everyone sticks to that story."

"Where does that leave Dr Zewali and me?" Maroun asked.

"You were suspicious of Bashir's motives and, in an official capacity, insisted on accompanying the expedition. You were both unaware of Dr Hanser's status at the time. It was only when Sarraj was killed and Minister Bashir disappeared, that you became aware of the whole dreadful business. Your word, together with mine, will exonerate Dr Hanser and her companions."

"Won't you be blamed too?" Marc asked.

"Everyone knows I was merely the Minister's secretary, nothing more. When I became aware of what was going on, I went to Dr Zewali and told him. I could not report to the Egyptian authorities, as I was uncertain as to how far the corruption extended."

Daffyd looked at Captain Massri, who sat quietly in the shadows, smoking a cigarette. "What about you, Captain? You're a military man and were under Sarraj's command. What's your opinion?"

Massri hesitated. "It is difficult for me to speak of such things. I am a loyal army officer, you understand? It is my career and people who speak out against their commanders have few prospects. However, Colonel Sarraj is dead and I do not believe he will be missed. He was ambitious and ruthless, and...I have heard rumours that...no, I will not say it out loud. Let me just say that President Nasser was once an army colonel, until a coup put him in power."

"Sounds like Sarraj and Bashir were two of a kind. Neither will be missed."

Massri nodded his agreement. "I must report back to Edfu, but I am not sure what I should say. They were my men that died, and I bear some responsibility for their demise."

"It was my understanding that Sarraj commanded," Nazim said quietly. "There is little a conscientious officer can do in the face of a direct order from a superior officer. Besides, Captain Massri, you were wounded in the attack that killed your men, so you cannot be accused of shirking your duties. I would be happy to make a statement to that effect."

"Thank you, Mr Manouk. I also have to explain the two men who died of fright."

Nazim smiled mirthlessly. "Would you care to explain how two fine men were attacked by a ghost and died? Far better they died combating Egypt's bandits while on active service, don't you think?"

"That is true," Massri conceded.

"You see?" Daffyd said. "We are piecing together a coherent account of what happened. Minister Bashir discovers a description of a lost tomb in Egypt. He packs off the British team so they won't interfere, and hot-foots it down to Egypt to plunder it. Here he discovers the description is inaccurate, so he asks questions of the museum experts and has his co-conspirator Colonel Sarraj kidnap the principals of the British team while they are holidaying in Libya. Sarraj forces the captives to reveal what they know and sets off with an army guard to plunder the tomb. The museum officers have, in the meantime, suspected his felonious intent due to the loyal revelations of Bashir's secretary, and accompany the army expedition to safeguard any discoveries. They barely find the tomb when they are set upon by bandits who are driven off at the expense of all the army personnel with the exception of Captain Massri, who is wounded. Minister Bashir goes missing..."

"But he's not missing," Muammar said. "They'll find his body in the shaft when they excavate it."

"Exactly. He took shelter in the cave and it collapsed on him, killing him, but we don't know that--only that he's gone missing."

"You think they'll believe it?" Marc asked.

"If we show a united front."

"What about the thugs who attacked me in my house?" Zewali asked. "You said the police would track down who sent them. How will that affect the story?"

"Sarraj didn't want the museum director watching him, so he tried to remove him," Daffyd suggested. "If the police don't make the connection, keep quiet. It was just local thieves breaking in."

Zewali and Massri contemplated their parts in the cover up, and whether any revelation could show them up in a lie. They looked at each other across the fire and first the captain, and then the scientist, shrugged and acquiesced.

"It's a reasonable story. I think I can convince my superiors," Massri said.

Zewali nodded. "I still intend to excavate the tomb, Dr Hanser. Its discovery is a wonderful thing and I cannot allow it to remain hidden. It is a part of Egyptian history."

"I understand your motivation, Karim," Dani said.

"Then we're agreed?" Daffyd asked. "Is there anything we've overlooked?"

"What about Nick?" Marc asked. "He's a news hound. Is he going to be able to control his desires to splash the truth all over the Sunday papers?"

"Why don't you ask him then?" Nick said. "Instead of talking about me as if I'm not here."

Marc flushed. "All right then--what about it?"

"First, I'm a freelance journalist, not a reporter for the Sunday rags. Second, I've agreed to submit anything I write to Dani and Daffyd for their approval before I publish. I'll keep my promise. Is that good enough for you?"

Marc nodded. "If it's alright with Dani..."

"It is," Dani said.

*   *   *

The next morning, they drove down to the river and took the ferry across to Luxor, where their story was put to the test.

Dani, Daffyd, Marc and Muammar gave themselves up to the police and were promptly arrested and jailed. Nazim and Dr Zewali testified that the Libyan and English people had been kidnapped and brought to Egypt against their will. The matter was referred up to the highest levels of government, and an investigation was instituted into the part Syrian Minister Ahmed Bashir had played and his connections with Colonel Michel Sarraj. Dani and her friends were released into the custody of Dr Zewali, until the British Consulate could provide temporary travel documents. The Libyan Embassy would provide similar documents for Muammar al-Hadi.

Nazim came under suspicion as Bashir's secretary, but Dani gave him a glowing character reference and Dr Zewali, a respected member of the Egyptian scientific community, testified on his behalf, declaring that the plot to plunder ancient artefacts would not have come to light without Mr Manouk's selfless actions.

Captain Massri reported to the commander of the Luxor army barracks and found himself held for questioning. General Gamal made a special trip down from Cairo and questioned him at length about Colonel Sarraj's actions. After a few days, the General launched a full enquiry into the Colonel's business dealings, arrested Lieutenant Azib, and learned a lot more about Sarraj's intentions, including his political aspirations. Captain Massri was sent back to his unit in Edfu. The police did make the connection between the thugs who broke into Zewali's house and Ali Hafiz, and the agent, who had survived Dani's defence, quickly implicated Colonel Sarraj in yet more wrongdoing.

Dr Karim Zewali and Dr Hosni Maroun put together an expedition to return to the green mountain to excavate the tomb. While they were gone, Nick came round to Zewali's house armed with tape recorders and notebooks, ready to hear the full story of Scarab. The five of them sat around a large dining room table, and Zewali's housekeeper kept them supplied with coffee and snacks, as well as three meals a day, while Dani recounted the story of the discovery in Syria. Muammar sat in on the sessions, interested in how the whole enterprise had started.

Nazim had turned over everything that had been confiscated from the British expedition, so Dani was now in possession of the details of the inscription. She was surprised that Nick was so interested in the account and said so.

"I would have thought your readers would be more interested in the modern day search for the tomb, rather than a long account of dead people."

"I think many will be," Nick said. "But the account is the guts of the story. Of course I want to know how you found the chambers and what you thought, and how you got into Egypt, but I'm fascinated by Scarab too, and I want her story."

"One thing worries me right there," Marc said. "You want to know how we got into Egypt, but if you print the true story we get into trouble."

"I know, and there are ways round that. I've promised I won't say anything that will compromise you, and I really want to know."

"We trust you, Nick," Dani said. "What exactly do you want to know?"

"Everything."

It took several days, working through the journals, poring over photographs of the inscription itself and the artwork on the walls of the chambers, and listening to the tapes made while Dani translated. They took it in turns, working twelve hours a day or more, only stopping for meals, toilet breaks and writer's cramp. When the last words had been copied, the tale brought up to date, Nick threw down the latest stub of pencil and regarded the pile of filled notebooks on the floor beside his chair.

"That is one hell of a story."

"A bit long for an article," Daffyd said. "Even a series of articles."

"Hmm." Nick leafed through the last notebook thoughtfully. "There is another option. I've often thought about writing a novel but I couldn't think of a decent story. Well, you've given me that. I could write this up as a novel--if you had no objection, of course."

"The finding of the chambers and the tomb? Or Scarab's story?"

"Both. You couldn't write one without the other."

"Would you use our real names?" Marc asked.

"No, and that brings me back to your passage into Egypt. I'd use different names to protect your reputations."

"They'd still know it was us," Daffyd said. "How many British expeditions investigating Neanderthal migration routes get chucked out of Syria?"

"Yes, but that's the beauty of a novel as opposed to a scientific article. It's a fictionalised account, so nobody can be quite sure what's true and what's made up. All you'd have to do is deny it and there's nothing anyone could do. Naturally, I'd be as accurate as possible, but I can include all those magic bits and gifts of the gods that I'd have to gloss over in a scientific article. I can tell the whole story."

"Can I think about it?" Dani asked.

415

"Of course. It will take me some time to get this mass of data into some coherent form. Keep in touch, and I'll let you know when I'm ready to start writing."

*   *   *

Dr Zewali returned--in a bad mood. "We could not find the damn thing."

Daffyd poured him a cup of coffee and took it to where the archaeologist sat glowering in an armchair. "I wouldn't have thought a mountain--even a small one--was easy to lose. Didn't you have the map coordinates?"

"We had them, and we followed the tyre tracks back for half a day, and then they just petered out."

"Still, dead reckoning should have got you to familiar territory."

Zewali sipped his coffee. "You'd think so, wouldn't you? When we got to the place where I was almost certain it should be, it wasn't. There wasn't a mountain, green or otherwise. No sign of a camp, no abandoned jeep, no mass grave. Nothing."

"You must have mistaken the place."

"When I say nothing, we did in fact find the corpse of Colonel Sarraj. It was lying on the surface as if even the desert did not want him. That is how I know it was the right place, but the mountain was gone, taking with it the tomb. If I hadn't seen it for myself, I'd doubt its very existence."

"A mountain doesn't just disappear."

"The earthquake," Dani said. "The last big one. It must have swallowed up the tomb."

"The gods answered your prayer," Marc murmured.

Zewali grimaced. "It will be there somewhere. The earthquake merely altered the terrain in such a way as to obscure the site. We'll send out another team, and another, until we find it."

"Good luck," Dani said politely.

*   *   *

Their travel documents came through, courtesy of the British Consulate, so they bade farewell to Dr Zewali and Dr Maroun at the museum, and travelled with Nick and Nazim up to Cairo. Nick was accompanying them back to England, but Nazim was returning to Syria.

"Are you going to be alright?" Dani asked. "Now that Bashir's out of the picture?"

"The Ministry has made it plain that my career has been somewhat tainted by my association with ex-Minister Bashir. I have decided to take early retirement and plan on buying a small property near Jarabulus on the Turkish border. I'll grow olives and perhaps even write my memoirs."

"Scarab's gold will come in handy then."

Nazim looked startled. "You know about that?"

Dani smiled. "Scarab said you could take according to your need."

"So she did."

"On that note," Marc murmured. He pulled out the four small bars of gold he had removed from the tomb and passed one each to Daffyd, Muammar and Nick. He put the fourth one back in his pocket. "Everyone needs a souvenir or to recoup expenses."

Nick whistled and stroked the gold. "I'm never selling mine."

"Nor me," Daffyd said.

"I might have to," Muammar said, "But we'll see."

"What about Dani?" Daffyd asked. "Doesn't she get one?"

"I have my golden scarab." She took it out and held it in the palm of her hand, where in gleamed in the airport concourse lights.

"I can't imagine how I ever mistook it for a rock," Nazim said.

The airport tannoy echoed and screeched, but they heard enough to know their flight had been called. They said their goodbyes to Nazim and walked across the tarmac to the waiting aircraft. Nick and Marc chattered between themselves, eager to be back in England, but Dani and Daffyd hung back, as if reluctant to leave Egypt.

"It'll be good to get back, lass, especially now that Bashir's been discredited. I imagine your suspension will be overturned and you'll be reinstated without prejudice."

"And you. Back to lecturing."

"Our lives returning to normal."

"Or as normal as they'll ever be. Things have changed, Dafs..." Dani gave Daffyd's hand a quick squeeze, "...for all of us."

"What about Scarab? Is she still with you?"

"I'm just plain Dani Hanser now. What you see is what you get."

"Oh, I do hope so." Daffyd grinned.

Dani blushed.

They crossed the remaining tarmac and stood at the foot of the stairs, looking up at the smiling stewardess.

"And Scarab?" Daffyd asked softly. "Where is she?"

"She's reunited with Khu after three thousand years. I'd say that was a happy ending."

"An ending? I wonder..."

Epilogue

The man and woman walked over springy turf, a cool wind in their faces and the sun warm on their backs. Spreading out to their right, fields burgeoned with wheat and barley, the ripening ears waving in the gentle breeze; vineyards as far as the eye could see, the vines heavy with dark grapes. In pastures, cattle grazed--powerful bulls and beautiful fat cows with calves at their sides--black ones in one field, red in another, and white in a third. To their left, reed beds swayed in the breeze, the wind playing with the feathered tops and ruffling the stretches of cool water that lay between them. Fish jumped in the limpid waters and flocks of ducks and geese exploded upward as they passed, wheeling in the clear blue sky and landing again behind them. The man breathed in, taking in lungfuls of clean air so free of dust that it smelled sweet in his nostrils. The green of the grass and reeds was unblemished, of such a rich hue it made him want to weep for the joy of it. Sunlight warmed him, a gentle heat that comforted and soothed, and silence enveloped him save for the gentle sigh of the wind, the muted squabbling of wildfowl in the reed beds, and the distant lowing of contented cattle.

"Where are we?" the man asked.

"Don't you recognise it, Khu? No, of course, how could you? You have been in service to the gods for untold years. This is Sekhet Aaru, the Field of Reeds."

"But...but what of judgement? What of the weighing of the heart?" Khu looked around fearfully as if expecting the dreadful beast that ate the hearts of the wicked to haul itself out of the clear waters.

The woman smiled. "You are already here, dear Khu. You need have no fear."

Khu looked at the young woman who walked beside him. She wore a pure white linen kilt that contrasted sharply with her unblemished copper skin and her firm breasts were bare, scarcely moving as she walked. Stitched onto the edge of her kilt was a small blue scarab. He frowned, trying to remember.

"I should know you. The blue scarab means something."

The woman smiled. "It will come to you."

Khu nodded, accepting. "Where are we going?"

"Everywhere...and nowhere. But for now, to that city."

Khu looked ahead and saw gleaming white walls rising like clouds in the clear summer sky. The tops faded in the distance and the whiteness was so intense that every colour seemed to reflect back to his eyes. He gasped with pleasure and awe.

"What is the name of this city? What king rules here?"

"You may call it Men-nefer if you wish, for enduring and beautiful describes it perfectly, but no king rules here save the One, of whom the Nine of Iunu are but an aspect."

"I don't understand."

"You will."

As they drew close to the city, they found that a narrow stretch of water separated them from the white walls. The woman led Khu to a small, narrow-beamed boat and bade him climb aboard. She pushed off and, taking a slim pole in her strong hands, sped them across the water. The boat grounded on the far shore and Khu leapt out, offering his hand to the young woman.

"I know you," Khu said as their fingers touched. "Almost."

She smiled and gestured toward the huge gates that lay spread wide, inviting him to enter. As he walked forward, Khu became aware of people all around him, though a few moments before he had been certain the city was deserted. Men, women and children walked or ran, talking quietly and earnestly, or chattering and laughing in high spirits, and when faces turned toward him, Khu saw that they were smiling. He felt their welcome as something tangible and his heart went out to them.

The woman led Khu further into the city. Beyond the towering white walls lay broad avenues between stone buildings, great open plazas and parks with soaring palm trees, flowering shrubs of a hundred different colours and scents, and fountains of crystal clear water.

"This is...is the place of the blessed."

"Yes."

Khu turned to the woman and smiled. "I know you. You are the young girl who came to my village."

"I was indeed, dear Khu. Who else was I?"

"A...a princess, a queen, a king? A...my wife...Scarab?"

"Yes."

"But you look so young and I...I am..."

"Young too, my love."

Khu looked at himself in a pool of water and touched his youthful, unlined face in wonder. "How is this? I was an old man...then I...I died. Now I am in the Field of Reeds?" He stared at his reflection in the pool of water, then up at the young woman standing before him. "We are married. I remember that."

"A man and a woman were married, but they were Khu and Scarab."

"That is who we are."

"No, that is who we were." Scarab took Khu's hand and squeezed it gently. "We are no longer married, dear Khu, but that does not change my love for you."

"I have always loved you."

"And I you, but I am no longer Scarab, and you are no longer Khu."

Khu looked puzzled. "If I am no longer Khu, then who am I?"

"You will remember when you are ready."

Khu looked about him at the clean, bright city and its parks, at the throngs of smiling people without a trace of hunger or disease. "I have been here before," he murmured. Then he pointed. "That man--I think I know him."

Scarab beckoned and the man walked over, greeting her with a quick embrace before studying Khu.

"I wondered when you would return to us. Welcome."

"Thank you. Do I know you?"

"We shared a life once," the man said.

"I...I have not lived for a long time. I cannot remember your face, but I recognise something in you."

"You recognise the inner flame of being. This face belonged to my last life. The one you remember is this..." The man's features blurred and swam, before solidifying once more.

Khu gasped and involuntarily took a step backward. "Tjaty Ay. You!" He turned to Scarab with a look of consternation on his face. "How can he be here in the Field of Reeds? Surely when his heart was weighed, his black deeds must have..."

"He judged himself," Scarab said, "And atoned for his deeds in his next life."

Ay smiled. "My next three lives. I was an evil man then."

Scarab embraced Ay. "Ah, but you should have seen him in his last life," she told Khu. "He was a man who helped others. He gave of himself selflessly. If you had known him then, you would have loved him. As I did, for I was one of those he helped."

"I...I find this hard to understand."

"It will come to you."

Ay smiled and walked away, becoming lost in the throng of people.

"Who else is here?" Khu asked.

"Everyone you knew, and countless others."

"My parents? My brothers and sisters? Our daughter Dania?"

"Dania inhabits an earthly body at the moment, as does your mother, but yes, you'll see the others soon."

Scarab took Khu by the hand and led him out of the park, through the crowds of people and into one of the tall buildings. Great cavernous halls filled with light receded beyond the limits of his sight, and were lined floor to ceiling with shelves, packed with scrolls. In the spaces between the shelves, people talked or read scrolls, discussing the contents and making notes.

"So many scrolls? What is this place?"

"The Hall of Records. The lives of every person who ever lived are written on these scrolls." Scarab took a scroll from a shelf, seemingly at random, and unfurled it. "Here is your last life, Khu--every thought, every deed, every word you uttered."

"Everything? No scroll could possibly be large enough."

Scarab laughed, the sound refreshing him like running water in the desert. "Neither the city nor this building; neither this scroll nor the bodies of the people you see around us have any physical meaning, dear Khu. They are present in those forms to comfort you until your mind can grasp the truth."

Khu scanned the scroll in his hands, but he was not reading. Rather, he focussed on a phrase Scarab had uttered. "My last life?"

"You have lived before, Khu, and will live again--if you choose. How can any man perfect himself in just one life? Or any woman?"

"You said this city was ruled by the One. Who did you mean? One of the gods?"

"All gods are part of the One. And every god that we knew was once as we were, men and women walking the earth. They have perfected themselves and now guide us so that one day we may join them."

The Hall of Records faded away around him, and Khu found he was alone, walking through verdant gardens and beside tumbling brooks, to where a group of some twenty people stood in a circle. He smiled as he approached them for he recognised them all, not by their outward appearance but by the inner flame of their being. His father was there, his brothers and sisters, a man who had been Nebhotep the physician, Jesua the Shechite, Jeheshua the Khabiru, as well as men who had been kings when last he walked upon the earth. Akhenaten was there, Smenkhkare with his arm around Tutankhamen, even Ay and the old king Nebmaatre Amenhotep. The man who had been Khu greeted them all one by one, recognising what each person meant to him and what he meant to them. Scarab was there too, and his mother, and his daughter Dania.

"Scarab said you were living a life."

"When she said it, I was," Dania laughed. "Since then I have lived a full and rich life."

"In so short a time?"

"There is no past and future," his mother Asenath said. "Only now."

Full understanding flooded over Khu, and he felt a warm and comforting sense of well-being, of having come home to his loved ones. His consciousness expanded and merged with the other beings around him, becoming one with them all. Time ceased to exist.

*   *   *

Two souls and a guide existed together.

"Are you ready?"

"Yes."

"Will you choose, or will you be guided?"

"Both."

"This is the man best suited for you." Images appeared. A man walked and interacted with others, scenes of a life played out, from birth through to death.

"Will I be with..."

"Yes. She will be your wife again. See?" The images changed as a woman entered the scenes, altering the destination of several lives. "Any other changes you would make?"

"Perhaps...?"

"Your life would be harder."

"But more worthwhile. If this happened...or that..."

"Yes. Good choices."

"Who would my parents be?"

"They are part of our group, living now. They hold the names Marc and Jenny Andrews."

"And her parents?"

"They live too, and are known to you. Dani and Daffyd Rhys-Williams."

"I am content."

"And I."

"Then let it be so."

The End of the Story of Scarab

You can find ALL our books up at Amazon at:
https://www.amazon.com/shop/writers_exchange

or on our website at:
http://www.writers-exchange.com

JOIN ONE LIST. GET FIVE FREE BOOKS.

Join the Writers Exchange E-Publishing readers' list and *immedaitely* get a free novel! A new download link to a novel in each of our five main genres (Romance, Fantasy, Science Fiction, Mystery, and Historical) will hit your inbox every week!

http://bit.ly/WEE-Newsletter

You'll be kept up to date about our giveaways, new releases, and blog highlights.

About the Author

Max Overton has travelled extensively and lived in many places around the world-- including Malaysia, India, Germany, England, Jamaica, New Zealand, USA and Australia. Trained in the biological sciences in New Zealand and Australia, he has worked within the scientific field for many years, but now concentrates on writing. While predominantly a writer of historical fiction (Scarab: Books 1 - 6 of the Amarnan Kings; the Scythian Trilogy; the Demon Series; Ascension), he also writes in other genres (A Cry of Shadows, the Glass Trilogy, Haunted Trail, Sequestered) and draws on true life (Adventures of a Small Game Hunter in Jamaica, We Came From Königsberg). Max also maintains an interest in butterflies, photography, the paranormal and other aspects of Fortean Studies.

Most of his other published books are available at Writers Exchange Ebooks, http://www.writers-exchange.com/Max-Overton.html and all his books may be viewed on his website: http://www.maxovertonauthor.com/

Max's book covers are all designed and created by Julie Napier, and other examples of her art and photography may be viewed at www.julienapier.com

If you want to read more about other books by this author, they are listed on the following pages...

A Cry of Shadows
(Paranormal Murder Mystery)

Australian Professor Ian Delaney is single-minded in his determination to prove his theory that one can discover the moment that the life force leaves the body. After succumbing to the temptation to kill a girl under scientifically controlled conditions, he takes an offer of work in St Louis, hoping to leave the undiscovered crime behind him.

In America, Wayne Richardson seeks revenge by killing his ex-girlfriend, believing it will give him the upper hand, a means to seize control following their breakup. Wayne quickly discovers that he enjoys killing and begins to seek out young women who resemble his dead ex-girlfriend.

Ian and Wayne meet, and when Ian recognizes the symptoms of violent delusion he employs Wayne to help him further his research. Despite the police closing in, the two killers manage to evade identification as the death toll rises.

John Barnes, the detective in charge of the case, is frantic, willing to try anything to catch his killer. With time running out, he looks desperately for answers. Will John get them before it's too late?

Publisher Book Page: http://www.writers-exchange.com/A-Cry-of-Shadows.html

Amazon: http://mybook.to/ACryOfShadows

Adventures of a Small Game Hunter in Jamaica
(Autobiography)

An eleven-year-old boy is plucked from boarding school in England and transported to the tropical paradise of Jamaica. A shy and dreamy boy, he has one great love in his life--butterflies. He discovers that Jamaica has a wealth of these wonderful insects and sets about making a collection of as many as he can find. Along the way, he has adventures with many other creatures, from hummingbirds to vultures, from iguanas to black widow spiders, and through it all runs the promise of the legendary Homerus swallowtail, Jamaica's national butterfly.

Other activities intrude, like school, boxing and swimming lessons, but he manages to inveigle his parents into taking him to strange and sometimes dangerous places, all in the name of butterfly collecting. He meets scientists and Rastafarians, teachers, small boys and the ordinary people of this tropical isle, and even discovers butterflies that should not exist in Jamaica.

I was that young boy. I count myself fortunate to have lived in Jamaica in an age very different from our present one. I still have some of the butterflies I collected half a century or more ago, and each one releases a flood of memories every time I open the box and gaze at their tattered and fading wings. These memories have become stories--stories of the Adventures of a Small Game Hunter in Jamaica.

Publisher Book Page: http://www.writers-exchange.com/Adventures-of-a-Small-Game-Hunter.html

Amazon: http://myBook.to/AdventuresGameHunter

Ascension Series A Novel of Nazi Germany
(Historical: Holocaust)

Book 1: Ascension

A small boy discovers that being a Jew in Germany can be a dangerous thing. Fear prompts Konrad Wengler to put his faith aside and he tries desperately to forget his heritage.

He fights in the Great War and is wounded, becomes a policeman in his tiny Bavarian town, where he falls under the spell of the fledgling Nazi Party. He joins the Party in patriotic fervour and becomes a Lieutenant of Police and Schutzstaffel (SS).

In the course of his duties as policeman, he offends a powerful Nazi official, who starts an SS investigation of this troublesome police Lieutenant. When war breaks out, he joins the Police Battalions and is sent to Poland where he has to witness the atrocities being committed upon his fellow Jews.

The SS investigators have discovered Konrad's origins and follow him into Poland. He is arrested and sent to Mauthausen Concentration Camp. Suddenly, Konrad must face what it means to be a Jew and fight for survival. He has friends on the outside, a wife and a lawyer, but will they be enough to counter the might of the Nazi machine?

Publisher Book Page: http://www.writers-exchange.com/Ascension.html

Amazon: http://mybook.to/Ascension1

Book 2 Maelstrom

Konrad Wengler has survived his brush with the death camps of Nazi Germany, and has been reinstated as a police officer in his home town despite being a Jew. He throws himself back into his work, seeking to uncover the evidence that will remove a corrupt Nazi party official, but underestimates his enemy. The Gestapo have their own agenda, and despite orders from above to eliminate this troublesome Jewish policeman, they hide him in the Totenkopf (Death's Head) Division of the Waffen-SS.

Now Konrad must fight to survive in the snowy wastes of Russia as the tide of war turns against Germany. He experiences tank battles, ghetto clearances, partisans, and death camps (this time as a guard), as well as the fierce battles where his Division is badly outnumbered and on the defence.

Through it all, he must try to live by his conscience and resist taking part in the atrocities happening all around him. He still thinks of himself as a policeman, but his desire to bring the corrupt official to justice now seems far removed from his present reality. Konrad must first survive if he is to find the necessary evidence.

Publisher Author Page:
http://www.writers-exchange.com/Max-Overton.html
Publisher Book Page: http://www.writers-exchange.com/Maelstrom.html
Amazon: http://mybook.to/Ascension2

Fall of the House of Ramesses

Book 1: Merenptah

Egypt was at the height of its powers in the days of Ramesses the Great and the young king confidently predicted that his House would last for a Thousand Years. Sixty years later he was still on the throne and one by one his heirs had died and the survivors had become old men. When he at last died, he left a stagnant kingdom and his throne to an old man - Merenptah. What followed laid the groundwork for a nation ripped apart by civil war.

The northern tribes rebelled and joined forces with the Sea Peoples, invading from the north; while in the south the king's eldest son, angered at being passed over in favour of the younger son, plotted to rid himself of his father and brother. An ageing king takes to the field to fight for the House of Ramesses.

Publisher Book Page: http://www.writers-exchange.com/Merenptah.html
Amazon: http://mybook.to/FOTHR1

Book 2: Seti

Merenptah is dead after only nine years on the throne and his son Seti is king in his place. He rules from the northern city of Men-nefer, while his elder brother Messuwy, convinced the throne is his by right, plots rebellion in the south.

The kingdoms are tipped into bloody civil war, with brother fighting against brother for the throne of a united Egypt. On one side is Messuwy, now crowned as King Amenmesse and his ruthless General Sethi; on the other, young King Seti and his wife Tausret. But other men are weighing up the chances of wresting the throne from both brothers and becoming king in their place. The House of Ramesses crumbles under the onslaught.
Publisher Book Page: http://www.writers-exchange.com/Seti.html
Amazon: http://mybook.to/FOTHR2

Book 3: Tausret

The House of Ramesses falters as Tausret relinquishes the throne upon the death of her husband, King Seti. Amenmesse's young son Siptah will become king until her infant son is old enough to rule. Tausret, as Regent, and the king's uncle, Chancellor Bay, hold tight to the reins of power, and vie for complete control of the kingdoms. Assassination changes the balance of power and Chancellor Bay attempts a coup...

Tausret's troubles mount as she also faces a challenge from Setnakhte, an aging son of the Great Ramesses who believes Seti was the last legitimate king. If Setnakhte gets his way, he will destroy the House of Ramesses and set up his own dynasty of kings.
Publisher Book Page: http://www.writers-exchange.com/Tausret.html
Amazon: http://mybook.to/FOTHR3

Glass Trilogy
(Paranormal Thriller)

GLASS HOUSE, Book 1: The mysteries of Australia may just hold the answers mankind has been searching for millennium to find. When Doctor James Hay, a university scientist who studies the paranormal mysteries in Australia, finds an obelisk of carved volcanic rock on sacred Aboriginal land in northern Queensland, he knows it may hold the answers he has been seeking. And when a respected elder of the Aboriginal people instructs him to take up the gauntlet and follow his heart, James, Spencer, an old friend and an award-winning writer, Samantha Louis, along with her cameraman and two of James' Aboriginal students, start their quest for the truth.

Glass House will take you deep into the mysteries that surround the continent of Australia, from its barren deserts to the depths of its rainforest and even deeper into its mysterious mountains. Along the way, the secrets of mankind and the ultimate answer to 'what happens now?' just might be answered. Love, greed, murder, and mystery abound in this action-packed paranormal/thriller.

Publisher Book Page:
http://www.writers-exchange.com/Glass-House.html
Amazon: http://mybook.to/Glass1

A GLASS DARKLY, Book 2: A dead volcano called Glass Mountain in Northern California seems harmless - or is it?

This is the fascinating setting of this mesmerising epic, the second book of the Glass Trilogy. Andromeda Jones, a physicist, knows her missing sister Samantha is somehow tied up with the new job she has been offered. Federal forces are aware that something is amiss, so Andromeda agrees to go on a dangerous mission and soon finds herself entangled in a web of professional jealousy, political betrayal and greed.

She helps construct Vox Dei, a machine that ostensibly is built to eliminate wars. But what is its true nature? Who is pulling the strings?

The experiment gets out of control, dark powers are unleashed and the danger to mankind unfolds relentlessly. Strange, evil shadows are using the Vox Dei and Samantha to try to get through to our world, knowing the time is near when Earth's final destiny will be decided.

Publisher Book Page:
http://www.writers-exchange.com/A-Glass-Darkly.html
Amazon: http://mybook.to/Glass2

LOOKING GLASS, Book 3: Samantha and James Hay have been advised that their missing daughter Gaia and Yowie nursemaid Cindy have been located in ancient Australia. Dr. Xanatuo, an alien scientist who, along with a lost tribe of Neanderthals and other beings who are working to help mankind, has discovered a way to send them back in time to be reunited with Gaia. Ernie, the old Aboriginal tracker and Garagh, leader of the Neanderthals, along with friends Ratana and Nathan, all characters from the first two books of the trilogy, will accompany them.

This team of intrepid adventurers have another mission for the journey along with aiding the Hayes' quest, which is paramount to changing a terrible wrong which exists in the present time. Lauded as the 'Australian Jurassic Park' *Looking Glass* is a mixture of Aboriginal mythology, present day UFO activity and pure science. It guarantees to please any reader who enjoys well researched, action packed and mind blowing events.

Publisher Book Page:

http://www.writers-exchange.com/Looking-Glass.html

Amazon: http://mybook.to/Glass3

Haunted Trail A Tale of Wickedness & Moral Turpitude
(Western: Paranormal)

Ned Abernathy is a hot-tempered young cowboy in the small town of Hammond's Bluff in the Dakota Territories in 1876. In a drunken argument with his best friend Billy over a girl, he guns him down. He flees, and wanders the plains, forests and hills of the Dakota Territories, certain that every man's hand is against him.

Horse rustlers, marauding Indians, killers, gold prospectors and French trappers cross his path and lead to complications, as do persistent apparitions of what Ned believes is the ghost of his friend Billy, come to accuse him of murder. He finds love and loses it, he finds gold in the Black Hills and must defend his new-found wealth against greedy men. Finally, he comes to terms with who he is and what he has done. Ned confronts the ghosts of his past and returns to Hammond's Bluff, where a shocking surprise awaits him at the end of the haunted trail.

Publisher Book Page:

http://www.writers-exchange.com/Haunted-Trail.html

Amazon: http://mybook.to/HauntedTrail

Scythian Trilogy
(Historical)

LION OF SCYTHIA, Book 1: Alexander the Great has conquered the Persian Empire and is marching eastward to India. In his wake he leaves small groups of soldiers to govern great tracts of land and diverse peoples. Nikometros is a young cavalry captain left behind in the lands of the fierce nomadic Scythian horsemen. Captured after an ambush, he must fight for his life and the lives of his surviving men. He seeks an opportunity to escape but owes a debt of loyalty to the chief, and a developing love for the young priestess.
Publisher Book Page:
http://www.writers-exchange.com/Lion-of-Scythia.html
Amazon: http://mybook.to/Scythian1

THE GOLDEN KING, Book 2: The chief of the tribe is dead, killed by his son's treachery; and the priestess, the lover of the young cavalry officer, Nikometros, is carried off into the mountains. Nikometros and his friends set off in pursuit.

Death rides with them and by the time they return, the tribes are at war. Nikometros is faced with the choice of attempting to become chief himself or leaving the people he has come to love and respect, returning to his duty as an army officer in the Empire of Alexander.
Winner of the 2005 EPIC Ebook Awards.
Publisher Book Page:
http://www.writers-exchange.com/The-Golden-King.html
Amazon: http://mybook.to/Scythian2

FUNERAL IN BABYLON, Book 3:
Alexander the Great has returned from India and set up his court in Babylon. Nikometros and a band of loyal Scythians journey deep into the heart of Persia to join the Royal court. Nikometros finds himself embroiled in the intrigues and wars of kings, generals, and merchant adventurers as he strives to provide a safe haven for his lover and friends. The fate of an Empire hangs in the balance, and Death walks beside Nikometros as events precipitate a Funeral in Babylon.
Winner of the 2006 EPIC Ebook Awards.

Publisher Book Page:
http://www.writers-exchange.com/Funeral-in-Babylon.html
Amazon: http://mybook.to/Scythian3

Sequestered
By Max Overton and Jim Darley
(Action/Thriller)

Storing carbon dioxide underground as a means of removing a greenhouse gas responsible for global warming has made James Matternicht a fabulously wealthy man. For 15 years, the Carbon Capture and Sequestration Facility at Rushing River in Oregon's hinterland has been operating without a problem--or so it seems.

Annaliese Winton is a reporter, and when mysterious documents arrive on her desk that purport to show the Facility is leaking, she investigates. Together with a government geologist, Matt Morrison, she uncovers a morass of corruption and deceit that now threatens the safety of her community and the whole northwest coast of America.

Liquid carbon dioxide, stored at the critical point under great pressure, is a tremendously dangerous substance, and millions of tonnes of it are sequestered in the rock strata below Rushing River. All it takes is a crack in the overlying rock and the whole pressurized mass could erupt with disastrous consequences. And that crack has always been there...

Recipient of the Life Award (Literature for the Environment): "There are only two kinds of people: conservationists and suicides. To qualify for this Award, your book needs to value the wonderful world of nature, to recognize that we are merely one species out of millions, and that we have a responsibility to cherish and maintain our small planet."

Awarded from http://bobswriting.com/life.html

Publisher Book Page: http://www.writers-exchange.com/Sequestered.html
Amazon: http://mybook.to/Sequestered

Strong is the Ma'at of Re Series, A Novel of Ancient Egypt
{Historical: Ancient Egypt}

Book 1: The King

If there was one thing that filled Ramesses III with pride, it was that he was descended from Ramesses the Great. Elevated to the throne following a coup led by his father Setnakhte during the troubled days of Queen Tausret, Ramesses III set about creating an Egypt that reflected the glory days of Ramesses the Great. He took on his predecessor's throne name, he named his sons after the sons of Ramesses, he pushed them toward similar duties, and he thirsted after conquests like that of his hero grandfather.

Ramesses III assumed the throne name of Usermaatre, translated as 'Strong is the Ma'at of Re' and endeavoured to live up to it. He fought foreign foes, as had Ramesses the Great; he built temples throughout the Two Lands, as had Ramesses the Great, and he looked forward to a long, illustrious life on the throne of Egypt, as had Ramesses the Great.

But it was not to be. Ramesses III faced troubles at home; troubles that threatened the stability of Egypt and his own throne. The struggles for power between his wives, his sons, and even the priests of Amun, together with a treasury drained of its wealth; all forced Ramesses III to question his success.

Publisher Book Page: http://www.writers-exchange.com/The-King.html
Amazon: http://mybook.to/StrongIsTheMaatOfRe1

Book 2: The Heirs

Tiye, the first wife of Ramesses III, has grown so used to being the mother of the Heir she can no longer bear to see that prized title pass to the son of a rival wife. Her eldest sons have died and the one left wants to step down and devote his life to the priesthood. Then the son of the king's sister/wife, also named Ramesses, will become Crown Prince and all Tiye's ambitions will lie in ruins.

Ramesses III struggles to enrich Egypt by seeking the wealth of the Land of Punt. He dispatches an expedition to the fabled southern land but years pass before the expedition returns. In the meantime, Tiye has a new hope: A last son she dotes on. Plague sweeps through Egypt, killing princes and princesses alike and lessening her options, and now Tiye must undergo the added indignity of having her daughter married off to the hated Crown Prince.

All Tiye's hopes are pinned on this last son of hers, but Ramesses III refuses to consider him as a potential successor, despite the Crown Prince's failing health. Unless Tiye can change the king's mind through charm or coercion, her sons will forever be excluded from the throne of Egypt.

Publisher Book Page: http://www.writers-exchange.com/The-Heirs.html

Amazon: http://mybook.to/StrongIsTheMaatOfRe1

Book 3: Taweret

The reign of Ramesses III is failing and even the gods seem to be turning their eyes away from Egypt. When the sun hides its face, crops suffer, throwing the country into famine. Tomb workers go on strike. To avert further disaster, Crown Prince Ramesses acts on his father's behalf.

The rivalry between Ramesses III's wives--commoner Tiye and sister/wife Queen Tyti--also comes to a head. Tiye resents not being made queen and can't abide that her sons have been passed over. She plots to put her own spoiled son Pentaweret on the throne.

The eventual strength of the Ma'at of Re hangs in the balance. Will the rule of Egypt be decided by fate, gods...or treason?

Publisher Book Page: http://www.writers-exchange.com/The-One-of-Taweret.html

Amazon: http://mybook.to/SITMOR3

The Amarnan Kings Series, A Novel of Ancient Egypt

SCARAB - AKHENATEN, Book 1:

A chance discovery in Syria reveals answers to the mystery of the ancient Egyptian sun-king, the heretic Akhenaten and his beautiful wife Nefertiti. Inscriptions in the tomb of his sister Beketaten, otherwise known as Scarab, tell a story of life and death, intrigue and warfare, in and around the golden court of the kings of the glorious 18th dynasty.

The narrative of a young girl growing up at the centre of momentous events - the abolition of the gods, foreign invasion and the fall of a once-great family - reveals who Tutankhamen's parents really were, what happened to Nefertiti, and other events lost to history in the great destruction that followed the fall of the Aten heresy.

Max Overton follows his award-winning trilogy of ancient Greece (Lion of Scythia, The Golden King, Funeral in Babylon) with the first book in another series set in Egypt of the 14th century B.C.E. Meticulously researched, the book unfolds a tapestry of these royal figures lost in the mists of antiquity.

Publisher Book Page: http://www.writers-exchange.com/Scarab.html
Amazon: http://mybook.to/ScarabBook1

SCARAB- SMENKHKARE, Book 2:

Scarab - Smenkhkare follows on from the first book in this series as King Akhenaten, distraught at the rebellion and exile of his beloved wife Nefertiti, withdraws from public life, content to leave the affairs of Egypt in the hands of his younger half-brother Smenkhkare. When Smenkhkare disappears on a hunting expedition, his sister Beketaten, known as Scarab, is forced to flee for her life.

Finding refuge among her mother's people, the Khabiru, Scarab has resigned herself to a life in exile, when she hears that her brother Smenkhkare is still alive. He is raising an army in Nubia to overthrow Ay and reclaim his throne. Scarab hurries south to join him as he confronts Ay and General Horemheb outside the gates of Thebes.

Max Overton's series on the Amarnan kings sheds new light on the end of the 18th dynasty of pharaohs. Details of these troubled times have been lost as later kings expunged all records of the Heretic king Akhenaten and his successors. Max Overton has researched the era thoroughly, piecing together a mosaic of the reigns of the five kings, threaded through by the memories of princess Beketaten - Scarab.

436

Publisher Book Page: http://www.writers-exchange.com/Scarab2.html
Amazon: http://mybook.to/ScarabBook2

SCARAB - TUTANKHAMEN, Book 3:

Scarab and her brother Smenkhkare are in exile in Nubia, but are gathering an army to wrest control of Egypt from the boy king Tutankhamen and his controlling uncle, Ay. Meanwhile, the kingdoms are beset by internal troubles and the Amorites are pressing hard against the northern borders. Generals Horemheb and Paramessu must fight a war on two fronts while deciding where their loyalties lie--with the former king Smenkhkare or with the new young king in Thebes.

Smenkhkare and Scarab march on Thebes with their native army to meet the legions of Tutankhamen on the plains outside the city gates. The fate of Egypt and the 18th dynasty hang in the balance as two brothers battle for supremacy and the throne of the Two Kingdoms.

Finalist in 2013's Eppie Awards.

Publisher Book Page: http://www.writers-exchange.com/Scarab3.html
Amazon: http://mybook.to/ScarabBook3

SCARAB - AY, Book 4:

Tutankhamen is dead and his grieving widow tries to rule alone, but her grandfather Ay has not destroyed the former kings just so he can be pushed aside. Presenting the Queen and General Horemheb with a fait accompli, the old Vizier assumes the throne of Egypt and rules with a hand of hardened bronze. His adopted son, Nakhtmin, will rule after him, and stamp out the last remnants of loyalty to the former kings.

Scarab was sister to three kings and will not give in to the usurper and his son. She battles against Ay and his legions under the command of General Horemheb, and aided by desert tribesmen and the gods of Egypt themselves, finally confronts them in the rich lands of the Nile delta to decide the future of Egypt.

Publisher Book Page: http://www.writers-exchange.com/Scarab4.html
Amazon: http://mybook.to/ScarabBook4

SCARAB - HOREMHEB, Book 5:

General Horemheb has taken control after the death of Ay and Nakhtmin, and forcing Scarab to marry him, ascends the throne of Egypt. The Two Kingdoms settle into an uneasy peace as Horemheb proceeds to stamp out all traces of the former kings. He also persecutes the Khabiru tribesmen who were reluctant to help him seize power. Scarab escapes into the desert, where she is content to wait until Egypt needs her.

A holy man emerges from the desert, and demands that Horemheb release the Khabiru so they may worship his god. Scarab recognises the holy man and supports him in his efforts to free his people. The gods of Egypt and of the Khabiru are invoked and disaster sweeps down on the Two Kingdoms as the Khabiru flee with Scarab and the holy man. Horemheb and his army pursue them to the shores of the Great Sea, where a natural event or maybe the hand of God alters the course of Egyptian history.

Publisher Book Page: http://www.writers-exchange.com/Scarab5.html
Amazon: http://mybook.to/ScarabBook5

SCARAB - DESCENDANT, Book 6:

Three thousand years after the reigns of the Amarnan Kings, the archaeologists who discovered the inscriptions in Syria, journey to Egypt to find the tomb of Smenkhkare and his sister Scarab, and the fabulous treasure they think is there. Unscrupulous men, and religious fanatics, also seek the tomb, either to plunder it or to destroy it. Can the gods of Egypt protect their own, or must they rely on modern day men and women of science?

Publisher Book Page: http://www.writers-exchange.com/Scarab6.html
Amazon: http://mybook.to/ScarabBook6

TULPA
(Paranormal Thriller)

From the rainforests of tropical Australia to the cane fields and communities of the North Queensland coastal strip comes a tale of the horror than can be unleashed by playing with unknown forces.

It starts with a fairy story to amuse small children, but when four bored teenagers and a young university student in a North Queensland town become interested in an ancient Tibetan technique for creating a life form; all hell breaks loose...literally. A seemingly harmless experiment unleashes terror and death and soon the teenagers are fighting to contain a menace that grows exponentially. The police are helpless to end the horror, and it is left to the teenagers to find a way of destroying the menace, aided by two old big game hunters, a student of the paranormal and a few small children. But how do you destroy beings that can escape into an alternate reality when threatened?

Publisher Book Page: http://www.writers-exchange.com/TULPA.html
Amazon: http://mybook.to/TULPA

We Came From Konigsberg, A Novel of Nazi Germany
(Historical: Holocaust)

January 1945, and the Soviet Army is poised for the final push through East Prussia and Poland to Berlin. Elisabet Daeker and her five young sons are in Königsberg, East Prussia, and have heard the stories of Russian atrocities. They seek to escape to the perceived safety of Germany.

This is the story of their struggle to survive, of the hardships endured at the hands of Nazi hardliners, of Soviet troops bent on rape, pillage and murder, and of Allied cruelty in the Occupied Zones of post-war Germany. 'We Came From Königsberg' is based on a true story gleaned from the memories of family members sixty years after the events, from photographs and documents, and from published works of non-fiction describing the times and events that are described in the narrative.

Elisabet Daeker's sons, and subsequent daughters, all have families of their own, and have carved out meaningful lives for themselves in far-flung parts of the world. One thing they all claim, though, is - we came from Königsberg.

The Amarnan Kings, Book 6: Scarab - Descendant by Max Overton

Winner of the 2014 EPIC Ebook Awards.
Publisher Book Page: http://www.writers-exchange.com/We-Came-From-Konigsberg.html
Amazon: http://mybook.to/Konigsberg

Kadesh, A Novel of Ancient Egypt

Holding the key to strategic military advantage, Kadesh is a jewel city that distant lands covet. Ramesses II of Egypt and Muwatalli II of Hatti believe they're chosen by the gods to claim ascendancy to Kadesh. When the two meet in the largest chariot battle ever fought, not just the fate of empires will be decided but also the lives of citizens helplessly caught up in the greedy ambition of kings.
Publisher Book Page: http://www.writers-exchange.com/Kadesh.html
Amazon: http://mybook.to/Kadesh

You can find ALL our books up at Amazon at:
https://www.amazon.com/shop/writers_exchange

or on our website at:
http://www.writers-exchange.com

Made in the
USA
Columbia, SC